Luring them in . . .

The low sensual beat pulsed across the floor as people danced, wrapped around each other so that their bodies became just one entwined shadow.

Kendall could feel the excited throb of his pulse, hear it as she shimmied a little closer and wrapped her arms around his neck. His hands shifted from her sides to a little lower, one resting dangerously close to her butt. Against her belly, she felt his sex stir and she had to fight to keep the female interest on her face.

Not that she wasn't excited. She was plenty excited, the heat of the chase on her, ready to culminate. All she had to do was finish him.

She tipped her head back, staring up at his face and using that to shift away from him just a little, forcing a seductive smile onto her lips and watching with hidden amusement as he fell for it, smiling what she assumed was his charming smile as he stroked his hand up and down her back.

All Kendall wanted to do was to take his head between her hands and wrench it until she felt his neck snap. Even the thought of all that hot blood pumping under his skin didn't arouse her hunger. She suspected he would taste vile. But she wanted him dead, dead and cold in the ground . . .

HUNTING
THE HUNTER

SHILOH WALKER

BERKLEY SENSATION, NEW YORK

THE BERKLEY PUBLISHING GROUP
Published by the Penguin Group
Penguin Group (USA) Inc.
375 Hudson Street, New York, New York 10014, USA
Penguin Group (Canada), 90 Eglinton Avenue East, Suite 700, Toronto, Ontario M4P 2Y3, Canada
(a division of Pearson Penguin Canada Inc.)
Penguin Books Ltd., 80 Strand, London WC2R 0RL, England
Penguin Group Ireland, 25 St. Stephen's Green, Dublin 2, Ireland (a division of Penguin Books Ltd.)
Penguin Group (Australia), 250 Camberwell Road, Camberwell, Victoria 3124, Australia
(a division of Pearson Australia Group Pty. Ltd.)
Penguin Books India Pvt. Ltd., 11 Community Centre, Panchsheel Park, New Delhi—110 017, India
Penguin Group (NZ), Cnr. Airborne and Rosedale Roads, Albany, Auckland 1310, New Zealand
(a division of Pearson New Zealand Ltd.)
Penguin Books (South Africa) (Pty.) Ltd., 24 Sturdee Avenue, Rosebank, Johannesburg 2196, South Africa

Penguin Books Ltd., Registered Offices: 80 Strand, London WC2R 0RL, England

HUNTING THE HUNTER

A Berkley Sensation Book / published by arrangement with the author

PRINTING HISTORY
Berkley Sensation mass-market edition / July 2006

Copyright © 2006 by Shiloh Walker.
Excerpt from *Heart and Soul of a Hunter* copyright © 2006 by Shiloh Walker.
Cover illustration by Jonathan Barkat.
Interior text design by Kristin del Rosario.

ISBN: 0-425-21100-2

BERKLEY® SENSATION
Berkley Sensation Books are published by The Berkley Publishing Group,
a division of Penguin Group (USA) Inc.,
375 Hudson Street, New York, New York 10014.
BERKLEY SENSATION and the "B" design are trademarks belonging to Penguin Group (USA) Inc.

PRINTED IN THE UNITED STATES OF AMERICA

10 9 8 7 6 5 4 3 2 1

To my family, always

Mom, thanks for believing in me.

Jerry, thanks for being you. And to my babies—
I love you all so much.

A special thank-you to the people who helped
while I wrote this—
Angie H.
Valerie P.
Jeff S. via his wife, Shannon
Phillip P. via his wife, Jamie.

Thanks for all the help, guys.

Prologue

I⟨T⟩ was hotter than hell.

Sweat rolled down Kane Winter's face but he didn't dare move an inch. Less than ten feet from them were six men who would shoot both Kane and his partner without even blinking.

Well, that wasn't a big surprise, considering that one of the men was a drug dealer. Miles Lancaster was one of the most wanted men in America, and Kane and Duke Monroe were here to apprehend the bastard and haul his sorry ass to prison.

They'd been tracking this bastard for three months. Kane had known they were close. But he hadn't really planned on getting this close, at least not when they were so very badly outnumbered.

Closing his eyes, Kane held still. They'd already been talking for a good ten minutes. Couldn't be much longer— this kind of people wouldn't stay too long in an unsecured place.

They'd go and Kane could finally move, wipe away the sweat burning his eyes. Hell, maybe they'd be lucky and

Miles Lancaster would be the one to linger behind. Not very likely, but shit, miracles had happened before, right?

But the time to slip quietly away never came and what came next wasn't Kane's idea of a miracle. More in the realm of nightmare, although Lancaster ended up dead.

One minute Kane and Duke were crouching in the shadows behind cans of garbage, and the next, it was like hell had opened up right in front of them. Although Kane saw nothing, fear was suddenly choking him and it took everything he had just to stay still, stay quiet.

Silent screams tore through Kane, but he never made a sound as he stared in shock, trying to figure out what in the hell had happened.

Duke moved, and Kane flinched as he felt his friend's hand come up and rest on his shoulder. In a low voice, Duke murmured, "Get down, man."

Uh, down? He was already down, crouched on his knees in garbage that stank to high heaven. He'd lain in stuff that smelled worse than this before and he would again, but he didn't really want to. *Shit*, he swore silently, moving as quietly as he could as he started to shift to his belly.

Duke went to stand and Kane swung his head around in shock, before raising his Beretta and aiming at the men in front of them.

But they looked as stunned as Kane felt and none of them even looked Duke's way.

Instead, they were all staring straight ahead. At the mouth of the alley there was a slender man with a shock of red hair. He looked more like a boy than a man. Kane doubted the top of his head would clear the middle of Kane's chest, but there was something about his eyes that made Kane think the man was a lot older than he looked.

"My, my, my . . . yummy. Look, Miguel, it's a veritable feast." The boy/man's voice sounded lilting and sweet, almost like he was about to break into song.

Kane started to rise, but Duke hissed, "Stay down. Get ready to run."

Though Duke's words were pitched whisper soft, the

boy/man heard and he laughed. The sound was like a wind chime, and for some odd reason, it terrified Kane. "Oh, a bonus."

The men in front of them were in even worse shape than Kane. How in the hell could the sight of a doll-like creature make men quiver with fear? He didn't know, but that's exactly what was happening. Only three of the seven men were still standing. Four, including Miles, had fallen to the ground, hiding their heads like children hiding from monsters.

The two moved forward, the boy/man and the one he'd called Miguel. They were incredibly fast, and what little air Kane had in his lungs wheezed out as two of the three men standing went down. The boy/man tossed his red gold hair back, and Kane's gut twisted with fear as he watched the boy/man's lips peel back from his teeth.

I'm having a nightmare . . . That was the only thing that made sense, because that *thing* had fangs in his mouth. Inch-long gleaming incisors and Kane stared, frozen, as he moved, striking at the man pinned beneath him like a cobra. The man wailed in terror and in his mind, Kane echoed the sound. Falling back on his ass, Kane scrambled backward on his hands, his heels scuffing the ground.

His back hit the wall.

Duke still hadn't done anything. He stood there, looking at the two *monsters* and it was as if the terror thrumming the air left him totally unaffected. Suddenly Kane saw Duke's gaze slide to the shadows beyond the grisly scene in front of him, and then he glanced back at Kane and said once more, "Get ready to run."

Kane couldn't see his weapon, but Duke stood there, tense and ready to fight.

The only man left standing was backing away inch by inch, shaking his head. The hand gripped tightly on the Browning was trembling.

The boy/man lifted his head. Blood stained his mouth and Kane swallowed, watching as the attacker shifted his gaze from the man with the gun to the bleeding man beneath him. The injured man still whimpered, but the sounds were weaker. The boy/man caressed his face, almost lovingly, and then, he wrenched his head, the neck snapping like a twig.

Kane stared into dead eyes as the boy/man rose, moving toward the dealer with a smile on his face. "Drop the gun," the monster whispered.

The gun fell from a hand gone limp and the word *Run* echoed in Kane's mind, but as the thing advanced on the dealer, Kane couldn't move. Not a single inch. The dealer stood frozen as well as the creature embraced him like a lover, and sank his fangs into a bare, vulnerable neck. The man didn't even scream, didn't struggle, but Kane knew it wasn't because he didn't want to—his own mind was screaming at him to run, but he couldn't move a muscle.

The man called Miguel rose from his victim, and blood pulsed from the ragged bite in the victim's neck. It was Miles Lancaster—and judging by the ever slowing blood flow, he would be dead in minutes, maybe less.

Well, that will be an easy 500k if we can ever make it out of this alive, Kane thought inanely. The government might want the bastard alive, but the man who'd put up the bond for his release wouldn't give a rat's ass. Of course, Kane and Duke had to get out of here first.

Kane turned his head to glance at his partner and his mind went blank, then as realization hit, dread crawled through his system.

Duke's eyes were glowing. Reflecting light back at him like a cat's. Kane's gut twisted—he'd seen that look a time or two before. And if Duke was getting ready to shift, things were looking pretty damned bad.

Duke looked at Kane and whispered in a deep growling voice, "Run."

There was no other warning. Seconds later, Duke had shifted and his massive cat's body hurtled through the air. Kane ignored the order and just knelt on the ground, collecting the weapons that had fallen from Duke's body as his friend shifted.

Duke was a shape-shifter—not a werewolf, but a big cat. It still made Kane's mind reel every time he thought of it. And the few times he had seen it, hell, he was left questioning his sanity. Especially that first time.

For some reason, a memory of that day flashed through his mind, the day when he'd seen Duke shift for the first time. They'd been out running maneuvers and Monroe had stilled, looking around, his normally mild hazel eyes narrowing as he cocked his head, listening.

When he had looked at Kane, Kane could have sworn the teeth in his mouth looked longer. "Get the hell out of here, buddy," Duke had ordered, then his chest blossomed bright red, the sound of the gun fading even before they had fully realized what had happened.

Duke had dropped his eyes to his chest and growled, "Damn it, I fucking hate getting shot."

Kane had hit the ground as the bullets exploded all around them, staring at his friend as Duke dropped to his knees, throwing back his head and roaring . . . then a large, furred body had seemed to leap from within his skin. The cat had slanted another look at Kane, and then the thing had torn off in the direction of the bullets.

Twenty minutes later, Kane was still trying to convince himself that hadn't happened when the giant cat came padding across the sands toward him, cocking his head and staring at him with wide eyes.

Kane had watched in shock as the thing sat on its haunches and the fur melted away, like it was being absorbed back inside the thing's skin. When it was over, Monroe had been sitting there, wearing nothing but his now furless skin, watching Kane with a cocked brow. "You can freak out at any time, buddy."

And his chest was whole, completely unmarked.

It had been that level, almost amused tone that had kept Kane from doing just that.

Kane wasn't too sure anything Duke said *this* time would keep him from losing his mind, though. Duke was getting torn up pretty bad. Kane could see the thing on Duke's back, tearing through the thick fur, drawing blood. The air was heavy with the stink of it.

And if Duke went down—Kane was dead meat. Hell, he was probably dead meat anyway. Duke had pounced on the taller of the two, Miguel, and both of them looked like they might have done each other in. The shorter man had now focused on Kane.

From the corner of his eye, Kane could see Duke where he lay on the ground in an ever growing puddle of blood. Miguel lay a little farther away and he struggled to move, but it looked like Duke had hurt him just as bad.

Duke was down, bleeding and hurt. Sucking in a slow breath of air, Kane did his damnedest to clear his mind before focusing on the thing that was moving toward him. The fear clouding his mind retreated just a little and he rose from the ground, leveling his gun at the rosy-cheeked boy in front of him.

Damn it. The kid looked like he ought to be playing Peter Pan on Broadway or something, all big eyes and apple cheeks. But those eyes were evil.

For a second, the fear threatened to choke him again. *No,* Kane told himself, clenching his jaw. He'd been afraid before. He'd looked death in the eye before. He'd seen evil before. Having it look at him from the face of a child didn't really change anything.

Evil was still evil. He could either face it and maybe live, or he could give into that fear and die.

Kane really didn't want to die just yet.

"Put the gun down."

Kane just smiled and said, "I don't think so, buddy." He cocked it instead, aiming for the middle of the forehead.

The monster's eyes widened. "How unusual . . . what is your name, handsome?"

Kane couldn't miss the interest in the creature's eyes and revulsion snaked through him on several levels. The thing, while he might not *be* a child, still looked like one. And Kane had absolutely no interest in men, but something told him that this thing didn't care.

Faking bravado was easy. Keeping his voice level wasn't, but he managed to reply in a controlled voice, "I fail to see why that's any of your business."

A smile curved the monster's lips, and his eyes were dark, evil, and cold. That fear hammered at Kane again, but it was weird. It didn't seem to come at him from inside.

It was almost like the monster in front of him was causing it. Throwing it at him almost.

Swallowing, he focused once more, squeezing his hand tight around the grip of his Beretta. Steadying the gun, he aimed for the middle of that young, smooth brow.

Those eyes started to glow, taking on an eerie, deep blue color as the creature stared at Kane. There was nothing sane, nothing remotely human in those eyes. Kane's blood flowed icily through his veins and his heart skipped a beat as the monster moved just a little closer. "Put the gun down."

At the edges of his consciousness, Kane felt something odd pushing at his mind, like something—or someone—was trying to crawl inside his brain, but he didn't lower his Beretta. "No."

Those odd, glowing eyes narrowed. "I said, put the damned gun down!"

Like a cold wind, that voice rippled along Kane's skin and he shook with the chill of it, but he didn't move. "And I said, *No*," he repeated. His own voice was icy. He'd faced down some of the worst scum known to man and had fought and bled on the deserts of Iraq, aware every breath might be his last.

Hell, his best friend was a shape-shifter, and possibly bleeding to death right now. He'd be damned if he'd freeze from fear over some Tiny Tim lookalike.

Well, okay. This wasn't a kid. He wasn't even human. Kane was staring at a monster, he knew that.

Monsters were real. Kane had seen a lot of them in his line of work. But most of them were human. This thing that looked like a boy wasn't human. It was a monster. But Kane couldn't quite accept what his mind was telling him the thing was.

The fangs . . . the blood. The years he had known Duke hadn't quite prepared him for this.

"Well, well, well. Anton. He doesn't seemed to be all that impressed with you."

This new voice was low and husky, amused. But the golden eyes Kane found himself now staring into were anything but. The man, Anton, snarled with rage, his eyes narrowing as he spun to glare at the newcomer.

The fear that had seemed to eat at Kane's mind faded away the minute those evil blue eyes looked away from him.

There were two of them—another man standing next to a sleek, rather sexy woman. The man was tall with dark, dark skin, dark hair, dark eyes.

The woman's hair seemed dark as well—in this light, it looked close to black. But her skin was pale, almost gleaming in the dim light, and her eyes glittered gold. For one brief moment, Kane's gaze locked with hers, and her lips moved. *Sleep.*

Darkness pulled at his mind and he fought it with all the strength in his body. *Sleep?* he thought incredulously. "Like hell," he muttered, shaking his head and looking back at the thing in front of him. He wanted to walk out of here, get Duke out of here. Not get carried out in a body bag.

Those golden eyes narrowed—the push at his mind strengthened for just a moment and then it faded. There was a sighing in the air and she whispered, "I don't have time for you, mortal."

The next touch on his mind wasn't a gentle nudging or a light push.

It packed all the power of a sledgehammer, striking his mind, and light and pain exploded. Distantly, he heard himself bellow and then he fell to the ground as everything around him went black.

K ENDALL saw the man fall to the ground and she prayed she hadn't hurt him, but she didn't have time to coddle a stubborn mortal right now.

On the ground, a golden cat labored to breathe. It was giant, more than eight feet long, and unlike any natural cat she'd ever seen. But he wasn't natural. That was a shape-shifter lying there, struggling to live after either Anton or Miguel had damned near bled him out.

He isn't a Hunter, Kendall thought, *but if he lives, he damned well ought to be.*

But right now, she had her hands full. Behind her, she could hear Marc grunting as he fought the vampire that traveled with Anton. Marc, her trainee, hadn't yet fought a feral vampire hand-to-hand, and she hoped he was ready for this.

The vampire's name was Miguel. The shifter had done a great deal of damage to him, she suspected. She could smell the musky scent of vampire blood in the air, but from the way he was moving, he'd had enough time to heal many of his wounds.

God willing, though, he was still weak from the healing and Marc would be able to take him, because she'd have her hands full with Anton.

Tucking her worry out of her mind, she braced herself as Anton lunged.

Anton was a wily bastard, and crazy as hell. He'd managed to elude Hunters for more than fifty years, but this was it. He'd killed his last victim, and she was pretty damned sure he'd be really pissed off that it was a woman that had finally run him to the ground. Anton really hated women.

He was strong and fast, but that small body of his didn't have quite the strength he would have had if he'd been an adult when he'd been Changed. Kendall was faster and had more experience behind her.

Still, fear gave the younger vampire a strength that was damned near unnatural even for a vampire.

She screamed with rage as he sank his teeth into her forearm as she struggled to pin him down. The icy cold of a knife tore through her thigh and she jumped away, staring at him with fury as he waved a silver knife at her. "I picked up a few of your tricks, Hunter whore," he rasped at her. "I'm going to stab you in the heart with this. And while you're dying, Miguel will rape that nasty, ugly body of yours. He likes women more than I do."

Kendall sneered at him, sweeping out with her injured leg and kicking the knife out of his hand. "You'll have a hard time stabbing me with it when you can't hold onto it."

Anton howled with rage, lunging at her. He caught her around the middle, taking her down. Kendall gritted her teeth, holding back her scream as he fisted his hands in her hair and pounded her head back against the pavement. It cracked under her head and she smelled her own blood. Instead of trying to pry his hands away, she reached up, slamming the ball of her hand against his nose. He swore at her, but didn't let go.

Narrowing her eyes, she murmured, "You asked for it, little bastard." Dropping her control, she let her own power roll through the air. Anton had been using a vampire's power of fear on the humans earlier, and he had been doing a damned fine job of it.

But his gift paled in comparison to hers.

Like a storm, it thundered through the air, and Anton struggled to beat it back. But it took only seconds for him to falter.

His hands fell away from her hair and he tumbled limply away from her body, whimpering pathetically as he curled into a ball.

Rising, she nudged him with her toe and murmured, "Now you understand how they felt, don't you, Anton?" Drawing in a shuddering breath, she reined the power back in, concentrating until only Anton was affected.

From the corner of her eye, she saw Marc rise from the ground, still maintaining his human form although his eyes glowed, red striations swirling through the dark brown irises. On the ground, the vampire was dead. The hilt of a knife protruded from his heart and Kendall could see small wisps of smoke and smell burnt flesh.

Vampire flesh really hated silver.

Anton lay sobbing on the ground, and the sounds were pathetic.

Kendall sighed sadly. Even though she knew what a terrible man he was, pity filled her.

He'd been so young when he'd been changed. But he had chosen to become a monster. Nobody had made him become a rapist, a killer.

She released him from the prison of fear and waited until his sobs faded and he rolled onto his back, staring up at her with eyes full of rage and hatred. "Will you lay there or stand up and take your sentence like a man?" she asked quietly.

"Who are you to judge me?" he spat, rising to his knees.

Arching a brow, she stared at him for a long minute. "You know who I am."

He rose slowly, his body tensed, ready to flee. A slow smile curved her lips. "You can't get away this time, Anton. It's over."

Drawing a silver blade from the sheath at her waist, she said soberly, "You've been found guilty of crimes against humanity, Anton Le Blanc. Your sentence is death. May God have mercy on your soul."

She muffled his scream of death against her palm as she plunged the silver blade into his heart, rotating it. Before they left, though, they'd have to burn the bodies. Vampires were a weird lot. Unless the hearts were destroyed, powerful vamps could sometimes come back with the moonrise.

Although she just might make Marc do that part. What were trainees for, if you couldn't give the messy work to them?

And besides, she still had the human to deal with, and the bleeding shifter. Casting Marc a glance, she nodded toward the shifter and said, "Take care of him."

Resting her fingers on Anton's brow, she touched her mind to his and found nothing. He was well and truly dead. But protocol demanded the body be destroyed. And they didn't really want somebody cutting up a vampire's body trying to find the cause of death.

Well, that was pretty obvious. He had a gaping hole in his chest. But still . . .

Shoving the morbid thoughts out of her head, Kendall rose from the ground and moved over to the human, studying him with curiosity.

Just human. Nothing remarkable about him, save for what was probably a very thick head.

As she knelt beside him, her eyes lingered on the lean lines of his face. Okay, she couldn't exactly say *nothing* remarkable. Even asleep, he looked very remarkable. A grin curved her lips. He looked rather bitable, in more ways than one.

His hair was cut a little too short for her taste, but it suited the lean, almost savage lines of his face. His mouth was full, one she wouldn't have minded spending a little time tasting, under different circumstances.

Hard to judge his height with him lying down, but he wasn't too tall. That was nice. Kendall was pretty short. Only five two, and tall men made her feel claustrophobic. But there was lean, controlled power to this man that was evident even now.

She'd seen how easily he held his gun. A warrior. Kendall had known a lot of them in her lifetime, both mortal and other. This one was definitely a warrior.

But beyond being a very good-looking guy, he was just human. How had he resisted her commands?

He was still breathing, thank God. The power she'd used to put him under could have killed him, and in the back of her mind, that fear had gnawed at her even as she dealt with Anton.

Skimming her fingers along his brow, she let her mind touch his as she laid a false memory down. As stubborn as he was, it was possible it wouldn't hold—but there was an intelligent mind inside that thick skull. She'd seen it in his eyes, could feel it even now. And intelligent humans tended to resist what their minds couldn't explain.

Even if the memory didn't hold, surely he wouldn't go around babbling about giant cats and vampires.

But what in the hell was she supposed to do with him now? What had the shifter been doing here?

She had an idea why this one was here. She had seen the gun. She'd seen enough drug deals gone wrong. This one here was either a cop or something along those lines—was there a partner there, among the dead? She didn't know.

One thing was certain.

She couldn't leave him here.

Too much blood, no way to provide answers. With a tired sigh, she glanced toward Marc. It was going to be a very long night.

PART ONE

CHAPTER I

Two Years Later

THE nightmares were getting worse.

    The sheets twisted around his naked limbs and a fine film of sweat covered his entire body.

Trapped in the cage of his own mind, Kane stood helplessly, watching as a geyser of blood erupted, soaking the tawny golden coat of a giant cat. A cat that stared at him with Duke's eyes.

Then the cat was dead and it changed, back to Duke's body. And over him, there was a woman. Her eyes were golden, her mouth downcast as she stared at the dead man at her feet.

She lifted her head, and when her eyes met his, she smiled.

In her mouth, instead of incisors, he saw two long, glistening fangs.

He awoke with a start, jackknifing up in bed. Air sawed in and out of his lungs raggedly as he stared around him, bewildered.

"Just dreaming," he muttered, shaking his head.

The dream had been haunting him ever since he'd woken in that damned hospital.

A few days of his life gone. Told by the doctors he'd been found lying unconscious in the parking lot of the emergency room, Kane had spent nearly a week in a coma. And when he woke up, it was to find out that Duke was dead.

The police had ruled that he'd been killed when he stumbled upon a drug deal. Stumbled, my ass, Kane had fumed as he read the report. Even when he told the cops that Duke was a bounty hunter they had just stared at him blankly.

Duke had been found unarmed in the same alley where Kane and Duke had been watching Miles and company. Unarmed. No. No way, no how. Kane and Duke didn't do unarmed.

According to the report, Duke had been shot execution style. A .32 caliber slug was removed from his skull. He'd been wearing a T-shirt, blue jeans, tennis shoes.

That wasn't what Kane remembered. Duke would have been nude. His clothes had been shredded when he shifted. Not that Kane could say *that*. But they didn't go on jobs like that one wearing street clothes. They'd been wearing black, all black utilities, and if Duke had been killed in that alley, and Kane knew he most likely had, it had been from blood loss.

What in the hell had happened that night, Kane didn't exactly know, but the bottom line was that somebody had murdered his best friend.

Somebody had messed with evidence, somehow. Falsified a police report.

And that woman had something to do with it.

He didn't know how.

And he didn't know who she was.

But Duke was dead. And that bitch was going to pay for it.

With a tired sigh, he climbed from bed.

Sleep was long gone now. Might as well pack up and head out. There wasn't much of anything left around here for him to find.

Time for a new hunting ground.

* * *

THE low, sensual beat pulsed across the dance floor, the lights low, as people danced, wrapped around each other so that their bodies became just one entwined shadow.

Kendall could feel the excited throb of his pulse, hear it as she shimmied a little closer and wrapped her arms around his neck. His hands shifted a little lower from her sides, one resting dangerously close to her butt. Against her belly, she felt his sex stir and she had to fight to keep the female interest on her face.

Not that she wasn't excited. She was plenty excited, the heat of the chase on her, ready to culminate. All she had to do was finish him.

She tipped her head back, staring up at his face and using that to shift away from him just a little, forcing a seductive smile onto her lips and watching with hidden amusement as he fell for it, smiling what she assumed was his charming smile as he stroked her back.

All Kendall wanted to do was take his head and wrench it until she felt his neck snap. Even the thought of all that hot blood pumping under his skin didn't arouse her hunger. She suspected he would taste vile. But she wanted him dead, dead and cold in the ground.

Instead, she was playing this little fool's game and letting him think that she was interested, interested in going to a motel with him, letting him put his hands on her . . . letting him kill her.

A Hunter of the Council, Kendall was not particularly interested in being his next victim. And she was pretty damned certain that she could give him a few scary surprises if he tried to pull anything. She wanted to, with an intensity that should have frightened her.

But she couldn't kill him and just get rid of his body.

The cops had a man in the jail they thought was guilty. Porter Jenkins was a little weird, but he wasn't a killer. He just had the bad luck to be seen near not one, but two of the dead girls' apartments . . . and he just a little weirder than the

cops liked. In a small college town like Hanover, weird people tended to take the blame for a lot of things, when the
only thing they were guilty of was just being odd.

Kendall had smelled the blood and death on this man the
moment he sauntered through the doors, a half smile on his
lips, surveying the crowd before him. A dozen other guys
had come through that door, with that exact same look, but
they were just on the prowl, looking for sex, looking for
fun . . . or drugs. There was a dealer here—a pretty, perky
woman who looked more like a college coed than anything.

Part of her felt like she needed to handle that, but the
larger part knew that she needed to deal with the problem at
hand. That problem's name was Aaron Meyer and his hand
had slid down to cup her ass now.

For three weeks, she had been trying to track him down,
with no luck. The residents of this small Indiana town had
been living in terror for a couple of months now, and the cops
had no clue who was killing the pretty young college girls.

Aaron Meyers was either very lucky, or very brilliant, because he'd evaded not just the police, but her. And she didn't
have to follow the rules that often hamstrung the police. But
still, it was like the killer vanished after each crime, leaving
next to nothing of himself behind.

There was no blood trail to follow, and without that,
things were a little harder. Since Kendall wasn't a witch, the
killer would have to be closer in order for her to sense him.
Now if he was a vamp, or almost any paranormal creature,
different story . . . she could sense them from miles away
and would have homed in on him within days, if not hours.

Of course, another vampire could possibly sense her as
well, but even when they did, they couldn't outrun her for
too long.

The hand on her ass squeezed just a little and she made
herself stare at him with wide eyes, wetting the curve of her
lips with her tongue as she forced out a shaky sigh.

As she lifted her eyes and looked at him from under her
lashes, she saw the smile on his face and smiled flirtatiously
back. Inside, her belly was roiling. Damn it, he stank.

Blood and death surrounded him, clung to his skin like a shroud.

The hand on her ass stayed firmly in place and his other hand was cruising up her side. As his thumb brushed over the lower curve of her breast, Kendall's control snapped.

Damn it, I've had enough of this.

Plastering a sly smile on her face, she leaned against him and crushed her breasts against his chest, rising on her toes and pressing a kiss against his neck.

His breath stirred her hair as he murmured, "What do you say we find someplace a little quieter?"

"I thought you'd never ask," she purred. *And that's the truth,* she thought disgustedly. Much more of his cold hands, and she'd have been ready to tear them off at the wrists, and feed them to him.

He caught her wrist in his hand, and she blanked her face to keep from snarling at the possessive gesture as he led her through the crush of people. The minute his face was turned, Kendall grimaced, forcing the tension in her shoulders to relax.

I can do this. She just had to get him to take her to the hotel, let him paw her a little, and then she could knock him out, preferably with a large blunt object that would leave him with the world's biggest headache. Maybe grind his balls into a pulpy, useless mass with the heel of her shoe on her way out the door.

After that, call the police . . . he'd be taken in. Kendall would leave an anonymous tip about the trophies he was keeping in his house, the police would arrest him for the murders and let Porter Jenkins go.

THE woman slid through the crowd, following the man in front of her with a grim little smile on her pretty face.

Where in the hell did he know her from?

It had been plaguing him from the first second Kane had seen her, but he'd be damned if he could remember where he'd seen that lovely face before. Using his cell phone, he shot a few pictures of her. He'd figure it out sooner or later.

Right now, though, he didn't have time to sit there and figure it out.

There was a vampire in here somewhere, and whoever in the hell it was, the vamp was old, so old it made his teeth ache. Over the past year, he'd been hunting them, picking up a feel for things like this.

Old meant one thing, strong and powerful. The older ones tended to be the ones that had the money, which was a good thing.

His bank account was getting low—if this one didn't have some jewelry to pawn or money Kane could swipe before he burned the body, he'd have to take on a few *paying* jobs soon.

Killing vampires was a damned rewarding job, but not always a paying one. He had no qualm taking money from one of the dead freaks once he'd finished them off, but most of the younger vampires weren't as well off as TV or literature made them out to be. The last one he'd taken care of had less than fifty bucks on him. And the older ones were pretty hard to catch.

Turning away from the woman, he started to scan the crowd, looking for the bloodsucker.

But then his eyes shut. *Shit*.

Bloodsucker.

Slowly, he turned back around and stared at her, fury starting to brew in his gut, watching as her hips swayed from side to side.

Vampire.

Fuck.

It was her . . . the woman that had haunted his dreams ever since Duke's death.

His friend had been dead for two years now. That first year, Kane had damn near drank himself into the ground, convinced he was losing his mind as the vague bits of memory did little more than haunt him at night. None of it had really seemed real, not then.

Not until that night . . .

But then it happened. He had stumbled out of a bar and

heard something. A woman's scream. It was a wonder he hadn't gotten his own throat ripped out. The vampire had been young. That was the only way he could figure it out. Kane hadn't had a single weapon on him and he'd gone for the only thing he could find, a splintered section of a two-by-four that was laying on the ground.

The vampire had moved like the wind, but as Kane slammed him across the face with the piece of wood, memories from that night superimposed themselves and he was seeing that slender boylike vampire again as he attacked one of the drug dealers, and the other, Miguel, attacking Duke.

Rage had flooded him and it gave him strength and speed. Still, the vampire had almost killed him. Kane had ended up on his back while the vampire snarled and spat at him. As he rushed toward Kane, Kane jerked up the two-by-four, the jagged edge pointed out.

The vampire hadn't stopped in time and it had impaled him right through the chest.

That had been it—as he climbed from the ground, his clothes stained with blood that was too dark to be human, he'd known.

This was what he had to do.

Kill the people that had killed Duke. The people that had tried to hurt the woman he found sobbing and bleeding on the ground.

In the past twelve months, he'd killed seventeen of them. Most of them hadn't been as easy as that first one, which had been pure, dumb luck.

Now he hunted. He prowled the streets at night until he found what he was looking for, and then he hunted.

He knew how to hunt. Before Duke had been killed, that was what they did. Two of the most respected bounty hunters in the States, they went after the criminals that others wouldn't touch.

But Kane hadn't been expecting to find *her*.

He'd come here to get a few drinks, hopefully get laid. Not hunt.

But a small smile curved his mouth as he watched her.

Answers . . . she would have answers. Of course, he was going to have to get to her before she got loverboy out the door and tore his throat out.

As he wove through the crowd, he kept her in his site. Blood pulsed through his veins slow and heavy, pooling in his groin until his cock ached. It wasn't really any surprise, not considering he'd been studying her for the past twenty minutes.

She danced like some women fucked, all body language and sultry looks.

The woman was sex personified.

The wine red pants she wore were all but painted on, riding low on her hips, the stone in her navel flashing, her hips swinging back and forth as she followed after her partner.

The shirt she wore laced between her full, round breasts, ended inches above the waistband of her pants and dipped low between her breasts, revealing a naked strip of skin between its edges. She'd piled her thick red hair into one of those knots on the top of her head, with loose tendrils spilling down to frame her heart-shaped face.

Hell, yes, sex personified.

Part of him hoped he'd find something different in her eyes when he faced her. Something other than the monster he was used to seeing when he killed a vampire.

But Kane knew better.

After executing close to twenty of them, he had no illusions about what they were. Killers, plain and simple, and despite the fact that this woman looked entirely too kissable, she would be the same.

Death, nothing more. She was death in a pair of fuck-me shoes and tight clothes that revealed every ripe curve of her body. And he didn't have sex with killers.

Kane watched as she tipped her head back and smiled at her date. The blond guy dipped his head low to murmur in her ear and then they started making their way to the door.

He moved through the crowd, keeping sight of her by the thick red locks that spilled from the loose knot atop her head. For a moment, he lost sight of her in the crowd and a snarl crossed his lips, but then the people parted and he saw her again, just under the exit sign as she smiled demurely up at her dance partner.

He shifted and moved through the crowd, just a few feet behind them. Just a second before they would have slid through the door, the woman stilled.

Shit.

Her head lifted, cocked as though she was listening to something the others couldn't hear. She stopped, resisting the flow of people around her as she turned her head, staring all around her, searching the faces around her, a watchful, intent look in her eyes.

Narrowing his eyes, he stilled himself as her gaze swung his way. As her eyes met his, he tried to force a casual smile, but it fell flat and he just stared at her.

Busted . . .

A frown crossed her face as she slid her tongue out, staring into his eyes for a moment. Did she recognize him? He had no idea. It had taken him a moment to place her face, but if he could figure out who she was, she could sure as hell do the same with him.

But there was no recognition in her gaze—just an awareness, a watchful, intent look that any other predator would recognize.

The guy in front of her tugged on her hand and she turned and looked at him.

Whatever the poor schmuck saw on her face was enough to make the man's eyes narrow, something scared flit through his eyes. And then he jerked away, snarling something at her before he took off running down the street. As he disappeared into the shadows, the woman propped her hands on her hips, shaking her head in disgust.

She spun around and met his eyes and he felt the effects of her gaze like a punch in the gut. Damn it, she was beautiful.

How could that delicate, soft woman have killed people? Killed Duke?

Murderers shouldn't look that good.

Shouldn't look so sweet and kissable.

Her face was heart-shaped, a cute little nose that tilted up at the tip, high cheekbones, and a wide, mobile mouth. The loose strands of hair spilling down from the knot on top made him wonder just how easy it would be to make the rest of her hair fall down.

No. A murderess shouldn't look like that.

Taking a step forward, he moved his hand to the gun at the small of his back, but she spun away from him, and before he could even blink she disappeared down the street.

*B*LOODY *hell.*
   Standing in the door of the club, she met Aaron's eyes and watched as the knowledge bloomed there.

His thoughts were plainly read and she almost laughed at the one phrase that circled through his mind: *Cop-bitch.*

Nothing terribly original, but she hadn't really expected that either.

"Cop-cunt . . . you got lucky," he sneered arrogantly.

A smile curved her lips as she purred, "Lucky?" Kendall flashed fang prettily, watching as the nerves bloomed into fear. He spun away and took off running, sliding in and out of the people entering the bar. She started to go after him, but she felt those eyes on her neck and stiffened, turning back around. Who was watching—

That man—the one she had seen watching her from time to time in the bar. He had a killer's eyes, the flat, empty gaze of a man who had killed before and would again.

Not a murderer.

But a hunter.

She recognized that in him, for that was what she was. Birds of a feather . . . the phrase circled through her mind as she looked at him through the smoke-filled air.

For one brief second, she saw her death in his eyes, but she spun away and took off, following the rank scent of fear that trailed behind Aaron Meyer. That bastard had killed four women in the past six months.

She'd be damned if she let him kill another one.

* * *

THE hunt took a little more than she'd planned, since the mystery man had broken her focus and she let the mask she showed to the world falter and drop, showing Aaron Meyer the predator, when he had thought she was the prey.

But all's well that ends well. Eh, not that it had ended too well. Four women dead. The papers had speculated on the brutality of the murders, but they hadn't even skimmed the surface. Touching his mind had left her feeling dirty.

And since she ended up placing him under a compulsion, she felt like she had been swimming through a pool of shit, and the stains it had left weren't likely to ever fade away completely.

Not all the monsters were of the Hollywood variety. Or even like her.

Some of the most foul, perverted creatures she had ever met were humans, neither shifter, nor vampire, nor magick bearer. Just human . . . nasty, evil human.

Job done, Kendall returned to her hotel, turning on the TV before going to stand at the window, watching as the horizon slowly lightened. Sunrise . . . she loved sunrises.

For the past seventy-two years, she had been able to tolerate watching the sun rise, and as time passed, her tolerance for the purity of sunlight increased. Now she no longer had to fear bursting into flames if somebody managed to toss her into the light for a minute or two.

It had happened before, packs of ferals hunting down the Hunters and using the vampire's natural weaknesses against him. That very real fear was the reason so many vampires still preferred to keep underground during the daylight hours.

Not Kendall.

She'd spent too much time in darkness, and before the sun started to sting her sensitive skin, she had every intention of enjoying as much of the sunlight as she could. So for nearly thirty minutes, she stood at the window, watching the sky bleed from blue to lavender then gold, all the clouds a wispy pink.

By the time the sky was summer blue, though, her skin was pink and starting to burn.

Twenty-nine minutes, she mused. With a sardonic smile, she thought maybe by the time she saw another century pass, she could tolerate the sun for a couple of hours.

When the news came on, she closed the curtains, securing them thoroughly and shoving a chair under the doorknob before cuddling against the headboard to watch. The chair wouldn't keep out anybody stronger than a mortal, but she wasn't worried about keeping anybody out.

She just wanted to be awake should a fight come.

A slow smile spread across her lips as the reporter stared soberly into the camera and said, "The reign of terror in Hanover has ended. The police were given an anonymous tip about the identity of the killer, and when the they went to question him, he confessed and turned himself in without a fight. His car fits the description of the vehicle one of the victims was last seen entering, a car that is similar to that of a man who was just released this morning. Porter Jenkins, it seems, is no longer a suspect . . ."

The reporter droned on, never once cracking a smile as she gestured over her shoulder to the police department, but Kendall tuned her voice out and just smiled, closing her eyes and cuddling into the blankets with satisfaction.

Job done. He'd be spending some good, hard time in prison. The compulsion she had placed within his mind would weaken and fade, but it would take years. The threads of his mind were weak, easily subverted, and it would take a long time for his personality to reassert itself, years before he started to question why in the hell he'd made a confession.

And Kendall had the feeling, pretty boy that he was, once he got inside a prison, he'd come to understand feelings of helplessness and terror.

Fitting punishment.

It was with a smile that she settled down to sleep, completely unaware of the man that was hunting *her*.

*   *   *

K ANE Winter stood at the bar, losing his patience, although no sign of it showed on his face. Blank, impassive stares tended to disturb people more than angry ones.

"She was here, last night, with a tall blond guy," he repeated, edging the picture a little closer to the guy manning
the bar. "Had a surfer boy look to him."

Giving the picture a cursory glance, he lifted one shoulder, the stud in his left nostril reflecting light back at Kane
as he said, "Don't know her. I know the regulars. She's not
one of them." With a small smile, he said, "Girl that looks
like that will catch some notice." Then he cocked his head,
a thoughtful look entering his eyes as he asked, "Tall blond
guy? Looks like Malibu Ken?"

Kane cracked a grin at the description of the surfer boy
the vampire had been dancing with. "That would be him."
He reached inside his jacket and drew out one of the digital
pictures he'd printed out that morning—this one was a pro-
file of the woman and Malibu while they pretended to dance.
"Malibu Ken?"

"Yup." Now both of the bartender's brows shot up, disappearing under the shag of his matte black hair. "Now *he* was
a regular."

Hot satisfaction jolted through Kane and he reached into
his pocket, laying a twenty down on the bar by the picture,
waiting until the bartender's eyes met his. "Got a name?"

Now the bartender grinned, looking every bit as young as
Kane suspected he was. "Sure do. And that's the easiest
twenty bucks I ever made. Name's Aaron Meyer. And I can
even tell you where to find him."

Kane let go of the twenty and the kid pocketed it before
lifting a hand and pointing over Kane's shoulder. "He's in
the Clark County jail. Admitted to killing four girls."

Kane turned to stare at the TV screen as a reporter gestured behind her to a building. There was a picture in the
corner of the screen, a photo of a blond man. Across the bot-

tom of the screen, Kane read, *Madison man admits to rap-ing, killing four girls in Hanover.*

Hours later, he'd read through several newspaper reports and every article online. There was no mention of a woman. No redhead partner in crime, no lovely, delicate, nameless victim.

Clenching his jaw, he stood up and started to pace the room. She wasn't around here any more. If she was . . . hell, he would have felt it. It had been an edgy feeling that guided him to that bar, and that edgy feeling was the same one he followed when he was tracking down the vamps.

She was long gone, Kane suspected, and he had no clue where to look for her.

Aaron Meyer's face stared up at him from the newspaper and Kane paused, staring down at it. Well, he might not have a clue.

But maybe this guy would. Or at least a *name*.

Checking the time, he scowled. No way he'd get into see him tonight. Wearily, he dropped down on the bed, flopping back and staring up at the ceiling. *Damn it all to hell.*

Early the next morning, he drove down the two-lane road that led from Madison, Indiana, to Jeffersonville. The courthouse and jail were housed in the same building, and as he jogged up the steps, he was surrounded by cops, lawyers in their suits, and civilians dressed in everything from the bright orange of jail uniforms to suit and tie.

After signing in, he was left to pace the waiting room as he waited for Aaron Meyer to come out.

A name. That was all he wanted. Now an address would be wonderful, but just a name would be great. With his con-nections, he could feed a name into a computer and if there was any information on her, he'd have it in minutes. But re-alistically, he wasn't expecting much.

How likely was it she'd given him a real name?

Maybe he'd get lucky. Damn it, he had seen her last night for a reason. Not just to have her slip through his hands. Trying to chase after her had been like trying to catch smoke, elusive, impossible.

A guard appeared at the door and beckoned and Kane fell into step behind him, following him down a hall. "You a reporter?" the officer asked.

"No. Private investigations, trying to find somebody for a client. She was seen with your suspect. Hoping maybe he has some information, and he's feeling cooperative enough to share it," Kane lied smoothly.

The officer laughed as he stopped in front of a door and opened it, gesturing inside to the single chair facing the viewing glass. On the other side, Aaron Meyer sat in shackles, an armed guard at his back. "Oh, he's cooperative. Driving his lawyer nuts. He tells us everything we want to know." Then the officer scowled, disgust flashing in his eyes. "And some things we don't want to know. He's a sick bastard. Hope your client didn't spend much time with him. If she did, you may never find her."

Kane clamped his mouth shut around the question that had been forming in his mind as the guard stepped out and closed the door. Over the viewing glass was a sign that informed him that his conversation was being recorded. Taking the picture out, he held it up to the glass and said, "You were seen with this girl. Know who she is?"

Aaron smiled pleasantly. There was a look in his eyes—blank, almost dead. Like a doll's eyes. "Her name is Kendall. We danced a few times." Then his eyes got cloudy and he reached up, rubbing his temple. "We were going to my house. I was going to knock her out. Tie her up. Have some fun. They always scream so loud . . ."

Kane felt a cold chill run up his spine as Meyer smiled vaguely. *They always scream so loud.*

"They?" Kane asked levelly.

"The girls. Girls scream better than the boys . . . though I've played with some boys before, too. I just take a few of them, you know. Have a little fun. They break so easy. But she didn't . . . she was just gone. Just gone . . ." Meyer murmured, reaching up and touching his fingers to the glass, staring intently at Kendall's picture.

"Got a name for her? Anything besides Kendall?"

"Kendall. She just told me Kendall . . . and then she was gone."

Suppressing a snarl, Kane said, "I got that part. Gone before you could tie her up, have some fun listening to her scream."

"Oh, that's not the fun part. That's just a bonus. The fun part is seeing the look in their eyes when I hurt them. I really like that look," Aaron murmured, dropping his hand away and tucking it back in his lap.

Fuck. This guy was a damned loony toon. So far, insanity wasn't figuring into his case, but Kane knew a crazy bastard when he saw one. And this guy might as well be standing at a busy intersection wearing nothing but shoe polish and a sign that said, *I am the One, the savior to the world.*

He knocked for the guard and cast one last look over his shoulder at Aaron Meyer. "How did you all catch him?" he asked. "Better question, how did you *not* catch him before this? That guy is nuts. And I'm not talking Hannibal Lecter, brilliant but psycho nuts either."

A slight smile cracked the guard's impassive face and he said, "An anonymous tip. Led us right to him—from what I've heard, it's like the guy is pulling a Sybil, first he was acting just as cool as a cucumber when the investigating officers went to his house, and then once they started finding the grim trophies, he confessed. Just as pretty as you please. We keep waiting for the other shoe to drop, but so far, nothing. This has been the most uneventful major crime we've had in this area for a long time, if ever."

Kane flashed the picture at the officer and asked, "You ever seen her?"

The officer studied the picture briefly and just shook his head. "No, not familiar. You find her, let the investigating officer know. He may like to have a word with her, seeing as how she's wrapped pretty tight around Meyer there. *If you* find her. Have to wonder if that bastard has other victims we don't know about. That's the third time he's mentioned *boys,* but we've yet to find any male victims that fit."

Kane nodded and assured him, "Will do." Of course, he was lying. Once he found her, she was not going to be in any condition to talk to the police. "What about this anonymous tip?"

"Nothing to tell there. Call came through the desk and the woman wasn't on the phone no more than a minute. The girl in Dispatch that talked to her said she sounded young, but not a kid. Low voice. Nothing distinctive. Call came from a pay phone at a gas station. Nothing caught on film, and the attendants at the station don't remember seeing anybody using the phone."

Kane fell silent as the officer led him back out. He murmured the obligatory appreciation before he started back down the hall, the low hum of the florescent lights buzzing in his ears.

"So close, yet so far away," he murmured, leaving the county building behind as he strode out into the bright sunlight.

Lifting the picture, he studied her face again. "At least I got a name." With a soft laugh, he added, "Might be nice, though, if it had come with a last name."

CHAPTER 2

A WEEK had passed since she'd taken Aaron Meyers off the streets. She'd had three days of peace . . . and now she had a trainee with her.

She was familiar with him—the shape-shifter had been injured by a feral vampire sometime back. A year, maybe? Kendall couldn't keep track of time anymore.

Duke Monroe was a little unusual. He wasn't a werewolf, wasn't an Inherent wolf either. Not a wolf at all. The form he shifted into was that of a giant cat. He looked like a mountain lion on steroids. He didn't have to wait until a full moon to shift, but the moon did have some pull on him. He didn't have to change with it, but he'd told Kendall that he tended to get a little distracted then.

Maybe that would explain why he kept getting that vague, wild look in his eyes. It was well past sunset when they left the hotel, and the moon was shining high in the sky. Duke stood staring up at it for a long moment, almost mesmerized.

Kendall sighed. He may not be a werewolf, but the moon made him weaker. She'd be damned if she'd take him out Hunting like this. He needed to hunt, to run, to find a bunny rabbit or a deer or something. Taking him out on the streets like that was just asking for trouble.

He was still staring up at the moon when she climbed into her car. She waited patiently until he climbed in. This was why she didn't want a partner. Shape-shifters were almost as bad as witches—too fey, almost like they heard voices that nobody who wasn't like them could hear.

As they headed out of town, Duke finally seemed to realize where, and maybe who he was, looking around him curiously. "I thought we were going downtown," he murmured.

With a smile, she said, "You're no good to me right now, Duke. No good to me or to yourself. No way I can take you Hunting when you're all but worshipping the moon."

Duke gave her a sheepish smile. "It's been a little while since I changed. The moon makes it harder . . ." His voice trailed off, lids drooping.

Kendall murmured, "So I see. I'm not much on orders, but here's one for you. Stop going so long—I don't know *why* you haven't been shifting much, but if this is what the full moon does to you, you can't keep it up."

Duke smiled a little. "I'm fine."

Kendall quirked a brow. "If I were to take you around somebody hurt and bleeding, what little control you have just might snap. And that's what we do, deal with hurt and bleeding people."

Duke had no comment to that, and within fifteen minutes, they were past the Gene Snyder Freeway and she pulled off on the side of the road. Smirking at him a little, she asked, "I assume you can find your way back to the hotel?"

As he opened the door, Duke flashed her a wide grin. That was her only answer as he was gone in seconds. A moment later, she felt power ripple through the air and she smiled as she heard the mighty roar echo through the night.

With that problem solved, she turned her attention to the matter of her own hunger. Kendall had to feed. Hunger had been gnawing at her belly, and she couldn't keep ignoring it.

She'd been through Louisville often enough, but in the

past few years it had changed a lot. She hadn't ever been to this nightclub. It was situated in the middle of Fourth Street, between two giant neon orange guitars. There were several bars in there, but she liked the looks of this one. The men at the door turned several people away, but she sauntered in without a problem and made her way to the bar.

A drink would be nice. And then a dance partner . . . some good-looking man, a few slow dances, and then she'd lead him into one of the shadowed areas and feed, or maybe outside. A smile curved her lips as she felt somebody sliding into the chair beside her.

But she went stiff as she turned and found herself staring into a pair of bottle green eyes. *Shit.* Still, she smiled at him, tossing her hair back as she accepted her rum and Coke from the bartender.

Only sheer will kept her from dropping it though as the man leaned toward her and drawled, "I didn't know vampires could drink that stuff."

Lifting it to her lips, she sipped at it, refusing the urge to toss it back and demand another. Arching a brow at him, she gave him a quizzical stare. "Pardon?"

He grinned at her. "So how did Meyers end up in jail? He piss you off?"

Chilled to the bone, she studied him. She knew his face from somewhere. But she had no idea where. "Do I know you?"

He shrugged. "Not so much. But don't worry, we'll take care of that. The name is Kane. Might want to remember it—it's likely going to be the last name you hear."

Kendall laughed, sitting her drink back down. She shifted on the stool, bracing her body. "You're an arrogant one, aren't you?"

He knew what she was. She didn't know exactly how, but he knew. And he didn't like her. She'd run into his kind before, the kind who assumed vampires were like something out of *Buffy the Vampire Slayer* or out of Bram Stoker's books—all vampires were monsters, soulless creatures intent on nothing more than killing to feed their ravenous hungers.

Kane shrugged. "Not really."

Coolly, she asked, "You have any idea what kind of mess you're asking for?"

The slow, confident smile that spread across his lips made a chill run down her spine. There was a knowledge in his eyes, and she didn't like it one bit. "Cleaning up messes is what I do best."

She just stared at him. What in the hell had she gotten into? He was mortal— and she couldn't feel any evil inside him. That was too damned bad. If he'd been evil, Kendall could just take care of him . . . and feed. But the empty ache of hunger in her belly would just have to remain a little while longer. Because she couldn't kill him.

But she couldn't linger around here either.

She rose slowly, aware of the fact that he watched her with the eyes of a predator. "Well, sweetheart, this is one mess you'll have to pass on."

It wasn't always wise, using her abilities in a crowd like this, but this was just not a good place to be right now.

She slid through the bodies, winding her way to the back of the bar. The shadows were a little deeper there and she drew them around herself, cloaking herself in them as she searched for another exit. Not hitting the front door, no way.

There was an employee door, though, and she made her way to it, looking all around her. Kane was watching the wrong way, moving away from her with a look of disbelief on his face.

With a slight smile, she opened the door and found herself in the kitchen. A stocky red-haired man with a chef's cap glared at her. "Miss, you can't be in here."

Three or four pairs of eyes turned her way and she smiled, making sure she met each of their gazes. "I'm not in here. You didn't see me. Nobody came through here."

"I'M sorry, sir. I didn't see anybody. Nobody came through here."

Kane resisted the urge to growl. He'd heard that line from

every damned person he'd talked to. Just like last week, she'd disappeared, as elusive as smoke.

Hours later, he finally gave up. The bars around him were closing down and damn it all, he hadn't had so much as one beer, a single bite to eat . . . and the main reason he'd come to Fourth Street, well, that hadn't happened either.

He'd come here with the express intention of getting laid, and instead of finding a lady to help him with that goal, he'd ended up searching for a woman who disappeared like smoke.

Driving back to the hotel, he rubbed at his bleary eyes with one hand before glancing at the clock. Past five thirty. His stomach growled demandingly but he was too damned tired to find an all-night place.

He'd just go to the hotel and crash. Sleep . . . eat when he woke up. And then he'd start looking for the mysterious Kendall once more. Look for her, find her, and then finish her off before she even realized he was there.

D IGGING the keys out of her pocket, she headed for her car. Behind her, she could still hear the low throb of music, and the scents of life that filled the air were driving her crazy.

But she didn't have time to feed. She needed to get away from that man—*Kane*—before he managed to get on her tail again.

At that thought, an odd flicker of heat moved through her, followed by images that made a different sort of hunger surge through her.

"You've lost your mind," she muttered, shaking her head.

But the images haunted her thoughts as she headed back to the hotel, and another long night plagued by hunger.

K ENDALL stared, stupefied at the man closing in her. There was just no fucking way.

How did he keep finding her like this?

He was *human*. He wasn't a vampire, a werewolf, *anything* . . . just human. He couldn't possibly be tracking her by scent the way a vampire or wolf could. He wasn't a witch, so he couldn't be using magick.

But whatever means he was using to track her was just as efficient, as evidenced by the fact that she had no more entered the bar than she had sensed him.

It was that sense of purpose emanating from him that had warned her. Many vampires could read minds, but it wasn't exactly mind reading she used. Mind reading, for the most part, required being a little closer to the intended victim than she planned on getting.

Their senses were hyperacute, hearing, sight, smell, taste . . . instinct. And the deadly purpose that seemed to surround this man was what had warned her.

He needed to practice acting like a sheep a little more.

And she needed to figure out how in the hell he was doing this. Before he got too close to her, Kendall took off, working her way through the crowds. Once she got off of Fourth Street, the crowds lessened and she started to jog, intent on putting some distance between them.

She felt him though, closing in on her. Hissing out a breath, she ducked into an alley between a little Indian restaurant and a parking garage. Sliding her gaze upward, she checked out the old-fashioned fire escape and then glanced around her one more time.

Leaping upward, she closed her hands around the metal edge and pulled herself up. There, she watched and waited, and sure enough, within seconds, he was at the mouth of the alley.

She didn't like the look in his eyes. Not at all.

Even in the dim light, she could see the grim smile on that carved mouth, his hand idly caressing the knife at his hip.

The sight of that smile set her heart pounding, apprehension pooling in her belly. The saliva dried in her mouth as she started to feel the first edge of fear, something she hadn't felt in a long time.

Closing her eyes, she focused on breathing. Even though

she didn't need oxygen, there was something soothing about the simple act of drawing air in, and holding it for a moment before slowly blowing it back out. Her heart slowed back to its normal pace.

Sliding into a light trance, she forced her chaotic emotions to calm. He couldn't see her here. It was too dark. The streetlight at the mouth of the alley was out and there were no lights coming from the businesses around them. She could hide in the darkness and wait him out.

Hell, what she *needed* to do was face him and find out why in the hell he wanted her. But he had her death in his eyes, and she knew what was likely to happen if he became too much of a threat. Her instincts would kick in and one of them would end up dead. And Kendall doubted it would be her.

Smart or not, fast or not, he was a human and he was trying to face down a three-hundred-year-old vampire.

Within seconds, he was as lost in shadows as she was, and only her extraordinary night sight made it possible for her to see him. No mortal should be able to move like that, she mused.

He glided through the alley below her like a poisoned wind, silent and deadly.

She could hear the steady beat of his heart, his calm, easy breaths. Not afraid at all. Huffing out a slight breath, she sulked a little. Damn it, she was a damned vampire . . . and she was afraid of this mortal.

Below her, Kane stilled, cocking his head and listening. The words *oh, shit* made a brief trek through her mind but she didn't say them. Stepping back away from the railing, she hid in the deepest of shadows. Vampire magick made them seem deeper than they truly were and she should have felt safe and secure in the darkness.

But as she watched, he lifted his head and looked up, exactly at the spot where she had stood.

There was no way he could have heard that tiny sound. Was there?

He's human! If he was not human, she would have been able to tell. The scent of his blood, the way he breathed and moved—something would have told her. But no human should have heard that small exhalation.

As she watched a small smile curled his lips, and then he moved on. Within seconds, he was lost to the darkness and her heart started to slam against her ribs as she tried to find him.

She dragged her hands over the tight braid she'd captured her hair in and spun around, nervously pacing the small space.

Kendall had the oddest feeling—he had seen her. He knew exactly where she had been standing, the entire time.

"He's playing with me," she muttered. The idea pissed her off completely and she snarled, tensing the muscles in her body and then leaping for the edge of the roof. Her fingers bit into the old brick and she hauled her weight up.

The hair on the back of her neck stood up, and seconds before the arrow came flying out of the night, she let go, falling back into the concealing shadows. Her fangs dropped and the pace of her heart kicked up as she stared through the shadows.

Oh, she saw him now.

He hid in the shadows almost as well as she did—so well that all she saw was the glitter of his eyes as he searched the shadows for her. "Tricky bastard," she said quietly, arching a brow as she rose from her crouch on the fire escape.

Crossing her arms on her chest, she leaned against the wall, never taking her eyes from the shadow that hid in the darkness. "That's okay, buddy. I can wait awhile," she whispered.

K ANE knew his arrow hadn't hit.

The bitch hadn't gone on the roof, but he didn't think she'd left the tiny landing of the fire escape either. Would she stay there, a sitting duck?

He wasn't sure—she was a smart thing. She hadn't even seen him earlier, he knew that, but she'd known he was there in the bar.

Yes, he decided, she was still there, watching and waiting. Measuring him, most likely.

He didn't close the distance though—Kane was starting to suspect she wouldn't be as easy to kill as some of the other vamps he'd faced. He was at a distinct disadvantage right now—closing the distance could mean getting his own neck ripped wide open.

Idly, he stroked the crossbow in his hand, staring into the darkness where she hid. He could simply shoot—in his gut, he could hit her, he knew, even without seeing her.

But he didn't. Shooting blindly was likely to end with her dead. And he didn't want her dead just yet. He had to see her . . . had to know. None of the others had mattered as much, but she did.

He had to know why she'd killed Duke.

"That's okay, doll," he said, flashing a toothy smile in her direction. "You can't wait forever."

Nearly two hours later, he had to admit she sure as hell was patient.

Edginess rose inside him. So damned close—she was so fucking close—but his gut kept screaming at him not to close the distance, not to shoot.

His fingers tightened on his crossbow and he imagined just firing, shooting arrow after arrow until he'd pierced her black heart. He just . . . couldn't, though.

A scowl darkened his face as his hand fell from the crossbow.

A slight sigh in the air made him stiffen and he squinted, staring through the shroud of darkness, trying to see her again. He knew she was there; he could feel her.

But she continued to wait there even as dawn edged closer.

Finally he rose out of the shadows and stepped forward. "Sun's rising. Even though part of me wants to kill you personally, that will work just as well, doll," he said, keeping his voice low.

There was a shift of movement above him, and then she leaned forward for just a second, showing her face in the faint light of the moon, just long enough for him to see her lid drop in a slow, flirtatious wink. "Sun isn't as deadly to me as you probably think. Not anymore."

And then, as he watched, she *backflipped* onto the roof, like some gymnast on steroids. Before he could even raise his crossbow, the bitch was gone.

Damn it, she was playing with him.

Hours later, he was still fuming over it. Slamming his fist down on the counter of the small kitchenette, he muttered, "Fuck!"

If she could move that fast . . . why in the hell was he still alive? She could have closed that distance between them and ripped out his throat before he even knew what was happening.

Brooding in the silence of his hotel room, he paced, wearing nothing but a black pair of pants. They were a variation of the uniform, called battle dress uniform or BDUs, that he and Duke had worn in the Army. Instead of the multishaded green, it was solid black, but cut the same.

Running his hands through his hair, he linked them behind his neck as he replayed those last few seconds in the alley over and over in his mind.

"Hell, I fired a damn arrow at her. You'd think she would be a little pissed," he muttered, jerking the fridge open and grabbing the half-empty carton of milk. He drained it and tossed it in the garbage before turning to stare at the door.

Half of him wanted to grab his bag and head back out there. Search the city until he found her.

And it would be a waste of time. He hadn't *found* her any of these times. She was just there. Always where he was, always when he was.

Rage brewed inside as he stalked through the small confines of the hotel suite. Kane shucked the pants, letting them fall to the floor. The long silver chain on his neck glinted in the light as he dropped onto the edge of the mattress, bracing his elbows on his knees and leaning forward, staring into nothingness.

Hunting this woman was driving him nuts.

DUKE watched her with bemused eyes as they sped down the interstate.

"Weren't you the one fussing at me for not changing before the full moon? Something to do with control?"

Sliding him an irritable glance, she just shrugged.

"You haven't fed."

"I'm aware of that," she said shortly. It had been damned near a week since she'd fed at all, and nerves were eating away at her reserves.

"And doesn't being hungry push your control a little hard?"

Narrowing her eyes, she slid him a look. "I'm more than three hundred years old, Duke. I can control my hunger a little better than most."

"But why should you?"

Scowling, she said, "I don't have a choice. I tried to feed last night and the night before and I was . . . interrupted."

In a terse voice, she relayed the information about her new stalker as they headed for a different area of town. The people they would be Hunting weren't likely to be found in a ritzy bar. They headed for the projects. Kendall had been keeping her ears open, and there was an increased drug problem in the west end, as well as a rise in reports of sexual crimes.

There, they'd Hunt, and she'd finally feed.

"Why is he tailing you?" Duke asked when she finally finished.

"He wants me dead," she replied wryly. They took the exit off I-64 and she slowed at the stoplight at the bottom of the ramp before meeting Duke's eyes for a brief moment. "That's all there is to it."

"But why?"

With a sad smile, she said, "I'm not human—for some people, that's enough."

Duke fell into silence as they drove into a gravel-filled parking lot. The bar was a lot more rundown than the ones on Fourth Street, and the air was ripe with the scents of sweat and blood. And if she wasn't mistaken . . . cocaine.

A grin tugged up the corners of Duke's mouth and he said, "Well, there will be some people here who are okay with us not being human." As he spoke, Kendall followed his line of sight and they both watched as through the shadows, one man was pinned to the ground while three other men circled around him.

Kendall gestured toward them. "Be my guest—I'm going inside." There was something in there . . . her eyes stung a little from the smoke that poured out as she opened the door. The smoke was thick enough to choke somebody, she thought, wrinkling her nose a little as she headed for the bar.

Her stomach wrenched at a familiar smell. Blood . . . it stank of fear. It wasn't fresh. Somebody had been hurt in here. Recently. The air was stale with all the fear she scented.

She propped one hip on the edge of a bar stool, leaning against it and trying not to think of how long it had been since this place had been cleaned. The floor was littered with cigarette butts, peanut shells, and a million other things. The surface of the bar felt sort of greasy under her hand, the way something felt when it hadn't been wiped down in a long, long time.

But she plastered a smile on her face and asked for a Bud when the bartender looked her way. At least *that* she could drink from the bottle.

"Well, aren't you a pretty thing . . ."

Duke watched as the man shoved himself up from the ground, his legs unsteady. At least he was on his feet, though.

"You need to get out of here."

The guy just mumbled under his breath as he stumbled away. He wouldn't call the police. People in neighborhoods like this usually didn't trust the police enough to even think of contacting them.

His sharp ears heard the back door opening and then Kendall's voice. Two men . . . one stank of blood. Not his own. He'd made somebody bleed. And had fun doing it.

The other three men that Duke had taken care of were still unconscious. They'd likely be that way for a good long while. One of them might never wake up. Duke's sharp sense of smell could detect excessive blood, although there wasn't any on the ground. Brain bleed, he figured. He wasn't particularly sorry about that. These men had been asking for trouble for a long time, and the guy who had the worst injuries had been getting ready to gut the man who was still running away.

Sliding in the shadows, Duke leaned back against the wall, curious about watching her work.

She was the first vampire he'd ever met, although he didn't remember much of the night she'd found him two years earlier. He'd known they existed, just hadn't ever seen one.

And Kendall was the first vampire they'd paired him with.

All new Hunters had to spend time in formal training—in the States, they went to Excelsior. To the general public, Excelsior was a school for the troubled and gifted. In reality, it was home to paranormal creatures that would become Hunters.

After about six months in Excelsior, they'd decided he really didn't need them and had paired him off with a were-wolf. That hadn't lasted overly long, about four months—Duke wasn't a werewolf, but he was too much an Alpha in his own right to tolerate another one very well.

So they'd brought him back to the school and after a few more weeks, they paired him with a pretty red-haired witch in West Virginia.

Now that had been going well enough, but Lori's husband hadn't cared for Duke.

That had lasted about a year and then some obscure message came for him to return to Excelsior. He was there a week and then he was sent here, told to wait for Kendall. Why her, he wasn't sure, but he figured it had something to do with her being a female. Women didn't set his nerves on edge quite the way men did, and so far, they were getting along fairly well.

And she was damned easy on the eyes.

Apparently the two men with her thought so, too. They were too busy staring at her to even realize they had an audience. They also weren't much on foreplay, either.

The minute they had her in the alley, one moved behind her. The second his arms came up to pin hers, Duke had the pleasure of watching her go from flirt to fighter. Her head slammed back and Duke heard bone and cartilage crunch. The scent of blood filled the air as the man fell down howling, his hands covering his busted nose.

"I bet that hurt," Duke murmured quietly, wincing a little.

"Bitch!"

She ducked as the man in front of her tried to swing at her and came up behind him, silent as a whisper. Duke felt her power roll through the air as she struck, her fangs sinking into his neck. Duke suspected she was sinking into the man's mind as well.

The man hadn't even screamed, just whimpered, his eyes glazed with terror. The feel of power in the air swelled, and then it was gone. The man fell bonelessly to the ground, sobbing like a baby. "Remember what I told you," Kendall said obliquely. And then she focused her gaze on the man who'd tried to grab her from behind.

"Didn't anybody ever tell you it's not nice to grab people?" she asked, squatting down behind him.

"Get away from him."

Duke froze at the sound of that voice. *Familiar* . . .

*   *   *

KENDALL fought the urge to snarl as she stood and turned, facing the blond moving toward her. His hair was almost colorless in the faint light and half of his face was in shadow.

But she knew who it was.

Kane . . . her very dedicated stalker.

"But he's *such* a charming man," she drawled, tongue in cheek. Glancing down at the man who stared up at her with wide eyes, she smiled a little. *Be still . . . I'll deal with you in a minute,* she whispered into his mind. He just cringed and said nothing.

"And that's why he's bleeding? Why his friend is laying there with two bloody holes in his neck?"

Kendall shrugged. "They were looking for a little more than a dance."

"Then you shouldn't have come out here with them."

Kendall grinned. "But if I hadn't, then the next woman they brought out here might not have been able to get away like I can."

"So it's altruistic, what you do?" Kane said flatly. "Like I'm going to buy that. I've seen you in action."

Arching a brow at him, she asked, "And where on earth did this happen? You've got a familiar face, but I'll be damned if I can remember where I saw you."

"A couple of years ago. The night you killed my best friend."

Kendall felt something inside her still. She'd killed a lot of people. She was well aware of that, and the blood on her soul didn't rest much easier just from knowing the people she'd killed deserved death. There were a lot of people who'd want her dead if they knew what she did—even if she was human. She wasn't, so that made the problem a little trickier. But she wasn't going to let some man kill her because she believed in doing her job. "I'm afraid I don't know who you are talking about . . . but I don't kill unless I have to."

"And what constitutes having to? Being hungry?" he demanded, taking another step closer.

That was when she noticed what he held in his hand, that fucking crossbow. "No. I don't kill because I need to feed."

"Then what was it I just saw?" he demanded.

Narrowing her eyes, she took her gaze away from the crossbow just long enough to sneer at him. "It's called justice. That man reeks of so much blood and pain, it almost makes me sick. And he's nowhere near dead. I barely took enough to weaken him. But he'll think twice before he tries to pull this with another woman."

"So now I'm expected to believe you're a vigilante? A killer with a cause?" He snorted, shaking his head. "You killed my friend. I was there. I saw your face right before you did something to my head. And when I got out of the hospital, Duke was dead."

Her eyes narrowed. Time spun away as she remembered a night years earlier, when she and another Hunter had tracked down a feral vampire named Anton. There'd been a human there, one who resisted her mental commands . . . the night she'd found a shape-shifter and taken him to a Healer to save his life.

"You," she whispered.

"Son of a bitch . . ." the low whisper came from behind her.

Duke moved from the shadows, and when he stepped into the light, she watched the man in front of them go pale, his hand falling limply to his side as he stared at the shape-shifter.

"You . . . you . . . Duke?"

"Hell, Kane, what are you doing?"

"I saw your grave. You . . . you . . . you're dead." His gaze flickered back and forth between Kendall and Duke and her heart went out to him as she saw the anguish in his eyes. Anguish, disbelief . . . hope.

Duke glanced down at his body and then back at Kane with a small grin. "I feel pretty alive."

Kendall tensed as Kane swung his arm back up, aiming it at Duke with a blank expression. "You're one of them—she bit you, changed you."

Duke just laughed. "I'm a shape-shifter, Kane. I can't

be made a vampire. Just doesn't work that way. And I'm just *me*."

"Then why in the hell did you let me think you were dead!" Kane roared. He pivoted, and Kendall flinched as he flung his crossbow into the wall. As he spun back to face them, his eyes all but glowed with fury.

"He didn't have a choice," she said quietly. Reaching out, she laid a hand on Duke's arm, silencing anything he might have said. "You're right about one thing—he *is* one of us, but you have no idea who we are."

CHAPTER 3

THE bright florescent light glared down on them as the three sat down at a battered, scarred table at the all-night joint. The scent of food in the air did absolutely nothing for Kane as he leaned back, staring at Duke's face.

Alive. How in the hell was the bastard alive?

Duke shot him a narrow glance. "Quit staring at me like you expect me to turn into a ghost."

Kane scowled. "It's a not a ghost I'm worried about."

Across from them, the pretty redhead sneered. "He's more likely to turn into a ghost than what you expect."

"I'm not a vampire," Duke said quietly.

Kane turned his head, focusing on his friend's familiar face, a face he hadn't ever expected to see again. "How am I supposed to believe that?"

"Because I'm telling you."

"Why did you just disappear?"

Duke shrugged. "Like Kendall said, I kind of had to. These people . . . they are like me. Shape-shifters, were-wolves . . . and vampires. People who are different. I don't have to hide what I am from them. And we can make a difference. But I had to leave my life behind. The one I live now . . . well, I sometimes have to do things the law would frown on."

"And how does faking your death change things?"

Duke shrugged. "It wasn't just faked. Duke Monroe doesn't exist—no fingerprints on file, no physical description, nothing. There's no way I can be linked to Duke Monroe." He cracked a grin as he added, "Well, unless somebody who knows me sees me."

"No fingerprints . . .?"

Kendall smiled. "A lot of people disappear around us. Those who need safety find it. Those who need anonymity, for work, for whatever reason, they find it."

Kane glared at her. "You can't just make a person disappear."

She smiled, one elegant brow lifting as she studied him. "You want to bet?" Leaning forward, she held his gaze as she said quietly, "The lives we lead don't leave much room for a lot of luxuries. Friends, lovers, families, unless they are like us, they can be used against us. They become innocent casualties, and we don't like that."

"You make it sound like war."

"It's a lot closer to war than you'd like to think," she said huskily. Remembered pain lanced through her, and she prayed none of it showed on her face. "It *is* a war—and it's been going on for centuries. And it will continue to go on as long as this world turns."

Kane looked away from her, and she leaned back in her chair, watching his face as he looked at Duke. "This is how you want to live? Just leave your life behind like that?"

Duke was quiet for a long time and finally, he said, "I don't know if *want* is a good word. But it's what I have to do."

"*Why?*"

Later, Kane would remind himself that he'd asked. As Kendall argued in low tones with Duke, Kane leaned against the racy convertible. It was fire-engine red and without a doubt, one of the sleekest cars he'd ever seen. No surprise it belonged to Kendall. It was as smooth and sexy as its owner.

Right now, said owner was glaring at Duke, her hands fisted and propped on her hips. Their voices were far too quiet for Kane to hear a word they said, but he had a pretty good idea what they were arguing about.

As he sighed and shifted his stance against the car, Kendall turned on her heel, glaring at him.

Kane just lifted his brows, meeting her gaze silently. "I don't entirely believe everything you told me," he finally said.

She snorted, shoving a hand through her hair. Kane's eyes drifted to the silky dark-red strands and he wondered if they were as silken-soft as they looked. "Do you really think I *care* if you believe me or not?"

With a slow smile, Kane replied, "Well, you probably should. Because the only thing that kept me from putting a bolt through your chest was seeing Duke. And if I start thinking he's turned into a bloody monster—"

She started to laugh, her head tipping back, exposing the long, smooth line of her throat. "For the love of God, do you really think I'm going to be scared of a *human*?"

Kane narrowed his eyes at her. "Everybody can die, Kendall. Even vampires."

The laughter died as suddenly as it started as a chill rolled through the air. It felt like the temperature had dropped thirty degrees in seconds as she stood there staring at him with eyes that had started to glow and swirl. "You have no idea what you're facing."

Kane shrugged. "Another vampire. A splinter of wood through that heart and you're as dead as the others I've killed."

Tension rippled around them and Kane felt something pushing at the edges of his brain. She was trying to push inside his mind—she'd tried it before, as had several others. When he didn't do whatever in the hell she was trying to force on him, the pressure increased. His lids flickered as the shadow of pain started to bloom inside his mind, but he still held her gaze.

Seconds later, she lunged.

Kane brought his arm up.

At the sight of the Beretta in his hand, she froze. Her eyes narrowed as she stared at him. "Guns don't kill me, Kane."

He lifted one shoulder in a shrug. "No, but it will hurt you. And if I put a couple of bullets in your brain, or in your heart, it will slow you down. A lot. And then I can get my crossbow and put an arrow in your heart. *That* will kill you." Cocking his head, he studied her for a minute. "Aren't you going to try to make me put the gun down?"

"Kane, what in the hell are you doing?" Duke asked. His voice was weary and tired, but Kane didn't dare take his eyes from Kendall's face.

"I have to know, Duke. And you have to prove it to me."

"Know what?" Kendall voiced the question.

Duke, Kane suspected, already knew the answer. "I have to know why he walked. Why he let me think for two fucking years that he was dead."

All the tension in the air evaporated and Kane felt the temperature return to normal. He lowered his arm, finally looking away from Kendall as he slid his gun back into the holster at the small of his back. Across the parking lot, he met Duke's eyes and quietly said, "You were like a damned brother to me. We bled together—saved each other's lives a dozen times. *Why?*"

Duke shook his head. "I don't think I can explain it, Kane. But I can show you."

*Y*EAH, *I can understand why it couldn't be explained.*

Fear had lodged in Kane's chest, a cold, slimy weight that made breathing damned near impossible. He stood in the shadow cast by an old building, hardly able to see a damned thing, but that was an improvement.

There had been a light, but somebody had shot it out. Next to him, huddled into a tight ball, was a teenaged girl. Her face was cut and bleeding, bruised from a myriad of hands.

Duke and Kendall had led him on what seemed like an

aimless walk through the rougher part of Louisville, and impatience had simmered inside him as the silence stretched out. When they'd started to run, Kane had fallen behind and by the time he had caught up, the fight had already started.

There were people out there, but low growls punctuated the air, and he knew there were more than just humans. In the dim light, he caught sight of a furred body leaping through the air. It wasn't the pale golden color of Duke's cat form either.

It had looked like a . . . like a wolf. He had damned near run away before he had even gotten to them. The closer he had gotten, the harder it was to move, or breathe, or even think. He couldn't explain it—but it was like something was trying to keep him away. Make him afraid, make him want to run. It had been sort of like the night the vampires had come upon him and Duke all the months ago, but Kane had been able to think a little then. Able to move, able to function.

He couldn't now. His gun was still holstered at his back and his hands hung limply at his sides. It took everything he had inside him not to fall down beside the girl and sob like she was doing.

There was a yelp, followed by a thud, and suddenly, he could breathe again. The bands of terror that had been wrapping around him loosened and he sucked air in desperately as he knelt beside the girl. She cowered, cringing away from him, terror-stricken.

She was bruised, battered from head to toe, and she stank from sweat and blood and Kane didn't want to think of what else. Unable to think of anything else to do, he stripped off his shirt and tucked her inside it, murmuring quietly to her.

All around them were sounds of battle. Kane didn't know how anybody could see to fight at all. He could barely make out the pale circle of the girl's face and beyond them, all he could see were shadows lost in even darker shadows.

Another gunshot sounded in the night, followed by a squealing scream that ended abruptly. Silence fell and Kane went still, drawing his gun as he stared into the night, wishing to high heaven he could see better.

Then suddenly there was a light, a beam of it coming from the shadows and moving toward him. Lifting his gun, he aimed at the circle of light.

"Here."

When the light came hurtling toward him, he caught it out of reflex and turned it so that it shone in Duke's face. His friend was bloodied, four long cuts marring his face, starting at one temple and slashing down diagonally to end at his jaw. "Holy shit," Kane muttered.

Duke ignored him as he moved toward the girl. She caught sight of him and started trying to scuttle away, deep, ugly sobs ripping from her.

Kendall came up out of the darkness, moving up behind the girl. She touched her fingers to the girl's shoulder and Kane felt that . . . power, something indefinable, move through the air and then the girl slumped, her eyes closing.

Before she could collapse backward, Kendall caught her. At the look on her face, Kane's heart clenched. There was a bruise on her cheek—it hadn't been there earlier, but it looked days old already. A lone tear spilled down her cheek as she stared at the girl, falling unheeded as she brushed the girl's hair back.

"How did you know she was here?" Kane asked, his voice low and rough.

Behind him, Duke sighed. "We just do. That's just part of us."

CHAPTER 4

Kendall stared broodingly into nothingness.

It had been close to a week since the night she'd let Duke convince her to take his human friend out on a Hunt with them.

She hadn't seen him since, although she knew Duke had spent some time with him. That had been a few days earlier—they'd left Louisville since then and headed to Nashville. So far, this had proven to be as good a training ground now as it had been two decades earlier.

Duke didn't really need a trainer, she mused, dragging her eyes away from the brick wall she'd been contemplating as he finished dispatching the two drug dealers. Kendall moved her eyes to the child at her feet, managing to bank her fury—but just barely.

One of the dead men in the alley had been bartering his twelve-year-old daughter for drugs. One of the other dead men was the dealer who'd been interested. The only reason the other two dealers were alive was because they had shown no small amount of repulsion when the man had offered the girl in payment for drugs.

Kneeling, Kendall stroked a hand down the girl's hair. Her tear-stained face was relaxed and peaceful—the compulsion that Kendall had placed on her mind made sure of that. It also made sure the girl wouldn't remember any of this night.

Her mind was serene as Kendall linked with her briefly. There was nothing of power in the girl's mind.

If she'd had any kind of psychic gifts, any kind of supernatural power, Kendall could have taken the girl to Excelsior. Now they had to investigate what was going on in her home, and if her mother was the scum her father was, they'd have to find her a new one.

They'd done it before—a lot. It came with its own set of problems, creating a new identity for a child who could likely be seen all over the news. Her appearance would likely have to be changed some and a story fabricated to convince her of the necessity of what they were doing.

Sometimes, entire families were placed elsewhere—a mother with young kids who was trying to get away from a violent, criminal husband. The Hunters rarely trusted leaving the families behind. If one parent ended up dead or missing, they'd learned the hard way the remaining parent was often made a suspect.

Hearing footsteps, she glanced up to see Duke approaching. In the deep tan of his face, his eyes glowed and swirled with power, glittering, vaguely unfocused. Fights stirred up the blood lust—it was a problem that Kendall faced herself. Feeding was a little more of a problem for him, though. Although the shifters weren't forbidden from feeding on the people they killed in a Hunt, disposing of a body that had big missing chunks of flesh was a little hard.

His control was excellent though. She watched as he closed his eyes and dragged air into his lungs. The power floating around him seemed to make the surrounding air waver a little, and then it faded away into nothingness. When he looked at her again, his eyes were calm and sane. "Is she going to be okay?"

Kendall smiled a little. "Once we get her to somebody

that cares for her, she will be." With a shrug, she said, "The memory of this night is gone. She won't remember that her dad tried to sell her."

Memories, unwanted, unwelcome, started to run through her mind and Kendall shoved them back. There was an ache in her heart, but she didn't have the time or the luxury to soothe it.

As if there was even a way to do that. Shaking her head, she rose, dusting her hands off on her jeans before starting to kneel and take the girl. Duke was already there beside her though, his mouth grim, his eyes dark and unreadable. "I'll get her," he murmured.

Seconds later, they were sliding through the shadows, leaving the dead bodies and the other drug dealers behind them. The dealers were tied up—in a few more minutes, Kendall would make a call to the cops.

Both had enough coke on them to land them in jail for a pretty decent amount of time, and it was possible when they got out, they'd make a change for the better. Duke had certainly put the fear of God into them. They'd been staring at him wide-eyed with fright, not even noticing Kendall moving behind them.

"You two always move like that?"

Kendall's eyes narrowed. When Kane came out of the shadows, she stopped in her tracks and stared at him. "What in the hell are you doing here?" she demanded.

Duke shifted the girl he was holding and Kendall glanced at him. "Duke, get her home, figure out what the situation is. I'll meet you at the apartment in a few hours."

Duke's eyes narrowed. Kendall just lifted a brow at him. No, he didn't really need to be trained, but she was in charge. He returned her stare for a few more minutes and then slid Kane a glance. The two men held each other's gaze for long minutes and then Duke was gone, moving silently through the night as Kendall looked back to Kane.

"What are you doing here?" she asked shortly.

He shrugged, and Kendall found herself studying the width of his shoulders for a long moment. When he spoke, she jumped a little, feeling blood rush to her cheeks as she looked back to his face. His eyes were close to black in the dim light, but she had no trouble reading the heat there. Entirely too aware of her, and how aware she was of him.

Licking her lips, she shifted around, relying on the shadows to hide her face. She could still see him. The question, though, was why was she seeing him at all? "You never told me what you were doing here," she murmured.

Kane shrugged again. Her eyes narrowed as she saw the black strap of his bag over his shoulder. He'd had that bag every damned time she'd seen him. His bag of tricks. No doubt he had his crossbow tucked inside and plenty of bullets for the gun she knew he carried. He'd cleaned it recently. She could smell it.

"And I'm also curious why you're lugging that bag around."

Kane glanced at it before looking back in her direction. She could see him searching the shadows for her and she knew the minute he found her. Damned human—how could he do that? "Working."

Lost in her own thoughts, it took a minute to figure out what he was talking about. "Working?" she repeated. "Working how?"

But she had a bad feeling she already knew. He hadn't been hunting her when he'd found her. He'd just discovered her. How many others had he discovered?

He started to move toward her and Kendall felt her heart slam against her chest. Damn it, there was something about the way he moved—it made her want to find out if he moved like that all the time. The way that shirt stretched across his chest made her want to peel it away and explore the hard muscles underneath. And his jeans . . . her mouth went dry as she studied the way the denim cupped his sex, molded to long, powerful thighs.

Inside the lace of her bra, she felt her nipples peak, pressing against material that suddenly seemed too rough, too abrasive against her sensitive flesh. He crossed into the shadows where she stood, away from the circle of light on the sidewalk.

"It's sort of freelance work," he murmured. "I move around a lot. Go where I'm needed."

He was standing entirely too close. The heat of his body seemed to reach out and tease her, and his scent was hot and male, flooding her head, making her mouth water. Worse, he was stirring up hungers she had forgotten she even had. Her voice husky, she asked, "Doing what?"

He smiled at her. Oh, she suspected he could barely see her face, but he seemed to have an instinct as to where she was. His voice dropped and she had to suppress a shiver at that low, rough sound. "Whatever needs to be done."

Kendall forced a smile. "I get the weirdest feeling that you're avoiding answering my question."

Kane reached up and Kendall tensed as he cupped her cheek. His palm felt entirely too good against her skin. Slowly, she inched away, and as she moved his hand fell to his side. "I'm doing what I'm good at," he murmured.

She moved out of the shadows, circling around until she stood behind him. He turned, searching for her, and when he saw her standing there in the light, his eyes roamed over her body. How could somebody staring at her feel so damned arousing, she wondered helplessly. Closing her eyes for a minute, she forced herself to focus. Focus . . . *on what*?

He shifted and the motion made something inside his bag shift around. That soft, slight sound caught her attention and she found herself staring at his bag. "You're out hunting for vampires," she said flatly.

Kane smiled. "You're a quick one."

In a chilly voice, she said, "That's a livelihood that is sure to get you killed. And not all vampires deserve to get an arrow shot through their heart."

Kane's mouth curved up a little. "I haven't had the pleasure of meeting any . . . well, save you. As to my life expectancy, I'll take my chances. You do what you have to, right?"

Kendall shook her head. "But this isn't what you have to do," she said flatly. "It's what *we* have to do. You're human. Go live like one. Get a real job."

Kane moved toward her again, moving in a circle around her. "You know how Duke said he couldn't really explain it, but he was doing what he needed to do? I understood. I didn't understand how he could just leave his old life behind, but maybe I just didn't think about it hard enough. Or in the right light, because I did the same thing. I left my old life behind and I never even questioned the need for it. It was just what I had to do. Just like this is what I have to do."

"And how in the hell do you know you're hunting the right kind of vampires?" she demanded icily, slowly turning as he paced, keeping him in her line of sight.

He countered softly, "How do you?"

Rolling her eyes, she said, "I just know. It's what I do."

Kane grinned. "I may not be a Hunter—no superhero cop or anything—but I know what I'm good at. I know what I'm supposed to do."

Slowly, Kendall shook her head. "This isn't something you want to start, Kane. This isn't a life. You don't want to live like this. We sleep, we Hunt, we kill. After so long, that's all you know. It's what people like us do. It's what we're good at. It's all I'm good at."

Her breath froze in her chest as he stopped in front of her, staring down at her with eyes that burned. His hand came up, cupping her cheek once more as he lowered his head. She felt the warm touch of his breath on her face as he murmured, "I doubt that's all you're good at . . ."

When his mouth covered hers, she groaned. The taste of him was every bit as enticing as she'd imagined. Hot, smoky male, entirely too appealing, entirely too addictive. His tongue slid across hers as his hands slid down her sides, grasping her hips and bringing her close against him.

Against her belly, she felt the heat of his cock. A responding pulse echoed in her and liquid heat started to flow. She could feel the hunger throbbing as he pulled his mouth from hers, kissing a line down her chin, across her collarbone.

Desperate, she clenched her thighs together in response to the aching in her pussy, and she felt him chuckle against her skin. "That won't help, sugar . . . maybe this will." His thigh pushed between hers and lifted until she was riding the hard-muscled length. Instinctively, she rocked her hips and hot, streaking pleasure arced through her.

The blaring sound of a car horn caused her to jerk away from him, watching the red taillights as they disappeared into the night. A cool breeze drifted by as she stood there staring at him, and she shivered a little. Startled, she realized she was sweating. *Sweating* . . . hell, she couldn't remember the last time she'd got her heart rate up to what humans called normal, and he had her sweating.

As she stood there watching him, his tongue slid out, tracing over his lips. "You taste better than anything I've ever imagined," he whispered gruffly. As he took a step toward her, Kendall felt her heart quiver in her chest. "I want more."

Kendall shook her head. "No . . . that's not a good idea."

Kane smiled slowly. "I think it's the best idea I've had in a very long time. You bothered me, you know. A lot. Even before I figured out who you were, the night I saw you dancing, you bothered me. Just looking at you made me hot—and furious."

She felt frozen in place as he closed the distance between them once more, edging her back off the street, back into the shadows of the alley. "How could somebody that looked like you be a killer? Didn't seem fair."

Kendall forced herself to laugh. "I am a killer, Kane. Just not the cold-blooded kind you thought. And wouldn't life be lovely if we could recognize them just by the way they look? If they had horns or dark rain clouds hanging over their heads. Doesn't work that way."

His eyes held hers as he reached up, catching a lock of hair in his hand. "Maybe." Winding it around his hand, he drew her closer. "And I don't think you're a killer—a fighter, yes. I know—I'm the same way. And none of that matters."

His mouth took hers again and Kendall collapsed back against the wall as he leaned into her. His weight crushed her and through the layers of their clothes, she felt him again, the hard, throbbing length of his cock. Her sex grew slick and wet as she imagined feeling that pillar of flesh pushing inside her.

A whimper escaped her. He shifted against her and she quivered as he cupped her in his hand, rotating the heel of his palm against her clit. Through the denim and silk that separated his flesh from her, the heat of his hand teased and taunted.

Arching against him, she slid her hands up his chest and buried them in the silken strands of his golden hair. Against her ear, he muttered, "I want you naked." Tipping her head back, she stared into his eyes, unable to think of a damned thing to say.

He didn't seem to need words, though, as he trailed his fingers up and down her zipper. Kane circled his fingers once around the button before sliding it free. His knuckles raked against her skin as he slid the zipper down. When he slid his fingers inside the waistband of her panties, she whimpered, and when he pushed one finger inside the swollen, wet folds of her pussy, she screamed into his mouth.

Kane swallowed her scream down as he slowly pumped his finger in and out. Then he pulled back, catching the plump lower curve of her lip in his teeth, biting down gently. Feeling his eyes on her, she forced her lids to lift. His hands shifted and as he started to strip her jeans down her thighs, she almost let him.

She could smell him, hot and male, the pulsing of his heart a siren's song that was threatening her sanity. Her fangs had slid out, and as she stared up at him, he lowered his mouth to hers, angling his head. The sharp edge of one of her incisors nicked his flesh and she whimpered as the hot, rich wine of his blood flooded her senses.

With a vicious jerk, she pulled away, shaking her head, muttering under her breath, "No. I'm not doing this. No no no no no no." With hands that shook, she fastened her jeans, stifling a moan as the seam of her jeans slid slickly over the wet material of her panties. She was wet, she ached, and she felt so damned empty.

But slowly, she turned and faced him. Her voice wavered as she said, "We're not doing this."

Kane had taken the position she'd been in, propping his back against the wall, hooking his thumbs in his pockets as he stared at her. "Why not?"

Lowering her brows over her eyes, she glared at him. "Because we're not."

Waving an arm around, she snapped, "We're in an alley, damn it. People driving by? Hell, there's two dead bodies and a couple of drug dealers hog-tied a few hundred yards away."

Kane grinned. "Yeah, I watched. Nice work. I taught Duke that technique, you know. Grew up on a ranch."

Spinning away from him, she pressed the heels of her hands against her eyes. Suddenly, she remembered why in the hell the lack of a man in her life rarely bothered her. They were frustrating as hell, annoying, obnoxious . . . but he smelled so damned good . . .

Clenching her jaw, she started to stalk down the street. It wasn't five seconds before she heard his light footsteps behind her. Her back stiffened and her steps slowed, but she forced herself to keep walking. Maybe if she ignored him, he'd go away.

A minute later, her sharp ears detected the sound of sirens. They weren't close—it would be a few minutes before they got to the area. But she doubted Duke had called, which meant somebody had found the bodies and the restrained drug dealers.

"Out of my damned mind," she whispered, driving a hand through her hair and gathering it in a loose tail at the nape of her neck.

That was the only explanation.

He'd flustered the vampire.

Kane couldn't help but grin a little as he watched her march down the street. Her hips swung back and forth with her furious pace and he was damned glad nobody was around as he studied her ass.

It was a perfect ass—rounded and soft. His palms itched. Her skin was soft. Silken-soft. And she made the softest, sweetest little sounds in her throat when she was excited.

He wanted to know how she sounded when she came. Did she scream? Did she moan? With a slow smile, he made himself a promise. He'd find out. And if he had anything to do about it, he'd find out before the sun rose, because he had an odd feeling that as soon as she could, she'd slip out of town. And Kane would have to wait until fate brought them together again.

While fate seemed determined to do that fairly often, he'd be damned if he waited a few weeks to touch that soft skin. It was what he'd ached to do that night he'd seen her in the club, but his honor wouldn't let him make love to a woman he believed was a cold-blooded killer. It was unthinkable. And while he'd been accused of being a cold bastard himself, he also couldn't have sex with a woman he planned on killing.

That problem solved, he intended on getting her in bed— okay, *anywhere,* against a wall, on the bench seat of his truck, even a shadowed alley would have suited him.

He wasn't sure why she'd torn away from him so fast. He'd felt that brief pain as her fangs cut his tongue—a slow smile curved his lips and then a soft chuckle escaped him. Well, that would have explained it if *he* had been the one to jump away as if he'd touched fire. Why it had bothered her so bad, he didn't know.

If that's what it was though, he was in trouble. Because he planned on kissing her again, as often as possible. If he could get her to stop walking.

That wasn't an option right now though. In the distance he could hear the wail of police cars fast approaching. She'd probably heard it long before him and that would explain why she was walking at that brisk pace.

She could always run. The police would never see her, he suspected, if she unleashed that full speed.

Part of him wondered why she didn't run. The rest of him was glad she didn't. Kane really didn't want her disappearing just yet.

Digging into his pocket, he pulled out his keys and jogged closer. Closing his hand around her arm, he smiled as she flashed him a livid look. "Come on. My truck is just around the corner. You don't really want to be found in the area, do you?"

She dropped her eyes to his bag and said, "I could handle it better than you could. I'm not carrying an arsenal in a backpack."

Arching a brow at her, he responded, "It's a duffle bag. And I'm a licensed bounty hunter. All I'd have to do is tell them I'm working."

"And if they ask who you're looking for?"

Kane smiled. "That's the beauty of bounty hunting. There's criminals all over the world. I know where to look for the information." With a shrug, he added, "Plus it pays good. Sometimes I bring somebody in for the reward when I'm low on cash."

They rounded the corner, and she then stood there, staring at him with indecisive eyes as he unlocked his truck. Kane suspected she might have continued to stand there indefinitely if a car hadn't turned down the street. The sedan moved on past them but Kendall tracked it with her eyes for a long minute and then she turned to stare at him.

"Fine. You can take me to where we're staying." Her tone was low, almost a sulk, but she climbed into the truck.

Kane leaned in over her on the pretext of dropping his bag onto the floorboard by her feet. He mused that if she pressed against the seat any harder, she just might disappear inside it. He edged a little closer and he heard a swift intake of breath as he moved his face along her neck, breathing in the soft scent of her skin. "You smell unbelievable," he whispered.

Before she could respond, he pressed a kiss against her neck and then withdrew and closed the door. Climbing in, he started the truck, and as they pulled away from the curb, he listened to the sirens wail.

No more than a street or two away. Relying on previous knowledge of the streets, he headed north, taking them on a

swift route into a more populated part of the city. Within
three minutes, they were surrounded by traffic and he
breathed a little easier. Even though he had no doubt he
could offer a feasible story to any cop that pulled him over,
he didn't want to try it if it wasn't necessary.

Kane slid Kendall a look as they slowed at a stoplight.
"Where you are staying?" he asked softly.

"We've got a place on the south side of town. Get back on
65 for now."

"We . . . hmmm, oh, yeah. I forgot about Duke." A way-
ward thought passed through his mind, one he didn't really
care for. The question had barely formed, and he wished he
could take it back as he asked, "How long have the two of
you been working together?"

"Not long. We hooked up right before we saw you in
Louisville."

"Hooked up?" Kane slid her another look, but he couldn't
see her face. She'd turned her head to stare out the window
and her hair had fallen to conceal her face.

Kendall's only response was another one of those soft,
humming sounds. The silence that followed damned near
drove him out of his mind.

Blowing out a breath, Kane realized she wasn't going to
volunteer the information he was looking for. A throbbing
had started in his temple and it only worsened as he finally
asked, "Is he the reason we stopped?"

Distracted, it took a minute to understand what Kane was
asking. "Yes. Part of it." Damn it, she had to get away from
him. He smelled too good, and the small taste of his blood
still lingered on her tongue, making her crave more. They hit
the interstate and she glanced at the sign. "Not the next exit,
but the one after. Go right."

The pulsing of his heartbeat seemed to sing to her and she
barely heard him ask, "How serious is it?"

Hungry, confused, she glanced at him with a frown, trying to figure out what in the hell he was talking about.
Duke . . . he'd been asking about her training Duke. "Serious enough. It's something I have to do," she finally replied.

Kane fell silent and tension mounted in the truck until it was all but choking her. When they exited the interstate a few minutes later, she let out a soft sigh of relief. He turned right and she gestured at the stoplight. "Turn left there. It's the third street after that."

"Why in the hell didn't you say something?"

The harsh, angry tone of his voice had her back stiffening, and she turned her head to glare at him coolly. "I didn't realize it was any of your business."

That haughty look on her face made him want to howl. *None of my fucking business. I just had my fucking tongue halfway down your throat.* He turned the corner without slowing down and the squealing of the tires only seemed to add to the edgy anger inside him.

"End of the street," she said, but Kane was already heading there. It was the only dark, silent house on the street so where in the hell else would she be staying?

Slamming on the brakes, he turned his head to stare at her. Her face was in shadow—he could barely make out the soft bow of her mouth, the gentle curve of her jaw as she turned to look at him.

"Thank you," she said coolly, reaching for the handle. As she opened the door and slid out, light from the cab splashed on her face.

Holding her gaze for a minute, he realized there was an ache in his heart. Out of his reach . . . and he wanted her entirely too damned much. She closed the door and turned away. Hitting the button for the window, he waited until she turned to look back at him before he said gruffly, "Tell Duke I'm sorry."

PART TWO

CHAPTER 5

Just another dream. Logically, he knew that, but he couldn't seem to make himself wake up. Kane was walking down a city street. It looked familiar to him, vaguely, but he couldn't remember what city it was or when he'd been here.

It was silent.

Too quiet.

Cities the size of this one took on a life of their own, the heartbeat of life pulsing through them. There was always something going on, always people, even in the darkest hours of night.

But this place was empty.

More than that, it felt *wrong*.

Like something dark had happened here.

The sound of his heels on the pavement sounded abnormally loud as he continued to walk. He was looking for something. Wasn't sure what. But something . . .

He felt something like a raindrop hit his head. Followed by another, and another . . . reaching up, he touched his fingers to his hair. Something viscous, too thick for water. He stood in a circle of light cast by a streetlight overhead and slowly, he looked at his fingers.

Blood. He knew the feel of blood on his flesh, knew the scent of it. Slowly, he lifted his head, and as he stared upward, another drop of blood fell. He stepped out of the way right before it hit him in the face and watched as it fell and splattered on the ground.

It grew. That one drop of blood spread and spread, until it puddled around Kane's feet and turned the concrete of the sidewalk into a river of red.

He didn't know how he came to be on the fire escape. He didn't remember jumping, but now he was climbing upward. He climbed and climbed until the ladder ended.

There was a window before him, painted dark as though to keep the sunlight out. Reaching out, he touched his fingers to it, and at that light touch, it shattered. He was left standing there, shards of black glass at his feet, as he stared in through the window. There was a body in there.

Time seemed to fade out again and he went from standing on the fire escape to standing beside the body.

He knew those mild hazel eyes. Rarely had he seen them not smiling. Duke had always seemed to find something to smile about. Not now though. Death had claimed him and left his face a cold mask.

His neck was a ragged, ugly mess—Kane had seen people who had been killed by vampire bites. Only a couple, thank God, and he'd saved a few people from a similar fate.

Didn't make it any easier though.

Hell, nothing could make this easy. This was Duke—his best friend. They'd been in boot camp together, in Iraq together. When they'd left the Army, they'd done it together, and they'd been together those first few months as they tried to figure out what they were going to do with the rest of their lives.

Duke had been the one to stumble on bounty hunting. A friend of his dad's had been running a bail agency and he'd offered Duke a couple of jobs. Those hadn't paid as much. But Duke had liked it.

He'd gotten Kane into it, and as a team they were good at it. Very good—it took less than a few years to establish a reputation as some of the best.

And they'd both loved the money.

Now Duke was dead. Not just dead, though. It seemed worse than that. It was almost like he was empty. Like everything that had made him Duke had been killed before his body had died.

The very air around him seemed fouled and Kane couldn't help but wonder what in the hell had been done to his old friend.

Staring into Duke's still face, Kane felt his heart lodge in his throat. The sting of tears was unfamiliar, but when they started to roll down his face, Kane just let them fall.

Time passed and it seemed like he stood there over his friend's body for an eternity. Frozen, unable to move. Then Duke moved.

Just his eyelids, dropping down over his eyes, but then they lifted. He stared upward at Kane and horror flooded him as Duke started to rot. His flesh went ashen, then gray, his features thinning out, and skin started to peel away from his bones.

"Find her."

Kane jumped as Duke spoke. He whispered it again, "Find her . . ."

Duke started to sit up, his hand lifted toward Kane.

Just as his fingers started to brush Kane's leg, Kane awoke.

His breath wheezed out of his lungs in a painful rush as he sat up in bed, staring ahead of him while those last awful images played over and over in his head.

Fuck.

A cold sweat soaked his entire body and his heart was slamming against his ribs with a force that almost hurt.

The dreams had been getting worse. For quite awhile, but the past month, they'd been awful, so much so that he didn't even want to sleep. Dreams where he saw Duke suffering, hurting . . . being tortured.

This was the first time he'd dreamed his friend was dead.

His chest burned and ached. "These dreams are going to drive me nuts," he muttered. Climbing from the bed, he moved to the window, staring out into the night.

It was time to go.

He'd been in St. Louis for close to two months. He'd taken a contract and had a decent amount of money to go on for awhile. The world was also shy a few more vampires. And something he assumed was a werewolf. He hadn't ever seen one in that half wolf, half man form, but he didn't give a damn what it was. What he'd cared about was the woman he'd seen sobbing and fighting beneath the thing.

She had been alive as the paramedics gently moved her onto the stretcher. Kane had stood in the shadows, watching her with worried eyes as the paramedics stabilized the blood flowing from a dozen places.

She'd still been sobbing and crying as they moved her into the ambulance—her sobs tore at his heart and Kane wanted to do more, but that would have involved talking to cops. Normally he wouldn't have worried that much—but how in the hell could he possibly explain her injuries? Rape, what looked like very large dog bites, wolf hair under her nails.

He was done here for now. Something else was calling him, and he didn't like the dark, heavy feel that hung in the air around him. Something bad was getting ready to happen.

It took less than thirty minutes to gather his stuff together. There wasn't much. Clothes, a couple of books he'd picked up, and his weapons. The weapons were the most important. He could always buy more clothes, and he'd bought the books months ago and still hadn't gotten around to reading them.

The weapons, though, they were damned important. Many of them were specialty pieces, knives made from silver, titanium cuffs, the arrows for his crossbow, tipped again with silver. He had yet to try to special order silver bullets for his guns, but regular ammo did a decent amount of damage. Slowed most of the creatures he hunted down for a minute, which gave him time to get to his crossbow or one of the knives.

A few other things, a little more commonplace, were matches, lighter fluid, and a simple BIC lighter. These things *burned*, vampires and werewolves, like setting fire to wood soaked in gasoline, just that quickly. And they burned down to nothing but dust.

Not bone, not charred corpse. They burned and burned until there was nothing but ashes. Once Kane had learned that, getting rid of their bodies suddenly became a whole lot easier.

Checking his bags, he made sure everything was accounted for. His two guns, a Beretta and a Kel-Tec P32 waited on the bed. He secured the Beretta in a holster designed to rest at the small of his back. The Kel-Tec went into an ankle sheath and he rolled the leg of his jeans down, automatically checking to make sure it wasn't visible.

Casting a look around the room, he tossed the keycard on the dresser and left in silence. It was early. There was one clerk at the desk and she was dozing. Kane smiled a little as he heard a soft snore escape her mouth as he headed out the door.

The streets of St. Louis still weren't very busy, but as it pushed closer to six, that would change. Kane wanted to be out of the city before that happened. The traffic around here *sucked*.

He climbed into the truck, putting the small rolling suitcase with his clothes behind the seat. The bag of weapons he kept on the seat beside him. So far, nobody had come after his ass over the monsters he'd been killing.

But he wasn't going to count on that luck holding forever.

K ENDALL leaned against the wall of the bar, certain she was going to go nuts from sheer boredom.

She'd had a vague plan when she and Duke came to this bar, but it had been very vague. A girl in the hospital, the scent of blood and drugs in the air. But so far, the men she'd come here looking for hadn't shown up.

And there was not much else here. Hell, they'd been prowling the streets for more than a week with nothing to show for it. Part of her wanted to leave, but another part . . . well, she couldn't. A little voice kept whispering in her mind, *Stay . . . stay . . .*

But bloody hell, she was bored.

Damn it, she'd never been in a city this size where there was nothing to Hunt. Duke didn't seem to mind, she brooded, watching as her ex-trainee, now partner, danced a petite blonde around the dance floor.

Kendall had a feeling she'd be going back to the hotel alone tonight. Duke had been behaving himself a little too long. It seemed shape-shifters had quite a bit in common with werekind. Not just the shape-shifting, either. They were both constantly horny, it seemed.

And it seemed when Duke went more than a few weeks without getting laid, it was almost like he'd gone too long without shifting. And when he started looking at her with that hot, intent look in his eyes, Kendall knew it was time he found a woman.

Not that Duke wasn't a good-looking guy. He definitely was, and that look definitely made heat streak through her. But she didn't want to sleep with him. Even if he hadn't been her partner.

It wasn't any surprise where her thoughts started to lead.

The memory of a pair of bottle green eyes swam through her mind. And that thought did more than make heat streak through her. It exploded through her with an intensity that stole her breath.

"Bloody hell," she whispered, turning away from the dance floor. Pressing her palms flat against the wood of the bar, she closed her eyes and tried to convince her body that she didn't have to react that way.

A year—it had been a fucking year since she had seen him, and she still had to fight this wave of lust every time she thought of him.

A hand touched her shoulder and she stiffened, trying to school her features a little before she turned and stared at Duke. The blonde was leaning against his side and wouldn't meet Kendall's eyes, her cheeks flushed.

"We're going to go," Duke said quietly. He cocked his head, his eyes narrowing as he studied her face. "You okay?"

Baring her teeth in a semblance of a smile, she said, "I'm just wonderful."

His eyes continued to study her thoughtfully and Kendall felt blood rush to her cheeks in a flush as a slow, understanding smile began on his lips. "Get lost," she said shortly as she pointedly turned her back.

Duke laughed softly and seconds later, he was gone, his arm wrapped around the woman at his side.

Kendall caught the eye of the bartender and pointed toward the whiskey he'd served one of the other patrons at the bar. He nodded and a few minutes later, Kendall had her hand wrapped around the glass, staring broodingly into the amber liquid.

It would make her head swim a little, but nothing like the punch it packed on humans. No forgetfulness, no graying fog to cloud the desire churning through her veins. But she could always hope.

Tossing it back, she shivered a little as it ran down her throat like liquid fire. It hit her belly and warmth spread through her system.

The warmth the whiskey brought was almost as good as the warmth that came from having a lover touch her.

Almost . . . but not quite.

"Damn, you're a cute little thing."

Kendall closed her eyes, sighing tiredly as a hand came up to rest on her shoulder. *My fault,* she mused silently as she turned to stare up at the tall, scruffy-looking man in front of her. *I had been bitching about being bored . . .*

The whiskey hadn't done anything for her.

But as she recognized the man in front of her, adrenaline started to flow. His face was a little more handsome than it had been on the sketch flashed on the TV screen, but the darkness she felt inside him made her skin crawl.

He stank.

She smelled blood. She smelled drugs. The ripe stench of a woman's fear. It clung to the man, all but painting the air black around him.

As he started to tug her through the crowd toward the dance floor, Kendall smiled.

Well, at least she wouldn't be bored for a little while.

K ANE stood outside the bar, staring at it dubiously. A dive. A classic redneck dive. On the outskirts of Cincinnati, the pile of cinder blocks was painted black, maybe an attempt to make it look nicer than it was. It was the sort of place a man went when he wanted to get drunk or get in a fight.

And he really didn't think it was a place any sane woman would go.

But there was no denying who was in there. The edgy excitement that had been prodding at him for the past week since he'd headed out of St. Louis was only caused by one thing.

His gut was leading him to Kendall.

It had been a year since he'd seen her, but he could still remember the way his body went on edge the closer he got to her. He didn't even have to see her to know she was in there.

How he knew, Kane really wasn't sure. With a quirk of his lips, he wondered if maybe it was a north–needle thing, with his cock pulling him toward her the way a compass always pointed north.

Broken glass crunched under the heels of his boots as he crossed the parking lot. As he opened the door, a wave of bluish smoke billowed out, followed by the unmistakable scent of marijuana. Mixed with the body sweat, alcohol, and fried, greasy food, it made up a miasma that would have made some people sick.

The smoke stung his eyes a little as he stepped inside, scanning the crowd. *Oh, hell yeah. A dive.* The clientele ran from the shirtless to leather motorcycle jackets—there were heads shaved bald and others that had long greasy hair that likely hadn't seen a comb in months. If ever.

There were a few women here and there, but most of them were the brassy dyed-blonde type, poured into jeans two sizes too small and blue eye shadow clear up to the brow.

But there was one that stood out.

She was out on the dance floor, swaying to the band's very bad rendition of "Brown Eyed Girl." Kane damned near swallowed his tongue as she spun in a slow circle, letting him see what she was wearing. Jeans that were all but painted on, a halter top that looked like it was made out of chain mail.

Nothing under it. The golden metal links shimmered against the ivory of her skin, and Kane felt his mouth go dry as he thought he glimpsed a soft, rosy nipple before her partner turned her back around. As she swayed sinuously against her partner, the smooth muscles of her back flexed. Again, she spun around, placing her back against the guy's chest, sensuously rotating her hips as she bent her knees, making love to that god-awful music. Kane could see bare flesh under the gaps of her halter and he felt lust tear through him with vicious intensity. It bit and clawed at his belly like a tiger gone mad.

Several other guys were noticing her too. Three moved up and she smiled a teasing smile as she accepted one hand and rose from her little dip on the floor, her legs straddling the man's, her pelvis stroking against his thigh. Her partner moved up behind her, crowding his hips against her denim-covered ass.

Kane had the hard-on from hell. He was hard-pressed not to go over to her and yank her away from the men crowding around her. Yank her away, turn her over his knee, and paddle that fine-looking ass.

And cover her—all around, greedy male eyes were watching her, watching that shirt as it moved and shifted on her torso, teasing them with brief glimpses of soft, pink nipples.

Damn it, he ached. Even thinking of her was enough to make him hard, but this . . . this was worse. Vicious in its intensity, the lust had wrapped a choke hold around his throat and he could hardly breathe beyond it.

He wanted nothing more than to grab her and strip her bare, fuck her until she screamed out his name.

And he had no doubt the men around her did, too.

But he stayed in the shadows. There was a cool, calculating look in her eyes that none of the men seemed to notice.

She wasn't here looking to get laid, the way they were probably thinking. She was here after a target. Or targets, Kane realized some time later as he watched her tease and flirt with the two men she'd primarily been dancing with. As one of them tried to coax her to the back door, she pretended to resist for a little bit, ducking her head coyly and shaking it. One of them urged a beer into her hand and she drank, once more dispelling the myth that vampires didn't drink anything beyond blood.

When they tried to move her to the door again, she went, smiling a nervous little smile, ducking her head, and tucking a lock of hair behind her ear, holding one man's hand as he led her out. The other guy, a big, bearlike man with a grizzled beard and a tattoo of a skull on his cheek, followed, his eyes on Kendall's ass, a greedy look in his eyes.

Kane slid out the front door and made his way around the building, ears pricked, listening carefully. The music was fainter, but still loud. As he drew closer, he could just barely hear her soft laugh. The low rumble of male voices was harder to hear, and getting fainter. As he rounded the edge of the building, he saw them guiding her out of the circle of light cast by the single streetlight.

Damned idiot. What in the hell is she thinking, he thought surlily. As one man went flying through the air about ten feet away from him, Kane decided thinking probably wasn't a priority for her. Or maybe she just thought along a different path than he would have expected.

Kane squatted down by the man, studying the blood that

matted his beard and painted garish splatters along the tattoo of the grinning skull. Breath whistled through busted teeth, and the man's eyes were closed. Unconscious, he decided, watching the slow, steady rhythm of his chest rising and falling.

He figured the bastard might have internal bleeding, but considering the greedy, predatory look he'd seen in the man's eyes, Kane wasn't overly worried. They hadn't brought Kendall out here with the idea of a walk in mind. And she'd known it.

Rising, he slid through the cars, wincing instinctively when another bastard crashed into the car right in front of him. The guy came up swinging though, lunging back toward Kendall. Kane moved up behind him silently and caught him in a choke-hold, watching as Kendall turned around with a coy smile. "Did you bring more friends . . ." her voice trailed off and the laughter there faded as she saw Kane.

"Oh." Her tone was flat, bored, and her eyes were as blank as a sheet of paper. "It's you."

"Hello, Kendall," he said quietly. Shifting his grip, he shoved the man to the ground so that he landed in front of her on his knees. "This your date?"

She shrugged, still staring at Kane, not even glancing at the man as he rose. She sidestepped around him and studied Kane, circling around them, but not moving closer. "He's not really my type."

Kane saw the knife gleaming silver in the moonlight. "Kendall, watch out!" he shouted, but the knife was already cutting through the air. Kendall spun around in a blur of motion, just a blur of red hair and pale skin. He saw her catch the roughneck's arm, just the white flash of her hand flying up, and then the man was on the ground with his arm twisted behind, her fingers wrapped around his wrist, squeezing until man's skin under them went white.

The knife fell. Kendall didn't even notice it as she knelt down beside her prey, stroking a hand down his neck. "What were you planning to do to me, Eric?" she whispered softly, her voice warm and sweet, almost hypnotic.

"Let go of me," he muttered, his face red. He grimaced, baring his teeth, as she tugged on his wrist.

Kane could swear he heard the bone grinding.

Kendall chuckled and let go of his hand, stepping away. "There . . . one chance." Her lips twisted in a mean little smile and she said, "That is probably one more than you gave every last woman you raped in this parking lot."

Eric paled. "What the fuck you talking about, bitch?"

Kendall saw it, though, that flicker of acknowledgment, of fear in his eyes. Tuning Kane out, she focused on Eric's face. He stank of blood. Semen. Women's sweat . . . the scent rancid. Human sweat didn't smell like that. Unless they were frightened. Terrified.

"What am I talking about?" she repeated, arching her brows. The thoughts in her mind were anything but welcome, but Eric's mind had been like an open book, and the longer they'd danced inside the bar, the more pages she'd been forced to read. "What am I talking about . . . hmmm . . ."

She pretended to ponder that as she moved in a slow circle, watching him through the corner of her eye. She stopped by the spot where the grass met the gravel parking lot, staring at a patch of grass about twenty feet away, just behind the two large dumpsters. "The last one was right there. You slipped her a roofie. I can still smell it . . . she bled so much," she murmured. She slid Eric a sidelong glance. "Not that you care."

"I don't know what in the fuck you're talking about," Eric spat. But she could see the lie in his eyes, taste it in the air as she breathed in.

"Forget her already? Her name's Anne. She had a fight with her boyfriend and came here just to piss him off. He's very protective, and she knew he would freak if she came to a dive like this. Alone." She smiled and said, "I should be really nasty. I should go and get *him*. That boyfriend of hers is one pissed-off individual."

Eric sneered. "Like I give a shit. That little piece of ass was just begging for it," he spat. Then he clamped his lips shut.

"You two wasted too much time playing with her, didn't you?" Kendall asked. "When she woke up, you were back on top of her and she went crazy. Screamed. You hit her to shut her up. And then you liked it." She smiled as her fangs dropped. "Just as much, probably, as I'm going to enjoy this."

Then she lunged for him and he went down under her body, bucking and kicking, trying to punch her, but she caught his fist just before it would have hit her face and she crushed it. Her other hand was against his mouth, muffling his scream.

Lowering her lips to rest against his cheek, she drank in the hot, ripe emotions of fear that poured from him. "Now," she purred. "You know how she felt. Helpless . . ."

Dropping the reins of control, she smiled against his cheek as fear rolled through the air and took his mind. "Confused . . . scared for her very life." Chuckling, she sat up, brushing her hair back from her face as he started to mewl and bawl like a baby.

Her lids drooped as she gathered herself and leaped into his mind, using the power of hers to bore deep inside.

You'll confess. You'll go to the police, she ordered silently as he stopped writhing under her, staring at her slackly. His mind was malleable. Pliant; she could mold it like a piece of clay.

Drool dribbled out of the corner of his mouth. Wrinkling her nose in disgust, she rose away from him even as she continued to whisper silently inside his mind. *You will never touch another woman like that again. Without consent, using drugs to keep her quiet . . . none of it. It's over. Because if you do, I'll know.*

Now that part was a lie. She wasn't omniscient, and even if she was, all the men she'd done this to, if she tried to keep track of them, there would be no room in her mind left for her own thoughts.

However, there were so many men and women she'd told that little white lie to, and not one of them had ever doubted her.

She broke the connection with Eric, turning around and scanning the parking lot. Kane was still standing there, watching her with faint apprehension. Ignoring him, she strode past and found the other man by his scent. The air was ripe with blood, although the only blood she could see was drying under his left nostril. The cut on his temple had already stopped bleeding, but it had left streams of blood on his face.

They were damp still, but it wasn't enough blood to account for all that she smelled.

Internal bleeding. She suppressed a sigh. "It would be a lot easier on my conscious if this didn't happen so much."

A low laugh had her head flying around and she narrowed her eyes as she saw Kane moving closer. The light was dim, but it was bright enough to catch the gold strands threading through that shaggy mane of hair.

"He's scum. I recognized that the minute I saw him in the bar—what's it matter if he dies or not?" Kane asked, his lips lifted in a sardonic smile.

"Life matters," she said quietly. She looked down and watched as the man below breathed his last. "Life always matters."

Rising, she cast a quick glance over her shoulder. The entire encounter had lasted less than ten minutes. But still too much time. "I have to get out of here. Sooner or later somebody will come out here, either to neck, fuck, or get high," she said shortly. "What are you doing here?"

He shrugged. "Looking for you."

Arching a brow, she managed . . . just barely . . . to keep from launching herself at him as she responded, "Well, you found me. And one of these days you're going to tell me just *how* you keep finding me."

Turning on her heel, she headed for her car. He fell into step behind her, and she tensed unwittingly, feeling his eyes move over her almost like a caress. Trying to relax the tension in her shoulders, she dug the keys for her car out of the tiny little purse she had hanging on her hip, the strap going diagonally down her chest, between her breasts.

"Maybe it's me, but it's kind of weird thinking of a vampire driving a car," he said dryly.

She cocked a brow at him. "I can't fly."

"So that's another Hollywood thing?" he asked.

Smiling sweetly, she said, "No. Some of us can. I just can't."

The dumb look on his face was rather amusing. Smiling to herself, she unlocked the car.

"What does that mean? *You just can't?*" Glancing across the roof of her car at him, she saw him standing at the passenger door. *Looks like I have a hitchhiker,* she thought absently, still wondering what in the hell he wanted.

"I know some people who can draw. Does that mean all humans can make pictures like Picasso?" she asked with a smirk.

She could see his brows drop low over his eyes, almost hear the wheels spinning in his head as he thought that out. "So some of you can do things others can't?" he finally said.

"Boy, aren't you the bright one," she said, tongue in cheek. Climbing into the car, she started it as he opened the door and slid into the seat next to her.

"You been around awhile. Thought you got stronger as you got older. But you can't fly. Will you ever?"

"Not unless it's in a plane," she said, putting the car into reverse and wheeling out of her spot. She checked the highway before she peeled out of the parking lot, slinging gravel behind her as she went.

"What about the guy back there?"

Checking her rearview mirror, she forced a casual shrug. "He had internal bleeding. Rupture somewhere. A lot of blood—he was dead from the minute he walked outside with me. I could stay and answer a lot of tedious questions and dance through some red tape. Or I could just bail."

"People saw you leaving with him."

Amused, Kendall said, "Not a single one of them will remember come morning. And that's not the kind of joint to have video security."

A scowl crossed his face, and she had to suppress turning her head to stare at him. He looked unbelievably sexy, that mouth of his drawing tight, lids drooping. Dangerous. He looked dangerous.

Jerking her eyes back to the road, she focused on it. She didn't like dangerous men. The way they scowled, and stalked around, and growled . . . her heart slammed against her ribs. Her mouth dry, she swallowed and tried to think past the fog of lust that had suddenly clouded her mind.

"So they don't remember you?" he demanded, interrupting her jumbled thoughts.

She just smiled.

"People can't just forget every time they see you," he muttered, shaking his head.

"That's what you think," she said with a shrug.

"How come I haven't? Didn't you try it on me?"

Kendall sighed, shoving a hand through her hair. "I *have* tried. Apparently your skull is too damned thick. You shouldn't have ever remembered seeing me, and your memories of Duke, well, you shouldn't have remembered much about him at all—kind of like the memories you have of being a kid." Sliding him a sidelong glance, she added, "Most humans, though, their minds are easily clouded. Not the nicest thing to do, fog a person's memory, but people can't know about us. Too dangerous, for them and for us."

He fell silent and she tried to tune his presence out, tried to cool the hot puddle her belly had become, tried to dispel the sexual tension that had turned her thigh muscles to putty and had her pussy clenching eagerly.

Easier said than done. Twenty minutes later, the lights of her hotel were gleaming on the horizon and Kendall felt like little more than a hot, buttery pool of need. Her gums ached and the sexual heat was so hot, spiraling out of control, and now the hunger was rising.

Damn it, why did he have to show up again? And *now*? If she'd fed, dealing with him would have been a little easier.

But seeing him in the parking lot had made all thought flee, and all she could think of was him.

She wanted to feed, wanted to fuck . . . and not just anybody.

The scent of Kane's body had filled her head and she felt half drunk on it. Ripe and hot, he smelled of man, earth, and the wild scent of the woods.

Damn it, she was crazy.

Kendall couldn't think of anything she wanted more at that moment than to fuck the man who had once tried to kill her.

She parked in a darkened area of the parking lot, backing in automatically. Quick getaway. Always had to be ready for a quick getaway. Climbing out of the car, she leaned against it and folded her arms against her chest, listening as Kane got out. The gravel crunched under his feet as he came around, moving to lean against the concrete base of the broken streetlight.

"So to what do I owe this pleasure?" she asked, curving her mouth into a mockery of a polite smile.

Kane shifted and the soft white cotton of the henley he wore stretched across the muscles of his chest. That heat inside her belly seemed to expand and she had to bite back the whimper that rose in her throat.

She could hear his heart beat, all but taste the rich wine of the blood that flowed in his veins.

As he continued to stare at her in silence, she arched a brow at him, keeping her face blank. In a bored tone, she said, "I'm waiting, Kane. If you have something to say to me, then say it."

He cracked a small smile and she had to wonder why this man, this mortal, of all the men she'd known made her feel this way. "Where's Duke?" he asked quietly. His eyes rested on her face—in light this dim, he shouldn't have been able to see her well, but she suspected he saw her entirely too well.

Lifting her shoulders in a restless shrug, she responded, "He was at the bar earlier. We weren't planning on finding much—he ended up going home with a woman he saw there."

He arched a brow, studying her. "A woman—and you're okay with that?"

"Why wouldn't I be?" she asked, running her tongue along the surface of her teeth. Her fangs were still in their sockets, but her gums were itching. She wanted a taste of him.

Badly wanted a taste.

She muttered to herself, *Why in the hell do you always want what you can't have?*

K ANE couldn't see her that well—just the glitter of her eyes, the white flash of her teeth when she smiled. But he could smell her.

The subtle fragrance of her body drifted to him on the gentle breeze, flooding his senses. It woke a hunger inside him that was just too much, on the point of shattering his control. His skin felt tight and hot, too damned small for the need that raged inside him, and the longer he stared at her, the more intense it got.

His cock ached and his palms itched to hold her, to pull her against him and touch all those soft curves. Damn it, he wanted her.

And he couldn't have her.

There was little in life that was as frustrating as wanting something that he just couldn't have.

Jamming his hands into his pockets, he closed them into fists. The urge to reach out and touch her was almost unbearable. Focusing on her words, he said, in a tight voice, "You don't have a problem with your lover going home with another woman?"

"My lover," she repeated. Her voice had an odd, flat tone to it, and then she started to laugh. As that rich, husky sound echoed in the night, Kane narrowed his eyes, watching her.

The longer she laughed, the more irritated he got. Kane had to resist yet another urge—strangle her, spank her—

something to make her stop laughing while he tried to figure out what in the hell was so amusing.

Kiss her.

He wanted to haul that sleek, powerful little body against his and cover that smart-ass mouth with his, plunging his tongue into its satin depths, and gorge on her.

She'd taste sweet. He knew it. And addictive . . . just the scent of her body was intoxicating. The taste would be so much more. *Dangerous . . . dangerous . . .* Kendall was the sort of woman that got inside a man's soul and never left. He didn't need to have her more deeply imbedded in his being than she already was.

Finally, her laughter started to fade and she studied him closely. Those eyes saw entirely too much, he suspected. "Go home, Kane."

With a slight smile, he replied, "I don't really have one, babe. You ought to understand that."

She took a step closer to him, letting him see her face a little better. There was a sadness in her eyes, and she sighed, shaking her head. "Maybe I do. What I don't understand is why you're doing this. You chose it. It chose me —I have no choice."

"Maybe I don't either," he murmured. "I may not be able to control people's thoughts and I'm not as strong as five men combined, but I hunt. It's what I'm good at. It's what I've always been good at."

"Then go back to doing what you used to do. Not this, Kane. Not our life."

He smiled a little. "I can't."

Her eyes narrowed, and he felt a chill run through the air. The once muggy, heavy air suddenly felt frigid. "You need to, Kane."

"Stop it, Kendall. Your tricks aren't going to work on me."

"I can *make* them work—is that what you want, Kane? Want me to blast inside your mind with no regard to whether or not it damages you? I did it once. Don't make me do it again." Her head cocked and a cold smile curved her lips. Her eyes gleamed at him with power. "I can make you forget, Kane. Don't doubt that. Not just me, or Duke. But everything . . . even your own name."

As he stared at her, Kendall felt shame move through her. *Damn it, Kendall, what in the hell are you doing?* How could she even think such a thing, much less threaten it?

To keep him safe . . . That little voice whispered in her mind. The thought of him dead, bloodied on the ground, drained of life, loomed in her mind, and she squared her shoulders. Staring at him with an arrogant smile, she asked, "Are you scared?"

He moved up, towering over her. His scent flooded her head and Kendall had to muffle the moan of want that rose in her chest. "Of you? Not exactly. What you are . . . maybe a little."

His hand cupped her neck, pulling her against him as he lowered his head to murmur in her ear, "If that's what you think you need to do, go ahead—but that's the only thing that will make me stop doing what I have to do."

She felt his breath warm on her face as she lifted her gaze, staring up at him. It was somewhat intimidating—she was short, barely five-feet-two, and with Kane right at five-foot-nine, it put her on eye level with his neck, the throbbing call of his blood just a breath away.

"You know what *really* has me scared?" he whispered.

His hand came up, coming to her face, and Kendall shuddered. Dragging her tongue along her lips, she tensed. Was he going to kiss her?

Bloody hell, she hoped so. She couldn't remember wanting anything quite the way she wanted to feel his mouth on hers again.

His mouth was just a breath away, and his words drifted across her skin as he whispered, "I'm afraid of what Duke would try to do to me, if he had any idea what I wanted to do to *you*."

As he spoke, he pressed his mouth gently against hers, and the image that leaped from his mind for a long time made no sense. Duke and her, Duke's mouth on hers, while

Kane stood by in the background, staring at them with rage written all over his face.

Kendall gasped out a breath as she pulled away, staring at him with confusion. "Duke . . . and me . . ." she whispered, right before she started to grin.

Tipping her face back to the sky, she started to laugh. "Oh, man . . ." she giggled. Turning away, she walked over to her car, leaning against it as the giggles got worse. "Oh, man. That's good. Duke . . . and me."

Kane watched her as she laughed, feeling alternating waves of heat and irritation move through him. "I keep making you laugh—so glad to know I amuse you." Studying her, he realized she'd never actually admitted outright that her and Duke . . .

"Me and Duke," she repeated. Mirth sparkled in her eyes and she pressed a hand to her belly. Probably hurt from how much she was laughing, Kane thought sourly. "Oh, that is rich."

"I'm going to take a big risk here," Kane drawled. "But there's nothing between you and Duke, is there?"

She grinned at him. "Oh, I wouldn't go *that* far. He's a great guy—kind of quiet, but definitely somebody you'd want at your back in a fight. Funny as hell. And I do have to admit, his ass looks very nice in those jeans he likes to wear," she commented.

What exploded in him at that moment was indescribable. Hunger, a possessiveness that he couldn't explain, relief . . . and that was just the tip of the iceberg. Savage glee flooded his veins as he started to move around her, round and round. Her eyes lifted, and as her gaze met his, he stopped in front of her, just a breath away.

As their eyes met, all signs of laughter, of amusement, drained out of her face and her big eyes suddenly darkened with an unmistakable look of arousal, hot, potent, female arousal.

Memories of that kiss they'd shared all those months ago flooded his mind. That small taste he'd had still lingered on his lips—and she didn't belong to his best friend. That was all he cared about. He'd wanted to gorge on her and couldn't. Or so he had thought.

He *could* have her.

And damn, he thought, he would. Cupping her chin in his hands, he lifted her face to his as he whispered, "You have no idea what hearing that does to me."

Slanting his mouth across hers, he buried one fist in her hair. Her lips parted under his as she gasped, and he pushed his tongue inside the hot, wet cavern. Sliding his free hand down her back, he brought her body in line with his. The soft rise of her belly cuddled the aching length of his cock.

Kendall moaned into his mouth and Kane felt the hot lash of satisfaction. She felt it, too. He didn't know how he was so certain, but he was.

There was a pressure against his mouth, just under the curve of her lips, and then an icy sharp pain, followed by the coppery taste of blood in his mouth. He barely even took notice, but seconds later, Kendall had pulled away from him.

Rage tore through him at the loss of her body against his. He started to reach for her, but she lifted a hand, whispering harshly, "No."

The moonlight splashed across her face, and Kane saw the dark stain on her mouth, and the gleaming white of her incisors. As he watched, she shuddered, spinning away. "Get away from me, Kane," she rasped.

A slow smile arched his lips. "Why?"

She tossed him a cool glance. "I haven't fed. You look entirely too appetizing. Now go *away*."

"Appetizing, huh?" he mused, reaching up and stroking his chin. Studying her closely, he let the wide grin spread across his face. "I do have to admit, you look pretty delicious yourself."

Kendall's response was that sexy little sneer he found so enticing. "You seem to forget—when I say appetizing, I actually mean *eating*," she drawled. Her eyes dropped to his neck, and he was suddenly never so aware of the pulse of blood running through his veins.

Kane ran his eyes down the sleek lines of her body, imagining what she looked like without that skin-hugging top, the painted-on jeans. His eyes lingered low—he heard her sharp intake of breath. Softly, he whispered, "So did I—of course, I'm focusing on a different part of the anatomy."

As her eyes widened, Kane closed the distance between them. Watching her from hooded eyes, he waited for her to move away, but as he reached up and closed his hands over her hips, she just stood there, staring at him with wide eyes. Lowering his mouth, he whispered into her ear, "I'm going to take you places you've never even imagined."

A⊤ those roughly spoken words, part of her wanted to laugh, to scoff. But all she could do was whimper with want. He made her hot. He had from the very beginning.

When he pressed his mouth to hers, Kendall arched against him. His hands pressed against her back, hard, calloused, and so warm. Her body, always so cool, started to warm against his and the heat felt almost as delicious as the length of his cock pressed against her belly.

Damn it, his taste—he tasted so alive, so male. The scent of his skin flooded her head, sandalwood, pine, and under it the rich wine of his blood. She shivered as he pulled away from her mouth, kissing a hot trail across her cheek, down her jawbone, along the line of her neck.

When he raked his teeth across the sensitive skin there, she cried out. Hot, molten need flowed through her veins like lava.

A loud, raucous noise echoed in her ears, followed by a soft curse.

"Room," he muttered. "Where's your room?"

I'm not doing this, Kendall thought, even as she fished the keycard out of her pocket, gesturing silently to the room down at the end. *Nothing's changed, not one thing . . .* But that wasn't exactly right.

Things might not have changed for her, but they had changed for him. He'd been holding back that last time. And he wasn't now. Her breath left her in a shaky sigh and she realized she didn't even want to argue with him.

"Down there."

Kane took the key from her then swept her up in his arms. That gesture sent excitement coursing through her—it had been too long since a man had made her feel like a woman. Too long since she had felt like anything other than a Hunter. Just a weapon, a tool . . . nothing more.

Oh, but Kane. Even the feel of his hard, muscled arms under her back and knees had her heart pounding. Her head was spinning by the time they reached her door. Kendall gasped as his hand fell out from under her knees—her body trailed against his and she stared up at him hungrily as he leaned into her.

His mouth pressed against hers while he fumbled with the keycard and the door opened at her back as he stepped away. Kendall stumbled inside, thrown off balance by the buzzing in her head, the heat surging through her body, the memory of his mouth on hers . . . and hunger. Hunger was driving her mad.

But she didn't know what she wanted more—the feed.

Or the fuck.

His hands caught her, steadying her body, bringing her against him. Lifting her eyes, she stared into his dark gaze while he slid his hands under the hem of her shirt, slowly stroking upwards with the palms of his hands pressed flat against her skin.

The metal links that made up the shirt clinked together musically as it pooled around his wrists as he slowly moved his hands upward. When his roughened palms touched the curve of her breasts, Kendall thought her legs were going to give out from under her.

His mouth took hers and she moaned as he pushed his tongue past the barrier of her lips. Under the shirt, she was naked, and she had never been so glad she'd foregone bra and panties as his fingers sought out her nipples, plucking and teasing each crest.

Burying her hands in the tousled golden silk of his hair,

she pushed her tongue into his mouth as her fangs slid out. But Kane took control of the kiss, stroking his tongue against hers. Once more, one of her fangs nicked his tongue, and when blood welled, she whimpered, sucking delicately on his tongue and shuddering as a few drops spilled out, gliding down her throat like some rare, golden vintage.

He pulled his mouth away, his hands leaving her breasts. Kendall's mouth pursed into a sullen pout, as she lost both his touch and his taste. But then his hands closed around her head and he whispered, "Do it right, sweet," as he guided her mouth to his neck.

"No," she whispered, but her heart wasn't in it. She was hungry, and he felt so warm . . . Damn it, did he know what he was doing?

As his pulse throbbed against her lips, any weak protest she might have made died and she struck, her fangs piercing his golden skin. His blood splashed hot and rich into her mouth and she shuddered.

There was a harsh jerk at her neck as he wrenched open the clasp that held up the chain mail halter she wore, then the metal puddled around her waist and cool air kissed her flesh. Wrapping one arm around his head, she held him tight against her, straining to keep her grip on him. His hands closed over her ass, and as he lifted her up, she wrapped her legs around his hips instinctively, clutching at his body.

His mouth closed over the aching tip of one nipple, and she pulled her mouth from his flesh, screaming out his name in sheer delighted shock. He worked her nipple, using teeth and tongue and lips, suckling, biting, until she was squirming and bucking in his arms.

Between her legs, she felt the hard column of his cock and she rubbed against it. She was wet—she could feel the cream gathering between her thighs, soaking the crotch of her jeans as she moved against him.

"Your body . . . you're getting so hot," he whispered against her flesh. "So damn soft. How can you be this soft?"

Kendall suspected the answer to that might be that she was melting . . . damn it, she was melting. Had to be the answer. The heat flooding her body was unlike any she had ever felt.

Opening her eyes, she sucked in air as the world spun around her. No, the world wasn't spinning, the room was, because Kane had spun around and was carrying her to the bed.

She bounced once against the mattress, planting her hands behind her and watching as Kane stripped off his jacket, tossing it aside. There was a leather shoulder holster and she arched a brow as he unbuckled that, draping it over the spindly chair. A knife sheath was strapped to his ankle, and when a second small, compact gun came from his other ankle, she started to grin.

"I don't know that I've ever had sex with Rambo before," she mused.

Kane lifted his head, strands of golden hair falling into his eyes, shadows falling across his face. A slow smile curved his mouth and he murmured, "Well, I know I've never had sex with a luscious vampire before, so this will be a different experience for both of us."

Oh, yeah. Her heart was pounding faster than it had in a very long time, and her loins ached. Every time she shifted, the crotch of her jeans rubbed against her clit, the seam biting into her pussy—a sweetly painful sensation. The smile died on her face as she stared at him, the hard-muscled wall of his chest, the muscles that shifted and bulged in his arms, the hungry, predatory way he stared at her.

Her heart stuttered in her chest as he reached up, touching his fingers to the tiny puncture wounds in his neck. "How much did you take?"

Her mouth was dry as she responded, "Just a little. You'll never miss it."

The bed dipped under his weight as he braced a knee on the mattress. A moan shimmered out of her as he touched his fingers, stained with his blood, to her lips. "Can you take more? Safely."

Wordlessly, she nodded as he slipped his fingers inside her mouth. Curling her tongue over one, then the other, she sucked the blood away.

"Good . . ." the word was muttered into her hair as he bent over her, bringing his other knee up on the bed, one knee on each side of her hips, hunkering down over her, burying his face in her hair.

Slowly, he pulled his fingers from her mouth and Kendall felt her heart lodge in her throat as he wrapped his arms around her, holding her against him for a long moment.

I'm in serious trouble here . . .

Those words circled through her mind briefly, but then he moved, one hand coming up to fist in her hair, arching her face up to his as he took her mouth.

Nobody had ever kissed her the way he did. A conquering, a seduction, a claiming all in one. And something about the way he handled her, the way it felt when his eyes moved over her face, her body as he brushed the material of her shirt away, peeling the tight jeans off her body.

Treasured. How could this man that had tried to kill her just a year ago make her feel so treasured?

So safe . . .

So wanted.

His jeans rubbed abrasively against her legs as he kissed a hot trail down her body. She shivered as his hands cupped her ass, lifting her up. A hot puff of air caressed the naked folds of her pussy as he blew on her right before he lowered his mouth to her.

With a scream, she arched off the bed as he stroked his tongue along the narrow slit, then pushed inside. The pressure building inside her exploded in one hot, furious geyser. Kane muttered against her flesh and the vibrations of his words teased already sensitive nerves as she rocked against him. "That's it, sweet. Ride my mouth, come again . . . damn, you're sweet."

Dazed, she whimpered as he slid one finger, then a second inside her as the climax rolled through her. "You're not done yet, Kendall. Nowhere near. Come again."

She moaned as he pumped his fingers inside the hot, slick depths of her sex, shifting his angle and moving up so that he could nuzzle and tease her clit with his tongue and teeth.

Fisting her hands, she tugged on his hair and begged, "Come up here—I want to feel you inside me."

"I am inside you." As he spoke, he rotated his wrist as though to emphasize his words.

"Please!" She arched her hips, greedy for more, loathing the thought of him leaving her, but aching for more than just his fingers.

He chuckled against her, lifting his head as she tugged on his hair. "Guess I better . . . unless I want to end up bald."

Blood rushed to her face and her hands fell away. A few locks of hair came with her hands and she flinched, looking up at him. "So—"

Her muttered apology was muffled against his mouth as he kissed her gently. Lifting up, he jerked open the buttons at his fly. "Don't be sorry," he rasped, his eyes locked on her face.

He shoved his jeans down, and she dropped her gaze to watch as his cock sprang free, thick, hard, a bead of fluid leaking free, trickling slowly down the ruddy flesh.

"Damn, the way you look at me," he grunted as he covered her body with his, slanting his mouth across hers. Her taste was in the kiss and she flushed to the roots of her hair, trying to turn away from his mouth. "No," he whispered as he wedged his hips between her thighs. "Taste yourself. You're so sweet, so hot. I could feast on you for days."

As his tongue breeched the entrance to her mouth, she felt the broad rounded head of his cock nudging against her pussy. His lips left her—he pushed up, bracing his elbows beside her head and staring down at her. That look was almost as intimate as the feel of his cock sliding inside her. Caught in that dark green gaze, Kendall had never felt so exposed, so naked.

His voice was guttural as he murmured, "I've dreamed of this . . . even when I thought I was dreaming of a killer—oh, fuck!"

Kendall cried out as he buried his cock balls-deep inside her, a sharp little pain tearing through her middle, tears burning her eyes for a moment. "Kane," she sobbed, her hands curling into fists. Unconsciously, she tried to pull away, closing herself off from him. It *hurt* . . . the sensation of his cock burning and stretching the tight tissues of her pussy.

"Damnation . . . you're tight as a damned fist," Kane whispered raggedly, stroking one hand soothingly up and down her side. "Damn it, Kendall."

She stared up at him, forcing a smile. "Uh, it's been a while." She tried to think back and realized she couldn't even remember. More than years. Probably in the realm of decades.

His hand stroked up her side as he pressed his forehead to hers. Kendall felt her heart clench at the sheer tenderness of the moment. Like warm silk stroking down her cheek, he kissed away the tears and her body calmed just a little, her hands skimming up his chest, curling over his shoulders. "Just relax," he whispered as his mouth took hers again.

Kane started to move, slow, short strokes that teased her body into relaxing completely under his. Swiveling his hips against the cradle of hers, he moved so that he caressed her clit with each slow movement.

It seemed like no time passed at all before she was moaning under him, lifting her hips to meet him as he moved against her. Sweat started to gleam on his skin, her own body absorbing the heat from his until she was burning inside. Damn it, he was so deep—felt so tight.

"That's it, baby," he moaned against her lips, sliding his hand down and cupping her ass, bringing her tight and hard against him, grinding her against him.

Kendall shuddered convulsively when he trailed his fingers between the cheeks of her ass, pressing against her. "Kane!" He chuckled, lowering his head and raking her neck with his teeth.

"I've been dying to hear you scream my name, just like that." He pushed his weight up onto his hands, staring down at her with hooded eyes for a long moment before he trailed his gaze over the length of her body. His gaze lingered on her breasts before sliding down to watch as he shafted her slowly.

One hand came up, trailing down the middle of her body, one roughened finger circling over her nipple. He plucked it between finger and thumb and she moaned, feeling each slow, deliberate stroke echo down in her pussy.

Staring up at him, Kendall watched spellbound as he smiled at her, a wicked, hot smile. Those fingers left her nipple, trailing down her middle, circling over her navel, tugging lightly on the hoop there before moving down.

As he started to stroke her clit, she shrieked out his name. His touch became fast and more deliberate, but he kept stopping just shy of that one touch that would let her come. Arching up, she gasped out, "Damn it, let me come."

Kane smiled at her. With one flick of his wrist, he had sent her screaming into orgasm, sobbing out his name as she came. The muscles in her pussy clenched around him, the convulsions so hard and tight, her entire body shook from it. Her eyes were open but she saw nothing but light, bright glorious light.

One second she was screaming out his name, and then the next, her lips were pressed against his skin, while he muttered against her temple, "Do it, Kendall—let me feel it again."

Feeding while in the frenzy of climax was one of the most erotic, arousing things a vampire could do—and the most dangerous. His blood filled her mouth, hot and spicy with arousal, as her fangs sought out and pierced where she had bitten him earlier.

He withdrew, and if Kendall hadn't had her mouth pressed against his neck, she would have cried out at the loss as he pulled away. But then he slammed back into her, hard, deep, and she could feel the hot pulse of semen as he came deep within her.

It went on and on, his cock jerking within her pussy as he came, his blood pumping from the two small holes in his neck—it was his faint whisper, "Kendall . . ." that suddenly brought her back to herself.

Horrified, she loosed her grip and shoved him off of her, watching as his eyes slowly closed, a smile on his lips.

CHAPTER 6

KANE was sluggishly aware of her, her voice harsh and angry, her hands gentle as she lifted him—water being poured down his throat. *Drink, damn it!*

Her fingers against his throat . . . darkness, then the whole thing started all over again.

When he awoke, it was daylight. No light shone inside the room through the thick curtains, but he knew. His internal clock told him it was close to noon . . . had Kendall left him? Where did she sleep?

"You're awake."

Her voice was odd. Tight. Turning his head, he saw her reclining in the single chair the room boasted, as far away from the window as she could get, the dim light from the lamp casting its light on her face. Crooking a sheepish grin at her, he said, "Sorry. I don't usually pass out after making love to a woman. At least, not right away."

She didn't smile. In fact, he saw a tightening around her eyes, her mouth, and his gut started to churn. Shit. She was going to kick him out. Damn it, he couldn't stand the thought of leaving her—

"You don't usually damn near bleed to death after making love to a woman," she said flatly.

Kane scowled at her. "What?" He tried to think back to what she was talking about, but his mind was muddled, and hazy. He remembered the slick, hot satin of her pussy, how tight she was, how she screamed out his name . . . but the details were dim, almost dreamlike. And her teeth . . . the sharp, sweet little pain as her fangs pricked his flesh . . .

"It's a very bad idea to encourage a vampire to bite you when the vampire isn't in control," she said shortly. "I damn near bled you to death."

Kane just blinked at her.

Kendall glared at him, coming out of the chair in a flurry of motion, her voice low, cold . . . fuck, what was that? The room suddenly seemed thirty degrees colder and that crazy fear seemed to be pushing at his mind again. His skin chilled, roughened by goosebumps as she stalked over to him.

Shit, was she trying that mind control crap on him again? he wondered. What was she up to? But as she moved closer, all he could see in her eyes was pure, undiluted fury.

"You dumbfuck, didn't you *hear* me?" she snarled.

Clenching his jaw, he forced his eyes away from hers as he sat up slowly. Once his eyes left hers, the icy cold wasn't quite so intense and the fear retreated entirely.

Swinging his legs around, the sheet tangling around his hips, he planted his feet on the ground and just stared at her.

"I heard you," Kane said. Reaching up, he touched his fingers to his neck, feeling nearly healed skin. "So basically I'm short a pint or two of O negative. Nothing rest, food, and water won't bring back."

He had to grin at the sputtering sound she made, flicking his eyes to her face for the briefest of seconds. When the fear didn't wrap a choke hold around his neck, he continued to stare at her. "You are a dumbass," she finally muttered, spinning away from him.

That was fine. The back view of her was just as good as the front view . . . her sweet little ass curving under the tight fit of her jeans, her long back smooth and naked under the skimpy shirt she wore.

"Dumbass, dumbfuck," he mused, shaking his head. "Those aren't exactly the sweet nothings a man wants to hear after having some of the best sex of his life. Well, it might actually have *been* the best sex, but the memory is a little blurred." Grinning wolfishly at her, he asked, "Can we do it again?"

Kendall whirled back around to glare at him, folding her arms across her breasts.

She was so cute when she was thinking hard. Or pissed. Or flustered . . . what was she? He couldn't tell. All he knew was that she was standing there with her arms folded over her very pretty breasts, tapping her bare foot on the ground, and glaring at him with eyes that glowed warm and golden in the dim light. Her lip curled up and Kane felt heat flood his system at that sexy little snarl. "You're running a bit low on blood, pal. I doubt you could get it up."

Kane chuckled, wrapping one fist in the sheet and pulling it aside. Cupping his balls in his hand, his lids drooped, and then he stroked his hand upward, closing it in a loose fist around the thick pillar of flesh.

Her eyes dropped to his groin and his cock jerked under her stare. "Wanna bet?" he teased softly.

"Anybody ever tell you that you are a fickle bastard, Kane?" she asked hoarsely.

He pumped his hand up and down his length once, twice, before his hand slowly fell away and he rose. Crossing over to her, he hooked his arms over her shoulders, nuzzling the dark red of her hair as he whispered, "How's that?"

He heard her swallow right before she whispered, "There was a time about a year ago when you wanted me dead. Now, you seem to want me fucked. Don't you call that fickle?"

A muscle in his jaw ticked as he stepped away, staring down into her eyes stonily. "That was when I thought you were a killer, when I thought you'd killed Duke—"

She was always pale—but it seemed at the mention of his name, she paled even more. "Duke . . . oh, *shit!*"

Kane's eyes narrowed. "You said there was nothing . . ."

She turned away from him, stalking to the phone and lifting the receiver. Fury brewed in his gut at her obvious dismissal, but as he took a step closer, he saw something in her eyes.

Fear.

She continued to stand there, the phone pressed to her ear. Her other hand was opening and closing in a fist and her entire body was tense. Her eyes moved to his. "We always check in with each other the next morning if we split up." Her eyes closed for a long moment and then she looked back at him. "He didn't call yesterday morning and I was so damned worried about you—I forgot about him."

Dread curdled in his gut—coupled with fear as he remembered the dreams that had guided him here.

"When did you last see him? At the bar?"

Kendall nodded. "There was a woman there—blonde, shy. Wouldn't hardly look at me."

Kane scowled, remembering how he'd thought a woman would have to be damned near insane to go inside that joint, especially alone. Unless it was somebody like Kendall.

Arching a brow, he asked curiously, "Was she human?"

Kendall nodded. "Yes—there's not too many non mortals around here. We've hardly seen any."

With a thoughtful frown, Kane said, "That's kind of weird, isn't it? From what I've been able to tell, most of you like the bigger cities."

One smooth shoulder lifted in a shrug. "More anonymity here. We need that."

"Cincinnati is damned big." A wave of weakness struck him, and Kane felt his head start to swim. On watery legs, he crossed to the bed and lowered himself back down. A slow smile pulled up his lips as he saw Kendall staring at his lap. Under that watchful stare, Kane felt his flesh stir once more. As his blood started to pound and heat, his cock stiffened until it was jutting upward.

Reaching over, he flipped the sheet back over his lap. "What do we do about Duke?" he asked quietly.

Her gaze flew up to meet his and he could have sworn her cheeks flushed just a bit. Then she shook her head a little, and when she looked at him, the fires of lust in her eyes had been banked. "*We* don't do anything," she replied levelly. "He's my partner. I know he's your friend, but you aren't a part of this."

Softly, Kane argued, "But that's where you're wrong." Her eyes narrowed mutinously, and Kane lifted a hand. "Listen to me—did it ever occur to you there's a reason I can always find you when I need you?"

"Of course there's a reason . . . it's so you can be a pain in my ass."

Wolfishly, Kane smiled at her. "But I haven't even gotten around to touching your ass yet. Well, not as much as I want to, and certainly not enough to give you a pain there." Then his face sobered. "I've been having dreams, Kendall. They've been getting worse for the past few months. They're about Duke."

There was something a little unnerving, Kane decided, about having somebody like Kendall watching him in just that way. "What kind of dreams?" she asked, her voice low, almost whisper soft. Her eyes remained locked on his face, her stare focused and unblinking as the golden irises started to swirl and glow.

"He was dead in the last one." Kane dropped his gaze to his hands. "I looked at his face and knew somebody killed him because of what he is, and that person wasn't going to stop with just him."

"Human?"

Lifting one shoulder in a shrug, he murmured, "I don't know. Doubt it. He looked . . . I don't know if I can explain it, but I looked at him and it was like I could almost see through him. Like he'd been hollowed out."

H
E wouldn't go away. She did damn near everything she could think of to convince him.

Hell, she'd even tried coercion on him, and with his running low on blood, Kane shouldn't have been as strong. Kendall really wasn't sure what made him so resistant to the subtle mind control vampires used, but there was definitely something.

She knew she could simply stop holding back, but that wasn't something she wanted to try. A vamp's mind magick could be entirely too destructive—she wanted him safe, not mentally shattered.

"Damn it, do you have to be so damned stubborn?" she snarled, watching as he washed down a couple of iron supplements followed by a glass of orange juice.

The acidity of the juice would be reflected in his blood—already his body chemistry had changed a little, and the low-level hunger seemed to fade just a little more. Hopefully it would keep the temptation at bay until she managed to chase him away.

But the slow, confident smile on his lips told her something she didn't want to know.

Kane wasn't going anywhere.

"You can't help me," she said testily, watching as he tugged on his boots and started tucking away his various weapons. A gun at the small of his back. The long, deadly knife at his hip. Another gun in a sheath at his ankle.

He just lifted one shoulder in a shrug. "Maybe, maybe not." His mouth thinned out and his eyes chilled as he met her glare steadily. "But it's my best friend that's missing. You ever walk away from your friends, Kendall?"

Closing her eyes, she turned away from him. Sighing, she shoved a hand through her hair. "You're such a pain in the ass," she whispered.

Grabbing her keys and purse, she slid outside, listening to the light fall of his footsteps behind her. A few minutes later, he slid into the passenger seat across from her and Kendall started the car.

"Where are we going?"

Sliding him a look, she said, "Burger King. You need food."

His mouth twisted a little. "I don't know that I'd call that food."

She smiled sweetly. "I can drop you off anywhere you like."

Kane gave a low, husky chuckle. "Burger King would be just fine. Where to after that?"

"Back to the bar. See if we can find the woman Duke was with."

"Good—I need to get my truck."

Kendall snorted. "You actually think it's still there?"

He flashed her a wide, wicked grin. "Oh, I think there's a good chance it will still be there. I did the security myself. And the type of guy that frequents that dive you were at probably isn't the kind of guy that's going to have the electronic know-how needed to bypass my security."

Kendall only shook her head as she turned into the parking lot of the fast-food restaurant. "You know, one of these days somebody is going to do something that makes you a lot less cocky. I just can't decide if I want to see it or not."

THE black SUV was there. Kane just smiled as he popped another French fry in his mouth. A small, mischievous part of Kendall kind of wished the damn thing had been gone—or vandalized.

But the black exterior looked as new as if he had just driven it out of the showroom. Parking next to it, Kendall climbed out of her car and leaned against it while Kane went to unlock it. He used a fob, and it seemed to her there were a lot more buttons on that fob than she had on hers. Of course, a lot of modern technology still confounded her. She could drive and use a telephone, liked watching TV—*Law & Order* was a personal favorite. But there were a lot of vampires that abhorred any and all technology. If they had to go someplace and the less than traditional means of transportation were needed, then they had somebody drive them.

But even though she dealt with the technology of the current time pretty well, there was no way she could figure out what in the hell all those buttons and beeps were for.

She was still shaking her head when he opened the door a minute later. When he came out, he had another duffle bag in his hand and just met her eyes with a smile as he tossed it into the floorboard of her car. "Clean clothes."

"And what about your truck?" she asked mildly. "I don't think the owner wants it here indefinitely."

"I'll put it in storage tomorrow. Follow you back to the hotel for tonight."

Kendall sighed, reaching up to massage her temples. "I really don't like this," she muttered as she shoved away from the SUV. He fell into step beside her and his hand cupped her neck.

"That's okay, darlin'. I kind of do."

The bar was as picturesque tonight as it had been two nights ago. Cigarette butts littered the ground and glass crunched underfoot as they crossed the parking lot. The ripe smell of body sweat permeated the night air, and, faintly, she could still smell blood.

The two men from that night. The scent of their blood would take a few more days to fade away completely, although no human could possibly smell it.

"You sure nobody is going to connect you to those guys?" Kane asked.

Distracted, she glanced at him as she slowed down by the door. It was open, a burly, bearded dude wearing jeans and a leather vest, sans shirt, sat on a stool by the door, taking crumpled ones and fives from the patrons. *People actually pay to listen to this crap?* she wondered.

It sounded like cats screaming in the throes of death. Really, *really* bad.

Forcing her mind away from the music, she focused on Kane and his question. "Yes, I'm sure. And likely even if somebody *did* remember me, these people aren't going to call the cops."

"I'd almost rather they did," Kane muttered, shaking his

head as they closed the distance between them and the guy at the door. "Might be safer."

Kendall smiled a little at that. Well, that was true. If by some small chance somebody here did remember her, and was friends with the men she'd dealt with, they'd probably get a little testy. But it wasn't very likely to happen. And if it did, it wasn't anything she hadn't handled before.

Kane, on the other hand . . .

Guns and knives wouldn't kill her. Fists wouldn't. But they'd do Kane a lot of damage if the two of them got cornered. Silently, Kendall told herself, *I'll just have to make sure that doesn't happen.*

There was nothing to worry about, though.

Even the bartender that had been looking down the front of her shirt that night stared at her now with no recognition in his eyes. As she slid onto the bar stool, his eyes started to wander south, but then Kane joined her and the man's eyes promptly returned to her face.

She slid Kane a glance, but his expression was blank, a small smile on his lips.

They waited until the bartender brought them their drinks and then Kendall reached out, resting a hand on his arm. He stilled, and when she stared into his eyes, they were vague, almost confused. Smiling gently, she said, "I'm looking for somebody. Can you help me?"

He nodded, staring at her with a rapt gaze.

"Thank you." Leaning closer, she focused a little harder and made sure her hold on his mind was complete. "There was a blonde lady here, two nights ago. Young, pretty. She didn't look like she belonged here. Do you remember seeing her?"

The bartender spoke, his voice soft and slow, "There was a pretty lady—looked like a Barbie doll."

Kendall smiled. "Yes, that's her. Do you remember the man with her? He's a friend of mine. Tall, white-blond hair. Hazel eyes. They left together—do you remember him?"

"That was a scary dude. Take you apart with his bare

hands. Could see it in his eyes," the bartender said. Something he had seen about Duke had bothered him and his face grew agitated, his eyes clearing a little as adrenaline started to flow through him.

"Duke's a pussy cat," Kendall said with a soft laugh, projecting calm thoughts into his mind. As he relaxed a little, she patted his arm. "Do you remember seeing either of them again?"

He shrugged. "Not the dude. And not here."

"You saw the girl, then?"

He nodded. "She walks a lot. Seen her lots."

"W HAT in the hell did you do to him?" Kane asked as they slid outside a few minutes later. He wiped the back of his wrist across his eyes—they both reeked of cigarette smoke, and his eyes burned from it.

With a shrug, Kendall dug her keys out of her purse. "Asked him some questions."

Kane snorted. "That's not all. He was as eager to please as an honor student on the first day of school."

Her eyes met his as she rounded the car. Folding her arms, she rested them on its roof, propping her chin on them. "I wouldn't really know how eager that is. I didn't go to school, technically, until I'd been a vampire for three years. And Excelsior isn't your average school." Then she pushed back from the car, shrugging her shoulders casually. "But I get the point. It's called mind control, Kane. You know, the thing that doesn't work on you? It's the same way I'm able to make people forget they ever saw me. I can get people to answer most any question I ask them. There are other, less admirable ways to use it, as well, but that's generally not something a Hunter does."

"Like what?" he asked, following her actions as she slid into the car. As she started the car, the light from the dashboard painted her features with a silvery glow.

She met his eyes levelly, and the sadness in them made him want to punch something. Instead, he reached out and traced the bow of her lips, waiting for her to answer. She sighed and the soft breath of air felt like a caress on his hand. "You really don't want to know."

Leaning forward, he rested his elbow on the console between them. "Yes, I do," he murmured. Tracing his fingers across her cheek, he held her gaze. The thick, soft silk of her hair tempted him and he slid his hand down, around the back of her neck, and captured a fistful of the deep red strands, arching her face up to meet his.

Her eyes started to glow as she stared up at him. The sadness was still there, but there was also hunger starting to gleam, and the scent of her body seemed to get stronger. She didn't answer him, but Kane had totally forgotten that he'd asked her anything to begin with as he stared into her face.

Lowering his head, he slanted his mouth across hers and pushed his tongue inside. The ripe, sweet taste of her reminded him of peaches. Groaning, he reached out and hauled her against him, pulling her slender body over the console and into his lap.

She whimpered low in her throat as he cupped one breast in his hand. His cock throbbed against the curve of her hip. Reaching down, he cupped her in his hand.

There was a horn blaring in the distance. She stiffened in his arms and Kane groaned, tightening his grip on her for one long second before letting her go. Falling back into the leather, he ran a hand through his hair, watching her through brooding eyes as she slid back into her seat.

Kendall's eyes glowed dark and golden against her pale skin, her mouth swollen and shiny. He heard a soft shuddering sigh, and his eyes dropped to her chest, watching as her breasts rose and fell as she breathed in. Growling, he spun away. "Damn it, what in the hell are we doing?" he muttered.

Kendall sighed. "We can't keep doing this. Duke is missing. He's in trouble."

Gravel crunched as a truck turned into the parking lot, and both of them briefly turned their eyes to watch as it drove around the back of the cinder block building. Once it was out of sight, Kane looked back at her. "Are you so sure he's in trouble?"

Kendall just arched a brow. "He hasn't shown his face in more than twenty-four hours. He didn't check in. And you show up because you've been having weird dreams where he's dead. How can you *not* think he's in trouble?"

A wry smile creased his face. "I was usually the one causing problems."

Kendall scowled. "Trust me. You still are." Jamming the key into the ignition, she started the engine before looking back at him once more. "Come on. Lets see if we can't find where this girl likes to walk a lot."

T HERE wasn't a pretty blonde walking anywhere that Kendall could see.

And she couldn't smell or feel anything off.

But in her gut, she knew Duke was in trouble.

Muttering under her breath, she propped her elbow on the window as she racked her brains. *What in the hell do I do now?*

They drove around half the night without any luck. Sliding Kane a glance, she asked wearily, "Was there anything in these dreams of yours that might help us? Anything that looked familiar to you?"

Kane just sighed. "Not anything that I can point out to you. Hell, I can't even tell you if they were more than just dreams. They just kept . . . kept happening. Wouldn't leave me alone. I had to do something about them." He turned his head, stared out the window. "It wasn't here—whatever happened in my dreams, it wasn't here."

He fell into silence for a minute and then looked at her. She could feel the weight of his stare as she drove down the road and turned her head briefly to meet his gaze. "What?"

"Don't you have any way of tracking him or something?" Kane asked quietly.

Kendall sighed. "It's not always that easy. If he'd been hurt *there,* likely there would be a blood trail. That's strong, that's powerful, I could follow that. I can still vaguely smell him there, but once he got into a car, I can't follow that. There's not a strong enough scent path just from him. There has to be something more." Slowing at a stoplight, she propped her elbow on the door and rested her temple on her fist.

A witch. That was what she needed.

The light turned green, but she never even noticed as she slowly lifted her head up, staring ahead without seeing anything. A slow smile edged up the corners of her mouth as she thought, *Well, hell, why didn't I think of that sooner?*

Blinking, she came out of her daze and saw the green light. Pressing down on the gas, she drove through the light and turned right on Colerain, heading for I-75. "Let's go back to the hotel. I need to talk to somebody."

But by the time they were there, the somebody she wanted to talk to was already there, with his back against the door, his head down, chin against his chest like he was sleeping.

Of course she knew he wasn't. Vax Matthews wasn't the kind who'd let down his guard long enough to take a catnap in public.

Kane stood tensely at her side, his eyes trained on the dark-haired man still lounging at her door. There was an otherworldly aura to Vax that she suspected Kane could sense.

With every step they took, he grew tenser and tenser. When she saw his hand edging toward his back, she moved in front of him and called out, "Having a nice nap, Vax?"

Her ex-trainee lifted his head. Storm-cloud gray eyes met hers and his teeth flashed white in the coppery gold of his face. Those gray eyes were the only sign of something other than Native American blood flowing through his veins.

But nobody, not even Vax, really knew where he came from. Vax didn't know much of anything about his parents. He didn't talk about it, but from what Kendall had been able to put together, he'd been raised in an orphanage in Kansas City until he was five or six, and then he'd mostly lived on his own there, scrounging the way a homeless child did back in the 1800s.

Like a lot of the Hunters, there was tragedy in Vax's life. And like a lot of them, he'd moved past it. His eyes warmed as he smiled at Kendall, and she grinned at him. "I'm not even going to ask you what in the hell you are doing here," she drawled.

"You don't look very surprised to see me." Vax looked briefly at Kane before looking back at her, cocking his head. His hair, thick and raven-wing black, spilled over his shoulder, gleaming in the dim light.

Kendall laughed. "Vax, I learned a long time ago to stop being surprised by anything you did or said. You witches are all crazy."

Vax gave her a look of mock innocence, arching black brows over his eyes as he laid a hand over his breast. "Crazy? Why do you say that?"

Kendall just sighed, turning to meet Kane's distrusting gaze. "This is Vax Matthews. He's a Hunter—sort of."

Eyes narrowed, Kane asked, "How is one a Hunter, *sort of*?"

Vax smiled. "I'm retired."

Arching a brow, Kane said blandly, "You look a little young to retire."

Vax just chuckled. "I look pretty good for my age. Not quite as good as Kendall, but still."

Kendall just rolled her eyes and shook her head. Nudging Vax aside, she dug her keycard out of her hip pocket and opened the door to the hotel room. "Why don't we talk inside?"

Both of the men hesitated behind her, and Kendall turned to stare at them, arms crossed over her chest. Vax had a very, very long history of not trusting strangers and he didn't give people his back, but every instinct Kane had was raised, and he wasn't turning his back on Vax either. Tongue in cheek, she said, "You know, you two could always step inside back to back."

Vax grinned at that. Kane still had that steely look in his eyes, and it didn't lessen any as Vax walked past him into the room, whistling as though he didn't have a care in the world.

It didn't seem possible, but Kane's eyes seemed to get even harder as Vax paused by her and brushed his hand down her hair. "You look as lovely as ever, Kendall."

"And you're as much a flatterer as ever, Vax," she replied dryly, taking one small step away. It was just a little step, but it wasn't one she had ever taken before. She and Vax had shared a bed, and often, in the past. He knew her, and he knew her very well, better than anybody else. That one little step told him everything he needed to know. With a slow smile, he just nodded and moved away.

But not without a wide grin at Kane.

Kane's brows dropped low over his eyes, and he stepped toward Vax with a growl rumbling in his throat.

Shit, Kendall thought, moving between them yet again. "What are you doing out of Montana, Vax? And in a city, no less?"

The witch strolled across the room and flopped down on the rigid armchair, draping his long, rangy body on it like a cat. His eyes met hers across the room and he said, "Looking for you."

Too used to him to be aggravated, Kendall replied sweetly, "Honey, I gathered that. After all, you're talking to me. What I want to know is *why* are you looking for me?"

"Because I needed to talk to you, of course," he said patiently.

"Vax, you are a major pain in the ass." Kendall sighed and leaned against the wall, still keeping her eyes on Kane. His hand had finally fallen to his side, but she knew he could have that gun in his hand in an instant. Damn Vax—he was playing with fire and he probably knew it. A bullet wouldn't kill him, not that he'd ever let himself get shot, but she didn't want to see how ugly it could get just because Vax had a devilish streak inside him.

He opened his mouth, and judging by the look in his eyes, whatever he planned on saying wasn't going to be helpful. Narrowing her eyes, she focused on him and thought, *Shut the hell up*.

Vax just grinned. Then he turned his attention to Kane, his face sobering. "You really are human."

K ANE had thought the gray-eyed bastard was, but there was something about him that was *odd*. Shoving off the wall, Kane glared at him and asked, "What in the hell are you talking about? What else would I be?"

Vax, at least Kane thought that was what Kendall called him, shrugged his shoulders. "I wasn't sure. But usually mortals aren't much help in our fights. Don't know why you should be any different."

Kane just stared at him.

Vax stared back at him levelly and the silence stretched, growing heavier and heavier. It was Kendall that broke it when she asked wearily, "Vax, what in the hell are you talking about? Why are you here?"

Vax blinked, lowering his lashes, almost like he was sleepy, but when he lifted his lids, his gray eyes were glowing. Kane hissed out a breath as what looked like tiny bolts of lightening lanced through the depths of the man's stormy gray eyes. "Because I keep seeing your face in my head, Kane Winter, and you are all that stands between Kendall and death."

With that, he lowered his head, staring at the floor for a moment. When he looked up, those eerie gray eyes were normal once more, or as normal as they could get, that pale gray set against the deep gold of his skin. "It wasn't Duke they were after, Kendall. Duke was just the bait, a pawn. They took him because they knew you'd come looking for him."

"Who?" she demanded.

Vax only shook his head. "If I knew everything, I could find him for you. But I can't, because I don't." His gaze cut to Kane. "Kendall's mind magick doesn't work on you. Theirs won't either. There's darkness in this city, do you feel it?"

Kendall started to speak, but Kane interrupted her. "Yes, I feel it. It wasn't always like this."

Kendall shook her head. "There's nothing here, Vax."

Vax arched a brow. "There is. I'm not sure why you don't feel it. Hell, I don't really feel it now that I'm here. If I hadn't been having the dreams, and seen it through them, I wouldn't have known it was there. But there's darkness. They hide it. But Kane sees it."

Slowly, Vax rose and crossed the room, meeting Kane's gaze levelly. "Her life is in your hands. It's not an easy fight. It could have been, if it had been another Hunter that came here. But her heart will be involved in this, and not just because of you. If she dies, chances are, you will, too." A slow, nasty smile twisted his mouth as he added, "And if you don't, you'll wish you did."

Kane curled his lip in a sneer. His mind was full of questions, but he'd be damned if he'd asked them right now after the bastard had just threatened him.

Of course, he couldn't ask them later either.

Because just then, the man took a single step back and looked at Kendall. There was a smile on his face, a gentle one, full of love and a million unsaid memories. Then the air in the room seemed to tighten. Light exploded through the room and when it cleared, Vax was gone.

Kane stood there, staring at the empty space, while his mind tried to come to grips with what he had just seen.

Kendall had apparently seen this magick show before. She was pacing the room with long, jerky strides, those sexy legs of her scissoring back and forth as she muttered under her breath, "Dreams . . . all of this keeps coming back to dreams."

She turned on her heel to glare at him, her hair tumbling into her face. "I *hate* dreams. Nothing concrete about them."

Kane couldn't help it. She looked so frustrated, so adorable. Slowly, he closed the distance between them and lowered his head to kiss the tip of her nose. "Dreams aren't so bad—I had enough about you to drive me crazy. Even when I wanted to kill you."

She scowled at him.

Kane just laughed as he drew her against him and spun her around, walking backward until her legs bumped into the mattress. "I had dreams about you . . . ever since I saw you that night. I had them the entire time I was hunting you, and I have them still. I'll have them for the rest of my life. I see your face in my dreams—every time I close my eyes."

He held her gaze with his as he reached under the curtain of her hair, loosening the tie that held her shirt in place. It fell to her waist, catching for a moment on the full globes of her breasts. "I hated it at first," he whispered, lowering his head to skim his lips over the satiny skin of her breasts. "I was hunting for a woman that had killed my best friend, and I had dreams of her that left me aching, hot, sweaty. How could I want a cold-blooded killer? I hated myself, but I had them still—I understand why now. I knew, somewhere inside, you weren't a killer."

Her voice shook and she said flatly, "I *am* a killer. I've killed before, and I will again."

Sucking her nipple into his mouth, he curled his tongue around it, drawing her in deep, reveling in the scent of vanilla and strawberries that clung to her skin. As she moaned, Kane pulled back, just a little, laughing against her as she tried to pull him back to her. "Do you really think that matters right now? *This* does."

With those words, he cupped his hand over her mound, feeling her arch against him. Her flesh was cool—it had been like that earlier, too. But the longer he touched her, the warmer she became, until she all but scalded his hand with her heat.

"This matters," he repeated, pulling back so he could cup her breast in his palm, stroking the nipple with his thumb.

"Look at that . . ." her nipple, already drawn tight, but still pale, flushed as he touched her, deepening from soft, shell pink to deep rose in moments. "So pretty. You like feeling me touch you?"

Her voice was wry, a ghost of her former self, as she said, "If I didn't, do you really think you'd still be touching me?"

He chuckled. Slowly, he lifted his gaze to stare at her face. "How many times did Vax touch you?" he asked quietly.

The answer was there in her eyes. He'd suspected they'd been lovers, although part of him had hoped he'd been reading the signals wrong. But the way her face flushed deep pink told him he hadn't. Stroking the back of his knuckles across the top slope of her breast, he stared at her and waited for an answer.

The words came slowly. "It was a long time ago."

Kane smiled and trailed his fingers lower. Hooking the tip of his index finger in the low-slung waistband of her jeans, he whispered, "That's not the answer I was looking for."

She caught her lower lip in her teeth, and his fingers tightened on her waistband. "I trained him—then we were partners for years, Kane. Often enough."

Using his grip on her jeans, he jerked her against him. Kane fisted his other hand in the thick weight of her hair and arched her neck back, forcing her to look at him. Fury and jealousy ate at him at the thought of another man touching her. It was ridiculous. She was a vampire, centuries old. She'd had lovers before. She'd be alive long after he was dust in the ground; she'd have lovers after him. And he hated even thinking of it.

For a long moment, he held her gaze, and then he lowered his head, plunging his tongue greedily into her mouth. He felt the sharp edge of one of her fangs along the side of his tongue and the quick hot splash filled his mouth. Kendall vibrated against him, her body trembling, as she sucked on his tongue. The taste of blood faded and her head fell back, her eyes staring up into his, hot and hungry. "Damn it, you taste so good," she whispered.

"Quit trying to change to subject," he said, only half teasing. He whirled her around, pinning her against the wall. "Did he make you feel like this?" He slid his knee between her thighs, pushing up until she was riding him.

Kendall's eyes widened then her lashes fluttered closed. A soft whimper escaped her and she murmured, "No." Her hands tightened on his shoulders as she started to rock her hips, grinding her pelvis against his thigh.

L ust swirled through him like a riptide as he stared at her. The glittering ring in her navel glinted at him as she rocked back and forth, her breasts swaying with the motion. Her nipples were flushed a deep rose, almost the same shade as her lips, and diamond hard. Her flesh, normally so cool, had already started to warm, and he could smell her, that hot, indescribable scent of excited woman.

A smile curled his lips and he asked, "*No* what?"

Her lashes lifted and she met his stare. "No, he didn't make me feel like this. Nobody's made me feel like this . . ." Her voice ended on a broken sigh as she moaned, and her nails dug into his shoulders.

Slowly, Kane lowered his knee, letting her feet settle on the ground. She fell back, resting against the wall, her hands falling limply against her sides as he knelt down in front of her. Kane held her gaze with his own as he reached for the button on her low-slung jeans.

"I want you naked. I want to fuck you, hard and deep, and make you scream my name," he murmured as he dragged the zipper down slowly. It made a slow rasping noise that sounded terribly loud in the silence of the room. Kendall's breasts rose and fell shakily as she stared down at him.

"I want you to think of me every time you close your eyes," he whispered as he slowly smoothed the jeans down her thighs, taking the red lace of her panties as well. He had to stop when he reached her feet, so he undid the heavy metal buckle at her ankle that held her heels on. Glancing up at her, he grinned. "I have to admit, I love these shoes of yours."

Within seconds, he had her naked. Settling on his heels, he stared up at her. He stroked one hand up alongside her thigh before grasping her leg behind the knee and bringing it up over his shoulder, opening the already dewy folds of her sex.

He slid a glance up at her as he muttered, "It's my turn to eat now." Then he pressed his mouth against her pussy.

Kendall tasted her own blood as she bit her lip. His tongue circled around the nub of her clit before moving lower. Her knees buckled as he started to use his tongue to penetrate her, fucking it in and out.

He growled against her and the vibration of it had her quivering. Her belly felt like it was tied in hot little knots and each stroke of his tongue against her flesh made everything get tighter and hotter. Then he stroked one finger against the sensitive flesh between the cheeks of her ass, circling around the tender opening of her anus before pressing against it.

Arching against him, she came with a scream, reaching up and grabbing onto him. She dug her nails into his scalp as the orgasm tore through her. He held her against him as she came, his mouth pressed against her pussy, shifting just a little so that he could suck on her clit.

He groaned a little as she started to calm, and she felt him licking her, like he was licking the cream from her sex. "You taste so damned sweet," he muttered. "I can eat you for hours."

Her lashes fluttered and she looked down at him, breathing raggedly. "You're dangerous. You shouldn't be allowed around women," she whispered, closing her eyes again as she licked her lips.

"You'll just have to be my parole officer then," he told her as he stood up and hauled her against him. "Keep me away from them, make sure you keep them all safe."

"Who in the hell is going to keep *me* safe from you?"

Grinning roguishly at her, he cupped her in his hand, grinding the heel of his hand lightly against the pad of her pussy. "Do you really want to be safe from me?" he asked softly.

Her body shuddered a little, and she whimpered as she whispered, "Hell, no."

Slowly, he turned her around in his arms. Kendall stood still as he brushed her hair away from her neck, baring it. When he raked his teeth over the exposed skin, she felt her knees give way. He wrapped his arms around her waist, supporting her weight. Slowly, he eased them to the ground as he brought his lips to her ear. "I'm going to bend you over, right here, and fuck you like this," he told her.

Kendall gasped, her belly clenching as he took her hands, first one and then the other, guiding them to floor so that she was on her hands and knees. He smoothed his hands over her ass, trailed them over her back. She could feel him looking at her. Lifting her head, she looked at him over her shoulder, meeting his stare.

There was a hungry, predatory look in his eyes.

Running her tongue over her lips, she swallowed. Her fangs were down, not fully extended, but down enough that she could feel them. She was the predator, the Hunter—she shouldn't feel so damned turned on being in the weaker position, so why in the hell did she?

Because it was Kane.

Hell, anything and everything about him turned her on.

She suspected he could ask her to strip down in public and she just might do it.

"You look a little nervous," he whispered as he reached for the buckle of his belt.

Lowering her lashes, she forced a cocky smile. "Of you? Not likely."

He laughed. "Really? Not nervous at all?"

Kendall snorted and shoved up onto her knees, dusting her hands off delicately and shrugging her shoulders. "It's sex, Kane. Very spectacular sex, but it's sex. Nothing to be nervous about."

If she hadn't had her back to him, Kendall would have seen the look in his eyes. But she didn't. All she heard was the clank of metal links. "Really?" The cool tone of his voice warned her. And he moved fast, very fast for a human. He had one of her wrists cuffed before she had guessed he was up to anything. By the time she swung her head around to look at him, he caught her other wrist and fell forward, using his weight to take her to the ground. That movement took her leverage away, and he used that to get her other wrist cuffed to the first.

"Just sex, baby, let's have some fun with it," he teased lightly.

Kendall growled, jerking at the cuffs at her wrists. They weren't regular cuffs. She knew that. She couldn't see the metal to figure out what it was, but he wouldn't have used basic cuffs on her—he knew too much about vamps to even bother. "What in the hell are you doing?" she demanded.

He caught her hips and pulled her up, so that her ass was in the air. Her hands were cuffed at the small of her back, her upper body and face resting on the ground. "Getting ready to fuck you," he said gruffly. "Sex, right? Just sex—but I'm going to make sure you remember it for the rest of your life, no matter how much longer it is than mine."

She heard his zipper rasp, heard the underlying anger in his voice, and fought the urge to ask him to take the cuffs off. He wouldn't hurt her, right? She was nervous, though. And asking him to take those cuffs off . . . her pride wouldn't let her. She caught her lip between her teeth as she felt the broad head of his cock pressing against her.

"You're nervous now," he murmured. "You're shaking, trembling all over. But you're wet, so wet and so hot."

She groaned and arched, pushing back against him. Kane chuckled and pushed inside, just a little, pulling back before he'd even pushed halfway inside. He moved slowly, and when she tried to rock back against him and take more of him inside her, he stilled her motions by bracing his hands on her hips. "Be still," he murmured.

Narrowing her eyes, Kendall tensed her muscles and shoved back a little harder. She purred with satisfaction as he sank a little deeper inside her, but before she could pull forward and thrust back against, he pulled away and smacked her ass with the flat of his hand. He pressed against her again, but his cock cuddled against her ass instead of inside her. "My way," he whispered. "It's just sex, right, really incredible sex, so you can do it my way."

"Damn it, Kane," she groaned, pressing her face against the carpet, rolling her hips against him. "Please!"

"Please, what?"

She groaned in frustration. "I want you inside me," she rasped out, jerking against the cuffs at her wrists agitatedly.

"My way." Then he pushed inside again. Full and hard, thrusting in until he was in her to the hilt. "You're so tight, so soft. I love your pussy."

Slowly, thoroughly, he fucked her, stroking in and out until she was keening, sobbing. The need to come was explosive— tilting her hips, she tried to change the angle just a little. But Kane seemed to realize exactly where she was going, and he moved with her, changing his thrusts and moving a little more shallowly.

"You're a bastard," she muttered.

Kane chuckled and slid his hand up and around her hip until he could circle his fingers over her clit. A mini-orgasm raced through her and she arched back against him, rocking her hips against his hand. "I am, huh?" he teased, drawing his hand away. "And there I thought I was being considerate."

"Considerate my ass," she muttered.

"Considerate is the last thing on my mind when I think of your ass," he muttered. His hips started to pummel against her again, leaving Kendall gasping for breath.

That vicious climax started to build again low in her belly. Black dots started to dance in front of her eyes. The sound of Kane's hips slapping against her ass and the harsh sounds of his breath filled the room. "Damn it, I want to hear you scream," he whispered. "Scream for me."

She had no breath—how could she scream when she couldn't even seem to find her voice?

Kane's hand slid around her hip again. A harsh, broken scream fell from her lips as he started lightly stroking her clit. The orgasm tore through her, clawing its way through her as her entire body bucked and trembled. The climax ended almost as abruptly as it started and she sagged, wanting nothing more than to collapse against the floor.

But Kane wasn't done. His hands held her hips, keeping her up and open for him as he pounded against her, his cock swelling and throbbing inside her pussy.

Sweat dripped off of him. She felt it as it rolled from him, falling onto her, hot, almost scalding her sensitive skin. He felt so big inside her, stretching, almost bruising her sensitive flesh as he continued to fuck her. A soft groan escaped him, and he started to come, his cock jerking inside her.

Kane slumped forward, and he rolled to the side, taking her with him so that she was cuddled against the curve of his body, her hands still cuffed behind her back.

One brawny arm came around her, as he nuzzled her hair. His voice was low and rough as he murmured, "Don't tell me this is just sex, Kendall."

And for some reason, her eyes teared up.

CHAPTER 7

Damn it all to hell and back, he hurt. Duke opened his left eye. His right eye was swollen shut. It had been for the past two days and if they didn't stop pounding on his face, he didn't know if he'd ever open it again. Hell, what did it matter, he thought bitterly.

It wasn't like he'd ever leave here alive.

The little blonde bitch wanted something—not from him, exactly, but something out of him. In his gut, he knew that, but he wasn't really sure she needed him alive to get whatever it was she wanted from him.

She was there again, standing in the shadows of the room watching him with that scared, nervous look in her pretty violet eyes. It was that look that had suckered him into asking her to dance at the bar. How in the hell could it still draw him in? She was the reason he was here.

Damn her. She stiffened as she realized he was staring at her, and she started to back away. But Duke just closed his eye again, ignoring her.

Where was Kendall?

Was she looking for him? Well, that was a dumb question. He knew she was looking for him. But would she find him?

These people knew how to hide.

More than that. There was a whole world of wrong going on here, things they should have felt as they drew close to the city, but they hadn't. And these people were the reason. Somehow, somebody here was blocking the evil.

She was still watching him. He could feel her gaze on him, those dark, pretty purple eyes, so sad, so troubled. He couldn't figure out why she was still keeping up the act, though. He was here. She could drop the act. She could also leave him the hell alone.

Duke had had enough of lovely Miss Analise Morrell. But she wasn't going anywhere. He could smell her. The soft, sweet scent of her skin called to him as much now as it had that first night.

Fuck, had it just been three nights ago?

"Duke?"

Shit. Can you not even let me ignore you in peace? he thought wearily. Opening his one good eye, he stared at her coolly. "Get away from me," he said hoarsely. His throat was raspy and dry. Duke hadn't had a drink of water or a bite to eat since he'd left the bar. That wasn't good for a shifter. Shifters had a metabolism nearly double that of a human, and he had to eat a lot more and a lot more *often* than humans did. He'd probably already lost weight, and his throat felt as dry as the Sahara.

She seemed to know that, too. In one hand, she held a glass of water and as she held his gaze, she lifted it to his lips. But Duke just turned his head away. "Get away from me, Analise," he rasped, staring at the wall in front of him so he wouldn't have to see her face.

"Duke, you need water. Drink it. And I'll bring you some food once . . . once she leaves for the night," Analise said as she tried once more to offer him the water.

Duke jerked his head away almost violently. The glass bobbled out of her hand and fell to the floor, shattering at his feet. Staring angrily into her eyes, he rasped, "I said, get away from me. That bitch wants me dead, so why in the fuck does it matter if I'm thirsty and hungry?"

Analise backed away, staring at him with eyes he couldn't read. "Don't you care if you live or die?"

Duke laughed bitterly. "At the rate I'm going, death is just a day or two away." His wrists burned from the silver cuffs that had been used to chain him to the wall and he was weak from blood loss. Long, shallow cuts had been made all over his torso with a silver blade—the cuts would have healed if they'd been made with a regular knife, but the silver-wrought wounds didn't heal, they just bled and bled. Each time the blood started to coagulate, the bitch had cut into his flesh again and the bleeding had started anew.

The floor at his feet was stained red with his blood. He'd lost pints, he knew.

Between the blood loss, the lack of food and water, and the beatings, he was weak, weaker than hell. If he could change, he might have been able to get away, but there was a man that kept injecting him with something. Whatever it was, it kept him from changing. It did something to his body chemistry—altered his heart rate, did something to his adrenaline, and kept him locked in his mortal form.

Analise stared at him with fury in her eyes. "Please don't tell me that you don't want to live. I won't believe it. I *don't* believe it," she whispered, something replacing the ever-present sadness in her eyes. Anger. Rage. The passion burning in her eyes was bright and furious, impossible to miss.

He laughed sourly. "It has nothing to do with not wanting to live, doll. It has to do with accepting reality. I can deal with dying."

Her voice trembled with rage as she whispered, "But why *deal* with it if you can live?"

He arched a brow at her. "Live like you choose to? Let me guess, I can choose to live, turn into her lapdog . . . or cat. Do whatever in the hell she chooses, and in return, I can live. No, thanks. I'd rather die."

Analise swallowed, the sound almost echoing in the silence of the room. "I thought Hunters were supposed to fight."

"They do. And make no mistake, doll. A Hunter will come after me, and people here will die. That's good enough for me," Duke said wearily, leaning his head back against the wall. God, I'm just so tired, he thought.

Analise continued to just stare at him. "You're wrong. The Hunters don't see her. You're supposed to know when somebody like her is around, aren't you? But you didn't. Neither did the vampire you were with. Until you actually *saw* Catharine, you didn't even realize she was here. And she won't let your partner see her. Not until Catharine is ready to kill her."

"Kendall." Duke lifted his head and stared at Analise as fury began to build in his gut. That was what this was about. "This is about Kendall."

Analise lowered her lids, the thick fringe of golden lashes shielding her gaze from him for a long moment. "Yes. It's about Kendall. Cat knows her—wants her dead."

Duke sucked in a slow, painful breath. Breathing was torture. There were at least two, if not three, broken ribs on his right side. "Get me the fucking water."

Her eyes opened and she met his gaze. "So now you want to live?"

"I never wanted to die. But know this, Analise. If she hurts Kendall, I'll make damn sure I find a way to make you pay."

Analise laughed sadly. "I've been paying every single day since she found me, Duke. Don't worry about that."

With that, she turned around and walked away. When she came back a few minutes later with the water, she didn't say a word, and she wouldn't meet his eyes.

HE had the strength inside him, that was sure enough. It took a certain amount of strength to break past the illusions that Catharine's psychic power cast. It wasn't true magick, Analise knew that. Analise didn't understand true magick. But she did understand psychic power. She had it, after all. It was what had drawn Catharine to her.

And it was the only thing that protected Brad right now.

He had the power himself. And his own power was strong, entirely too strong. Cat wanted nothing more than to control the child, but so far, she hadn't been able to.

If Brad had been a normal child, it would have been child's play to control him.

But Brad was unique, in so many ways. And he wouldn't be controlled. Walking through the door to the room she shared with the nine-year-old boy, she met his eyes and forced a weak smile. "Hey, sweetie."

"You have to get him out of here, Ana. She's going to kill him."

Analise shook her head. "She won't. She's using him to bait a trap. Doesn't work as well if the bait is dead."

Brad rolled his eyes. "You're so naïve sometimes, sis. All Cat has to do is make this Kendall person *think* he is here, and she'll come. You'd do the same for me. Get him out. Tonight."

"Will you *hush*!" Analise pushed her hair nervously back and glanced at the door.

Brad laughed, and for one brief moment, he actually looked like the kid he was. "Like I'd let her hear anything I said. Don't worry. She can't hear me." His eyes darkened for a second, and then he added quietly, "Unless I want her to. Get him out of here, Ana."

Shaking her head at her brother, she said, "No. She'd take it out on you, Brad. I won't risk it. I'm doing what I can. I'll make sure he doesn't get any weaker, and when the opportunity comes for him to run, he'll be strong enough to get away. And he won't forget her face. His hatred of her will see to that."

For a second, Brad just stared at her, and she thought maybe he'd let it go, but no such luck. He shook his head and whispered, "And you think that's enough? You *brought* him here for her to kill. You're his one chance to get out of here and you won't do it."

Analise felt sick as guilt swirled through her. "Honey, I can't risk you," she said, her voice thick with guilt and grief.

"Me. It's always me," he muttered, shaking his head. After a minute, Brad shoved himself up off the bed, glaring up at her. In his rage, he started to levitate, his feet leaving the ground until he was hovering two feet above the floor and right in her face. "You can't keep doing this, Ana. You *can't*! I won't let you keep bringing people to her just because she threatens me. I can take care of myself."

Analise laughed sharply. "You're nine years old." But her laugh ended abruptly when she went flying through the air and landed on the floor with her back against the wall.

"I'm nine years old. And I'm stronger than *both* of you. I'm smarter than both of you. And I've got a hell of a lot more common sense than you do," he snapped. "You think I don't know why you stay with her? You could get away. You can hide from her. You've got the same abilities she does. You're almost as strong psychically as she is. It's the reason she wanted you. But you don't run because you're afraid she'll catch up with you, because you're afraid I'll slow you down."

Analise stood, slowly, shakily. Her head ached a little, like it always did when Brad used that incredible power of his. She'd been his only teacher in the past few years, ever since Mama had died. Catharine had killed her, a slow, painful death. Mama hadn't been as strong as Analise or Brad, but she'd tried her damnedest to protect them both. If Analise had listened, and run . . . Closing her eyes, she shoved the futility of those thoughts away.

"Brad, you don't understand. I'll do whatever I have to do to protect you. It doesn't matter what it is, or how long it takes. I'll do it."

Brad's eyes iced over. "Even if it means letting nice people die? Even if it means becoming like *her*?"

Analise felt a chill run through her— for a moment, it was like the ghost of her mother appeared in her brother's eyes. *You do the right thing, Ana. When you have a special gift, you have a responsibility and you do the right thing, no matter what.* "I have to take care of you, Brad."

Brad smiled at her, a cold smile that looked entirely too grown up for his young face. "Then lets get him out of here—all of us. He'll get us to the Hunters. That's where I need to be anyway."

Analise shook her head. "No. *No.* I won't let you go to them. Damn it, what good are they?" she demanded in frustration. Stalking up to Brad, she bent over until they were nose to nose. "Did any of them come to us when she killed Mama?"

Brad's eyes teared up and one fat drop rolled down his cheek. "No." His shoulders drooped for a moment and then he straightened them. "But they would have helped if they could have. They can't be everywhere. That's why I want to be one of them. The more Hunters there are, the more people they can help. Maybe I can save somebody else's mama."

With that, he turned away and walked over to his bed. He lay down and curled up on his side, tugging a ragged blanket over his shoulders, with his back pointedly turned to her. "You can't keep letting her kill people because of me, Ana. It's making you almost as bad as she is."

A NALISE froze as she slid out of the room where Catharine was keeping Duke prisoner.

Cat had woken early.

Ice blue eyes pinned Analise in place, and the water glass fell from numb fingers.

"What are you doing, Ana?" Cat asked quietly.

"Just giving him some water," Analise said quietly. "He's a shifter. They need more water than humans. You . . . you don't want him dying too fast, right?"

Cat's eyes narrowed. "That's a good one. I almost believe you."

The punch came too fast for Analise to try and dodge it. Blood filled her mouth and automatically, she swallowed it. When another punch came flying toward her face, she just sat there, taking it. A kick to her side, and then Cat was done. "You help him again, and next time, I'll beat your brother."

Slowly, Analise rose. "Leave Brad alone," she whispered.

Cat laughed. "You think to tell me what to do? Foolish little bitch, I *own* you. I own him. I can do whatever I wish to do with the two of you."

"You don't own me."

Analise flinched at the soft, steady sound of her brother's voice. Praying her voice wouldn't break, she quietly said, "Brad, go back to your room, baby. I'll handle this."

Brad ignored her as he glared at Cat from his doorway. "You don't own me. And you hit my sister again, you'll be sorry."

Cat started to laugh. "Are you threatening me, you little whelp?"

Brad just stared at her. Analise felt fear flutter inside her heart as she recognized the glow in his eyes, but Cat didn't know enough about Brad to understand that look. She took one step toward him, but then as she started to take a second, she went hurtling back through the air. She landed in a crumpled heap against the brick fireplace, blood trickling from a small cut on her forehead.

Across the room, Brad continued to stand there. There was a small trickle of blood under his left nostril. Excessive displays of his power always caused nosebleeds, but it took more and more power these days to cause the bleeding, and it stopped quicker and quicker. He just stared at Cat as she slowly shoved to her feet, her eyes glowing with rage. "You little bastard!"

Her eyes cut to Analise, and Analise tensed, lifting one hand. A glowing shimmery shield formed in front of her. It would keep Cat away from her for a few minutes, long enough to give her time to think, to plan. But it wasn't necessary.

A low, angry hiss filled the air.

Analise looked up.

Hovering in the air in front of Cat was a table leg. The low table had been smashed under Cat's weight when Brad sent her flying through the air. "If I can throw you in the air, I think I can shove a piece of wood through your chest," Brad said soberly.

His young eyes looked incredibly old in his pale face, but they were full of determination, and neither Analise or Cat doubted his words.

"You two will pay for this."

They both waited in tense silence until Cat left the room. Then Brad looked at his sister. "Now you have to get us out of here, Ana. We don't have a choice."

K ENDALL woke long before Kane did. Judging by the slow, steady sound of his breathing, he was going to sleep for a while yet. She climbed naked from the bed and padded into the small bathroom. Staring into the mirror, she studied her disheveled appearance with a bemused smile.

She looked like a woman who had been ridden good and hard.

That thought made her grin.

Well, she had.

Reaching up, she stretched her arms high over her head, and then winced as various aches and pains started to scream at her. Groaning, she moved to the shower and reached in, turning on the blast of hot water. She was loathe to wash his scent from her body, but she really needed to be able to move.

They had to find that girl tonight. Coiling her damp hair into a loose knot, she dug out a pair of jeans. After she slid them on over her naked hips, she grabbed a bra and fastened it on. But as Kendall started to reach for a T-shirt, her eyes landed on the simple white button-down that Kane had worn, sliding it on with a pleased sigh.

It smelled of him.

There was something about his scent that intoxicated her. Breathing it in was almost as satisfying as feeding on him.

And at the thought of feeding from him, her fangs started

to ache, throbbing inside their sockets. She didn't really need to feed; it was more like an urge. He just tasted so damned good. But feeding from him . . , that was something she couldn't do for a while.

Her body felt pleasantly full, not just from the blood she'd taken from him the other day, but the sex as well. She rode on the emotions she had drunk from him as they both came, and it energized and sustained her nearly as well as blood did.

Kane, on the other hand, needed to eat. He needed iron and fluids. She'd have to keep an eye on him and make sure he got plenty of both over the next few days to replace what she had taken.

Without looking, she knew the sun was still lingering in the sky. She could leave safe enough, but she wasn't leaving Kane alone, even just to get him some food. She wasn't going to risk leaving Kane alone. She was too damned edgy after Duke disappearing.

She could wait. He probably wouldn't sleep too much longer. Kane didn't strike her as the type to sleep the day— or the night—away. Once he woke, they could get him some food.

Sunset was close. Unable to resist, she opened the curtains, craning her head to watch as the sun painted the sky pink and gold and orange as it sank down below the horizon. By the time it had set, her skin was rosy and faintly itchy.

If she stood in the sun for an hour without any kind of protection, her skin would start to smoke . . . an hour and a half, she'd be covered in blackening blisters. If she didn't get inside after that, within another thirty minutes, an hour tops, she'd start to burn. A slow flame at first . . . but within moments, she'd burn as though somebody has tossed a lit match into a barrel of oil.

Nasty, horrible painful way to go.

She had watched it happen that way . . . once.

Before she had become a Hunter, before Agnes had freed her from her prison. Her master and sire, her *owner* had become unhappy with one of his servants, and he'd been dragged, kicking and screaming from his rest by three were-wolves, and they'd chained him outside in the courtyard.

All the vampires in the manor had been woken and forced to watch from within, protected by the shadows of the house and the spells of one of Dumont's witches. Still, her skin had been burning, angry red wheals breaking out all over her exposed skin. A vampire less than a year, she'd been vulnerable to the sunlight, and the magical shield hadn't been enough to protect her completely.

She should be scared to death of the sun. But as it sank down behind the treeline, out of sight, something forlorn moved through her. Resting her palm flat against the pane of glass, she closed her eyes, holding the image of the setting sun in her mind for long moments.

The blaring of a semi truck's horn pulled her from her reverie.

Sighing, Kendall let the curtain fall back into place as she turned away from the window. And laying on the bed, she found Kane, staring at her with dark, watchful eyes.

"So we just drive around," Kendall repeated, shaking her head. She propped her elbow on the door of the car, feeling the warm, muggy air blow through her hair.

Kane glanced at her before focusing back on the road. "We already swung by the bar. She's not there. I don't know what else to try. We don't have a name, a license plate number, anything, not even a picture. Just that she likes to walk."

Kendall groaned in frustration, absently tapping her fist on the door. This felt like such a waste of time. Part of what made her a Hunter, what separated her from other vampires, was an internal sense of danger. When there was something wrong, she could feel it. She was drawn to it.

And she didn't feel a damn thing here.

She turned left on River Road and glanced at the clock. Three hours. Three hours of nothing.

With a tired sigh, she headed north, away from the river.

Kane glanced at her. "Where you going? The guy said she likes this part of town."

Kendall slid him a level look as she replied blandly, "I haven't seen her yet, have you?"

The section of town she headed for was poor, older, but quiet. She'd been through here before, but she usually didn't have to stop. It was just . . . quiet.

Even before she turned down the street, Kendall started to question why she had even come here. A low-level headache started to throb at the base of her skull and she absently rotated her neck a little to try and relieve the pain.

There was a park at the end of the street but this late at night she knew it would be empty.

Empty. There's nothing here.

Might as well go back to the hotel . . . Kendall frowned a little even as the thought circled through her mind. "Can't," she muttered. "Got a job to do." Forcing her mind to focus, she concentrated on the long stretches of sidewalk on the right side of the road.

It took a few minutes to notice just how quiet Kane had gotten. How tense he was in the seat next to her. As she slowed at the stoplight, she glanced his way. His face was tight, a muscle ticking in his jaw, and his hand was fisted, pounding in a staccato beat on his thigh.

"What's wrong?"

He glanced at her. His eyes looked a little tense, a little distracted. "Don't you feel it?"

She shook her head. "I don't feel anything." Except the pain in her head. It was getting worse. And it was getting harder and harder to concentrate. *Damn it, what in the hell is wrong with me?*

His gaze rested on her face for a long moment and then he looked past her, staring through the window. When he continued to stare, she turned her head, following the direction he was looking.

Although her night sight was phenomenal, she had a hard time seeing the blonde sitting in the park across the street.

Hadn't she looked that way earlier? Why didn't she see the girl? Kendall blew out a soft breath as she drove through the light as it turned green. Keeping an eye on the blonde head, she turned left and turned off her lights, parking on the side of the road.

"That's her, I take it," Kane said.

Kendall didn't reply as she climbed from the car, closing the door quietly. Her mind felt kind of muddled, foggy, almost like she'd been drinking, or sleeping too heavily. Why hadn't she seen the girl?

She felt warmth at her back and then Kane's hand on her shoulder. It was weird—the moment he touched her shoulder, her mind seemed to clear. The pain in her head receded and clarity returned once more. Sucking a breath in, she stared across the distance that separated her from the girl.

Not only should she have seen the girl, she should have *felt* the girl. She should have felt her miles before now. The girl's soul seemed to scream out to her in the silence of the night. Full of pain, confusion, guilt—a soul in need of saving.

"What's going on?" she whispered quietly.

Kane's hand fell away.

But as soon as his hand fell away, the fog tried to close in around her mind again. Groaning, she pressed a hand to her temple again. "Damn it," she muttered, shaking her head.

Kane closed his fingers around her arm. "What's wrong?" Once more, the second he touched her, her mind cleared.

Kendall moved away from his hand and closed her eyes, shaking her head a little. It didn't help to clear the fog. Licking her lips, she slid Kane a glance and said, "I don't know." But she wasn't going to keep functioning with her mind so muddled. Sliding her hand down his arm, she linked her fingers with his. Ignoring the startled look on his face, she started across the street, heading toward the woman still sitting in the park on a swing with her head down.

Even when Kendall and Kane were standing over her, she still continued to stare down. Oh, the girl knew they were there. Kendall could feel her awareness.

Kendall suspected the girl even recognized her. And it didn't take Kendall any time at all to figure out why. She was all but shaking with rage as she stared down at the blonde. She could smell blood. Lots of it. Sweat, fear, and *Duke*. "Where is he?" she asked quietly.

At that softly voiced question, the woman finally lifted her head.

Kane's hand tightened around hers as they saw her face. The woman had a black eye. A nasty one. Kendall wouldn't be surprised if the bone surrounding the eye had been damaged. Her lip was puffy and swollen, and as she opened her mouth to speak, her lip split and blood started to flow. She swallowed and closed her eyes, like she was gathering the courage to speak.

"If I tell you, will you take us with you?"

Kendall wanted to hit the girl. Badly, desperately. Whatever had been done to Duke had been done because this little bitch had helped. But there was fear in the young woman's eyes. Fear and pain and guilt.

"Who is *us*?" Kane asked as Kendall just stared at the girl.

"My brother and me," the young woman said softly. "She killed our mom a few years ago. Keeps us around—uses me." A soft sob escaped her. "Uses me to bring her more toys."

"Toys?" Kendall asked darkly.

"Like Duke."

"Duke isn't a damned toy."

The woman flinched at Kendall's voice. Her voice wobbled as she whispered, "I know. He wanted to help me. Others . . . they see me and they just want . . . they want sex, but he—Duke wanted to help me. He was different."

Her voice was full of guilt and shock. Like she couldn't understand anybody wanting to help her.

That stilled Kendall. Even through her rage, she was still a Hunter. Always a Hunter. Swallowing, she closed her eyes for a second, focusing on leveling out the rage in her gut. Kane remained quiet, the rough, hard surface of his palm pressed against hers. When she opened her eyes, she looked at him first. He stared at her quietly in the dim light and just the sight of his face seemed to calm her further. That was something else she'd have to figure out later, but right now wasn't the time.

Once more, she looked back at the young woman sitting on the swing. Hell, she was hardly more than a girl. "What's your name?" she asked quietly.

"Analise."

"How old are you, Analise?"

Analise sighed and it seemed to make her entire body quiver. "Twenty-one," she whispered.

Twenty-one, Kendall mused. Kendall had only been nineteen when she'd been Changed. It seemed she could hardly even remember being human. She certainly couldn't remember being quite as vulnerable as the woman sitting before her. There was an air of frailty about her. She could see why Duke had been drawn to her. He would have wanted to protect her.

"What happened to Duke, Analise? Where is he?"

Analise looked up, and Kendall found herself staring into the woman's dark, fearful eyes. "Not far from here. And we don't have much time. She's going to kill him."

Kane asked softly, "Why hasn't she already?"

Analise never took her eyes from Kendall as she answered Kane. "She was having too much fun playing with him for awhile. But he never mattered to her. She wasn't interested in him."

Kendall's voice was low and raspy with anger as she demanded, "*What* was she interested in?"

"You."

The pain returned with a vengeance, throbbing inside her skull. Kane's hand fell away from hers, but the cloudiness didn't attack her mind again. It was Analise. Kendall didn't know how, but something about Analise clouded her mind and made it hard for her to think, to concentrate. Why it wasn't happening now, Kendall didn't know.

She turned away from both of them, staring off into the night as she struggled to drag air into her lungs past the constriction in her chest. Fuck, she was so damned pissed she could barely see straight.

All around her, she could feel it, like people screaming out at her in the night. Why hadn't she heard them before now?

Distantly, she heard Kane talking to Analise. "Why does this woman want Kendall?"

"So she can kill her."

Kendall laughed, a dry brittle sound. She'd already figured that one out. "Who is doing something to the city?" she asked quietly. "Duke and I were here for weeks, and we felt hardly anything. Nothing to Hunt, hardly any vampires, no shifters, nothing."

Analise was silent. Turning on her heel, Kendall stalked up to the girl, reaching out and grabbing the front of her shirt. Disregarding her injuries, Kendall jerked her up and glared into Analise's pale face. "You really want to answer me, darling," she said softly.

Analise swallowed. Kendall could see the woman's throat work, hear the rapid beat of her pulse as fear sped up her heartbeat. "It's me—I'm psychic. It's just . . . just part of my gift. I don't really know how to control that part of it. It's one of the reasons Cat never Changed me. She was worried about what vampirism would do to my gifts. Too unpredictable." Tears filled her eyes and Analise's voice broke a little, then trailed off altogether.

Kendall uncurled her fingers, and Analise slumped back down to the swing, the chains clinking musically together. Kendall licked her lips, her gut knotting. "Cat?" she repeated.

Analise glanced at her, and then away, just as quickly. "Catharine. That's her name."

Time seemed to freeze as Kendall stared at the pale woman in front of her, that name circling around and around in her head.

ST. LOUIS
1864

Kendall found herself kneeling down on the ground while Vax went chasing down the last two feral werewolves. A mile back, there was a scene that would live on in her memory for a very long while.

The werewolves had decided to have a meal. They hadn't chosen a herd of cattle or sheep either. They'd chosen the ranch owner's family. Why they'd taken this small baby with them instead of killing her there, Kendall didn't know, but she thanked God.

They'd killed the rancher, his wife and two small boys, but this little baby, for some reason, had been spared. Kendall lifted her, her heart wrenching at the sight of blood splattering the small white blankets wrapped around her.

"What's your name, precious?" she whispered, stroking back downy curls of butter yellow.

The baby stared up at Kendall and hiccoughed, tear tracks drying on her little face. Big blue eyes stared up at Kendall and she felt her heart melt. Gently, she ran her finger down the babe's cheek. When the baby turned and tried to catch Kendall's finger in her mouth, Kendall chuckled. "I'm sorry, pet. Nothing for you there. But we can find you something, I'm sure. Just give me a little bit of time, will you?"

EVERYTHING faded to black, and Kendall heard a voice, familiar, but it seemed so out of place with the memories crowding her head.

The voice, hard and male, kept saying her name over and over. Finally, strong, calloused hands closed over her arms and she gasped as somebody shook her. Black dots danced in front of her eyes and she blinked until they cleared. She looked up, staring into Kane's dark, worried eyes.

"Are you okay?"

"It can't be her," Kendall whispered, shaking her head.

"What?"

"It can't," she said patiently, licking her lips. "She's dead. She died a long time ago."

"Kendall, what are you talking about?"

Chains clinked together again, and they both turned to look at Analise. "She's talking about the vampire that has Duke. Her name's Cat. And she hates Mary. Wants her dead."

Kendall stilled at the sound of that name.

Kane turned to stare at Analise with puzzled eyes. "Mary? Who in the hell is Mary?"

Kendall sighed softly, lowering her head to stare at the ground, not really seeing the bare ground at her feet. "I am."

IRELAND 1701

The room was little more than a cell, less than eight feet long, and dark. Cold. The young girl on the bed lay shivering under the thin blanket, sleeping. There were dried tear tracks on her face, and an occasional sob escaped her even in sleep.

She'd cried herself to sleep every night for more than a month. Ever since a man had burst into the shop where she worked with her ma and dragged her kicking and screaming away from everything she'd ever known.

Da had sold her. To cover his gaming losses . . . sold her to that cold-eyed bloody Englishman. She hadn't seen Ma, her brother and sisters, or Sean . . . she dreamed of him while she slept, his dreamy blue eyes, the way his inky black hair spilled into his eyes. She hadn't seen Da either, but she never wanted to see him. Never again.

There was a loud noise. She jerked in the small bed, sitting up and cowering without even realizing what had woken her.

There were men in the house . . . voices. She'd heard some of them before.

When the door to her little room flew open, she shrank back against the wall, clutching the blankets to her chest.

The man in the doorway was one she had seen before, coming and going around the house that belonged to her master. He wasn't one of Frederick Smythe's friends, though. Smythe was scared to death of him.

"What do you want?" Mary demanded, her voice quivering.

The man smiled.

And when he did . . . his lips peeled back from his teeth, long, wickedly sharp teeth. Mary opened her mouth to scream, and he just laughed.

Blackness swarmed up, but that laugh, hideous and cold, followed her into her dreams.

Cold hands grabbed her in the darkness, burning pain in her neck.

The nasty, coppery taste as he forced blood down her throat. "Drink, pet . . . drink . . . DRINK!" The final word was a muted roar as she tried to spit the foul, thick liquid out. His hand, harder than iron, clamped around her jaw and forced her mouth closed, until she either had to swallow the blood in her throat or gag. She gagged at first, and his entire hand smothered her face; In response, she swallowed, choking on the blood that slid down her throat, burning her like fire.

The Change was brutal. Days of fever and hallucinations, followed by weeks when she felt as weak as a newborn kitten. There had been a while when she was certain she had lost her mind—times she prayed that that was what had happened.

But after months passed, she came to understand her new life was no hallucination, no dream, no product of a crazed mind. As she came to accept that knowledge, she began to crave death.

Mary remembered how often she'd long just to creep out of the room she was forced to share with Dumont, rush out and face the rising sun.

If she did, she could escape the rapes, escape the beatings, escape the pain. Burning under the pure light of the sun seemed almost bliss compared to the hell that was her life.

But something kept her from it. A hatred. Hatred that burned deep inside her, filling her, warming flesh that had long since gone cold.

She wanted death.

But she wanted his more.

She'd been a vampire for nearly three years when she finally got that wish. But it hadn't been her hand that had delivered the fatal blow. That was a regret she'd carry her entire life.

"Sweet, sweet Mary . . . do you really think you can beat me?"

She lay on the ground, a huddled heap of pale limbs, the skin of her back laid open by a whip, but with every second that passed, the flesh healed, knitting together, until it was whole and unmarked, stained only by the drying blood. She refused to answer— she didn't think she could beat him. But she wanted it, and if she gave up, she'd never find out. She could wait. She could wait, and get strong.

But sometimes, she wanted nothing more than to just rush out and greet the sun, and let it take her.

After what she'd seen today, watching as Dumont let the sun burn one of the servants to nothing more than a pile of ash, she wanted nothing more.

He laughed. Mary screamed out in rage as she realized he'd pushed inside her mind and heard every last thought.

"Now why would I kill you? You're such a fun little pet. Nearly three years and you've yet to break. My pets break so easily—but not you. Not you. Why are you so different?" His eyes, normally rather mildly blue, gleamed, glowing in the pale oval of his face.

"Go to hell," she gasped out.

He laughed. "Mary, sweet little Mary, you should really learn to watch that tongue . . . before I bite it off."

She swallowed the whimper of fear that rose in her throat, trying to keep him from seeing the fear in her face.

He moved closer and she flinched, wrapping her arms around her knees, pressing them to her naked chest. He reached out for her and Mary jerked, but when he pulled her to her feet, there was something in his eyes. Hunger. He was going to . . . to . . . she lost it, a scream boiling out of her throat, rage flooding her as she swiped out, raking her nails down his face, leaving bloody furrows behind.

"Bitch!" he bellowed, hurling her away from him.

Mary crashed into the wall and slid to the floor, but she forced herself back to her feet, the rage that pumped through her veins giving her a strength unlike any she had ever known.

He stood across the room, staring at her, his shoulders heaving up and down as he sucked air in. His eyes glowed above the bloody marks on his face. "You'll bleed for that."

But before he could cross the room, something moved through the air. Something warm . . . a breeze, smelling sweet, smelling of sunshine. Of spring time. There was a woman . . . Mary could hear her laughing. The voice that drifted through the air was low and husky, full of pleasure, full of something that made Mary's heart speed up in her chest.

Power.

The door blew open, and Dumont whirled around, glaring at the woman who stood there.

She was older, a frail-looking thing, not quite stooped with age, but the hair on her head was turning silver and lines fanned out from her twinkling blue eyes. Eyes the color of the summer sky, a color Mary hadn't seen in years. "I do believe she's bled enough for you, Victor Dumont. Many of these people have," she murmured.

"Get out, you old bitch," Dumont snarled. "Padrick! Liam!"

The woman laughed. "I am sorry, truly. But I'm afraid many of your servants realized they had prior obligations. Appointments in hell."

He snarled and lunged for the small woman. She was little, shorter than Mary, and her silver-streaked hair was worn in a fat braid that trailed over one slender shoulder. She was dressed in a plain white shirt and a dark skirt. And she just stood there as Dumont lunged for her. But right before he reached her, she smiled at him.

Mary stood there, dumbfounded, as Dumont froze in midair, hovering just inches away from the frail thing in front of him. "You're sentenced to death, Victor. For evils too great to number."

A look crossed Dumont's face. One of disbelief. Of abject terror.

"Hunter," he spat.

"That I am." Her eyes moved to Mary, and Mary swallowed at the smile that crossed the old woman's face. "And I recognize a kindred spirit. But first . . . let's take care of you."

"I'm not so easy to kill, bitch. For three hundred years I've walked this earth."

Agnes chuckled. "Well, then . . . you're almost as old as me." Something in her blue eyes glowed. It was like a fire . . . and Mary screamed as Victor Dumont's body burst into flames. Her screams mingled with his, chasing her into the dark veil that rose up to cover her mind.

"Wake up, Mary Kendall."

She didn't want to. Every time she opened her eyes, all she saw was more horror. Every time she left the solace of sleep all she felt was more pain.

"Child, you've known more pain than any one person should have to deal with. Wake up, now . . . let's get to healing some of that pain."

That voice was so gentle, so full of caring. But still . . . Mary didn't trust what her heart told her anymore. She tried to retreat back into sleep, but that woman, she just kept talking. "Come on out of it now, Mary. Open your eyes . . . talk to me."

Finally, she opened her eyes, pulling free from the embrace of sleep with a bitter sigh. "What do you want?"

"Hmmm. That's better. Well, now. What do we have here?"

Staring into those faded blue eyes, Mary felt something inside her that she hadn't felt in months . . . years. Concern. "What . . . what are you? Who are you?"

The woman smiled, and the lines around her mouth and

eyes deepened. "Ah . . . darling child, I think the question is . . . who are you?"

"KENDALL."

His hand tightened on her shoulder, and she shook off the fog of memories that kept swarming up to take her. It had been ages since she had thought of them. Hearing Cat's name brought them all back.

She didn't consider, not even once, it was somebody other than the Cat she knew.

It was Catharine . . . Cat. The child she'd found outside St. Louis more than a century ago. The child she'd raised as her own. The woman she'd failed to protect.

The woman she'd brought over after two men had raped her and then left for dead.

Cat hadn't been strong enough to survive the Change. It had driven her insane, but she'd hidden it well, entirely too well. It had taken Kendall years to find out just how insane Cat was.

And for the past century, Kendall had thought she was dead. She took a deep, slow breath, trying to find some measure of calm in the action. But there was nothing calming, nothing comforting in it.

Kane's hand slid down her arm and his fingers linked with hers. "What's going on, Kendall? Who is Mary? Who is Cat?"

"It's a long story," she whispered, shaking her head.

His lips quirked in a humorless smile. "Tell me the short version."

Glancing at Analise, she jerked her head toward the car. "Come on." As the girl fell in step behind them, she dug her keys out. "I was Mary Kendall. A long time ago. Mary—she died a long time ago. Cat . . . Catharine is somebody I thought died with Mary. I was wrong."

Kane continued to look at her expectantly, but Kendall didn't say anything, just unlocked the car door and stood aside, waiting for Analise to climb in. Kane muttered under his breath, "Well, I asked for the short story."

He walked around the car and slid her a look. "I expect to hear the long version."

Kendall started to slide in but he caught her gaze over the hood of the car. Something in his eyes made her pause, and she nodded jerkily. "Duke first," she whispered.

Enough people had died because of her. Because of Cat. She wasn't going to let another die.

Looking in the rearview mirror, she met Analise's gaze. "If Duke dies, I hope you realize, you go with him."

Analise nodded. "Just promise me, somebody will take care of my little brother."

Guilt ripped at Kendall. The brother played into this. A lot. She gave one sharp nod. "Can you hide yourself from Cat?"

Analise nodded. "Yes."

"What about Duke and your brother?"

"I . . . I don't know?"

Kendall sighed. "Great."

We're going to need backup.

There were a very limited number of people that she could count on to get here tonight. Glancing at Kane, she asked, "You have a cell phone?"

He arched a curious brow her way, but he tugged one from the clip on his belt and handed it to her. She scowled at it dubiously. "I don't know how to use those damn things."

Kane laughed. "What's the number, babe?"

Babe? She narrowed her eyes a little but rattled off the number to the young women's dorm at Excelsior. No phones were kept within the school itself. They kept getting zapped by all the magicks getting practiced within, but finally they'd installed phones within the dorms and offices.

And the voice that answered, thank God, was a familiar one. "Kelsey, I need you to get in touch with Vax. I need him here *now*."

Kelsey sounded alert and awake even though it was two a.m. in Virginia. "Something wrong, Kendall?"

"Everything is wrong, Kelsey. Just get Vax. I need him *here,* and I need him now."

"I'll get him." Kelsey hung up without another word.

Kendall had no sooner handed the phone to Kane than Analise told her, "Turn left."

Beside her, Kane tensed. Kendall heard his heart rate speed up, heard the change in his breathing pattern. Sliding him a glance, she saw him staring down the road with apprehension in his eyes. "Kane?"

"It was here," Kane murmured.

The dreams . . .

Analise didn't seem to notice either of them as she reached between the seats to point to a rundown apartment building. "There. She owns the entire building. We stay in the basement, but the rest of it is empty."

Analise never saw Kane move. Truthfully, until Kane's hand was wrapped around Analise's wrist, squeezing off the blood supply and pressing on sensitive nerves, Kendall barely even realized what had happened. Analise whimpered and then cut the sound off like she knew better then to let somebody know when she was hurting.

"I don't much like hurting females," Kane said.

Kendall didn't like the look in his eyes. Reaching out, she laid a hand on his arm. The muscles under her palm were tensed and hard, ready to snap a bone, to hurt. "Kane . . ."

He never even looked at her. "I don't like it, you understand me, Analise?"

Face pale, eyes dark with terror, Analise nodded.

Kane smiled. "Good. I'm glad you understand me. I don't like it. But I *will* do it."

And then he turned away, releasing her hand as he climbed from the car.

Kendall got out and held the seat forward as Analise climbed out, sliding Kane a nervous look. Kendall had to smile a little at that. Kane was human. Kendall was a vampire. She could snap Analise's neck with one flick of her wrist. And who was the girl afraid of?

Kane.

"Can you tell if she's in there?" Kendall asked quietly as they stepped up on the crumbling curb.

Analise nodded. "She's not. She's . . . uh . . ." Licking her lips, Analise tucked her hair behind her ear. "She's mad. She'll be out tonight late. Until she has to come in." Her voice dropped to a rough whisper. "She'll hurt people tonight. A lot of them."

Guilt and icy fear mingled in Kendall's chest, threatening to rise up and choke her. "Then now is as good a time as any to go and get Duke and your brother," she finally said, forcing the words out of her tight throat.

"Aren't you going to wait for me?"

At the familiar voice, Kendall turned and watched as Vax stepped out of the shadows. She couldn't even force a smile at him. "You got here fast."

He shrugged. "Well, isn't that why you called me? I move fast."

Both Kane and Analise were staring at him with wide eyes. Kendall made a mental note to try and explain flyers to Kane at some point. Some witches had a rather unique talent to move through time and space in the blink of an eye. Vax was one of them. He was also a warrior, which was one of the reasons she'd needed him.

Granted, he was technically not an active Hunter any more, but he'd still take a rare job now and then. Protecting a young child and an injured shifter would be right up his alley.

Turning his head, Vax stared up at the building with shuttered eyes. "So there's a party here?" He glanced at Kendall. "This place is full of bad vibes. But you haven't been feeling it, have you?"

Kendall shook her head. Jerking a finger toward Analise, she said, "Something to do with her."

Vax looked at Analise, and his eyes softened just a little. He moved toward her and reached out, touching her face. Kendall expected her to jerk away, but she didn't, just held still, trembling with fear. He cupped her chin, turning her face this way and that. "I'll take care of this later. Don't worry—it will be okay."

Kane growled a little under his breath and took a step toward Vax. "She's the reason Duke is in there."

Vax gave Kane a mild look. "I know that." Then he looked
back at Analise, his gray eyes darkening with pain. "But
there's more pain in that place than you've ever dealt with in
your life. When you deal with pain on a daily basis, you stop
thinking about right and wrong. Only one thing counts, and
that's survival."

Kane started to say something else but Kendall stepped
between them. "That's enough. We're here for a reason. To
get Duke and the boy out. So let's go do it."

She started towards the building and then paused. Speaking over her shoulder, Kendall said softly, "There's another
reason I needed you. There's an old friend of ours in here.
One we thought was long dead."

A tense, strained silence hung in the air, and then Vax said
softly, "Always good to see old friends."

Bitterly, Kendall said, "Not this one."

THE cloying stench of blood, sweat, and fear was almost
enough to make Kane gag.

People had died here. He could almost smell the rotting
stink of all the people who had been killed here.

Dear God, please don't let Duke be one of them.

Ahead of them, Analise opened a door, and her pale form
slowly disappeared down into a maw of darkness. Kendall
followed. Kane drew the Beretta, holding it loosely in his
hand as he started down the stairs. The stench got stronger
here.

Behind him, he felt Vax's silent presence. There was no
sound to give him away, but Kane knew he was there.
Damned quiet bastard.

Kane rounded the corner at the foot of the steps and
tensed as a shadow moved in the darkness. "Ana!"

"Damn it, Brad! You have to be more careful!"

Kane blew out a breath as he lowered his gun. There was
light here, dim, but at least he could see his hand in front of
his face.

And the pale, pint-sized kid standing in front of Analise. Dear God.

The boy ignored Kane. He moved to stand in front of Kendall, staring up at her with what looked like hero worship. "You're a Hunter."

Kendall flashed Analise a look as she knelt down in front of the boy. "Hey, sweetie. Brad, right?"

He nodded vigorously. "Did Ana bring you here?" he asked.

Kendall nodded. Kane caught a sheen of tears in her eyes and suspected she had to force the smile as she replied, "Yes, she did. What do you say, you want to come with us?"

The boy didn't seem at all disturbed by the violence that hung in the air as he stared at Kendall with that rapt look on his face. "You talk pretty."

Kane had barely noticed. That low, husky voice of Kendall's had always hit him in the gut, but it wasn't the timbre of her voice the kid was talking about, he realized. It was the very faint wisp of an accent there. It was rarely there. But it slid in from time to time, and even more when she was upset. He watched as Kendall smiled, a little easier. "Aye. 'Tis Ireland. That's where I came from, a long time ago. Maybe someday, I kin take ya there," she murmured, letting the lilting accent slip into her voice just a little more.

It didn't seem possible, but his eyes got even wider and he nodded. "Oh, that would be awesome. I've seen pic—"

Gently, Kendall said, "Have ya, now? But they can't even compare. We don't have time now, though. We have to hurry. You want to come wi' us?"

As though he sensed the urgency inside her now, his face went solemn and he glanced at his sister. "Ana, too?"

"Yes, Ana, too."

The smile that spread across his face was heart wrenching. In a whisper that Kane could barely hear, Brad said, "I knew it!" He took a deep, slow breath as though he was trying to calm himself down. Then he met Kendall's gaze straight on, and said quietly, "I always knew you would

come for us. I kept telling Ana, but she wouldn't listen."
Then he straightened, pulling his thin shoulders back and
up. "Come on. We have to get Duke. He's in bad shape."

Brad wasn't lying.

The room was dark.

And the smell in here was worse. The air was stale,
reeking of sweat, and blood. It hadn't known fresh air in
years, if ever. Across from the doorway, a man was
chained to the wall.

Kane barely recognized the thin, battered man.

He was literally chained, with manacles at his hands and
feet, chains through metal loops that were attached to the
wall. The manacles had the gleam of pure silver, and Kane
knew that under that silver there would be nasty, deep burns.

"Fuck, she's been starving him," Kendall whispered.

At the sound of her voice, Duke stirred, but he didn't so
much as open his eyes.

There were nasty bruises and cuts all over him, scratches
all across his face that were starting to heal, but they looked
like they had cut almost down to the bone. One eye was
swollen almost completely shut. Kane took one step toward
Duke, all but shaking with fury. "Sweet damnation. What
did they do to him?" he whispered.

Vax moved forward. "I'll get him down." Looking at
Analise, he said, "If there's anything you two want, get it
now. We're gone in less than three minutes."

"How can he look that terrible? It hasn't even been a week."

"It doesn't even take three days for a shifter," Kendall said
gruffly, a lone tear rolling down her face. "Their metabolism
is so high, they need twice the amount of food a human
needs. Humans take weeks to starve to death. Shifters, only
a fraction of that."

Analise still stood in the doorway, one hand resting on
Brad's shoulder. "I've given him water when I could. Cat
beat me for doing just that."

Kane slid an evil look at her. "Aren't you supposed to be
getting your stuff?"

Her hand tightened on Brad's shoulder. "I have everything that matters."

Brad looked at Kane. Those eyes looked entirely too adult for his young face. "Ana doesn't always do the best thing, mister. But everything she's done, she did because she wanted to protect me."

The clinking of metal drew their attention back toward Duke, and Kane went to help Vax as Duke fell forward. "Where are we going to take him? He can't be safe anywhere in this city," Kane said quietly.

"I'll handle it," Vax said softly. "Let's just get out of here."

Getting out of there sounded good. Very good.

CHAPTER 8

CATHARINE stood just inside the door, trembling with rage. Even though she had fed until she felt nearly ready to pop, her fangs had dropped and all she wanted to do was tear into somebody's neck. Just to bleed them, though. Bleed them.

Bleed *her*.

The *her*s though, blended in her mind. Analise and Kendall. She didn't know which one she was more pissed at. Both of them had been here. She could smell both of the bitches. As well as Vax, that mangy, witchy bastard who thought he was so damned righteous. Those fucking Hunters. Shit, how she hated them. All of them.

But Kendall, she was the worst. Thought she was so damned high and mighty. Holier than thou.

The scent of blood filled the air, and Cat looked down, saw the blood trickling from her fists. A scream of rage escaped her as she realized she had torn her own palms in her fury.

They were going to pay for this.

"Kendall, you are so fucking dead."

They hadn't just taken the cat. That was bad enough. She really liked toying with shifters.

But the boy . . . she had really, *really* wanted to break him.

What was worse, though, Analise had brought them here. She had to have helped them. Kendall wouldn't have found this place on her own. The bitch just wasn't smart enough.

"Should have bled her out." Forget Changing her. She would have whined and bemoaned her fate for centuries. Or just gone and stood in the sun as soon as Cat turned her back. Analise wasn't strong enough to see her true destiny as a vampire.

They were predators.

Born to hunt and to kill.

Fuck, she might have even tried to become one of those mangy Hunters. And that just would have been more than Cat could have handled, one of her offspring becoming a Hunter.

"I'll get her, though," she muttered, pacing the empty, open space of floor, her long legs scissoring back and forth. Her hair flowed back from her face as she moved. "Find that whiny brat of a brother of hers."

Now *he* was young. Too damned young. She knew from experience, if you turned them young enough, they rarely survived the Change—intact. If Cat brought Brad over while he was young enough, that powerful mind of his would be malleable, even though now it was anything but. Of course, it would take a hell of a lot to get close enough to bite him. Even sleeping, the kid had formidable protection. An injury. That was the only thing she could think of.

But that was doable.

Slowing to a halt, she stared out a window into the night. "Why didn't I think of that sooner?"

Yes. That could work. Hurt him, incapacitate him, and then she could drain him to the point of weakness and force the Change on him. Once he was Changed, she could inflict her will on his young mind. That would be a fitting punishment. Not just on Analise, but on Kendall as well.

Of course, she wouldn't stop there. Not for Kendall.

No.

Kendall had to die.

But first, she had to find Kendall.

Wherever Kendall was, she'd find her cat, the kid, and the traitorous bitch, Analise.

Now if Kane had known that the minute he turned his back the dark bastard was going to just *disappear* again, he might not have been so amicable about it.

He wasn't sure what he could have done, but shit.

And not only were Vax and Duke gone, but the little bitch was gone, too.

Now granted, the boy was gone, and Kendall assured him that Brad was safe, and that was a good thing.

But Kane still wanted some justice for what Duke had suffered.

"I think Analise suffers every time she looks at Duke."

Kane glared at Kendall over his mug of coffee. "Stay out of my head."

Kendall snorted. "I can't read your mind." With a shrug of her shoulders, she said, "I'm not sure why that is. Most humans have minds that are like an open book."

Her nose wrinkled as she added, "But yours is like a tome of ancient Greek. Not only can't I read it, I can't understand half of anything you do."

She lifted a steaming mug of tea and sipped a little before lowering it back to the table. "No, I wasn't reading your mind, darling. I was just reading your face."

Kane blew out a pent-up breath of air. "Where did he take them?"

Kendall raised one shoulder, a pensive look on her face. "Some place safe. Maybe to his ranch. Maybe to the school. Maybe to England. I'm not really positive. But someplace where Cat can't get to them."

Arching a brow at her, Kane asked skeptically, "Would she even try?"

"Oh, yes."

They fell into silence as the waitress approached, carrying a tray laden with food. She transferred the dishes from her tray, ignoring Kendall, but bending low over the table and treating Kane to an excellent view of her rather bountiful breasts.

"If there's anything I can do for you now, sweetie, let me know," she cooed, before she walked away, swinging her hips.

Kendall waited until the woman was out of earshot before she said, "Well, she's a friendly one, isn't she, sweetie?"

Kane grinned at her. "A ray of sunshine." He scooped up a forkful of eggs and popped them into his mouth.

"You look exhausted," he said softly.

She glanced up at him. "I feel exhausted."

"Well, it was a lot easier than I expected, but I'm worn-out just from the stress of it." He started cutting through the country ham, stabbing a piece of it with his fork.

She laughed, but it was a humorless sound. "Kane, it's not over. That was the easy part. But it's not over."

Kane stopped chewing the ham and stared at her. "It's not."

"It is for you. You helped me find Duke, and you can go back to whatever it is you want to do. But I can't stop until I find Cat."

Slumping back against his seat, Kane muttered, "Fuck."

Yeah, that part hadn't occurred to him.

But it should have.

Kane sat there for a few minutes, working on cleaning his plate, brooding and thinking. It took less than five minutes to come to a conclusion. No. It wasn't over. And he knew what he needed to do. Now he just needed to convince Kendall. But why did he have this odd feeling it was going to take a little bit of work to do that?

"Okay. So we go after her."

Feeling her eyes on him, he glanced up at her. Kane cut into a biscuit and slathered it with butter and strawberry jam as he politely asked, "What?"

"There's no *we*."

Grinning at her, he said, "Yes, there is."

"You can't come with me."

Kane shrugged. "Well, you can always try and leave me behind. But I'm pretty good at finding vampires on my own. You might have noticed that. And if you leave me behind, I'll just try to find her on my own. And I suspect you'd rather me not do that."

Kendall just glared at him. Even though that look was hot enough to singe, he just smiled affably at her as he went about cleaning his plate.

"You don't understand, Kane," Kendall said through clenched teeth. "She is nuts. Psycho."

"I *do* understand that, Kendall. I understand that pretty well. I saw what she did to Duke. And I don't plan on letting her do that to you."

"What makes you think you can stop her?" Kendall demanded.

Kane just shrugged, lifting one shoulder. "I don't know. But I know I have to try."

With that, he fell into silence. Across from him, Kendall stared into her mug of tea and fought for words to try to make him understand how foolish he was being. To convince him to trust her enough to do her job. Finally, she just said it flatly. "Kane, I'll find Catharine. She will die. But I won't take you with me."

His fork clattered to the table as he tossed it down, leaning back in the booth, crossing his arms over his chest. "You will."

Coolly, she said, "And I assume you think you can make me?"

Kane shrugged. "I know the rules of bargaining. I'm willing to bet you won't bargain risking my life—because if you don't take me with you, that's exactly what you are doing. Either take me with you . . . or I'll just go looking for her on my own."

Narrowing her eyes at him, she said shortly, "Like you could find her."

The sharp, cool look that entered his eyes raised a chill on her flesh. "I found you, sweetness, didn't I?" A satisfied smile spread across his face as Kendall dropped her face into her hands, groaning. "I've got a better chance of surviving it with you around. We both know that. But whether I live or die, I'm going after her."

"This is *my* job, Kane. *My* responsibility." The unspoken words *my fault* echoed through her head and guilt all but choked her as she stared at him. When the look in his eyes softened and his smile gentled, that made it worse.

"I know. But I've got a right to see this through, Kendall. I started this. I believe in finishing what I start—don't you?"

How in the hell could she argue with that? she wondered helplessly.

She couldn't.

No more than she could risk him going after Catharine on his own.

No.

He had her right where he wanted her—well and truly caught.

Kendall clenched her jaw; her hands closed around the thick mug of tea as she tried to calm the fear that flooded her. Fear, frustration . . . *trapped*. Damn it, trapped. No options, no choices, nothing.

Trapped . . . that feeling, regardless of what inspired it, was enough to bring back memories she'd fought long to destroy. The echo of a scream whispered through her mind and she clenched her hands.

The mug in her hands shattered, and as the scalding hot tea spilled all over her hands, she dropped her gaze to stare at the flesh. It pinkened, just a little, but vampires didn't have the same kind of reaction to injury that humans did. For one, healing was hyperfast. Certain chemicals and antibodies in their blood rushed to the site of any energy, and the body absorbed minor injuries like this the same way a sponge absorbed water.

Didn't keep it from stinging though. Flexing her fingers, she stared at her hands, barely hearing the startled exclamation from the waitress who'd been lounging against the counter.

It wasn't until the lady started patting at her hands with a towel that Kendall really heard her talking. Shaking her head, she focused on her words and forced a smile. "I'm fine . . . really. It's not a big deal."

"I can't imagine what made that cup break like that," the woman murmured, her eyes wide as she sopped up the tea from the table after Kendall pulled her hands away.

Kendall flicked her gaze to the woman's nametag before she said, "Holly, I'm fine. Really. Don't worry about it."

After the waitress left, Kendall tucked her hands in her lap, lifting her gaze to stare at Kane's eyes across the table. "I don't like this," she said quietly, her voice flat and cold. "Not at all."

His mouth curved up in a sardonic smile. "I kind of figured that."

Blowing out a sigh, she focused for a minute on the stinging in her hands. It was fading with every second, and by the time they left, there'd be no sign left of what should have been a nasty burn. "You do one thing I tell you *not* to do and I'll knock your ass out and leave you wrapped up like a Christmas present."

He crooked a grin at her. "I'll get out."

She smiled nastily. "Maybe. But not before I have a couple of big werewolves come and haul your ass to some place you won't be able to get out of."

One dark blond brow rose and he nodded slowly. "Okay. Understood."

"And if I tell you to do something, I want it done before I even look at you to see if you're listening," Kendall added.

Now the other brow rose and he stared at her hard. "Provided you don't try to tell me to walk away or something stupid like that, I can handle that."

She snorted and rose from the table, careful to keep her hands out of sight as she walked past the waitress. Behind her, she heard Kane tossing money on the table, and she pushed on outside as she called over her shoulder, "Like I'd be that naïve."

*   *   *

In the past thirty minutes, she'd responded to every question with as few syllables as possible. Oh yeah, she was pissed.

Kane wasn't surprised.

Hell, he'd expected that. Although he hadn't realized he would miss seeing her look at him, or smile, that dimple winking in her cheek, the way her eyes glowed.

He was right about this.

In his gut, he knew it.

It didn't matter that there was a nasty fear in his gut when he thought of walking back into that hellhole where they'd found Duke. He went icy just thinking about it.

He could imagine dying there. Easily. People had, he knew. That was not his imagination. People had died there, and it was no stretch to imagine he might be the next one.

But despite the fear it put in his gut, he couldn't walk away from this. No matter how much she said he could walk away, he knew he couldn't.

Some quiet voice whispered in his mind that he had to see this through. It was his only chance—Kendall's only chance. She could easily die going after that woman.

Vax had said, *Her heart will be involved in this.*

A look entered her eyes when she mentioned the woman's name, a grief, a rage—something that blinded her to rational thought. Kendall couldn't think clearly in regards to Catharine. He didn't know how he knew that, but it was just fact.

You are all that stands between Kendall and death.

Kane wasn't exactly sure how in the hell that was possible. He was just a man. A human man at that. He was strong, but he couldn't bench-press cars, and he suspected some of these paranormal creatures just might be able to. He couldn't whisk himself from one state to another, couldn't read minds—although some of the mental tricks didn't seem to work on him.

But what difference did that make?

Kane really didn't know. But he wasn't leaving Kendall alone to fight this Cat-bitch.

Whoever she was. Once, she had meant a great deal to Kendall. He could see that in her eyes. Every time her name was mentioned, grief welled up in Kendall's eyes.

That grief just might get her killed.

Maybe that was where Kane would come in.

He wouldn't let grief slow him down.

He shrugged off the thoughts circling in his mind as he told himself one simple thing. Together, they would find her, and they would make Catharine pay.

Together . . .

Unbidden, another word formed in his mind.

Forever.

His eyes narrowed as he repeated that word, mouthing it silently to himself. Forever had never been something he'd considered in life. For the past couple of years, his future had revolved around one thing. Hunting down Kendall, taking back the blood he had thought she had owed him. After discovering she wasn't who he had thought, just hunting down killers had been enough for a little while.

But his life had felt so empty.

He hadn't even realized it until he had her by his side.

And he didn't want to go a single day without her.

Not one.

He wanted her so bad, he ached with it. But it wasn't just a temporary thing, he suspected. Kane wanted *her,* for as long as he had life inside him.

Blowing out a breath, he slid a look at her from the corner of his eye and wondered how she had gotten under his skin so bad, so fast. They'd had a handful of days together, truth be told. Some really amazing sex. Then he recalled the last time they'd been together. What he'd told her. It was more than sex.

A smile tugged up the corners of his mouth. That was the truth. It was more than sex. When he slid inside her body, it felt like more than that. It felt like their souls were meshing as well. She felt like the other half of him.

The car slowed marginally, and he glanced up, seeing the bright splash of streetlights flooding the interior of the car as they turned into the hotel parking lot.

Brakes squeaked as she angled the car into a parking spot. Kane climbed out, thankful he had his own keycard, because otherwise he had a feeling he might be spending the night in the car.

Be optimistic. Maybe she's cooled down, he told himself.

Then he winced as he listened to Kendall slam the door behind her.

She was still very, very pissed off.

KENDALL wasn't pissed.

She was furious.

She was scared.

She was sick with fear.

A cold sweat had settled over her entire body.

But she wasn't pissed. Stalking down the hall, she jammed her keycard into the slot just above the handle on her door and jerked on it so hard, she heard something rattle inside. The little green light came on though and the door opened. That was all she cared about. She shoved it open and stomped inside without looking back at Kane.

She could feel Kane's eyes on her back, and she resisted the urge to turn around and snarl at him.

Damn it.

He'd backed her into this and she hated it.

But Kane Winter was a damned smart man. He knew when to hold his tongue, and the bastard didn't try to say anything that might cool her off, didn't try to charm her out of the mood she was in. Jerk. How could she bite his head off when he wouldn't give her an opening to do it?

She hadn't realized she'd been standing in the middle of the room, her entire body tense, vibrating with suppressed emotions, fury, grief, rage, too many to name until she heard her name voiced in a soft, gentle tone.

"Kendall?"

Swallowing, she turned and opened her eyes to stare at Kane, the concern she saw in his dark green eyes was like a splash of cold water in her face. Slowly, she turned away from him, walking over to the bed and collapsing on it, falling forward and burying her face in her arms. "Leave me alone, Kane," she said thickly.

Like somebody had just pulled a plug, all the fury had drained out of her, leaving nothing but fear and grief. There was too much of that, and it was seeking an outlet.

She wanted to cry, but she couldn't. Not now. Not in front of him. She was afraid that if she started to cry, she wouldn't be able to stop.

The tears wouldn't be held back though, and they started to flow silently.

The bed dipped with Kane's weight as he lowered himself to sit beside her. She stiffened at the soft murmur of her name, tried to stop crying, but the tears just kept falling, saturating the pillow as the knot in her chest threatened to choke her.

"Kendall."

With a violent jerk of her shoulder, she dislodged the hand he had placed on her shoulder. "Leave me alone, Kane," she whispered, her voice thick and rusty. "Just leave me alone."

S HE was crying.

Kane retreated to sit in the chair, staring at her slim form, his heart knotting inside his chest, every beat painful. What had caused this . . .

There was no sobbing, no violent shudders wracking her body, just silent tears that seemed all the more heart wrenching.

How did a woman go from such volatile fury to these silent tears in a matter of seconds?

Kane really didn't know, but he was pretty sure he would rather have the fury, even as disconcerting as it was. Still, he wanted to know what had caused it. Closing his hands into impotent fists, he stared up at the ceiling through the darkness.

There was such pain inside her. It had always been there. He'd seen it inside of her almost from the beginning, that sadness in her eyes, that grief. There was a pain in her eyes that ran so deep, it hung in the air around her like cloak.

Clenching his jaw, he closed his eyes, trying to force his body to relax, but he couldn't. Shooting out of the chair, he moved across the room and laid on the bed beside her, pulling her tense body into his arms. When she struggled against him, he buried his face in her hair and murmured, "Stop. I'm not going anywhere."

She could have forced herself away from him. A woman who could throw a man twelve feet wasn't going to stay someplace she didn't want to be. But a shudder wracked her body and she held herself still in his arms, tolerating his embrace.

Slowly, the tension in her body drained away and she relaxed against him. This close, he could feel the small tremors that wracked her body, and hear an occasional shaky sigh slip from her lips. Sliding one hand up, he stroked her hair out of her face, baring the gentle curve of her cheek. Skimming his lips over the satiny skin, Kane held her as the tears continued to fall.

They fell even after sleep claimed her and were still seeping out from under her lids as Kane gave into the exhaustion and followed her into oblivion.

"Y OU'RE awake."

At the sound of Kane's husky voice, Kendall closed her eyes. "Yes."

One muscled arm slid around her waist, tightening as he pulled her more snugly against him. "You had nightmares."

Nightmares . . . that seemed almost a tame word for what had tormented her. The memories were some she'd give damn near anything to wash from her mind. But maybe they were the penance she had to pay, for what she had done, what she had allowed to happen.

He sighed—she could feel the movement of his chest, the soft brush of his breath along her nape. "Tell me about Mary Kendall," he whispered. "Tell me about Catharine."

Kendall's eyes flew open and she struggled away from his embrace. He didn't release her easily—but she pried his arm away and sat up, scuttling away from him to brace her back against the headboard, drawing her knees to her chest. A rising sob threatened to choke her. As she battled it down, it ached within her throat, in her chest, a raw, hideous pain.

"Catharine is a lunatic. That's basically all you need you to know about her. And Mary . . ." her voice trailed off for a minute. Finally, she whispered huskily, "Mary Kendall is dead. Long dead."

Tears blinded her as he sat up, reaching out. She saw his hand moving toward her, and she held herself rigid as he cupped her cheek in his hand, his thumb stroking over her skin. "When did you die, Mary?" he asked softly.

The pain in her chest bloomed larger and a soft, muffled sob escaped her lips. Tears rolled down her cheeks and she turned her face away, unable to look in his eyes. "A long time ago, Kane. A very long time ago."

His arms came under her, but she didn't have the energy to evade him, and he drew her into his lap, cuddling her against him. The heat from his body slowly seeped into hers, warming her. She hadn't even realized she was cold—not until she felt his heat. But now, she started to shiver.

"Tell me about her."

Squeezing her eyes closed, she tried to block out his voice, tried to block out the gentle touch of his hands on her body. "She was a weak fool," Kendall whispered. "Too weak to run away, too weak to fight. She died because she was weak . . . and I was born."

"You've never been weak, Kendall."

His lips brushed her temple and she laughed bitterly. "You didn't know me, Kane. I *was* weak. I let them take me away from my home and I didn't try to run. When another came, a vampire, I let him Change me I lived, choking with fear, but did I ever try to run away?"

"There's a difference between being afraid and being weak."

"When the fear controls you, it makes you weak, Kane. Rising above it is a sign of strength," Kendall said darkly.

"Then that proves it—you're the strongest woman I've ever met, and the fact that you once damned near choked on the fear only makes you stronger," Kane said quietly.

Kendall didn't know what to say to that. She might be strong now. But she had lived in fear for so long. Then in ignorance.

She'd been blind. Blind and stupid.

And because of it, she Changed a woman who wasn't strong enough to survive it intact.

Catharine had come through a cold-hearted, crazy murderess . . . but Kendall suspected the weaknesses in Catharine had always been there. The flaws in her character had just been exploited, aggravated . . . brought to the fore during the grueling Changing process.

Catharine had become a killer. And because Kendall hadn't looked at her with objective eyes, the blood Catharine had shed was on Kendall's soul.

Strong—how could she possibly be strong? A strong woman would have made sure Catharine was dead. She wouldn't have just assumed. Hell, a strong woman would have just let Catharine go, not tried to Change her.

Kendall had Changed her, because she just couldn't say good-bye.

"I'm not strong, Kane," she whispered quietly as tears rolled down her face.

He cupped her cheek and arched her face up so that he could stare down at her. "How can you say that?"

"A strong woman wouldn't have done the things I've done."

Brushing her hair back from her face, Kane kissed her softly. "What have you done that's so awful, Kendall? You face monsters that would break the sanest of men and deal with nightmares I don't even want to imagine. What have you done that's so awful?"

Shame flooded her at the sure, certain sound of his voice. How could he be so certain of her? He barely knew her. Gently, she shrugged off his hands and backed away from him. Quietly, she said, "I'm not what you think, Kane. I have blood on my hands. Blood of innocents, because I wasn't quick enough, strong enough to stop their killer."

He was silent for a moment. When he spoke, his voice was low and gritty. "You can't hold yourself responsible for the actions of another person, Kendall."

Slowly, carefully, each movement almost painful, Kendall lifted her head and stared into Kane's brooding green eyes. The lean lines of his face seemed tighter and tension hung in the air around him. Quietly, she said, "I can. I can if I'm the one who brought Catharine over."

Turning away from the confusion in his eyes, she stared out the window, away from him so she wouldn't have to see his face.

The moment he understood, she knew. Kendall felt it as the air in the room was suddenly choked with anger, with rage . . . with disbelief.

"You *made* her?"

Leaning her head forward, she rested her brow against the window, letting it cool her heated flesh. She felt hot and sick all over with remembered shame and anger. *I should have known. . . .* Shoving that aside, she started to speak.

"Catharine was just a baby when I found her. Vax and I were still partners. It was outside of St. Louis. Two feral werewolves had attacked her family, killed everybody but her. They kept her alive, although we aren't really sure why. When they realized we were trailing them, they just dropped her and ran. Vax went after them. I stayed with her—and I kept her . . ."

Kendall kept it as short as she could, explaining how she'd raised the child as her own, loved Catharine as her own. Coddled her, protected her.

"Too much, I think," Kendall whispered, tears stinging her eyes. "She slipped out one night when I was out Hunting. Damn near smothered her with it. She wanted a night of freedom. But I'd done too good a job of sheltering her. She had no idea what danger was. The men saw a woman alone. They chased her. They raped her." Her throat ached—swallowing was torture. "I heard her screams as she woke up, tried to fight. They hit her. Beat her, damned near to death, while I was trying to get to her. I killed them—but it wasn't soon enough to save her. She was dying. I could either let her go . . . or I could bring her over."

Turning, she met Kane's dark, angry gaze. "I shouldn't have brought her over. She wasn't strong enough—but I didn't think of anything but saving her, in the only way I could."

Crossing to him, she knelt down in front of him. Her hair fell over her shoulder as she cocked her head, studying him. "So you see . . . I failed. Unless you know the human is strong enough to survive the Change intact, mentally, emotionally, you don't bring them over. And not only did I not look, I didn't care. It *is* my fault."

The silence of the room was oppressive as she rose from her crouch on the floor and walked away, slipping out of the room without another word.

CHAPTER 9

K<small>ANE</small> didn't know how to handle the emotions churning inside him.

There was a great hatred for the monster that had damned near killed Duke. A rage that made his hands clench into tight fists, made him want to beat something, tear something apart. A growl of fury ripped through his throat as he paced the room.

Kendall had made Catharine into a vampire.

I didn't care . . . It is my fault.

But he also kept hearing those words, spoken in a voice so thick with tears, he was amazed she'd been able to speak at all.

Part of him wanted to go to her and hold her tight, to kiss her, to strip her clothes away and love her until she forgot her pain, until she forgot her name. Another part of him wanted to grab her and shake her for letting that soft heart rule her head.

She'd sired a monster.

Dropping on the bed, he pressed the heels of his hands against his eyes. But when he closed his eyes, he didn't see darkness, he saw the small boy, his body so thin as he moved into the door and stared at Kendall, joy blooming as he realized somebody had come to save them from a monster.

And he saw Duke, chained to the wall like a fucking dog, his body broken and battered. Even Analise, her delicate face bruised from a vicious beating.

He now understood the phrase *seeing red*.

Everything in front of him seemed faintly tinged with it, and as he stared at the walls, he could almost see blood splatter on them.

How long has Catharine been doing this?

How long has Kendall been letting her kill?

The walls of the room seemed to be closing in on him.

"I've got to get out of here," he muttered. He put his boots on, sliding the silver knife into an ankle sheath before grabbing his jacket. On his way out the door, he paused long enough to jam his Beretta under his waistband at the small of his back.

Kendall's car was still in the parking lot.

He scowled at it and realized she was probably at the place he had planned on going. His eyes narrowed in fury as he imagined just what she might be doing there.

Damn near every time he'd seen her in a bar, she hadn't been sitting on a stool alone. No, she'd been all but making out with a man, getting it on with music. And Kane would be damned if he let some bastard lay a hand on *his* woman.

The bar was less than a half a mile away, separated by a stretch of busted pavement, a couple of gas stations, and some fast-food joints, all closed for the night.

Jamming his hands into the pockets of his jacket, he started down the road, his jaw clenching. Ahead, he could hear raucous music, and he saw the neon glow of a sign that badly needed repairing. *Liv mus c here 2 nite,* it said, flashing off and on.

Music and men, yeah, it was entirely possible he'd find her here, all right.

Of course, from the sounds of what was pouring from the bar as he drew closer, he wasn't sure he could call it music. It was loud, and it was rough, but that was about it.

He had to admit, part of him hoped he wouldn't find Kendall in there. He wanted to be alone, and he wanted a beer. No, screw that. Whiskey. He wanted to feel it burn down his throat. Just a little while of not thinking about the confusing jumble of thoughts in his head.

Yeah, he could go for that, a few hours to think through this and get a handle on things. Some of the tension knotting his shoulders eased up a bit as he decided to do just that. He almost headed back to the hotel, but something made him walk inside the bar.

His rage exploded as he stalked through the doors and saw Kendall.

Her long, pale arms wrapped around the neck of a boy who looked barely old enough to drink, her butt pressed up against his hips as she moved to the music. All she wore was a pair of those low-slung, painted-on jeans she loved, and a skinny strapped shirt that didn't even reach the waistband of her jeans. *Fuck.*

She hadn't even been out of the hotel ten minutes. What did she do, keep a change of fuck-me clothes in the trunk of her car?

The gold hoop in her navel flashed in the dim light. She had one slim hand resting on her hip as she swayed to the music.

At the sight of her, that constant low-level hunger flared to rampant life, and he could all but feel the blood as it drained out of his head, pooling in his groin as his cock lengthened and engorged, aching inside the confines of his jeans. Winding through the swaying bodies of women and men dancing, he made his way to Kendall, moving close enough that when Romeo spun her around and bent her back, she bumped into him.

Cutting the kid a cool glance, he said, "I'm cutting in. Get lost."

Kendall snorted, but the kid just laughed. There was a look in his eyes . . . one that Kane should have seen the minute he stepped through the door. *Would* have seen, if fury hadn't been blinding him.

Age.

This wasn't a fucking kid, no matter how young he looked. *Vampire.* It took only a second to sum him up, and even less to decide this was no Hunter. There was an air of . . . evil to him. Sliding his eyes to Kendall, he arched a brow and said, "Your taste in men isn't much better than your taste in friends."

Her eyes flashed.

With hurt, he thought before he shoved the idea out of his head.

"I'm busy, Kane," she said, her tone bored. "I've got things to do that don't include babysitting you."

Flashing her a cold smile, he said, "Too bad." Folding his arms across his chest, he glared at her, and it didn't take her long to get the point. He'd make a damned scene. Kendall didn't like scenes. Scenes were a little harder to erase from the memory, made it harder for her to slip away after . . .

Shit.

The cool assessing look he'd seen in her eyes before was there again. The look he'd seen in Hanover, right before Aaron Meyer had looked into her eyes and taken off running. Aaron Meyer, guilty of multiple rapes and murders. *Things to do* . . . yeah, I bet, he thought sourly. So she had come here with a job in mind. She had felt the damned vampire. He'd come here to get drunk.

She'd come here to work.

"I'll wait all night if I have to, Kendall."

He wasn't leaving her alone to get battered by a man again. Never mind that she could take it, and more, and heal before nightfall. A thought moved through his mind: *She's already taken too many beatings* . . .

Her lids lowered, shielding that golden gaze from him. But she turned her head and smiled at her dance partner. "He's a stubborn thing, Joseph. I'll have to finish this dance later."

The vampire wasn't so interested in letting her walk away, though. Closing bony fingers on her wrist, he kept Kendall from leaving as he summed up Kane with one dismissive glance. "He's not what a woman like you needs, sugar. People like us, we want something different."

Then his eyes slid to Kane, and a smile brightened his face. "Of course, we could have fun with this one."

Kane smiled coolly. "Try it, pal. You wouldn't be the first vamp I've wasted."

The look of disbelief on his face was almost comical. But Kendall's look was even better. Sheer, utter frustration, backed by the soft growl he heard coming from her.

"Kane." Her voice was a cold, stiff slice in the loud bar, one he had no trouble hearing.

The gangly, young-looking vampire snarled at Kane, trying once more to tug Kendall closer to him. Studying him, Kane got an impression of . . . power. Not that this one seemed a particularly strong vamp, but Kane almost felt as though he could *see* the vampire's age, the level of his power.

Younger than Kendall, although somehow Kane didn't suspect this man knew that. And nowhere near as strong.

When Kendall cut her eyes back to the vampire, looking first from his bloodless fingers wrapped around her wrist, then up to his eyes, Kane realized she had been hiding herself. Cloaking her own power, somehow. And now that fell away, revealing just what she was.

The vampire's eyes widened, his lids flickering as though to hide the fear that was brewing inside them. His hand fell away and he retreated one small step almost before he even realized it. After glancing at Kane, the vampire looked once more at Kendall, and apparently, what he saw on her face didn't please him because he took off running.

Kendall sent Kane one icy glance, and he was surprised the air didn't freeze around him. Before he could say another word, she slid through the crowd, disappearing among the throng of humanity like smoke on the wind.

She'd go after the vampire, Kane knew.

Leaving the dark, smoky bar behind him, he made his way outside, hands jammed in his pockets as he steamed in silent frustration. Couldn't catch up with her. He circled around the bar, searching for her, but he knew he wouldn't find her.

The odd protectiveness that rose inside of him was an emotion he really didn't know how to handle.

He *knew*, in his gut, that Kendall could take care of the man she hunted. Knew she could deal with it, probably better than Kane could ever hope. And while that knowledge burned a little, he could accept it.

But in his heart . . . in his heart, he wanted to protect her. To shield her against the violence that was her life.

Foolishness.

Simple foolishness—much like not paying too much attention to his surroundings. The vampire hadn't run too far.

Apparently, he'd backtracked and was even now moving closer to Kane.

He'd left most of his weapons back at the hotel, but he had his knife, and the gun at the small of his back. His knife was pure silver and would do a decent amount of damage. The gun was loaded so Kane wasn't exactly helpless, but first he had to keep the bastard from surprising him in the darkness.

Sweeping the dark area around him with his eyes, Kane searched for the man that watched him.

Although he saw nothing, Kane knew when he'd found the dark, deep shadows that the vampire hid in. It was like a tingling low on his spine. Slowly, Kane reached for the gun, staring into the darkness so hard it made his eyes ache.

"Don't you think you're kind of stupid coming back here? You should have run, fast and far as you could," Kane said levelly.

A cool laugh sounded in the air, echoing all around him. "Running doesn't do much good against a Hunter. You have to outwit them. Get them where it hurts . . . and you are what hurts her. After I kill you, she won't think as well. Then I'll kill her. I know people who'd give much to have the body of a Hunter . . . even a dead one. She's going to make me a rich man."

Kane snorted. "That's assuming you can kill her. And I don't think that's going to be as easy as you think."

The vampire sighed. The sound was slithery, like snakes, and Kane had to fight back the urge to shudder, to retreat, even a little. The lights of the bar behind him beckoned, and it took a decent amount of willpower to just stand there. The vampire could use fear—Kane knew that's what he was doing.

But Kane had stood in the face of fear that rolled from Kendall, like great waves crashing onto a rocky beach. And this was nothing compared to that.

"You're just a human . . ." As he whispered, the man stepped from the shadows, staring at Kane with eyes that glowed in the pale oval of his face. "Humans can't possibly hope to stand against one such as me."

Arching a brow, Kane drawled, "Dunno why the hell not. I've taken down one or two like you before. And you're using your hocus-pocus right now, and I'm still standing."

The vampire's lips peeled back from his teeth in a ghastly smile. "I don't sense a lie around you—hard to fathom, that you killed my kind. But they must have been weak . . . stupid. I'm neither."

Leveling his Beretta at the vampire, Kane grinned. "Well, I don't know. You're standing twenty feet away, and I've got a gun on you."

The vampire laughed. "A gun . . . a gun," he murmured, shaking his head, his eyes gleaming with amusement. "You think I fear a gun?"

Kane shrugged. "Well, you're not that old. Not as old as Kendall. And even a gun would hurt her, slow her, just a little. You, I imagine, it would hurt more. And if I load your head with every last bullet in this gun, it's going to do you more damage than you think."

A flicker of doubt crossed the vampire's face but then it was gone, like it had never been there. Kane knew what he'd seen though. As the vampire laughed once more, Kane just smiled at him. "You should really put that gun down," the vampire murmured.

And in those words, Kane felt that alien power pushing at his mind, but it was so much weaker than the power that Kendall had. Kane just smiled and said, "Nice try. But the mind control doesn't work very well on me for some reason."

Gravel crunched, and the vampire's eyes jerked to the left as Kendall came sauntering into the pale circle of light. A humorless smile curved her lips as she drawled, "That is because you've got a head like a rock."

She slid her eyes to the vampire and said, "Your tricks aren't working on him. Weren't you going to kill him in order to make me angry?"

The vampire curled his lip, sneering at Kendall. "He's your toy—you must have already put your mark on him. Otherwise, I'd *own* him."

Kane arched a brow at that but said nothing, keeping his gaze focused on the vampire. Kendall laughed. "You overestimate yourself." From the corner of his eye, he could see a slow smile curving up her lips. She gestured toward Kane with a pale hand. "Go ahead. Try for him. He's just a mortal, after all."

Kane scowled, flicking his eyes toward Kendall. What in the hell was she up to? But the second his eyes moved from the vampire, the vampire moved. Kane ducked to the side, avoiding the headlong rush by the merest inch. He could feel the air from the vampire's passing as he moved aside.

Leveling his gun at the vampire, he braced himself for another rush, but it never came. Kane wavered as he felt it, that dark, insidious power that Kendall welded.

Like a thunderhead, it broke open, and fear rained down on them. As the vampire fell whimpering to the ground, Kane pressed his hands to his face, grinding the butt of his Beretta against his temple, trying to focus on the pain. Kendall's hand brushed down his arm and the storm abated, just a little, enough that he could breathe, could think.

Lifting his head, he stared at Kendall and she smiled slowly. "Strong, stubborn man," she murmured before moving past him.

Kane sucked in air, feeling it squeeze past the tight muscles in his throat. Even though the fear had lessened a little, it was heavy, so damned heavy in the air. He staggered a little, collapsing against the brick wall at his back.

Through slitted eyes, he watched as Kendall moved to the vampire, her slender form so at odds with the dark, heavy fear that hung around her.

K ENDALL sighed as she knelt down by the vampire, balancing her weight on her heels as she studied his writhing form. "You should have just kept on running . . . I doubt I would have wasted too much time on you," she murmured. Her eyes moved briefly to Kane and the unspoken words drifted through her mind. *At least not yet . . .* Leaving a mortal companion alone in an area where she knew at least one vampire preyed wasn't something she would have done.

Of course, she'd never traveled with a mortal companion before. Never been an issue before.

A soft whimper on the ground drew her attention back to the vampire cowering on the ground. "Joseph . . . *look at me . . .*"

His eyes wheeled around, his pupils constricted to tiny black dots. He stank—of blood, of pain. She couldn't smell death, but this was a creature that thrived more on torture. She could feel it on him. Some creatures liked pain even more than death—death was the ultimate end to suffering. A man like this, he wanted his victims alive so he could play.

Touching her fingers to his forehead, she smiled as he flinched, trying to jerk away from her touch. "Hold still," she ordered, and he went as limp as a rag doll, drool leaking from the corner of his mouth, his eyes gleaming with tears. Focusing, she shoved inside his mind. Her belly wrenched with regret, but she didn't stop. Rifling through his mind, she went through his memories, seeking his sire. There was a taint on him that felt disgustingly familiar.

Too familiar.

As a face formed in his memories, her gut clenched. "Damn it," she whispered.

Kendall rose to her feet, staring down at him. Joseph

darted a glance at her, and as his eyes met hers, he sobbed a little. "Scared, aren't you? Don't much care for how it feels, I imagine," Kendall murmured, dusting her hands off, wishing she could wipe the tainted feel of his thoughts from her flesh.

Joseph just whimpered, like a scared child.

She laughed, a sad, bitter sound, as her fingers fell away from his brow. "That's too bad—you'll never know anything but fear."

As he wailed out, she snapped his mind, burying a seed of fear deep inside. "Go to your mistress . . . find her. Tell her who did this to you. Tell her this time I'll actually finish the job myself."

Joseph scrabbled back away from her, scuttling on his feet and hands like a crab. Tears, mucous, and sweat gleamed on his face, his nose running, tears streaming from his eyes. He jumped up, still sobbing in his throat, and then he took off running.

Kendall watched him for a moment, until the darkness swallowed him up, and then she sighed, her eyes closing. Shoulders slumped, she stood with her head lowered.

Weariness beat at her. She was tired—an exhaustion that went to the very bone. What she'd just done didn't make it any easier.

Her ears caught the sound of the door in front opening, and footsteps. Rising, she looked at Kane for a long moment and then she turned around, walking through the darkness as she circled back to the front of the bar.

The sound of his boots crunching lightly on the gravel echoed in her ears. Kendall could feel his eyes on her, but she never turned to look at him as she walked down the highway, focusing on the hotel in front of her.

They walked to the hotel in silence, and Kendall reached out, closing her hand around the doorknob, turning it. It didn't open. Fuck. The key.

Her head slumped forward, hitting the door. Behind her, she felt the warmth of Kane's breath on her neck, the heat of his body reaching out to warm hers as he moved up behind, reaching up one hand to close over hers. They stood like that for a moment and Kendall shuddered as hunger start to pulse through her.

Not to feed though.

She wanted to feel his hands on her.

Wanted to forget how weary she was, how angry she was. How lonely . . . Slowly, she tugged her hand out from under his, turning in the shielding circle of his arms, staring at the dark cloth that stretched across his chest. She shifted her gaze from his chest, to the long, tanned line of his throat, up to stare into his shadowed eyes.

His hand shifted and she heard a click as he pushed the keycard into the slot at the door handle, but she barely heard it above the pounding of her heart.

As the door pushed open, Kane's arms came around her and Kendall pressed eagerly against him.

His tongue pushed greedily inside her mouth, and Kendall sucked on it delicately, shivering as his taste flooded her system. Her feet left the ground as he lifted her and automatically, she closed her legs around his waist. The heavy door slammed shut as Kane moved away from it, turning to brace her back against the wall. The cool plaster pressed against her back, chilling her flesh even as his body warmed it.

Her nipples ached, the soft silky fabric of her bra abrading them.

Digging her fingers into the ridge of muscle at his shoulder, she hummed in her throat as he pulled his mouth away from hers, pressing a line of stinging, biting kisses against her neck before he boosted her up and closed his mouth around one nipple, the wet heat scalding her through the layers of clothes.

Kendall gasped out his name and buried her hands in his hair, the thick silk of it winding around her fingers. He shifted his attention to her other breast, nuzzling her gently before catching the tip of her nipple in his mouth and biting down gently. The feel of his teeth on her flesh drove her wild and she arched against him, screaming.

"Too many clothes," he muttered. The words barely made

sense in her fogged brain but the feel of hot male hands on her torso as he shoved her shirt up, *that* made sense. As he lowered her back down to the ground, she reached for her shirt, desperate to have it out of the way, but his hands closed over her wrists, guiding them gently back down. A soft mewl of frustration escaped her but she clenched her hands into fists and left them at her sides, lifting heavy lashes to watch him as he reached up, trailing one finger over the four small buttons that held her shirt closed.

Her breath tripped in her throat as he flicked them open, one after the other, until he could spread her shirt open. Goose bumps broke out over her flesh as he stared down at her—desperate, Kendall reached out for him. But once more, his hands closed over her wrists, guiding her hands back down. She groaned in frustration, closing her eyes and slamming her head back against the wall.

A low, husky chuckle escaped him, and she opened her eyes, staring at him from under the fringe of her lashes. That hard, sexy mouth curved upward in a smile as she stared at him, and he reached out, circling one finger over one silk and lace covered breast. "You're so impatient," he mused, tracing the rough pads of his fingers over the scalloped edge of her bra, moving toward the center of her body until he reached the clasp between her breasts.

He gave it a gentle tug and it gave, her breasts falling free as he smoothed the silky fabric aside. His hand gleamed golden against the paleness of her skin as he laid it against her breastbone, trailing the flat of his palm down her center then back up again. Her lids drooped closed once more as he cupped his hand over her breast, flicking his thumb back and forth over her nipple.

The already aching flesh seemed to grow tighter, burning under that soft, tormenting stroke. He pushed the shirt and bra off her shoulders, leaving her bare from the waist up. The heat of his body reached out to tease her as he pulled her up against him. Her breasts flattened against the wall of his chest as he bent down, slanting his mouth over hers.

She could feel the heat, the hardness of his cock. Greedily, she rubbed against him, the empty ache in her belly spreading until damn near every inch of her body ached and throbbed. "Kane, please . . . damn it, I need you inside me."

He chuckled, a soft puff of breath escaping him to caress her skin as he nuzzled her neck. "Inside you . . . here?" he asked as he slid his hand lightly grinding his palm against her sex.

"Yes. . . ." The word left her in a hiss as she arched against him, rubbing greedily.

The button at her waist fell open under his hands, and Kendall held her breath as he slid his fingers inside her waistband, trailing them along her skin, before closing his fingers over the tab of her zipper and drawing it down. "Inside you . . . inside you here?" he whispered as he slid his hand inside her jeans, pushing one thick, calloused finger inside her. She sobbed as his flesh rasped against her sensitive folds. "Inside this hot, snug little pussy?"

Her breath exploded from her in a rush and she sagged, all the strength draining out of her body. One big, hard arm came around her, bracing her weight as he pumped his finger in and out.

Kendall came in one hot, sudden burst, sobbing out his name. His lips crushed against hers, swallowing the gasping cries as she climaxed.

Her head was still spinning when he lifted her, carrying her to the bed. Quick, impatient hands stripped away her boots and jeans, and before she could even catch her breath, he came down on her, wedging his wide shoulders between her thighs and lowering his head.

Kane blew a hot puff of air on her dew-slicked flesh, and she moaned as he stabbed at her clit with his tongue. "Fuck . . . the taste of you, I can't get enough of it," he muttered, and the rough vibration of his groan against her had her shivering.

She rocked her hips up against him, his hands closing over the taut globes of her ass, lifting her against him. He teased her, working her with his tongue, with his fingers, until she was sweating, swearing, and begging him to let her come. Kane shifted, moving lower until he could push his tongue inside the clenching entrance of her vagina.

But he stayed just this side of that final touch that would grant her completion.

K ANE pushed up onto his elbows, staring up the long, pale line of her torso. A faint flush darkened her ivory cheeks, stained the elegant curve of her throat, even spreading down to her chest. And her eyes . . . her eyes were fogged with hunger.

Holding her gaze with his, he lowered his mouth back to the slick, dewy folds of her sex, rimming her entrance with his tongue. She trembled under the slow touch, fisting her hands in the sheets as she sobbed out his name. Dipping his tongue inside her pussy, he felt the small muscles inside her clenching around him. He shifted and moved up, until he could take the engorged bud of her clit in his mouth.

Catching it gently between his teeth, he sucked on it. Kendall's back arched, and he caught her hips in his hands, holding her as tightly as he could as she bucked and writhed under his touch. Stiffening his tongue, he stabbed at the sensitive bud of flesh and she exploded, screaming out his name and pumping her hips against his mouth as she came.

He moved then, covering her body with his, wedging his hips between the trembling muscles of her thighs and pushing inside her. Her climaxing body resisted the heavy invasion of his, the little spasms of her internal muscles milking his cock as he worked it inside.

Clenching his teeth, he pulled out just a little as he pushed up onto his hands, keeping his weight balanced between his hips and hands. With a groan, he sank completely inside her just as she started to still beneath him. "Damnation, you're tight," he grunted, rolling his hips against hers.

"Kane . . ." her mouth was red and swollen as she whispered out his name.

A small, feline smile curved her lips, and he chuckled a little. "You look pretty content there, pet."

Her lashes lifted and he found himself lost in the bottom-
less depths of her warm golden gaze. "Oh, I am," she purred,
arching up and rubbing her breasts against his chest. The
movement caused her silken tissues to caress his cock and
he growled, dropping his weight down on her. Her eyes flew
wide as he started to shaft her slowly.

The snug clasp of her pussy had eased just a little, but as
he fucked her, her body started to respond to his and those
muscles once more started clutching at his cock, squeezing
around him as he pushed inside, gripping around him as he
withdrew.

The smile died as her mouth formed a small *o* as she
moaned out his name. "I could take you five times a day," he
panted, lowering his head, nipping at the full lower curve of
her lip. "Every day—for the next hundred years, and it still
wouldn't be enough."

Slanting his mouth across hers, he kissed her, swallowing
her moan, pushing his tongue greedily inside her mouth. *A
thousand years,* he thought blindly. He needed her—too
much. Already, his balls were drawing tight against his body
with the urge to come.

Gritting his teeth, he rolled onto his back, taking her with
him and pushing her upright until she straddled him.
Kendall braced her hands against his chest and her head fell
back. Her breasts lifted, the small, tight little beads of her
nipples flushed a deep pink.

She rode him with slow, subtle moves of her hips, her
eyes closed, the deep red locks of her hair spilling down
around her shoulders, the ends flirting with the curves of her
breasts.

Kane slid one hand up her thigh, tracing one fingertip
around her sex, the tissues stretched tight around him. She
tensed under his stroking touch, and then she started to
pump her hips hard, working her weight up and down on his
impaling cock. Kane shifted his aim then, using his thumb
to circle around the hard nub of her clit.

As he did that, she wailed out his name and her entire
body went tense. She fell forward, bracing her hands beside

his head, her legs moving down to stretch out beside his. "That's it, Kendall," he groaned. "Ride me—hard."

She did, her hips slamming against his, her pussy slick and hot around his cock, squeezing around him with every stroke of her hips. Hot little tingles raced down his spine as she started to come again. His arms came up, banding around her torso and holding her flush against him as he started to thrust his hips up to meet hers.

They came together, his seed jetting from him to flood her depths as she spasmed around him, milking his cock with hot little convulsions, drawing his climax out until he could hardly breathe. As he emptied himself, she collapsed against him, her body shuddering atop his.

"A hundred years," Kane mumbled once more, and then he closed his eyes, giving into the lure of sleep.

THE pain in his head was obscene. He couldn't think past it. He was afraid. So afraid. He didn't know why.

But *she* would know.

He hadn't seen her in forever.

Not since she had left him. But he could find her.

That was just how it worked.

Whimpering, crying, Joseph shoved himself to his feet, stumbling along for a few minutes before he started to run.

He ran and ran for what seemed like hours. He stopped for a little while when he saw a giggling group of women leave a club. Hunger ripped through him. He wanted to feed. Had to feed. But when he staggered up to them, one of them pulled a bottle of mace from her bag and screeched at him, her eyes flashing.

Joseph sobbed and stumbled away. His ears hurt from her scream, and his hunger seemed to pale. No, he didn't need to feed that bad. He couldn't deal with that many people. Not without *her*. He needed to get to her. She'd take care of him. She'd make him strong again. Make him whole.

*   *   *

CATHARINE was still riding high on her fury at two a.m. Dressed in black leather pants and black brocade corset, she prowled through the bar, searching for a man to whet her appetite.

In a variety of ways. She wanted to fuck him, and then she'd drain him dry.

Leave him in the building for Kendall to find when she came back.

Because Cat had absolutely no doubt that Kendall would be back to look for her.

This was Kendall, after all. Holier-than-thou, ever-so-righteous Kendall. Hunter of the Council. That paltry Council. They thought they were so powerful. Out to protect the innocent, they claimed.

There were no innocents in this world.

Just sheep. Just fodder. Creatures like Cat were made for feasting on the fodder, but the fools on the Council were too damned weak and blind to see that.

Cat moved up to the packed bar and with one look, singled out a woman. The woman glanced up from her drink, and when Cat met her eyes, the woman simply got up and walked away. Even though people were standing three deep, not one person moved toward the vacated chair. Cat took the chair and smiled at the bartender and moments later, she had a glass of chardonnay. It wasn't quite as good as her preferred vintage, but until she found a decent man to feed on, it would do.

Within fifteen minutes, Cat decided her luck was finally changing. He was not quite six feet, but he had a nice ass on him, a great set of shoulders, and even better—there was a subtle scent of magick around him. Untapped, though. There were a lot of potential witches out there with magick trapped inside them that never even knew what they had. Many never would unless something brought it out.

Something sudden and violent. Cat smiled at him across the room. He'd been dancing with a brunette, but as he kept glancing at Cat, the brunette was getting more and more irate. He finally turned away from her altogether, and Cat

just smiled at the brunette before turning her attention back
to the man.

Yes, things were definitely looking up.

ONE small taste. Cat had to have one small taste before
they went back to her home and fucked like minks. She
didn't have long though. Dawn was only a couple of hours
away, and she wanted to feed and kill him, and she still had
to get to one of her other hideouts before the sun rose.

Damn Kendall's hide, anyway. Kendall didn't have to fear
the sun's rising the way Cat did. She could tolerate the sun's
rays for a short time. Cat still had decades yet before she
could, maybe even longer. And by the time Cat could tolerate even five minutes of dawn, Kendall would be even more
immune to the light of day.

Shoving those thoughts from her mind, she smiled at
Damon and tugged on his hand, pulling him into the narrow
alley between the club and the closed bookstore on the other
side. His eyes stared at her, fogged with lust, senseless with
desire. There was very little left of the intelligent man she'd
seen in the club less than thirty minutes earlier.

The second they were out of sight, she whirled, pinning
him against the wall. His hands clutched at her hips and she
let him press his lips against hers. Desire heated her belly—
for a moment, it startled her, the intensity of it. Damn, but he
could kiss. His tongue pushed inside her mouth, and if he
felt her fangs cut his tongue, it didn't bother him. The wine-
rich taste of his blood flooded her mouth and Cat growled,
jerking away from him.

Damon groaned, reaching for her again, but she just bat-
ted his hands away, rising on her toes as she fisted one hand
in his hair. Jerking his head to the side, she struck. He tensed
against her, but he didn't struggle. He wouldn't, not yet. Not
until his body started to realize it was dying, and then that
magick would break free and she could gorge on it—

The attack came from the side.

For a moment, she didn't even comprehend that the sobbing, whimpering creature pinning her legs to the ground was a vampire. The touch on her mind felt more like that of a frightened child. But the strength was vampire. Hissing, she flashed her fangs at the blond man and rasped, "What do you think you are doing?"

"Please, Catharine," the man sobbed. He looked up at her, his face wet with tears and mucous. "Help me—she's going to kill me."

Narrowing her eyes, Cat stared at him. Behind her, Damon staggered back against the wall, staring at the scene before him with disbelieving eyes. The fog from his mind cleared more with each passing second and finally, he started to stumble away.

Catharine heard him, but she was too busy dealing with the man clinging to her to stop him. "Get the fuck off of me," she snarled. When he didn't move, she struck out, clipping him in the temple with her fist. He whimpered and fell back, clutching his head with one hand, staring up at her tearfully.

"Who in the hell are you?" she demanded, rising to her feet. She dusted her clothes off as she waited for an answer.

He stared up at her woefully. "Joseph. You made me, Catharine. She . . ." His voice dropped to a terrified whisper. "*She* told me to find you. Tell you . . ." His voice trailed off again, and he hiccoughed. "She's going to finish the job herself this time."

Cat narrowed her eyes as she closed the distance between herself and the vampire. She remembered him now. Barely. He was a nobody, a nothing. He enjoyed causing pain, and that was good enough for her, but he'd never be a Master, wouldn't ever be strong enough to add to *her* strength, so he wasn't good enough.

And now Kendall had the nerve to use him as a messenger?

"Kendall sent you to me?" she repeated slowly, watching as he pushed himself up to his knees, reaching out one hand to her. She wrinkled her nose, sidestepping when he got too close.

"Don't know her name—Hunter. A Hunter. She told me. Find you. She said find you. She'll finish the job herself," he repeated.

Cat finally stilled and let him close his hands around one of hers. He pressed his cheek against her skin, and he felt almost feverishly hot, so very unlike a vampire. Her voice icy, Cat murmured, "She will, hmmm?"

Rage exploded through her and she tore away from him. He cried out, reaching for her again, but she spun around, kicking him in the chest. He fell back with a cry. Dropping to one knee, Cat struck out and closed her hand over his throat, tearing it open, severing it clear through to his spinal cord. Flinging the bloody mess to the ground, she watched the light in his eyes die.

As blood gushed from him, she turned on her heel and stalked away. *Damn it.*

"Kendall, you sure as hell know how to ruin a person's night."

CHAPTER 10

S HE slept.

Kendall hadn't slept at night for ages.

But, wrapped in Kane's arms, lulled by the soothing beat of his heart against her back, she slept and dreamed.

Senseless little bits of dreams that made no sense. Making love to Kane, then suddenly, she was back home, back in Ireland, and fleeing through the rain.

Monsters ran at her heels, howling and snarling. And when she turned to look at them . . . they were people. Dead people, the ghosts of all the people that Catharine had killed.

She awoke with a sob, jerking upright in bed, drawing her knees to her chest and pressing her face against them. A muffled sob tore from her throat, and she bit down on her lip to try to silence the rest of the cry.

Kane's hands came up, one working around her waist, hauling her back against him, the other threading through her hair until he could cup her neck. Once he had her body encircled by his, he started to rock her—and something about that gentle, comforting gesture shattered her. And she started to cry.

The tears burned out of her eyes, rolling down her cheeks, stinging like acid. The sobs tore from her throat with an intensity that bordered on painful. And throughout the storm, Kane held her, nuzzling her temple with his lips, murmuring to her, soft little nonsensical sounds that made no sense.

When she finally calmed, he pulled them back down on the bed and drew the blanket up over them. His hand came up, and she sighed as he brushed the tear tracks away. "What were you dreaming about, Kendall?"

She shook her head. "Nothing that made sense. Monsters. Guilt." Her voice sounded tight and hoarse, and speaking made her throat hurt. Bloody hell, she'd forgotten how bad a crying jag could tear one up, forgotten how weary it made one feel inside.

Kane was silent for a long moment, and then he rolled her over, pushing up onto his elbow so that he could stare down into her face. "Tell me about her."

Her eyes jumped away from his and she swallowed. "Her?" she repeated huskily. She knew who he was talking about—but damn it, she didn't want to talk about Catharine. Talk about how she'd failed—as a Hunter. As a person.

"Catharine. Tell me about her."

Closing her eyes, she tried to block out his voice, tried to lull herself back to sleep. It didn't happen though. And finally, she sighed. "I raised her. I took care of her . . . and I failed. If I had done a good job, been a decent parent, she wouldn't have become a monster."

Kane sighed, a soft, weary sound. Opening her eyes, she met his dark gaze, the harsh, hard lines of his face softening as he looked down at her. "Kendall, sweetheart, sometimes people are just born monsters. Nothing that happens to them makes them that way—they just are."

Pressing her lips together, she shook her head. "No. She was a good girl—would have been a wonderful lady. I failed her. I didn't make her strong enough, and when I didn't get there in time to save her, I Changed her. And she became a monster." Bitter tears slid out of her eyes, rolling down her cheeks to soak her hair. "And even then, I couldn't see it.

Couldn't see what she'd become—what I'd made her
into . . ."

ENGLAND 1884

Mary watched as Catharine slept.

*The first sleep after a Change was always the worst. Some
vampires never woke from it, just drifted on in sleep before
sliding into the silence of complete and true death. That
wouldn't happen with Catharine.*

She couldn't fail her so completely.

"She will wake."

*Mary lifted her head, staring wearily at the Hunter who
stood at the door. His name was Tobias. A powerful shape-
shifter, he'd served on the Council for decades. Agnes once
mentioned he was more than a hundred years old, and he
didn't look a day over twenty.*

*Tobias was an odd one, even among most Hunters. He
was a born shifter, although Mary had no idea what form he
took. There were whispers that his mother had been a powerful witch, other whispers that his father had been a werewolf. Many rumors, but Mary had never asked.*

*"It's been more than a day since we exchanged blood, sir.
She still sleeps."*

*Tobias shrugged. "Some sleep a little longer. I can sense
her soul—she hasn't let go of life. Those are the ones who
cross over—who don't rise as vampires. The ones who let
go. She'll wake." A look crossed his face and then his eyes
closed.*

"Tobias?" Mary asked, her voice shaky.

*He merely stared at her, his eyes shuttered, and his mind
blocked to her. She couldn't skim the thoughts within his
mind, couldn't read a damned thing from him. What had that
look meant? That look of . . . disgust, almost as if he wished
Catharine wouldn't wake.*

*"Possibly nothing," he finally murmured. "I don't know
yet. 'Tis too early. Rest, Mary. While you can."*

Catharine awoke the following moonrise.

Awoke starving, insatiable . . . for more than food.

The third werewolf staggered from the room, his eyes fogged with lust, two messy, bloody holes in his neck already knitting closed.

"More!" Catharine demanded. "And why didn't he touch me? My skin . . . it itches . . . I need—" She cut herself off before she could finish the sentence. But Mary knew what she needed.

Sex. That and feeding often went hand and hand, but Mary would be damned if she'd supply a lover for the newly Changed vampire lying in the bed. Catharine was like a daughter to her.

"It will pass," Mary murmured. "And Padrick couldn't give you what you need . . . he has a wife, a family. He wouldn't betray them."

"Then find me somebody who can!" Catharine wailed. Then her eyes narrowed, focusing on Mary's face. "Perhaps . . . perhaps you can help me."

Revulsion rolled in Mary's belly. She knew what Catharine was asking for. Yes, some women found pleasure in the touch of other women. Mary had never been one of them. More, Catharine . . . this was Catharine. Her baby. Her everything. Shaking her head, she said, "I can't help with that part, Cat. Only time can."

"Fuck time!" Catharine screeched, rising from the bed, her pretty face splotched ugly red in her anger. The erratic beat of her heart kicked up and she stalked toward Mary. "This is your fault—if you had gotten there sooner—and then, you made me into . . . into this! Sorry Hunter, you are. You were supposed to protect me . . ."

*T*hose words echoed in Mary's mind for weeks. Even as the first brutal hungers of the Change faded and Catharine became more like what she had once been, those words echoed in Mary's mind and guilt gnawed at her.

It was worse now. Catharine stood staring at the two Hunters that barred the way to Brendain, school to many

*younger Hunters, home to the Council. Catharine had come
to them, to appeal to them to let her enter these hallowed
halls. And they wouldn't even give her entrance.*

*"You are not a Hunter—not in your heart, not in your
soul," Tobias murmured, shaking his dark head. "I am sorry.
But you do not belong here."*

"Mary brought *me here."*

*Mary's face flushed with shame. Yes, she had brought
Catharine here, and Cat wasn't worthy. Averting her eyes,
she refused to meet the shifter's gaze, staring instead at the
deep gray stone of the walls that surrounded Brendain.*

*"T'was her responsibility—you seek to be a Hunter. It is
her duty to bring any possible candidate that requests it. She
cannot see who may become a Hunter—not yet. She is too
young. But we know. And you will not be a Hunter."*

*The witch standing at Tobias's side simply stared at
Catharine, but when the petite woman marched up to her,
Cat met her gaze with an arched brow. "Do* you *agree with
this . . . this* dog?*" Catharine snarled.*

"Cat!" Mary whispered, her mouth falling open in shock.

*"He is! A mongrel dog—and he thinks he can tell me that
I cannot enter here?"*

*The witch caught Mary's gaze and shook her head
slightly. "We but bring the messages, Catharine. And the
message we received was not to allow you entrance. Something dark hovers around you."*

*"Dark? I'm a bloody vampire—I drink of blood, born to
feed and live from the deaths of others."*

*Mary, shaken to the core, caught Catharine's arm. "We
are not like that. We are not animals, not monsters, not unless we choose."*

*Catharine jerked her arm away, and then her face
changed and she stared at Mary with beseeching eyes. "I
have to have this, Mary. If I do not have this, what do I
have? I'm nothing. Nobody. Forever."*

*   *   *

*T*en years had passed. Enough time had passed that Mary had almost forgotten what had transpired those first few days after Cat had been changed. And the memories of Cat's despondency after the Council had refused her had dimmed.

Cat was more like she had once been, a happy, sweet lady that Mary adored. They had settled into a routine of sorts. They lived outside of Marset, a small village just north of Brendain. This was Mary's territory—she'd been here for twenty years, ever since returning from America with Catharine, and she should be relatively content.

She wasn't, though.

She was worried.

Mary knew she needed to go home, check on Catharine, but inside her belly, there was a nasty fear.

Another murder.

Vampire, again. That was obvious by the victim, the way the man had been drained, and slowly, over a period of days. She hadn't particularly wanted to take his heart—but the few this feral vampire had Changed had risen as dark, tainted creatures. She couldn't risk another one loose.

So damned close to Brendain. What kind of madman hunted and killed this close to the home of the Hunters? It wasn't just Mary, the local Master, they faced, but all the Hunters that called Brendain home.

None of them could track the vampire. It was as though scent and trail had been wiped clean. The vampires had tried, the shape-shifters had tried . . . no luck.

Mary had heard that the witches wanted to know of the next murder—not to burn the body, because they wanted to try something.

And that was why she had come to Brendain, instead of heading to her small home after she had taken the poor man's heart. Marset and the area around it had become her own land—a small territory for certain, but none had any doubts it was hers. It had called to her, from the minute she crossed into it, crossing some indefinable boundary that separated an unMastered land from this one. This piece of land had been waiting for a Master—or a Mistress. Waiting for her.

But somebody was killing in her land. It was her responsibility to find that bastard, and stop him. Or . . . since that had failed . . . to enlist the help of those who could.

Moving through the silent halls of the manor house, she made her way to Agnes's chambers. The witch, even though she looked like quite the matronly sort, was one of the most powerful creatures on the earth. "Please, Lord," Mary murmured. "Let Nessa have a way to stop this monster. Let us find out who he is, where he lives, so that we may end this butchery."

It was nearing sunrise when Mary guided Agnes and another witch, his name Ezekiel, to where she had found the body. The ragged hole in the chest was no longer smoking, but the flesh was blackened, like it had been burned. It hadn't—not exactly. But silver on a vampire's flesh was almost like flame, and the flesh her blade had touched was charred.

She'd burned his heart, watching until it was nothing more than dust, before she'd left to find Agnes. Now, as the full moon shone down on his pale face, she felt ill inside. He was so young.

"You did what you must, Mary," Agnes Milcher murmured quietly. But there was just as much grief in her eyes as Mary felt inside. It didn't matter that they had walked this earth for decades, centuries—death never got easier.

"Did I, Nessa? How did I know he wouldn't rise a decent, honorable vampire? He could have been anything in life—we don't know that he would have been fouled with his death."

Agnes said quietly, "I know. I feel it—her taint. It's vile."

Mary stilled, lifting her head from her study of the dead man's face to study Agnes. "Her?" she asked, her voice trembling just a little.

"Aye. 'Tis a woman's touch I feel. And psychic power in the air—playing with our minds, she is. But I'm not so easily fooled."

Agnes knelt to the ground, and when Mary tried to question her further, the older woman had no response, just gazing into the ground as though the answers to the universe lay within the dirt.

"Psychic power can cloud the senses, Mary. That's why neither the vampires or the shifters can scent track our killer," Ezekiel said when Mary spun away from Agnes, blowing out a frustrated puff of air.

"So she is erasing her scent?" Mary asked doubtfully.

"No. It's still here—once Agnes is done removing the vampire's touch, we may be able to catch it. He was killed early in the evening—the scent should still be fresh enough to track."

And it was—but it wasn't possible. Mary could barely see for the darkness that swarmed up to overtake her vision. Shaking her head, she stared blindly at the spot where the man had been drained and Changed. "No," she finally murmured, her throat tight. The lone word felt like broken glass in her throat as she repeated it a second time. Blinking her eyes rapidly, she tried to clear the dark fog that obscured her vision.

Agnes shook her head, staring at Mary with concern. "What is it, child?"

Her sense of smell was acute, but it couldn't quite rival the abilities of a vampire. But the old witch knew that something was wrong. Terribly wrong.

"I smell something—blood. Soap . . . vaguely familiar," Ezekiel said, unaware of the turmoil in Mary's face.

"Zeke, hush," Agnes whispered. Taking a slow step toward Mary, she reached out a hand and murmured, "Talk to me, Mary. What troubles you so?"

The veil that had darkened her vision was abruptly jerked away, and she stared at Agnes's hand, but seconds before it touched her, she took off running, the blind denial still circling in her head.

No. It couldn't be. It couldn't. She'd go home, she'd see Cat sleeping soundly in her bed, and the taint of blood wouldn't cling to her.

There had been nights—the shocking knowledge she'd just had slammed into her face made those nights rise up and taunt her. Nights when Cat had come home, smelling of blood. Mary had shoved it aside. They were vampires—they fed on blood, was it any surprise that she caught the scent of blood on her friend from time to time?

But she had been blind.

She knew no other vampire that smelled of blood hours after feeding. No Hunter at least. The powerful stench of blood that she smelled on many a vampire was too often associated with violent deaths—like it stained the very air around them, ripe with fear and pain.

The ground flew beneath her feet. She'd left her horse behind with Agnes and Ezekiel. She hadn't even thought of mounting up on the animal—likely the docile mare would have thrown her anyway, in Mary's current state. Fear and rage had her fangs dropping, and she could feel the cold as it rolled from her in waves.

It seemed as though it took forever to reach her house, but she realized likely only minutes had passed. Bursting through the door, she headed for the cellar doors. The underground room where Mary and Cat slept was simple, but it was free from sunlight, and protected by more than just the solid wooden door in the floor. Spells set long ago by one of the witches from the Council protected them—kept all but those Mary had welcomed into her home from entering while Mary and Cat slept.

Cat blinked sluggishly as Mary came to a halt at her side, her breathing harsh and unsteady. Staring at the younger vampire with wild eyes, she fought against the crazed scream that was building in her throat.

Clenching her jaw, she kept the scream reined in as she drew in yet another draught of blood-ripe air. She knew the scent of that blood. She'd had it on her hands earlier when she removed the unrisen vampire's heart. "You fucking bitch," she rasped, her voice a cold, harsh whisper in the silence of the room.

Sleep still pulled at Catharine. Barely a vampire for a

decade, she couldn't resist her body's urge to sleep as the sun crept into the sky. "Mary . . . Mary, what's wrong?" she mumbled thickly.

Mary howled, her restraint shattering. Reaching down, she closed her hand around Cat's throat and lifted her body into the air, whirling around to slam the smaller woman into the wall. "What's wrong?" Mary demanded, her lips peeling back from her teeth, revealing fangs that all but ached with the urge to rip and tear. "What's wrong?"

She released Cat, letting her fall in a heap to the floor, curling her hand into a fist at her side as she whirled around. Carefully, she moved back one step, then another, staring at Cat, feeling her heart break as she finally saw the monster before her.

There was awareness in her eyes now, but Cat had always been a sly thing, and Mary could all but hear the wheels spinning in her head. Her control in shreds around her, Mary whispered, "Don't," as Cat started to rise, her face falling into pitiful, frightened lines.

Like somebody had jerked away a pair of blinders, Mary could see clearly, and what she saw beneath her sickened her, frightened her. "I had to kill an unrisen tonight," she said flatly. "We've had to kill far too many of our own kind over the past year. Too many that rose as mindless monsters. Too many ferals. There has never been this many so close to the heart of our land."

Catharine opened her mouth, but Mary slashed her hand through the air. "Silence!" she hissed. She felt something cold and deadly roll through the air, but barely realized it was coming from her. Cat cowered on the floor, covering her head with her arms as a whimper escaped her throat.

The sound of footsteps behind her had Mary spinning around. Agnes and Ezekiel stood in the doorway, staring at Mary, then at Cat. Agnes closed her eyes but not before Mary saw the knowledge there. Ezekiel stared at Cat, his pale gray eyes going cold with fury.

Mary turned back around, dismissing the two at her back. "Don't," she whispered as Cat tried to rise. The younger vampire froze—staring at Mary with wide, terrified eyes. "I smell his blood on you, Cat."

Cat's eyes narrowed. "You couldn't." There was a spark of knowledge in her eyes, something that made Mary's skin crawl.

"Why not? Because I never have before?" Mary demanded coldly. "Whatever it is you've done to cloud your trail doesn't work on witches, darling."

Cat's eyes flew to Agnes, and an ugly hate-filled scowl darkened her face. Mary barely saw her muscles tense before the vampire lunged for the old witch, but her body was already acting. Catching Cat around the arms, Mary flung the vampire across the room.

Waves of cold seemed to roll from her as she stared at Cat. "Do not move."

There was a surprised murmur behind her, but she ignored it as she stalked toward Cat. "You will not move again, Cat."

Her eyes glazed, Cat stared at Mary and repeated numbly, "I will not move." But then she blinked, and with it, the dazed look in her eyes cleared just a little. Mary watched as she jerked her eyes away and sucked in a breath of air, as though to steady herself. Cat squeezed her eyes closed, and when she spoke, her voice was low and ugly, "Get away from me, Mary."

Mary laughed. "I do not think so, sweeting. You committed horrible crimes—not creating more like us . . . but creating monsters and not staying by their side to make sure they came through intact. You don't make a vampire and just walk away, precious."

Cat sneered. "Intact? Like I was intact?" But still, the vampire wouldn't meet Mary's gaze.

"You're broken inside," Mary murmured softly, shaking her head. "I never saw it, not until now. Maybe I couldn't see it—or maybe I didn't want to. We don't allow our kind to turn into monsters, Cat."

Cat slid Mary one quick, sly glance before jerking her eyes back away. Slowly, she pushed to her feet, bracing her back against the wall. "And what will you do, kill me?" Cat taunted.

A sad, bitter smile twisted Mary's face. "It appears I must—after all, you're my responsibility. I made you—and you became a monster."

Cat laughed, a low, vicious sound in the dank, dark room. "A monster? Fool. I'm a wolf among sheep. I can go where I will and do as I wish—none of you have been able to even sense me these past months. But you think to stop me?"

She shoved away from the wall, but before Mary could grab her, an intense, blinding pain burst inside her head and she fell to her knees, clapping her hands over her ears in an attempt to block the pain.

Within seconds, it was gone.

But so was Catharine.

"How did this happen?" Ezekiel murmured as they sat down at the table on the main floor of the small house.

Agnes glanced over from the window she was be-spelling, her faded blue eyes cool and hard, her mouth a firm, flat line in a normally smiling face. "She is a latent psychic. That is the reason we wanted to be with you when the next attack happened. Psychics can use their powers to cloud your senses, but it doesn't work so well on witches. Something, either the trauma of her attack, or the trauma of being Changed, triggered that power. But the power and the Change, I believe, was too much for her, and some part of her, the part that makes a person decent, splintered."

"But how could she have hidden what she was?" Mary asked, half numb inside.

"That same power. A powerful psychic can often make you see what you wish to see—the trick to getting around it is knowledge, knowing that what you see on the surface is not what lies beneath it. She won't be able to fool you again, Mary. But she will be hard to track, hard to catch."

Ezekiel's mouth curved into a cool, humorless smile. "We shall just follow the path of bodies."

Agnes shook her head. "The girl is smart—she will not kill around here. She'll feed . . . but she won't kill. Not until she knows she's away from us. And she'll cloud her presence, the same way she hid her true self and all her killings from us for so long."

Curled up on the floor by the fire, Mary rested her chin on her knees, closing her eyes as she cursed herself.

"My fault," she finally murmured out loud.

"This is my fault."

"You couldn't know what she'd become, Mary," Agnes said gently.

At the sound of her name, she lifted her chin and stared blindly at her oldest friend. "No. Do not call me that name."

Agnes stilled. "Love, I know this is hard, but we will . . ." Agnes's voice trailed off as she met Mary's gaze.

Shaking her head, she looked at Agnes. "Mary is dead. Do not call me that name." Rising from the table, she repeated, "Nessa, this is my fault. I have to fix it."

"You could not have known what she would become," Agnes repeated firmly.

"Then I should never have brought her over. Not if I didn't know."

And neither Ezekiel nor Agnes could say much of anything to that.

*I*t took another ten years, and the help of her old partner, to track Catharine down. They'd found her in New York City. Neither Kendall nor Vax particularly cared for the large, loud city, but it teemed with life. Vagrants went missing all the time. Kendall hadn't sensed anything violent in the city, and she was positive Vax was wrong.

But he wasn't.

Standing just outside the abandoned building in a very poor part of the city, she stared at Cat, rage and grief warring inside her belly. Cat held in her arms a small, dirty *young child. The boy was so filthy, Kendall couldn't tell what color his hair was, but his pale blue eyes gleamed with terror as he struggled in Cat's grip.*

"Get away now or he dies, Kendall," Cat warned, jerking the boy's head to the side, preparing to strike. Kendall wasn't surprised that Cat was using a child to bargain with. But Cat hadn't counted on Vax.

Vax's eyes never left Cat's and he never made a sound, but Kendall heard his voice whisper in her mind. "Get ready, Kendall."

Kendall didn't ask what she was supposed to get ready for. She didn't need to. Whatever he was planning would work. In the years since Kendall had last seen Vax, his power had grown by leaps and bounds.

Of course, she really hadn't been expecting this. Kendall had blinked, and he was just suddenly gone. Then he reappeared standing next to Cat.

Bloody hell, he's a flyer, Kendall thought in dismay.

Cat shrieked out, trying to shove Vax away and clutch the child to her, but Vax simply struck out with one hand. Cat could either try to hold onto the child, or she could try to put out the fire that was suddenly eating at her clothes. As Vax leaped away, the building behind exploded in flames.

That was the last Kendall saw of Catharine.

K ENDALL fell silent, staring at the bland painting on the wall in front of her, feeling Kane's heat against her back, the strength of his arms around her. But she was still cold, too cold for anything to warm her.

"How long ago?" he asked softly, his breath stirring her hair.

"That was in 1904." Closing her eyes, she swallowed, feeling the tears as they trickled down her cheeks, cool against the chill of her flesh. There was no warmth left inside her, and for the first time in a very long time, she felt truly dead inside. "We thought she was dead. She fell back inside the house, and we just thought . . ." her voice trailed off weakly. Shaking her head, she forced herself to finish. "We thought she was dead. Vampire flesh doesn't tolerate flame very well. We burn like you wouldn't believe. Like wood soaked in oil. I don't know how she got out. But she did."

A bitter laugh escaped her as she pushed at Kane's arms. He only tightened his grip—she could get away from him, she knew, if she decided to really fight. But she didn't have the energy. Darkly, she muttered, "Some Hunter I am. I sired a damned lunatic, and when I finally tracked her down, I had to have help. When we thought she was dead, I didn't even make sure the job was done. I'm a complete failure."

His hand, the palm rough and hard against her face, cupped her cheek and she finally lifted her gaze, meeting his eyes slowly. "You're no failure. You haven't given up. A failure is somebody who gave up." His thumb stroked over the curve of her lip, and Kendall felt something wistful and sweet move through her heart as he stared down at her.

"We'll find her," he murmured as he held her gaze. "Together. And we'll stop her."

Her lashes lowered, shielding her eyes.

She'd already lost too much to Catharine. She could have lost Duke. Hell, she could still lose him. There was no guarantee he'd come through this. She'd lost her self-respect, her belief in her self. Her pride.

She didn't think she could stand to lose a lover—especially not Kane. How had he come to mean so much to her in such a short time?

Cuddling her head against his chest, she fell silent.

But in her mind, she whispered, *I can't lose you.*

K ANE knew what she was planning.
       It was as plain as that cute nose on her lovely face, but as she drifted off in his arms, he held his silence. And stayed awake.

She would wait until he was sleeping—and she'd try to leave him.

Her body was boneless in his arms and he relaxed long enough to bury his face in the deep red banner of her hair, breathing in the soft, subtle fragrance of her skin, letting it fill his head.

It was damned near an hour before he moved. Slipping away from her, he went to the bathroom, closing the door about halfway. If she woke up, seeing him move into the bathroom wouldn't be anything to make her suspicious. After taking care of the fullness in his bladder, he washed his hands and then moved on silent feet to stand in front of the door, staring through the narrow opening. Kendall still lay on her side, facing away from him.

He left the bathroom, keeping her in his line of sight as he moved toward the coat he had slung on the chair. The hardest part was going to be getting those titanium cuffs out of his pocket without making enough noise for her to wake up.

Or maybe he shouldn't worry about waking her up.

Making a decision, he took the bull by the horns and just took the cuffs out. As she opened her eyes sleepily, he gave her a wicked grin, strolling over to the bed and straddling her hips.

Her eyes widened slightly as she studied the cuffs he dangled from one finger. Pursing her lips, she studied him—Kane could hear the gears spinning in her head. Bending down, he bussed her mouth gently as he caught one wrist, then the other, shifting until he could draw her up into a sitting position, pinioning her wrists at the small of her back.

There was no headboard to cuff her to, and that would have been a waste of time anyway. She'd just jerk until the headboard broke. But with her wrists behind her back, she had less leverage. "What are you up to?" she murmured huskily as he drew back. Her tongue slid across her lower lip and Kane groaned, watching it disappear back inside the sweet, wet cavern of her mouth.

"You can't tell?" he teased as he settled back on his haunches, keeping his weight off her body.

Kendall shifted her wrists, making the reinforced titanium

cuffs jingle a little. Casting a look over her shoulder, she drawled, "Well, I have an idea or two."

With a wide grin, Kane said, "I bet you do."

He felt that biting hunger settle low in his gut as she continued to stare at him, a small smile on her pretty mouth, her golden eyes finally full of something besides that damnable pain he'd seen there far too often.

Too alone, he thought to himself. She'd spent far too much of her life alone, and he'd be damned if he walked away from her. Slowly, he reached up, trailing his fingers along the front of her shirt before releasing one button from its mooring. Then another, all the way down until the shirt hung open and revealed a pale strip of flesh between the edges, and the small band of lace that held the cups of her bra together.

Pushing the shirt off her shoulders, he let it fall down her arms, the deep red fabric pooling around her cuffed wrists. Her bra, fastening in the back, was a little harder to get out of the way. Flashing a slow smile at her, he reached for the knife he kept in his boot, tracing the flat of the blade along the curves of her breasts, just above the lace. Her flesh roughened under the cool touch of metal and she shivered.

When she looked up at him, her pupils had expanded, giving her a dazed, almost drugged look. Kane held her gaze as he slid the wickedly sharp tip of his blade between the bra and her flesh. After cutting through the lace there, he trailed the knife's edge along her skin, up to the straps that still held it in place on her shoulders. First one, then the other, he cut through each lacy strap, letting the scraps fall to the bed around her.

Her breasts lifted and fell as she took one slow, deep breath. Kane continued to trail the blade across her flesh, stroking the flat of it across one puckered nipple before laying the knife on the bedside table.

"Awful trusting for a vampire," he murmured, lowering his head to catch the other nipple in his mouth, groaning at the warm, sweet, female taste of her. "Cuffed . . . half-naked, letting a man touch that pretty white flesh of yours with a sharp knife."

Kendall whimpered as his mouth left her, she smiled and replied back, "Well, cuffed, with you holding the knife on me, what am I supposed to do?"

Kane shrugged as he ran his knuckles down the smooth skin of her torso, circling one finger around the button that held her jeans closed. "I don't know . . . fight?"

With a cheeky smile, she said, "But then you might stop."

Kane shook his head slowly. "No . . . I'm not planning on stopping anytime soon, darlin'. You're stuck with me." And that, he meant with complete sincerity. Lowering his head, he put his face into hers, whispering quietly, "I'm not going anywhere . . . and you're not going anywhere without me."

Kendall's eyes narrowed.

Kane pushed back, settling his weight on his heels as he crouched above her, holding her gaze. She stared at him with unreadable eyes. Her features had gone completely still, the life seeming to drain out of her in an instant. Long moments of silence passed. Then she blinked, and life seemed to return to her again. The muscles in her arms tensed, she tugged on her wrists and demanded, "Take the cuffs off."

He smiled, a serene, blissful smile. "You were going to slip away, weren't you?"

Her face remained blank. He saw the answer in her eyes. That warm golden brown started to glow, gleaming the way they always did when she was mad.

"That's what I thought," he murmured, stretching his length out atop hers, settling his hips in the cradle of hers and rocking his cock against her. Her lashes fluttered even as she tried not to respond.

"You're not leaving me, babe." He held her gaze for a minute and then lowered his head, closing his mouth around the pebbled flesh of her nipple and tugging it lightly with his teeth. "And you need to get something through that very pretty head of yours—if you try, then I'll just go looking on my own."

"Not if I leave you tied up," she snapped, even as her

lashes fluttered down. A soft moan escaped her lips and then she wrenched her torso, bucking her hips as she tried to dislodge him.

But Kane had grown up in the country—he'd spent a lot of time on horseback. He knew how to ride. Leaning forward, he put his face in hers. "You can't leave me tied indefinitely, sweetheart."

She gave him a saccharine smile. "No—just long enough for somebody to come and talk . . . or *put* some sense inside that rock-hard skull."

Kane grinned. "Well, the vampire didn't have much luck last night, did he? And you haven't had much luck anytime you've tried."

Kendall sniffed, lifting her nose arrogantly. She tried to shrug, but he figured it was a little hard to pull off with her arms bound. "Maybe I just need to try a little harder. And even if I can't do it, somebody else might have better luck."

Kane saw past the bravado in her eyes though, and he knew better. He could see the doubt in her eyes. Giving her a confident smile, he suggested, "Well, why don't you just give it one more try?"

"I don't want to do what I did that night," she said flatly.

Resting his chin between her breasts, he said, "Well, you don't need to knock me out this time. You just need to convince me that I don't have to go with you when you go hunting this psychotic vampire."

"You're telling me that I can use mind control and you aren't going to be mad."

An absolute stillness settled on her as she focused on him. Even her breathing seemed to stop. That was all the warning he had, and Kane jerked his eyes away, concentrating on anything but the feel of her beneath him, the need to stare into her coppery gold eyes.

He could feel it—the pulse of her power pushing against his brain. Closing his eyes, he focused on his anger instead of his lust. Images of Duke's battered body, the young boy that had been living in that filthy building. He made himself think of the pain he'd seen in Kendall's eyes. He'd see this through, damn it all. He didn't care what it took.

All the while, he kept feeling Kendall's power battering at his mind like a hurricane.

Gritting his teeth, he focused. In his gut, he knew he had to do this. Kendall wouldn't live through this unless he was with her. Not a Hunter, not Duke, not Vax, the weird, witchy bastard who stared at her with intimate, knowing eyes. He didn't know why he was so certain, but he'd be damned if he'd take the chance and let her go alone.

It was in the moment, as the waves of her control battered at his mind, that he knew—he was falling in love with her. It had started as an obsession, for all the wrong reasons, but even as she'd stood in a dirty alley by Duke's side and tried to explain why Kane had spent two years thinking his best friend was dead there had been a passion in her voice that had spoken to something deep inside him. *You're right about one thing—he is one of us, but you have no idea who we are . . .* Just those words, and that obsession of his had already started to become something more.

This was his woman. He didn't give a damn that he'd be old and gray in thirty or forty years, and she'd look every bit as young and lovely as she did now. He wanted every second of those years, and as many as God would grant him, so he could be with her, putting a smile in those sad eyes and holding her close as she slept.

"It's not working, Kendall," he said quietly. Lifting his lashes, he stared into her eyes, eyes that glowed and swirled with power. "You can't touch my mind. I don't know why, but you can't."

The pulsating waves of her power slowed and then stopped all together. A sigh escaped her and she closed her eyes. "Damn you. Why did you have to be so different?" Kendall murmured wearily. She shifted, rattling the links on the reinforced cuffs at her wrists.

Kane tugged the key from his jeans and unlocked her, tossing the cuffs down to the floor before he stretched out his length beside her. Skimming his lips over her cheek, he nuzzled the sweetly scented skin of her neck before lifting up to watch her face as he murmured, "I don't know . . . but I'm damned glad I am. You need me, Kendall. Even if you don't want to admit it yet."

Her eyes opened and he found himself staring into tear-bright irises. "That's the whole problem, Kane. I know I need you—and the thought of losing you scares me to death."

Against her lips, he whispered, "You're not going to lose me. Not to her. Not now. Not anytime soon, if I can control it."

He covered her mouth as he wedged his hips between her thighs, rocking against her. Hot, demanding greed filled him. Of all the women he'd touched, she was the only one that had him burning with a need to mark her, to claim her. Rocking back on his heels, he tore at her jeans, stripping them down her slender legs with hands gone clumsy with his hunger. The denim tangled around her ankles and he snarled, jerking impatiently until one foot came free. Ignoring the rest, he focused his attention on his own clothes, jerking open his shirt. Buttons went flying but he scarcely noticed as he fumbled the one at his fly free. Easing the zipper down over his aching cock, he groaned at the cool kiss of air on his freed flesh.

Moving up over her, he pushed against her, the head of his cock brushing against the dew-slicked flesh of her sex. "You're mine, Kendall," he murmured gruffly. "I'm not letting you leave me."

Her lashes fluttered closed as he pushed inside. "No . . . look at me." Kane stared into her desire-clouded gaze as he started to pump back and forth inside her. "I want to watch you. I'll never get tired of watching you."

She felt swollen and tight, her flesh heating around him. Gritting his teeth, he pushed up onto his hands, staring down at where they joined, the dark column of his flesh pushing inside the softly flushed tissues of her pussy. The sight of it made his body tense, his balls drawing tight against him, the need to come pounding inside him. Lashing the need down, he slowed his strokes until he was barely rocking in the hot, wet embrace of her sex.

Resting his forehead against hers, he murmured, "Don't come yet. Stay with me."

A moan shimmered out of her, and he felt the small convulsions start in her pussy. "Kane, please . . ."

"Stay with me," he repeated. The second she started coming, he was lost. He stilled within her, groaning raggedly as she rippled around his cock.

The tension slowly drained out of her body and the fragile curve of her ribcage rose and fell as she dragged air into her lungs. "This is torture, Kane."

Chuckling, he bussed her mouth gently. "No . . . torture would never be doing this again. That's why I'm not going anywhere. I want to be able do this all the time, anytime . . . as often as I want. And I'll want it a lot."

Kendall flexed around him, and he sucked in a harsh breath. "We can't do this when we're trying to catch a killer . . . what are we going to do, try to make her die of envy?"

"Well, that's not quite violent enough for me."

Her hands pushed lightly at his chest and Kane let her urge him away, falling onto his back. As she straddled him, her eyes stared down at him. She cupped him in her hand, and Kane rolled his hips upward to meet her touch. His cock jerked and throbbed as he hissed out a breath. "I don't know. I think I'd die a slow and painful death if I had to watch while another woman had you . . . had this . . ."

The hot, wet circle of her mouth closed around the head of his cock. "Sweet damnation," he grunted, reaching down and winding his hands in the thick silk of her hair.

She hummed softly and the vibration of it went shooting straight to his groin. Her eyes rolled up, meeting his over the expanse of his torso. The muscles in his belly clenched at that hot look and in self-defense, he closed his eyes as she started to move her head up and down.

Her tongue swirled across the rounded blunt tip, and he tried to use his grip on her hair to drag her head up and down. She resisted, holding her position as she continued to torment just the upper half of his cock, sucking on him, pulling away lightly to rake his sensitive flesh with her teeth.

"Fuck!" He surged upward, and with his movement, she fell back. Catching her in his arms, he rolled, trying to get her under him. He saw the edge of the bed, but it was too late to stop his roll and he shifted in midair, trying to keep his weight off of her as they fell to the floor. They landed on their sides and Kane grinned into her eyes, but it fell away at the stark hunger he saw there. Catching one thigh in his hand, he drew it up over his hip, pushing slowly inside her.

Her eyes fluttered closed, her head falling back. Kane buried his face in the curve of her neck as she closed around him, the slick tissues seeming to grab at his cock. Bracing one hand at the small of her back, he rocked gently until he had gone as deep as he could.

Her muscles squeezed around him, and he started to push harder against her, his teeth gritted. Shifting, he moved until he was straddling one of her thighs, still clutching the other in his hand as he pushed up on his knees. Her upper torso fell back until her shoulders rested against the floor, while her lower body was held in place by his as he started to shaft her.

As he thrust inside her, Kendall stared blindly up at him, whimpering under her breath. "Bloody hell, Kane," she breathed out. His cock jerked inside her and she screamed out his name, clenching around him. Low in her belly, she felt everything inside her going tight.

One big hand, warm and hard, smoothed over the curve of her rump, his fingers trailing down to the sensitive area between the cheeks of her ass. Kendall shivered at that touch, her teeth sinking into her lip.

"Come for me," he whispered, his thrusts growing rougher. Falling forward, he braced his weight over her on one hand, his other hand cupping one of her breasts. "Come for me. Come, Kendall, I need to feel it."

It tore through her as though it had teeth, the climax stealing away all thought, all vision as it wracked her body.

Blind, floating in darkness, she rode the orgasm as it broke over her like waves crashing against a rocky beach.

Inside her pussy, she could feel him throbbing, the heat of his seed flooding her. Distantly, she heard his ragged groan, as her eyes started to clear. He sank down, falling to the floor behind her and curling up against her. His arms came around her, drawing her into the curve and warmth of his body.

"You're not leaving me," he muttered against her nape.

She could hear the exhaustion in his voice, and a slow smile curved her lips. A tenderness filled her, her heart expanding inside her chest, aching. "No," she agreed, her voice thick with tears. "I'm not leaving."

CHAPTER 11

THE witch's eyes were faded, old, full of a weariness that made Vax ache with sympathy as he stared into them. "Agnes, what brings you to the States?" he asked gently as he lowered Duke's battered body to the bed beside the witch. Of course, that was a stupid question now that he thought of it.

She was sitting there, obviously waiting.

Waiting for Duke, it would appear. She didn't leave her native England often any more. She was mostly retired. And after five hundred years of serving the Council, she had earned it.

Powerful witches would live easily three or four hundred years. If their soul bonded with another paranormal, one of the longer-lived races like a vampire or a shifter, they lived as long as their mate did.

As far as anybody knew, Agnes had never mated. Nobody knew why—whether she simply never found the love of her heart, or if she'd lost him when she was young, before she'd become a Hunter.

But she was more than five hundred years old, and she

had retired from the Council decades ago. Living in seclusion in Cornwall, she spoke with a few select people.

If she was here, then she was here because she had reason to be.

"You look well, Vax," she said, her voice still the same as it had been when he'd seen her last. That had been close to a century ago. Her eyes twinkled merrily and she grinned at him wickedly. "If I was just a little younger . . . okay, a *lot* younger."

Vax chuckled. "Agnes, if you were younger, I'd probably either fall at your feet and beg for mercy or run screaming in terror. You're more than I could handle." And he spoke nothing more than the truth. Her features still held the echo of the beauty he knew she had been, but it was more than that. She had broken hearts.

Vax didn't like the idea of having his heart broken. Not at all.

One silver brow arched over faded blue eyes as she studied him. She knew every single thought that had just circled through his mind. Vax scowled at her. Shit. He hadn't had anybody read him that easily in, well hell, *ever.* "You will, lad. You'll have your heart broken and then some," she murmured, her gaze turning distant.

Then she shook her head, her eyes clearing as she turned to study Duke. "Bugger. She beat the bloody hell out of you, didn't she, lad?" She sat on the bed, reaching out to touch his forehead with a frown.

"Why isn't he healing any?" Vax asked quietly.

Agnes never even glanced his way. "Too drained. His body has no energy left for healing. It's conserving all his energy just to live." Agnes stroked a gentle hand down Duke's brow. Vax blinked, and during the micro second his lids were lowered, he saw a sparkling flash flow from her hand. Healing energy, seeping into Duke's flesh. "He will be fine, though. Aye, he will. You're a strong bastard, aren't you?"

Duke seemed to sigh, and some of the lines of pain around his eyes eased a bit. Agnes turned to face Vax. "Did you see Kendall?"

Vax merely stared at her.

The witch just smiled serenely at him.

Vax raised his eyes heavenward. This woman was enough to try the patience of a saint, he suspected. Dropping onto a chair across from the bed, he hooked his ankle over his knee and stared at her. "Briefly. Very briefly."

"She is well?"

Vax lifted one shoulder restlessly. "Well as can be expected." Brooding, he stared sightlessly at the Monet that adorned the wall across from him. "Cat is alive."

A quiet sigh drifted through the air. "I know."

Vax's gaze flew to the old witch. "You *know*?"

Agnes just nodded.

Slowly, he rose, staring at her with turbulent eyes. "Exactly how *long* have you known?" he demanded.

Agnes lifted one stooped shoulder in a shrug. "I don't exactly know. Time runs together once you get to be my age. A few years, no more. Started with just the odd dream. I brushed it off at first. Then Kendall brought this one in. The dreams started coming more often. And I knew."

"You didn't say anything."

There was an odd flicker in her eyes. "Sometimes things happen the way they do for a reason. Cat was meant to live, Vax. For a reason."

Vax growled, jabbing a thumb toward the battered man on the bed as he snapped, "And that man was meant to be beaten for a reason?"

Agnes replied softly, "He is alive."

"He could have died! And there was a damn kid in there and his sister; she looks scared of her own shadow. Cat's been out there for a century, torturing and killing people. Damn it, Agnes."

Vax could have bitten his tongue off as he saw the minute her control snapped. She rose from the bed with a speed a woman of her age shouldn't possess. The rather frail-looking matron of minutes ago no longer seemed to exist as she advanced on him, her voice a thunderous echo as she said, "Who do you think you are speaking to, *boy*? I did not put these events into action. I had to watch them play out, the same as the rest of us."

He opened his mouth to say something, offer an apology, maybe, he didn't know. Whether he could have said anything with the spit dried in his mouth, he'd never know, because a hand closed around his throat even though she was five feet away. That hand locked all the words in, and he couldn't say a damn thing.

"Bloody young fools. Always thinking with your heads. It doesn't always work to listen to your head, you know that, Vax?" Agnes murmured.

The hand around his throat loosened, and he collapsed to his knees, sucking in oxygen as he stared at her. She turned away and walked back to the bed, lowering herself delicately down. Crossing her hands in her lap, she looked back at him.

"This is the way it had to be. Whether we like it or not, sometimes, sacrifices must be made."

Clumsily, Vax shoved himself to his feet. His throat felt raw and his lungs burned from the lack of air as he stared at her. Holy hell, the woman looked like she should be sitting in a rocking chair, knitting something.

And she was fucking deadly.

For one second, his gaze flickered to Duke's face. Barely able to believe his eyes, he saw that most of the bruises were already gone from the shifter's face.

Vax swallowed. His throat screamed as he did it and he saw the satisfaction in Agnes's eyes. Oh, yeah, he'd pissed her off.

"Leave us now. I need to help this young Hunter."

Vax left. After all, how in the hell could he argue with her?

WITH Kane's bare skin pressed against hers, Kendall awoke in the dead of the night, feeling the presence of a killer, the presence of danger and death as something stalked the night.

No, not stalked, exactly.

Fled.

What made a Hunter a Hunter wasn't something tangible. It was an odd sense, something that made them aware of danger. Masters often felt it and sent their people out. Kendall was a Master without a land to protect since she had walked away from it all those years ago.

Now, she just felt it at random. It was more disconnected now, and often she felt like she was plucking at loose threads, but she got the job done.

Or she had been, until she came here. There had been odd little jobs here and there, but not anything that truly called to her.

Not until now. Except for Joseph.

But this was *more*. It was powerful, and something so full of some insidious rage it made her belly roil.

Rising from bed, she moved to the window.

This wasn't just any killer either.

In her gut, she knew who it was. It was Cat.

But why she was feeling her now, she wasn't really sure.

Cat was running. Hard and fast.

The sky was still dark. Sunrise was maybe two hours away. Resting one hand against the window, Kendall closed her eyes. It felt like there was a clock inside of her soul and it had just struck the midnight hour.

Time's up.

A lone tear trickled down her cheek as she turned away. The past hundred years, she had survived by thinking that the Cat she had known and loved was at peace. And it had been a relief, not to have actually had to have fought face-to-face with the woman she had known and loved.

But now she would have to fight her. Have to kill her.

Kendall was so caught up in her thoughts, she didn't realize Kane had woken up until he spoke to her. "Where are you?"

Startled, she spun around and stared at him.

"Hey," he murmured, pushing up on his elbow and staring at her with worried eyes. "You look like you've seen a ghost."

"I didn't know you were awake." Blowing out a breath, she crossed the room to him and lowered herself to perch on the edge of the bed. "I need to go out for a few minutes. I'll be back before sunrise."

That lopsided grin of his that she secretly adored appeared and he shook his head. "I don't think so, sugar. That wasn't the deal. If you're going out, so am I."

Scowling at him, Kendall shook her head. "I'm not *doing* anything." At least she didn't think she was. Cat wasn't going to stay out too long. She was too young to risk staying out much longer. It was pushing ever closer to dawn, and Cat would have to seek shelter soon.

When she went to ground, Kendall would be there. She wanted to know where Cat's hiding place was. Forcing a reassuring smile, she shrugged. "I just want to feed real quick."

Kane apparently didn't believe her. That grin remained firmly in place, and he nodded slowly. "Sure, darlin'. You can feed and on the way back, we can swing by some place and get me a bite before we crash for the day."

Sighing, Kendall rose. Damn it. Well, she sure as hell wasn't going to be doing anything now.

KANE swung his legs over the edge of the bed and stood. As he crossed the room to his own gear, he watched as Kendall tugged a pair of jeans from the drawer and slid them on. No panties. He grimaced, passing a hand over his already very interested cock.

No time for play, though. Without even looking at the clock, he knew they only had a few hours before the sun rose. If she really did need to feed, they only had a short time.

He could satisfy his baser appetites later.

And thinking about her naked under that tight denim, he'd most definitely need to satisfy those appetites. But first things first.

As he dressed, tugging on another pair of his ubiquitous

black BDUs, he wondered what she was up to. *Feeding, yeah right.* She probably *would* feed, since that was the line she had given him.

But that wasn't what she'd been planning.

Kane wasn't sure why he was so positive, but he could tell when she was lying to him. Just like he could tell when she was telling the truth. It was almost like the words felt different to him.

Actually, it had always been like that with him.

One of the reasons he had been such a good bounty hunter.

Now, one thing he was sure of, whatever was going on inside that pretty head of hers, it had to do with Cat. Cat was about the only thing that could bring that kind of sadness into Kendall's golden eyes.

Digging out a black T-shirt, he tugged it on and turned around to look at Kendall. She was sitting down, sliding her feet into a pair of sensible shoes for once, white tennis shoes, lacing them up, but once that was done, all she did was stare at the floor, her slender shoulders slumped.

She looked completely dejected.

Kane clenched his jaw. He had never been one to entertain fantasies about hurting a female. Even bringing one in on a job had left a bad taste in his mouth. But he wanted to hurt Cat. In a bad way.

If for no other reason than because she kept putting that pain in Kendall's eyes.

Turning away from her, he made himself focus on the job. Sliding his holster into place and grabbing his gun, listening as Kendall started to move around behind him. He slid the Kel-Tec into his ankle holster, the knife into the sheath, and then picked up his Beretta. He holstered it before he turned to meet Kendall.

She was standing silently behind him.

Forcing a smile, he said, "Ready?"

She just stared at him.

Kane opened the door and gestured. "After you."

*   *   *

CATHARINE felt it. The presence of a greater predator moving through the night. Her blood chilled in her veins and for a minute, she could hardly move. Whimpering, she pressed her back against the brick wall and clutched her head.

"Go away," she whimpered, shaking her head. "Just away."

There was no answer.

"Why is this happening?" Cat whined, stomping her foot. Bringing one hand to her mouth, she started to chew on a nail, staring out into the night. They *never* felt her. Even before she found Analise, her own psychic gifts created some sort of null. Bloody hell, that was why those fool Hunters never even realized *she* was the feral vampire killing on their sainted grounds of Brendain all those years ago.

So how come they could sense her now?

And Cat had a terrible dread in the pit of her belly that she knew exactly who was moving in so very close. She'd always meant to close in on Kendall. But it had been Cat's intention to make the first move. Not let Kendall move in on her. Cat had to have the advantage of surprise, had to have the advantage of her psychic powers. Otherwise, the older vampire would destroy her, utterly and completely.

Worry and fear ate at her as she shoved away from the wall and once more started to run. It felt more like fleeing, and that only made her angry. Damn Kendall to hell and back for making her feel fear. Cat hadn't been afraid of anything in a hundred years. She had been strong, powerful. Nothing had been able to touch her.

"Kendall's fault," she rasped, darting into an alley as a car turned down the street. If Kendall had saved her that night—flinching, she shoved the memory away, shying away from it. She refused to let herself think that maybe she shouldn't have left the shelter of her own home.

All Kendall's fault.

Worse, now she didn't even have her pets. Granted, Brad hadn't been much fun. Though he was just a boy, he had been too strong. She couldn't toy with him the way she had wanted. His mind was too powerful, too keen. He saw through all her tricks, all her games. Even in his sleep, when he should have been open to her suggestions, he was not.

Cat wasn't able to touch him. And as he got older, he only became more powerful. But Analise, now she was fun. The girl had no idea just how powerful her brother was, no idea just how useless Cat was against him. All Cat had to do was suggest a threat to him and the girl caved.

How Kendall was able to coax Analise to go with her, Cat had no idea. Analise had been completely cowed, or so Cat had thought.

There was a fire escape at the end of the alley and Cat leaped, bypassing the ladder and leaping to the landing with ease. Jogging up the steps, she reached the roof in seconds and cast a glance at the eastern sky. Still dark. She had a good two hours yet.

Her gut screamed at her to get hidden. Go to ground, a place nobody knew about, and hide.

But she didn't want to. Not with a Hunter breathing down her neck.

She paced back and forth, her hair billowing around her as she tried to make up her mind what to do.

She needed to feed. She was hungry, and if a battle was coming, she needed to be stronger. She'd expended too much energy fleeing, worrying, searching for Analise and Brad.

"Damn damn damn!"

KENDALL let the dealer drop to the ground without even glancing at her. Feeding usually brought her a little more pleasure than this, but it had seemed more like a chore this time around, something she did because it needed to be done.

As she'd fed, Kendall had placed the suggestion that the

woman go to the police and confess. The woman would accept whatever plea bargain was offered and she'd get clean. Hopefully by the time Kendall's suggestions wore off, the woman would realize life was better without the drugs and the dirty money she got by selling them to kids.

Staring off into the distance, Kendall continued to move through the darkness, unaware of Kane's narrowed gaze.

Behind her, Kane trailed after her with watchful eyes. He hadn't realized a predator could look so . . . fey. That was the only word he could think of that fit her right now. Those golden eyes had an otherworldly glow and her feet barely seemed to touch the ground.

She had hardly spoken a word. Not when she took down the dealer just as the woman started to swap some coke for money with a kid who barely looked old enough to be in high school and not after she'd fed.

Kane suspected she'd forgotten he was there with her.

He knew why.

There was something out there.

A vampire. Vampires made him itch. Kane wasn't exactly sure why, but he didn't even have to see one, or be in the same room with one to know one was nearby. They made him twitchy. The more powerful the vampire was, the twitchier he got.

He'd been damned twitchy the night he'd seen Kendall, thinking she was Duke's killer. Kendall was powerful. The vampire he felt now was just a mild itch on his spine compared to Kendall, but there was a different feel to the power, and he could feel something pressing against his mind.

It was not what he felt when Kendall was trying to use mind control on him. Just as useless, but different.

Psychic. Kendall had mentioned a witch when she was telling him about Cat, and the witch had said Cat was psychic. Exactly what was a psychic, he wondered?

He suspected Kendall's version of psychic wasn't the same as what he'd see on TV with a 1-800 number. But he'd have to wait awhile before he found out because his sexy vampire was still off in her own little world and drifting further and further away from him with every step she took. Not physically. She was only an arm's length away from him.

But she wasn't even aware of him. Kane reached out and trailed his fingers down her back, and she turned her head and smiled at him, but it was the smile she'd give a stranger, blank and polite. Then she was back to staring down the street.

Her steps slowed and she cocked her head, turning to stare down an alley.

"There you are," she whispered.

A chill ran down Kane's spine at the soft, eerie whisper. As she started to move down the alley, he reached out and folded his hand around hers. "Kendall."

She glanced down at his hand and then looked back at him. She blinked, and her eyes cleared a little.

"Remember your promise. We do this together."

That fey smile faded from her face just a little and she nodded. "I remember, Kane."

"Who are you looking for?"

Kendall didn't answer, just turned her gaze back to stare down the alley. He followed her stare, watching as her eyes climbed upward until she was staring at the top of the building. "She was here. Just a few minutes ago."

"Who was here?"

Kendall sighed, her slender shoulders rising and falling, slumping forward as though she carried the weight of the world on them. "Cat. Just a few minutes ago." Her lashes drifted down. "I can still smell her. She's afraid."

Useless anger tore through him, and he wrapped his arms around her, bringing her back against him. "She's not the woman you knew, Kendall. That woman is dead—all that's left is a monster."

Her hands came up, gripping one of his arms. Her nails bit into his forearm. "I know. The only thing I can do is finish it."

Kane pressed a gentle kiss to the crown of her head before letting his arms fall away. As she stepped away, Kane slid his eyes up, staring at the building. Cat wasn't there. The only vampire in the immediate area was Kendall. But part of him wished Cat was there. So he could pump her black heart full of the bullets and then slowly carve it out of her.

Kill her slowly and painfully.

Make the bitch suffer half as much as Kendall was suffering right now.

H<small>E</small> was worried about her.

Kendall knew it. She could practically feel it as she started down the alley.

But the closer she got to Cat, the more everything else faded into the background. The harder it was to think about anything else, even Kane breathing down the back of her neck.

Her gums ached until she gave into her instincts and let her fangs slide out. With her hands curled into loose fists and her muscles in the ready state, Kendall felt like she was going to explode.

Slowing to a halt, she stared up at the fire escape. Slowly, she licked her lips. If she had been here even five minutes earlier, she would have seen Cat as she fled up the stairs. Her hideout wasn't here. This was just the route she took to get to it. Cat would hide underground.

But she was close.

The air brushed her face as she jumped from the ground to the landing, leaving Kane below, staring up at her and muttering under his breath. She'd cleared the top of the building by the time Kane had figured out a way onto the fire escape. She could hear him, very quiet for a mortal, as she started across the roof.

Busted glass and cigarette butts littered the roof of the building. On the opposite side of the roof was a door. Near it sat a worn patio table and a couple of chairs. Somebody had made an attempt at a rooftop garden. Kendall could smell the roses—the scent of them teased some long forgotten childhood memory. The night was heavy with the scent of flowers, more than just those Kendall saw in front of her.

Roses, honeysuckles, lavender, jasmine.

The roses . . . Mum had loved roses.

Tears stung Kendall's eyes. So had Cat. They'd planted a garden together, her and Catharine. Closing her eyes, she let one tear burn its way down her cheek before shoving the memory aside and turning away from the small garden.

Did the sight of such things bother Cat at all? Kendall wondered.

As she stepped to the edge of the building, she stared down. Well, she had her answer; she just wasn't sure how to translate it.

There, at the base of the building, was a city garden. If Kendall just *looked,* it would have been a lovely a spot. But she couldn't just look. She both looked and felt.

Cat surrounded herself with flowers while she hid.

And at the heart of that garden was a maw of darkness. Some vampires had the gift of shadows. They could cloak themselves in them, making the shadows seem darker and heavier than they really were. Cat was one of these. Cat could make a room that was normally dim seem as black as the blackest of caves.

Although Kendall couldn't completely see through the darkness that Cat's gift cast, she could just barely make out the rough shape of a building, the faint gleam of light on glass.

There.

That was Cat's hole. That was where she went to ground.

Turning, she looked at Kane with a slow, satisfied smile.

K ANE couldn't see a damn thing through the darkness, but if Kendall insisted there was some place in the garden where Cat could hide, then he believed her. Pushing a hand through his hair, he glanced at the sky.

It was still dark, but dawn was coming. It couldn't be more than an hour before the sky started to grow lighter. "What do we do now?" he asked quietly.

Kendall stared into the night, a thoughtful look on her

pretty face. Finally, she shrugged. "We'll go get my car. I'll sleep in the trunk—"

That was as far as he let her get. Closing one hand over her upper arm, he pulled her back against him. "I don't think so, babe. It's summer. It's hot. That trunk is too damned small . . . and what in the hell are you laughing at?" he demanded, glaring down at her.

She grinned up at him, shaking her head. "Kane, it's not like I need the air. Hot weather, cold weather, they don't much matter to me anymore. It won't be the most comfortable I've ever been, but hell, I've done it before, and I've slept in much worse places. As long as it's dark and secure, I'll be fine. It will be dark. And you'll be there, so it's secure."

For one second, her trust distracted him. Just a second, though. Long enough for him to think about hauling her against him and kissing her senseless. But then he reminded himself what she was talking about. *Sleeping in a damned trunk.* "No." Shaking his head, he repeated it. "No. Not going to happen. Think of another plan, babe."

Kendall narrowed her eyes. "We're a little short on time to be thinking of many plans, *babe*. Sunrise is coming. She'll be trapped during the day. Come sunset, she'll run again. Which means I have to stop her *before* that. I can move for a little while before the sun sets, but just a little while. Which means I have to be *here*. I don't have time to move from the hotel to here. I need someplace safe, some place here."

"Won't she feel you?"

Kendall cocked a brow at him. "She already knows I'm tracking her. But if she knew how close I was, she'd still be running. So obviously not."

Crossing his arms over his chest, Kane held her stare levelly. "You are not sleeping in a damned trunk."

Kendall snarled at him. "Then damn it, what in the hell do you suggest?"

Smiling at her calmly, he asked, "How dark does it have it be?"

*   *   *

Tʜᴇʀᴇ were times when she really, *really* wanted to strangle that man.

She watched him disappear down the street, jogging easily like he hadn't been trailing after her for half the night.

Kendall absolutely refused to admit she hadn't really been looking forward to spending a day locked in the small, tight confines of her trunk. So what if it was the trunk of a luxurious Jaguar? It was still a bloody trunk.

Sleeping in the back of Kane's SUV was much more preferable. He kept blankets back there, and he assured her that the windows were tinted. She could pull the blankets over her head if the sun threatened, and Kane said he could find a place to park or just drive around the park. They didn't actually need to keep the park in eyesight. Kendall could feel Cat now. She just wanted to be close.

He was just so . . . so . . . so bloody *smug*. So damned sure of himself. How could he be so sure of himself?

Didn't he realize how fragile human life was?

Kendall certainly did. She looked at him and realized just how easily it would be over with for him. How quickly. He had but a handful of years left to him. Fifty or sixty even, if he wasn't killed by some vampire, or an accident . . . if he lived out his life to its fullest, he'd die an old man.

So little time.

It hurt her heart just to think of it. Tears stung her eyes as she realized walking away from him was going to leave a hole in her heart. How had he gotten under her skin so quickly? In all her years, nobody had gotten to her like he had.

"I don't like it, not at all," she muttered.

Drawing her knees to her chest, she rested her chin on them, staring into the darkness.

"Bugger," she sighed. Closing her eyes, she gave into the urge and let the tears fall down her cheeks.

She hadn't even lost him yet, and already she felt the pain.

"Don't do this." Reaching up, she wiped away the tears.

This was a weakness. Letting him inside her like this gave Cat a weapon to use against her. If not Cat, then somebody like her.

Kendall had survived this long simply by not having a weakness. She wasn't going to pick one up now. Closing her eyes, she sank to the floor of the roof and folded her legs under her. Centuries ago, she had been a student at Brendain, and there, she had learned how to fight, how to master her strengths, how to hide her weaknesses, and how to clear her mind.

It had once seemed such a waste of time to meditate, but she'd learned it was anything but.

Right now, she needed desperately to find the peace meditation offered. With slow, deep breathing, she emptied her mind.

It was a struggle, though—had it been so hard back then?

She focused on the sound of her heartbeat, the sound of her breathing, the scents of the night hidden underneath the scents of the city. A baby cried in the building next door. A siren wailed a few miles away. All around there were cars. The buzz of voices coming from radio and television.

But under all of it was life. People talking, laughing. Birds chirping, even the faint hum of insects.

The throbbing call of life.

The baby cried once more, and she focused on that sound. The low, soothing murmur of a woman's voice and the baby quieted. Innocence, youth. A reminder of why Kendall did what she did.

Time passed, and Kendall just let it drift by. Dawn drew near but she didn't open her eyes to look at the sky. Kane would be there.

Right now, she just wanted to refocus. Needed to *find* her focus, so she could deal with Cat.

As that thought drifted through her mind, a vision of Cat's face seemed to waver in front of her.

The distance that separated them seemed to spin away, and it was like the two women stood in the same room, a darkened room where only they existed. Whether Cat had forced herself in on Kendall's meditative trance, or whether Kendall had somehow forged the link, Kendall didn't know.

Kendall would deal with that mystery later.

As they faced each other for the first time in a hundred years, a hideous pain tore through Kendall's heart. Shoving it aside, Kendall blanked her face and met Cat's gaze.

Cat looked exactly the same, Kendall realized. But then she looked a little deeper and realized her mistake. There was something different.

In the eyes. There was nothing remotely human, nothing at all sane, left in Cat's eyes.

"Hello, Kendall."

"Hello, Catling."

"You took away my pets; I'm a little upset about that."

For a second, Kendall had no idea what Cat was talking about, and then it dawned on her. A memory of Duke's battered face flashed through her mind, and she had to fight not to snarl at the younger vampire. Clenching her hands into fists, Kendall just barely managed to keep her temper under control as she said, "People aren't pets, Cat."

Cat shrugged as she spun away from Kendall and started to pace the small room. "I think that's what's always made the two of us different, Kendall."

Dryly, Kendall said, "Well, there's a little more than just that, sweetheart."

"Oh, like you being a righteous prude?" Cat asked, casting Kendall an innocent look over her shoulder.

Kendall shrugged. "I was thinking more along the lines of you being an insane, murderous bitch."

Cat stiffened and spun around, glaring at Kendall. "You need to leave, Kendall. This is *my* home." Displaying just a little bit of the child Kendall still remembered, she stomped her foot imperiously and waved a hand toward Kendall, like she could just brush her away. "So just away. Go hunt somewhere else. This is my land."

"I'm here for a reason, Cat. I'll leave once the job is done." Kendall stared at Cat with grim eyes.

Cat just sneered at her. "You can't stop me, Mary Kendall. You couldn't stop me before because you were too bloody weak, and you won't stop me for the same reason. You're weak. Weak and soft."

Sadly, Kendall whispered, "That was true, once. But I can't let you kill anybody else, Cat. It has to end."

Cat laughed and shook her head. "It won't end, I'll be gone before you get here. Long gone. You won't catch me. For the love of God, you didn't even realize I was here until Analise started helping you. Where is the sniveling little bitch anyway?"

"At Excelsior by now."

Fury bloomed in Cat's eyes, and Kendall laughed. "You didn't really think I'd keep her in your reach, did you?"

"They won't keep her," Cat rasped, shaking her head. "She's been under *my* control for years. She brought me victims. She's just as much a killer as I am."

Kendall arched a brow. "She's not a killer. You had her convinced you would hurt her brother." Lowering her voice, Kendall asked, "But I've got to wonder. I talked to that boy. Now, I'm not psychic. But I can sense the power. And what I feel from him, it's amazing. You couldn't touch him, could you, Catling?"

Cat snarled at Kendall. Kendall braced herself for an attack, but it didn't come. Finally, Kendall realized that Cat couldn't touch her, not here. Wherever *here* was.

Smiling broadly, Kendall asked, "That's it, isn't it? He's too strong for you, isn't he? A little boy, and you can't get inside his mind. How old is he? Nine? Ten? Makes me wonder just how powerful you are."

Cat's face contorted into an ugly mask and she hissed, a sound that didn't sound even remotely human. "Like *you* are so powerful. All of you. Foolish Hunters. You don't know what power is." Her sky blue eyes narrowed down to slits as she stalked closer to Kendall. "Power is reaching inside yourself, finding the part of you that is truly evil and embracing it. Letting it become you. I've found that inside myself. I've let it become me and I've embraced what it's made me into, and it's made me powerful. Evil, that's what power is, Kendall. Damn Hunters, all you do is hide from it."

Kendall stared at Cat for a long second, and then she started to laugh. "Evil? Is that how you see yourself? Oh, Catling. Darling, you've done some terrible, wicked things in life, but what you are is *weak*. You didn't want to rise above that monster that lives inside the vampire. Something inside you shattered during the Change and you didn't want to fight it. Now true evil—I've seen that. I've faced it, and it's stained something inside me forever. You're miserable and pathetic, and the world will be better with you gone. Killing you will tear something inside of me, but you fall just a little shy of *true* evil."

Cat's face flushed with fury. Kendall felt pity move through her. All her life Cat had wanted to succeed at something. She wanted to make her mark somehow. Her life had ended before she had been able to do it as a mortal. She hadn't been able to do it as a Hunter. And she didn't have it inside of her to do it as the bad guy. After her death, only Kendall would mourn her. Only Kendall would remember her.

"It's over, Cat."

"If it's over," Cat whispered, "then I'll take you with me."

Kendall felt the tension in the air mounting, much like all the years ago in England, in the cold, clear predawn of morning when she had found the monster that lay below the surface Cat presented to the world. She knew a strike was coming, but she didn't know how to guard against it.

The tension mounted and mounted.

And then it was simply—gone.

The pain Kendall expected to feel exploding through her head never came. Cat still stood in front of her, staring at her with a dumbfounded look on her face. "So you lie from time to time after all," Cat said after a long moment.

Kendall shook her head. "I've never told you a single lie, Cat."

"The only thing that could keep me from using my power on you is if Analise was near and protecting you."

Arching a brow, Kendall just shrugged. "Analise is at Excelsior. Vax took her there himself."

An odd smile curved Cat's mouth, one that Kendall couldn't quite read. "Well, we'll just have to see about that, then, won't we?"

The tension mounted again, and though the pain didn't come, Kendall did feel herself flying this time. She sucked in air instinctively to scream, but couldn't.

And by the time she could, Kendall found herself laying flat on her back and staring straight up at the sky.

As she slowly sat up, her vision swam in and out of focus and her stomach started to roil nauseatingly. Bloody hell, could a vampire get sick? Kendall moaned, pressing one hand to her temple. Her head ached and throbbed. What in the hell had Cat done?

Cat shot up from the floor and screeched, her hands fisting in the butter gold of her hair. The sound echoed in the small underground room. She tore out fistfuls of her own hair and the pain only added to her fury. *She* didn't want to feel pain. She wanted to inflict it. On Mary Kendall.

How dare that bitch threaten her?

Worse, how in the bloody hell had Kendall been able to resist Cat's power? When Cat had sensed the presence of another vampire, something inside of her had told her it was her sire. Instinct, she supposed.

She'd reached out, trying to get an idea where the meddlesome bitch was at, and to Cat's surprise and delight, Kendall had been meditating. To meditate, one had to lower their guard. Not much, but it was just enough to let Cat slide inside Kendall's mind.

It *should* have been enough to let Cat take control.

So why in the hell hadn't she been able to?

The answer to that, Cat didn't know.

She'd even tried the psychic equivalent of a sucker punch on Kendall. Cat had hurt her before. She should have been able to now. The power she'd been building up should have hit Kendall hard, weakened her.

Not that Cat really *needed* Kendall to be weakened in order to beat her. Cat assured herself of that.

But Kendall deserved to feel weak and helpless. The bitch deserved to suffer.

But it had backfired on Cat. When she'd tried to strike out at Kendall, the power had flown out and Cat had waited to hear Kendall's agonized scream of pain. That pain would have fed Cat's power, almost as well as a vein.

The pain never came though, and instead, the power sank into the ground and left Cat drained. It was almost like Kendall had some sort of shield around her. But that wasn't possible.

Damn her. Cat started to pace, gnawing on a fingernail absently. She'd never known Kendall to lie. She hadn't actually been physically facing Kendall, so she couldn't determine if there were any physical signs that might tell if Kendall was lying, a change in heartbeat, breathing—or Cat could sense something psychically.

But she'd sensed nothing. And they hadn't been together physically. Just on a psychic plane.

So likely Analise was exactly where Kendall said she was. Excelsior. That infuriated Cat. Cat had tried to enter Brendain. Brendain was Excelsior's English predecessor.

Cat hadn't been good enough for those hallowed halls, but that little treacherous bitch was welcome in the home of the Hunters. As was her brother. But that wasn't any news to Cat. Cat had always known that would happen. That power that she'd seen so ripe inside of him would call to them—he would lead them to her. She'd planned to see the boy dead before he got much older. Too old and she wouldn't be able to use him as a bargaining tool against Analise anymore.

But if Analise wasn't protecting Kendall, who was? Kendall couldn't be doing it. She didn't have any kind of psychic power, just the mind control gifts that all vampires had. Cat knew that Kendall's gifts were powerful, but that shouldn't have been able to shield her against a psychic attack.

A sharp pain lanced through her finger, and she looked down, staring at her nail. "Bugger!" Fucking manicure was ruined. The nail had been raggedly chewed down to the quick and blood oozed sullenly. She licked the blood away slowly, her fangs emerging.

The hunger burned through her.

Cat needed to feed.

The failed attack on Kendall had weakened her.

Dawn was too close to risk going outside. But that didn't bother Cat. She could always bring prey to her.

CHAPTER 12

KANE parked in front of the dilapidated old building and climbed out. As he started down the alley, and for the back entrance, he felt something roll through the air. He stopped, bracing his back against the crumbling brick wall. Fuck, his head had always felt a little over full, but lately it was getting worse.

The pushing increased and he focused, concentrating on his breathing, on his heartbeat until they both slowed down and leveled out. As that happened, the external force that tried to take over his mind seemed to weaken and by the time he was steady again, that force had faded altogether.

Shoving away from the wall, he grumbled to himself, "I don't have time for this right now." Right now, he had to worry about Kendall.

He just hoped to hell this crazy plan of hers wasn't setting her up for pain. He was going to have to watch her like a hawk. Yeah, he had blankets in the back and she could settle down on the floor with one of them over her. And if worse came to worse, he'd just empty out the special storage unit in the back. Yeah, he might have some explaining to do if a cop saw his stash of weapons, but he *could* explain them, and all legally. He'd rather do that than risk Kendall getting hurt.

Kane still didn't like the plan.

Rounding the corner, he checked the dark alley as he moved toward the door. He liked this way much better than the very exposed fire escape. Not to mention the ten-foot leap it required to get onto the landing. Kendall had done it in the blink of an eye.

"This is my life," he muttered to himself. Kane shook his head. Just a little over two years ago, he and Duke had been very content as they chased down drug dealers and rapists.

Now he was paired up with a vigilante vampire as they hunted down a murdering vampire. If he tried to explain his life to the average person, they'd have him committed.

A grin flashed across his face as he jogged up the stairs.

His life had become insane. He could die in the next twenty-four hours. Kane was pretty damned certain he had lost his mind, thinking he had any chance of helping Kendall face a vampire bitch that had killed more people than Kane had probably saved in all his careers combined.

So why in the hell did it feel so fucking right?

Kendall. Plain and simple.

Every time he touched her, every time he kissed her, felt the soft satin of her skin under his fingertips, it felt perfect. Even just holding her while he slept made his entire life feel more complete.

Reaching a landing, he paused. *Shit.*

He slumped back against the wall. His head thudded against the graffiti-stained concrete, but Kane never even noticed. He was in love with her. He had gone past the falling point and was already there.

Completely and totally, irrevocably in love with her.

At his side, one hand closed into a useless fist. "Damn it."

Then a second later a grin split his face. What the hell. He had already known it was happening. What did it matter that it *had* happened?

What mattered was living through this, and convincing

Kendall that they belonged together. It didn't matter to him
that she would live on long after he'd turned old and gray,
that he'd be dust in the ground—well, it didn't matter to
him. He'd have to convince her whatever happened would
be worth it, so long as they spent what time God gave them
together.

Starting back up the stairs, he chuckled to himself. First
he had to see how she felt about him. If she didn't have similar feelings, he had to fix that.

But Kane was pretty sure she did. It wasn't indifference
he saw in her eyes when she looked at him.

And hadn't she already said the reason she didn't want
him with her when she faced Cat was because she didn't
want to lose him? That was a start, right? He cleared the last
two stairs with a jump, suddenly desperate to see her, to jerk
her against him and kiss her. He wanted to tell her; now
wasn't the time, though.

Kane didn't want her distracted from Cat. She needed to
focus on her target. But when it was over . . .

As he reached out to shove open the door, he felt it again.
The weird external force from before. It felt different though
this time. It was almost like it had a scent—a feel.

A woman.

This time, she was searching.

Searching for *him*.

Kane didn't know what in the hell this was. Grinding his
palms against his head, he focused. He dredged up some of
the goriest, grimmest memories as that external force tried
to shove its way inside his mind. This wasn't like what
Kendall had done years ago. She had wanted him to sleep.

This one was calling him. "No." Kane repeated the word
over and over again, slamming his head back against the
wall. The pain bloomed in his head and the fog there cleared
just a little.

The summoning increased, and desperate, Kane dropped
to a crouch, drawing his knife from his boot. He dragged it
slowly across his palm, hissing at the pain. Blood started to

trickle down his palm and wrist. "Get out of my head," Kane rasped.

There was a sense of anger and surprise, and the pushing increased, but Kane had better control now. Before the pain in his hand could fade, he closed his fist, digging his nails into the cut.

It wasn't just a calling now. This time, it was a woman's voice. Soft and sweet, it echoed in his mind as she murmured, *Come to me . . . I need you . . .*

Kane said flatly, "Get the fuck out of my head, bitch."

AGNES stared into the mirror, the surface clouded and fogged. Oh, he was a handsome one. And stubborn, she mused, pursing her lips as she listened to him snarl at Cat. "I wonder if I'm really needed at all."

But she wasn't going to risk it.

Reaching out, she picked up the silver knife on her dressing table and pricked the tip of her finger. A fat drop of blood welled, and she pressed it to the mirror. It glowed, the clouds fogging the surface swirling as the magick worked its will.

"A wall, Kane. Picture a wall. You have the power inside you, you just need the training."

She watched him stiffen. Saw the shock register on his face as he heard her voice. Could almost hear his internal battle as he tried to figure out what he was supposed to do. "Listen to me, boy. You've got a well of power inside of you. What you decide to do with it is up to you, so long as *she* doesn't get ahold of you. If she does, though, can you imagine the power it will give her? How much pleasure she'll have taunting Kendall with what she's done to you?"

That turned it. She could see it. His hands clenched into fists. "What do I do?" he asked stiffly.

"Just build a wall. All you have you to do is think of one, something strong and impenetrable. Something she can't get through."

Catharine was pushing at him again, Agnes sensed it. In the reflection of the mirror, she could see his face pale, feel the mental agony Cat caused.

There was more, a physical pain of some sorts. He'd hurt himself, caused some kind of damage to himself, something to focus on besides Catharine's call. *Smart lad,* Agnes murmured to herself.

A physical pain was the wisest course of action for somebody so untrained. Agnes whispered softly, "We have to get you trained, boy." Then she focused.

Doing what she could, Agnes buffered Cat's touch, but there was only so much she could do. But she did what she could, and she knew a bit about Cat's power.

Agnes was, after all, a witch. Witch power was a little different from psychic power. But Agnes knew enough and she knew when Kane had succeeded in shielding himself from Cat. The chaotic mess of his thoughts calmed and the riotous colors of his emotions had calmed out to a level blue. Blue, she should have known. He was a warrior, through and through.

Kane had been unconsciously shielding for awhile now. Agnes couldn't tell when his power had been awakened. Not his entire life. He'd been latent, otherwise his shielding would have been more refined than this. Something triggered the power though.

Agnes watched through the mirror. Kane's body slumped back against the wall as the tension drained out of him. "You did just fine, lad," she murmured.

He lifted his head as though he was searching for her. "Who are you?" he murmured.

"Just an old friend of Kendall's." A smile creased her lined face, and she chuckled. "A very old friend."

A scowl darkened his face. Agnes laughed. *My, my, my, Mary. What a sexy one you picked out.* Agnes had to admit her heart rate kicked up a little at the dark look on his lean, handsome face. Oh, but she did envy Kendall. Young, well, relatively speaking, with the love of her life right in front of her—instead of forever lost to her. "How about a name for this very old friend? She's only a couple of centuries old. She's bound to have made several friends."

Agnes laughed. As she reached up to touch the mirror, she murmured, "Oh, aye. But I'm older than Kendall. Much older, lad. And you'll be meeting me soon enough. Go on to her now."

With that, she swiped her hand across the mirror, breaking the line of blood and power that connected her to Kane.

CAT felt him break away from her with a suddenness that left her floundering. But instead of being infuriated, she was intrigued. Another psychic. And a man. If that rough, sexy growl of his was anything to go by, then he was definitely one she wanted.

"I'll find you, love," Cat purred, her lids drooping low. And she just might keep him around a while. His power was raw, with an untamed feeling. Untrained.

That one had potential. An untrained psychic would be so much easier to control than Analise and the hateful little brat Brad. That pathetic mother of theirs hadn't had much power, but she had known how to train them and had done a damn fine job of it.

But this one—a latent. Had to be. That was the only way to explain why a grown man would have that much raw power inside of him.

Cat wanted to know, though, how he had suddenly been able to cut her off. He should have come walking right to her waiting arms. That he hadn't, puzzled her. Part of her was tempted to try again, but her common sense interfered. She needed to feed. That was why she had reached out to begin with, trying to call somebody to her. When she had felt that ripe, rich power she hadn't been able to resist reaching for it.

Damn it, she wanted him. A sexual hunger burned alongside the vampire's hunger. Without even seeing him, Cat wanted that man. Blowing out a breath, Cat spun away from the door. The night was *not* going her way.

One thing was certain, though. She needed to feed. Kendall would come hunting hard and fast for her come sunset. Cat wasn't going to bet on having time to feed before Kendall got there. Although it would be such fun having a toy there to play with right in front of Kendall. Make her suffer a little.

Now that could be fun.

Using her mind, she reached out. There were people around, just now leaving bars, or rushing to work. The closest mind was a tired one, female sadly. Aching feet, sore back. Muttering about a bitchy boss at work and worried about an odd noise in the engine.

"Well, pet, soon you won't have anybody to complain about," Cat murmured.

The woman fell silent, and under Cat's unspoken command eased her car to the side of the road. The road was still quiet and nobody saw as she climbed from the car and walked into the park, crossing the grass. Cat stayed connected with the woman's mind, using the human's eyes and ears to make sure nobody saw or heard anything as Cat led her prey in.

Wouldn't do to have anybody see this woman walking into the park and then have a family member call the police just before Cat was ready to disappear. The woman came into view, and Cat smiled. She was young, her eyes wide and frightened. Cat could always make it so that her prey never even knew what was happening, but where was the fun in that?

There was so much more pleasure when they were terrified. Fear made the blood riper, gave it a wine-rich flavor that not even sex could equal.

Reaching out, Cat linked fingers with the woman and murmured, "Tell me your name."

Tears rolled down her face as she whimpered, "Marci. Please . . . please . . . please don't do whatever . . . it is you are going to do. I've got a little girl. I'm all she has."

Cat laughed. "Hush now, Marci. I'm just a little hungry— for now." But those softly spoken words pricked a conscience Cat had forgotten she even had. Without acknowledging why, Cat used her mind to silence Marci and keep her from talking as she closed the door.

Moving behind Marci, Cat brushed aside the shoulder-length hair and struck. As hot, rich young blood filled her belly, strength flooded her, and for a few minutes, the whispering ghost of the woman she used to be was silenced.

Not for long though. It only took a soft mental nudge to send Marci into a deep sleep. Should have just drained her, or broken her neck.

Every time she looked at the slender woman with the strawberry blonde hair, she kept seeing those tear-drenched hazel eyes and hearing that trembling voice, *"I'm all she has . . ."*

Cat had heard those words before. From a vampire. Cat hadn't known what Mary Kendall was. Oh, she'd known the woman raising her was different, but she didn't know what. Mary employed a nanny, Laura, who cared for Cat and provided schooling for her. Cat didn't know why she only saw Mary early in the morning and late in the evening, but Laura was always there.

But even with Laura and Mary, Cat was lonely, so lonely. Laura often took her to Brendain, and she played with the children there, but she knew she didn't quite fit in. Nowhere. Cat didn't fit in anywhere.

Late one night, while Cat was supposed to be sleeping, she crept from her bed, past Laura. Voices had awakened her. People often came to talk to Mary, but this voice was one that made Cat uncomfortable. Agnes didn't like Cat. The old woman hadn't ever said anything to Cat, but she could feel it. There was just something about the way the woman looked at her with those faded blue eyes.

It was *her* voice that had woken Cat. And it was Agnes that was speaking now. "Mary love, if you are truly so concerned about Catharine being so lonely, perhaps you should send her to London. I have a house in the city. Both Laura and the child would be very comfortable there. She could go to school there, be around more children her age—"

"Agnes, I cannot. She needs me." Mary's voice had sounded tired and weary, like she hadn't slept well. "I'm all she has."

Agnes had sighed and said nothing else. Cat had never been sent away to school. No, Mary had kept her there at home, and it was five more years, shortly after her twelfth birthday, before she learned exactly why Mary and all the others around her were so different.

There was a soft sighing sound and Cat brought her mind back to the present, spinning around to stare at the woman that was responsible for her walk down memory lane.

"Bloody hell," Cat rasped, clenching her hands into tight fists. This was the absolute last thing she needed. Long-suppressed memories of what her life had been like *before* she had been Changed. Of Mary Kendall. Not Kendall. Kendall was the hateful bitch that had let Cat down, the bitch that hadn't saved her. The one that hadn't made sure Cat had gotten into Brendain, instead cursing her into a life of uselessness.

Until Cat had saved herself.

"Your fault!" Cat hissed, taking one step toward Marci, rage boiling inside her. *"Your fault!"* But before the rage could spill out and she could leap on the sleeping woman and tear her apart, again the memory of Marci's tremulous voice, *I'm all she has,* echoed through her mind, and Cat spun away, and tears rolled down her face as she fell to her knees.

I̶T was relatively cool and dark in the parking garage adjacent to the Bethesda hospital. With her head pillowed on her arm, Kendall drowsed. She was too edgy for a deep sleep, but vampires could go days without that. When they were on a Hunt, a few hours of these light, drowsing naps were really all vampires needed to sustain them.

Well, she needed a little more.

Even though she slept, Kendall was aware of him, listening to the rhythmic sound of Kane's heart. It was that soothing sound that had lulled her into this peaceful light state somewhere between dreams and waking.

She heard him sigh, and the sound of it made her smile even in her sleep. He was bored. A man of action, Kane was. He was bored to tears, sitting in a parking garage while she slept in the cool darkness behind him. But he did it for her, keeping her safe. Her mind worked busily, even while she dozed.

Kendall would have been fine. All he would have had to do was park the car here. With his security system, nobody would steal the SUV. The heat would have been uncomfortable, but it wouldn't have bothered her that much.

Too much of a gentleman, although she imagined it would have annoyed him a great deal if anybody tried to tell him that.

She wanted him back here in this cool, darkened space with her. The windows were tinted so heavily a person could barely see inside —nobody would know if he climbed back there and lay with her while she rested. Kendall wanted to feel his arms wrap around her, his heartbeat against her back as she rested.

That was what she wanted——when he held her, she had all she needed in life.

The one thought hit her like a splash of cold water, and it jolted her right out of her resting state. Her lids flew open and she lay on her back, staring straight in front of her.

All I need.

What a bitter, sorry joke life had pulled on her.

This man had come to mean damn near everything to her, and she'd known him for such a short time. She was in love with him. And if she didn't succeed in killing Cat, she'd lose him.

There was no guarantee that Kendall was strong enough to stop Cat. She hadn't been before. She should have made *sure* Cat was dead that night. But she hadn't. Instead she had focused on the child they'd taken from Cat.

Others had paid for it.

Duke had paid. Analise and Brad had paid. Countless oth-

ers. Kane could suffer for it. All because Kendall had been
too weak. Because she couldn't even think of Cat without
remembering the child. And such weaknesses were just the
thing Cat loved to exploit.

The child Kendall had loved was gone. Perhaps even then,
Cat hadn't been what Kendall had thought . . . had hoped.

All those doubts and fears circled around inside her mind.
Slowly, she worked at blocking them off. Couldn't keep
them inside her like this—they made her too vulnerable.

She needed to focus, but there was no way she was going
to try meditation again, not after this morning.

Distantly, she was aware of Cat in the back of her mind.
She had been, ever since Cat had connected their minds this
morning. It was the first time, though, that Kendall had been
mentally aware of the younger vampire in a hundred years.

Not since the night of the fire. Cat had somehow damp-
ened that awareness that night a century ago, dulled it in
some way. But whatever had happened early this morning
had reawakened Kendall's awareness of the vampire she had
sired.

Rest, she told herself silently. *Just rest.*

Blanking her mind, she focused on the one thing that she
knew wouldn't cause her distress. The slow, steady sound of
Kane's heartbeat.

.

K ANE knew the second Kendall woke up. He waited for
her to say something, but she never did. Something was
bothering her. What it was, he didn't know and since she
wasn't in any hurry to talk about it, he guessed he wasn't
going to find out just yet.

She needed rest, though, not for him to ask two hundred
fifty-six different questions about why she had woken up in
the first place. Kane had been dozing off and on most of the
morning and right now, he was hungry. It was close to two
in the afternoon though. Too much sun in the sky for his
preference, even though Kendall had assured him if he

wanted to drive around, she'd be fine with the blanket over her head.

No, he'd just eat a granola bar for now and drink a bottle of water.

Later in the afternoon he'd run to the fast-food restaurant down the road and get a couple of tacos and a coke.

Damn it, though, he was craving a steak, a baked potato the size of Texas, and a salad. A couple of beers. A soft bed that he didn't have to pay for by the night and a few weeks uninterrupted that he could spend doing all sorts of unimaginable things to Kendall's soft, sweet body.

Reaching into the glove compartment, he grabbed one of the wrapped granola bars he kept on hand and tore it open. The bottle of water in the console was still cool, thanks to the air conditioner, and he drained what was left in it. He shifted in the seat and draped his left arm on the edge of the door.

The bandage he'd covered his palm with caught his eye and he stilled, flexing his hand a little. What was going on inside his head anymore? It wasn't his imagination, he knew that. There was something happening that logic and sense just couldn't explain, and it had been going on for awhile now, but lately, it was getting worse.

Hell, maybe that was the wrong way to put it. It was getting better . . . clearer . . . easier. Blowing out a frustrated breath, Kane clenched his left hand into a fist. The jolt of pain that arrowed up his arm did nothing to clear his clouded thoughts this time, though. This time, it was caused by his own confusion.

Kane really wished he knew what in the hell was going on. Part of him wanted to talk to Kendall about it. Even if she didn't know, chances are she'd know who would. But this was the last thing she needed right now.

After they dealt with Cat.

If he lived through it.

The thought that came to him next was odd. It was almost like it was coming from somebody else. He was going to live through it. Irrevocably changed forever, but he'd live.

So would Kendall.

The only question left though, was would they be able to live with each other, because he knew pretty damn well he didn't want to live without her.

The need to climb back into the back with her and just wrap his arms around her was almost overwhelming. He wanted to feel her against him, feel the slow, almost immeasurable beat of her heart, hear the occasional sigh she made while she rested. Kane just wanted to touch her, hold her while he could. Know that for now, she was safe and whole and here with him.

Lifting his gaze, he looked into the rearview mirror but he couldn't see anything behind the back seat. He could smell her though, the soft, sweet scent of her body.

Hunger rolled through him and Kane groaned, forcing it aside, making himself focus. He couldn't think when he had thoughts of that luscious body on the brain. For the next sixteen to eighteen hours, what he needed to think about was keeping that sweet body alive and well.

Sleeping was out of the question, but he had to clear his mind.

Closing his eyes, he shoved everything out of his mind but the job. He'd done this before. Used to be old hat—every time before he and Duke had gone out on a job, if something had been troubling him, he'd take awhile and clear his head. Didn't matter if it had been a bad day, or if he was tracking down a nineteen-year-old kid who had killed his dad because the old man had hit him one too many times. A job was a job.

Cat was just another job to do, and he'd do it just like every other last job that had been thrown at him.

She was just a little crazier, a little more bloodthirsty than average.

As he forced his tense muscles to relax, the hunger raging inside him slowly subsided. The chaos in his mind calmed, and without Kane even realizing it, his mind started to drift.

He saw a woman.

She was young. Barely more than a girl. There were dried

tear tracks on her face and she curled up against a wall, silent and still, staring in front of her. His field of vision widened and he saw what the woman saw. This other woman terrified the young woman. As Kane stared at her, he could understand why.

The woman was a blonde, her eyes a cool, icy blue. There was nothing remotely human in her gaze. There was hatred and fear and self-disgust, all swirling together in a riotous mess. As she paced back and forth, she kept sending the cringing girl evil glances, as though the girl was somehow responsible.

"Your fucking fault," the woman lisped. When she spoke, Kane saw the bulging incisors, a certain sign of just how enraged she was. Most vampires Kane had seen kept their fangs retracted unless they were feeding. Rage and lust brought them out. And Kane didn't think what he saw in her eyes was lust.

The woman on the floor sobbed, but she muffled the sound against her hand and buried her face against her knees as she tried not to make anymore noise. Now the vampire hardly even seemed aware of her as she resumed her pacing. "What did they do to me?" she muttered, reaching up and smacking the ball of her hand against her temple. "I don't care for this weakness inside me."

As she whirled around, her eyes landed once more on the terrified girl, blazing, glowing with rage, and Kane felt the useless anger build up inside him. *Leave her alone!* The words formed inside his mind, but he couldn't give them form. He couldn't talk. Couldn't move . . . where was he . . .

Even as he tried to figure out what in the hell was going on, the woman stilled. As she lifted her eyes and turned to gaze at him, Kane felt the power of the look clear through to his soul.

"Well, well, well . . . what do we have here . . . a wanderer," she purred.

There was something familiar about that voice.

It was the same voice that had tried to call out to him that morning. Before that old woman had whispered to him about a wall.

Before fear even had a chance to start to build, he stopped fighting and just replied, *Hello, Cat.* His words had no sound—he just thought them, but from the look on her face, he knew she heard him.

He could feel her surprise. "You know who I am."

Yes. For awhile now.

She cocked her head. "How curious. You can't possibly be a Hunter. They wouldn't send out one so untried, so untrained. You will be so easy—all you are is food to me. Why would they do that?"

I'm no Hunter. But I wouldn't die as easy as you think. And if I am just food—well then I'll make damn sure you choke on me as I go down.

Cat laughed. "Oh, aren't you a cocky one. Why don't you come to me now?"

Kane shook his head. *I don't think so.*

Cat's mouth curved into an evil smile. "Oh, but I do." She turned away, sauntering over to the girl. She looked even more terrified now. The sight of the woman talking to thin air had probably not done much for her state of mind. Kane stiffened as Cat jerked the girl to her feet, arching her neck in a way he knew must be excruciating.

"Either come to me . . . *now,* or I'll kill her. Slowly, painfully. And I'll make sure you hear her scream."

A soft sob escaped the struggling woman's lips as she fought uselessly against Cat. Cat lowered her head, nuzzling the woman's cheek. "So what is your answer, lover? Are you coming? Or do I kill her?"

No answer came.

Cat snarled as his presence disappeared as abruptly as it had appeared.

Damn him!

Something hot and wet splashed on her hand, and she jerked away from Marci as though the girl was on fire. Shoving her to the floor, she spat, "Get away from me!"

Turning away, she started to tear at her hair, digging her nails into her scalp. There were little voices inside there, soft mocking ones, the echoes of the conscience she thought she had lost so long ago.

Faces rose up to taunt her—so many people she had killed. So many lost lives.

"Kendall, you pathetic whining bitch, what did you do to me?" she hissed, kicking at a fallen bit of debris. It went flying across the room, hitting the stone wall with a force that made it crumble.

"Voices, too many voices. Are they even my own?" Cat muttered, shaking her head.

She sucked in a breath of air and tried to calm herself, but even that didn't help. All it did was bring in the scent of blood and fear.

Marci was hiding again, cowering against the wall, not even looking at Cat. As though that might help. Cat sneered. Hell, it might have, if Cat hadn't been so pissed off. But she wanted blood. She wanted a fight. She wanted fury and desperation and pain—she wanted Kendall, on her back, bleeding and pleading for mercy.

And Cat wouldn't give her any.

Then she wanted that man. She would hunt him down, fuck him, and feed on him. Hurt him a little. Not much, just a little. Maybe that power-rich blood would hush these damn voices inside her head and she could think a little.

Yes, she needed to think some.

She was going to have to run.

The Hunters knew she was here by now.

They wouldn't be here tonight, Cat didn't think. So she had to get rid of Kendall, find her man, and get out of town, tonight. "Got to move quick," she mumbled, nodding. Unkempt hair had fallen into her eyes and she shoved it back, staring wildly into the distance. She didn't see the gray stone walls of the old storage building that surrounded her, though.

She saw Kendall. On her back, clutching at her throat as

a fountain of red spilled forth. Cat would make her bleed first. Then she'd cut out Kendall's heart and burn it. Leave her corpse for the world to find.

The Hunters may well become the hunted. Once the mortals found out there were people like Kendall around, they wouldn't be able to Hunt as easily. Losing their anonymity would take away some of their power.

Cat smiled. She liked that. And killing Kendall would hurt them. Hurt that odious bitch witch, Agnes. Bloody hell, Cat hated Agnes. That old hag had always seen too damned much with her eyes, seen clear through Cat.

Now she could mourn Kendall, and Cat hoped it hurt her like hell. Maybe the grief would kill her.

Once Kendall was dead, Cat would find the psychic. Shouldn't be too hard. His power was swelling out of control. That alone would beckon to Cat almost uncontrollably once she had fed. It was just the hunger making her power so erratic.

Nothing else.

Cat gnawed on another nail as she tried to convince herself of that.

Nothing else.

The hunger rose to whisper tauntingly to her, *Go . . . feed us . . . she's just right there . . . so young, so ripe . . .*

But every time Cat so much as tried to move toward Marci, she kept hearing those words again: *I'm all she has.*

Damn it all to hell and back, she couldn't kill that girl. Might as well let her go. But she wouldn't. Kendall wouldn't know she wasn't going to kill the girl. And she'd make a wonderful hostage.

And maybe, just maybe, the man would come wondering in. Two hostages were even better than one. Especially when one had power . . .

For hours, Cat paced, gnawing her nails down to the quick and tracking the sun on its journey through the sky mentally. As afternoon turned to evening, she grew more and more agitated.

Hunger raged inside her. The sun burning outside kept her

caged, and she didn't dare try to draw another human inside to feed on, not so soon after grabbing this whining bitch. Cat couldn't waste her energy wiping her memory and letting her go either, so she was stuck with her, feeling those frightened eyes staring at her. Listening to that erratic heartbeat, the sobs Marci tried so hard to silence.

Just kill her—feed. You will feel so much better, the hunger crooned to her. The hunger, always the hunger. It was so seductive. It had risen within her like a siren's call the very first night she'd awoken as a vampire, and it hadn't taken long for her to give into it.

Oh, Cat had hidden it. At first, she left the lands of Brendain when she'd gone looking for more than just the willing throats offered by the weres, shifters, and witches that populated the area around the home of the Council. It hadn't been often, either. Once a month, maybe twice. Too often, and she knew Mary would find out.

Soon, though, the need to feel that wild rush had become more than Cat could bear. She'd been heading south to Brighton when she'd seen him, a young, handsome fool, stumbling home drunk after spending a little too much time at the inn with his ale. He'd been singing—her lips curved upwards as she remembered. His voice had been low and mellow.

Ah, he'd been a handsome one. Even drunk as he was. When she'd slid out of the darkness in front of him, the only thing she'd had on her mind at first was sex. Mary so hated it when she came home smelling of sex and sweat. Part of Cat could understand that, but the other part didn't care. That part was the winner that night.

He'd stared at her, startled as she moved closer and wrapped her arms around his neck.

"I must have had a bit more to drink than I thought," he murmured just as she covered his mouth with hers.

They barely made it into the grassy area beside the road before she jerked his trousers open. He stared at her with bemused eyes as she jerked up her skirt and the single petticoat she'd put on for the fun she'd planned that night. Smiling naughtily at him, she straddled him and took him inside, pumping her hips up and down, laughing as he groaned out, "Bloody hell, this is like no dream I've ever had in my life."

Cat laughed. "This is no dream, love."

He started to reach for her and Cat caught his hands, slamming them back down, pinning him to the ground as she started to ride him harder and faster. His eyes widened a little, but seconds later he was groaning again, arching up into her. She rode him until they both came, and still she continued to move against him, until he'd come a second time. Once she'd felt him empty inside her once more, she relaxed against him, cuddling against his chest and releasing his hands.

His arms came around her and Cat smiled. "That was nice."

He just laughed. "Aye, that it was. Does my dream lover have a name?" he whispered as he stroked her hair.

She just made a soft, humming sound under her breath as she turned her face a little more into his neck, licking at the pulsating vein there. He chuckled, murmuring, "You'll have to give me a moment, pet. You wore me to the bone."

Cat just smiled, nuzzling him again. "That's fine. You rest . . . and I'll . . ."

She struck then. She felt the shock roll through him, felt him stiffen. His arms clutched at her and his hands tried to pull her away. She caught his hands and pinned him down, her jaws working against his neck as the hot splash of his blood pooled in her belly. It was hot and potent, almost too heady from all the ale he'd taken in that night. Combined with the energy she still had buzzing through her from the sex, Cat almost felt drugged.

He continued to fight her, desperation giving him strength, and she had to put a little more effort into holding him down. Sinking her teeth harder into him, she groaned and started to pump against him again. Bugger—it made her belly heat, just feeling that fear inside of him. As her desire rose, something started to pour from her in waves, a scent that flooded that air.

The man underneath her wasn't immune to it. Even as he struggled, he reacted to her, his cock hardening and lengthening once more. He fought against her and fucked her at the same time. Tears rolled down his face and he begged her to let him go, cursed her and praised her all in the same breath.

It was the most intense moment of Cat's entire life. But before she reached climax, his struggles slowed, his heartbeat started to falter. Cat sat up, staring down at him. A few drops of blood flowed sluggishly down his neck as he stared up at her. "I'm not dreaming, am I?" he asked hoarsely.

Cat shrugged. "No."

His lids drooped. When they lifted, she suspected he wasn't seeing her at all. "Beth . . . where did you go?" A soft sigh left him, and then his eyes closed once more. A few minutes later, he stopped breathing altogether.

Cat didn't bother hiding his body. He'd be found sooner or later anyway. Brendan was twenty or thirty miles away. Hunters were always patrolling around her. He'd be found. Why bother?

She rose, staring at his handsome, still face. She hadn't ever actually drained anybody before. Oh, she'd fed on plenty of unwilling victims. Not that any of them ever remembered it. Her mental gifts were far above what even Mary knew. She'd surpassed what Mary could do months ago, not that Cat had let Mary in on that.

Wiping memories clean was child's play.

With a giggle, she nudged the leg of the dead man on the ground. Well, she wouldn't have to bother with this one, would she?

Cat sagged against the wall, bracing herself with her hand to keep from falling. She had laughed . . . lifting her head, she stared at her reflection in the mirror. She had *laughed*. If she had found joy in killing before, and often, then why in the bloody hell was it bothering her now?

And it was bothering her all right. Cat felt sick inside, sick to her very soul, and she couldn't even understand *why*.

Who was Beth . . .

That question circled over and over in her mind. The strength seemed to drain out of her, and she fell to the ground, burying her face against her knees and sobbing, deep wrenching sobs that hurt her throat.

Repeatedly, she asked herself, "How could I have laughed?"

But there was nobody there to offer her an answer, except the frightened woman who stared at her with both terror and confusion in her eyes.

CHAPTER 13

Agnes pushed inside Vax's room without even knocking. He growled at her as he opened one eye. Without so much as speaking, he flopped over on his other side, pulled up his blanket, and tried to go back to sleep.

"Get up, lad. It's time."

"Get out."

She just laughed. "You didn't really think your part in all of this was done, did you?"

"Part in what?" he grumbled.

"Kendall is going to need your help."

He groaned and sat up. He could say no to a lot of things, but not when it involved Kendall. "Kendall can fight her own battles."

Agnes smiled at him. "It's not the battle she'll need you for, lad. It's what happens after."

Vax scowled at her. "What are you talking about, you old witch?"

"You'll see in awhile, you young witch, now get up. It's almost sunset, and I don't move as fast as I used to."

Vax sighed but rose from the bed. The blankets fell away

from his nude body and he glanced down with a scowl before looking pointedly at Agnes. She just grinned at him.
"Give an old lady her entertainment, Vax. It's not like I get
much else."

And Vax actually blushed.

As he walked past, very quickly, toward the bathroom, he
heard her chuckling.

"Crazy old bat," he muttered, shaking his head.

It took less than ten minutes for him to shower, and when
he came striding out, his wet hair was slicked back into a tail
that streamed half way down his back. As he buttoned up a
white shirt over his still damp chest, he glanced at Agnes.
She was staring into space, but he had no doubt she was seeing something. Hell, Vax was a witch, but she sometimes
gave him the creeps.

After a few more seconds, she blinked and then turned her
eyes to his. "You ready?"

He dropped to the edge of the bed with a grunt. Jamming
his feet into a pair of boots, he laced them up. The night-
stand at the side of the bed held his weapons. He didn't carry
as many as some Hunters. As a witch, a great many of his
weapons came from inside, but he still liked to be prepared.
He stuck a silver knife into the sheath at his hip, a bottle of
garlic-laced water into a little pouch hanging from his belt
next to a nicely carved wooden knife. Looked a helluva lot
better than a wooden stake. Fire worked a lot better, but it
didn't hurt to be prepared.

Standing, he stared at Agnes and arched a brow. "Where
are we going?"

She smiled and walked slowly over to him. Holding out
her hand, she asked, "To Kendall. Will you do the honors?
I'm a little tired."

Tired, my ass, Vax thought sourly. *What in the hell are
you up to?*

Out loud, he just said, "You're a very aggravating woman,
you know that, Agnes."

She winked at him. "I think I have heard that a time or
two, lad."

Vax sighed. He'd seen close to a hundred and fifty years, and this woman still called him a lad. Shaking his head, he drew her closer. Focusing his mind, he summoned up a mental image of Kendall's face. It was a little trickier doing it the way he preferred to do, but he never liked landing right where a person was immediately. Never tell when he might be landing in a firefight, and with a five-hundred-year-old witch at his side, he definitely didn't want to do that. He didn't know if Agnes was feeling her age yet, but he wasn't taking the chance.

So he used a searching spell. The last safe place . . .

Time and space disappeared around him and both he and Agnes were flung into a vortex. Flying seemed to last forever and no time at all. It was almost impossible to explain to a person that hadn't ever done it. It was exhilarating and terrifying, breath-stealing and nauseating all at once.

When they had solid ground under their feet once more, Vax opened his eyes and stared around them.

A parking garage?

Scowling, he stepped away from Agnes and turned around in a slow circle. He'd seen Kendall in his mind. She'd been resting.

Why in the hell had she been resting in a parking garage? And where was she now? It was still daylight.

K ENDALL adjusted the sunglasses as they once more slid down her nose. They were too big, but that was good. Shielded more of her face that way. Sliding Kane a glance, she asked once more, "Are you okay?"

He looked at her. "Yes. Why do you keep asking?"

As they moved quickly across the old park, she shrugged. "You just look . . . tense."

At that, Kane laughed. "Hell, I look *tense*. I wonder why."

Kendall snorted. "Love, you came chasing after me with nothing more than a knife and a couple of arrows, and I'm every bit as dangerous as Cat is. Right now, you have me on your side and just as many weapons now as you had then. And you didn't look nervous at all when you were after me."

Kane grinned. "Well, part of me still couldn't decide if I wanted to kill you or fuck you. Maybe that's why I wasn't as nervous."

Behind the dark lenses of the sunglasses, Kendall just rolled her eyes.

Kane slid a glance at the sun still visible in the sky. "What about you?"

She shrugged. "I itch. Nothing major."

It helped that she had slid on a hat and a long-sleeved jacket Kane had unearthed from his SUV. That vehicle of his carried everything but the kitchen sink, she suspected.

Their steps slowed as they came within eyesight of the small stone building. Half of it was underground, a narrow flight of steps leading down to the door. Kane gestured to the trees and they headed toward them. Kendall sighed as the shade provided some relief from the unrelenting heat of the sun. Kane moved closer and dipped his head. "I'm going to circle around, see if there's another exit."

Kendall studied the sun's position and then nodded. "Fast." There was no way Cat would come out right now. It would be suicide for the younger vampire. Only vampires with a good two hundred years of age could tolerate sunlight like this. And Kendall needed the protection of the glasses, the jacket, and the hat. Without them, Kendall would have had to wait until later.

Still, even as certain as she was, she stood there nervously, fidgeting with the rolled-up cuffs of the jacket, shifting from one foot to the other until Kane came back into view.

He waited until he was right next to her again before he spoke, lowering his head until he could murmur into her ear. "No other doors. No windows. Something weird about that place. I keep feeling like walking away. And nobody else is around. All these trees, you'd think some people would be here, but the closest families are a good three hundred yards away, in the sunlight."

Kendall murmured, "It's Cat. Part of her magick. Nobody wants to be close to it." She could sense it, but it didn't control her.

"Does she know you're here?"

A humorless smile curved her lips. "Oh, yes." Cat had sensed Kendall some time ago. Kendall had felt the rampant fear flood the younger woman, the desperate helplessness. "She knows."

"Now what?"

But Kendall didn't have time to answer that.

The heavy metal door to the storage building came flying open. "Get the fuck away or I'll kill her!"

The front of the building lay in the shadows and Cat inched halfway up the steps, holding in front of her a sobbing, trembling woman.

Kendall snarled, shrugging off the jacket and tossing the sunglasses and hat to the ground as she moved forward. "Let her go, Cat. You know I can't let you walk away from this."

Most of Cat was hidden by the girl's body, but as Kendall drew closer, she could see half of Cat's face, and she gasped. Cat's eyes were red and swollen, wet with tears. The young woman in front of Cat lifted terrified hazel eyes to stare at Kendall. "Help me, please . . ."

Behind her, Kane whispered, "Oh, fuck."

At the sound of his voice, Cat tensed. Then her eyes widened. The girl fell forward as Cat's grip on her loosened. "Oh, look at what we have here!" Cat said, her voice going from an angry shriek to a cheerful chirp in seconds. "Hello, lover."

Kendall didn't spare Cat or Kane a glance as she focused on the young woman. She still lay sobbing on the stone steps. Kendall focused. She felt the girl's mind calm. Hopefully Cat was too focused on Kane to notice Kendall as she murmured silently into the girl's mind, *Come on . . . come to me.* The girl's eyes glazed as she started to follow Kendall's silent command.

"Mary, you always did have wonderful taste in men. Well, Vax was a bit of a hard-ass," Cat murmured as she stared at Kane with hungry eyes, completely unaware of Marci creeping away.

Kane's voice was level as he replied, "If you're calling

him a hard-ass because he wasn't impressed with you, then consider me in the same category, sugar. You're not my type."

Cat smiled at him, her dimples flashing at him. "What is your type, love?"

Kendall tried to block their voices, watching as the woman on the ground continued to creep away, her eyes rapt on Kendall's face. *That's it, honey . . . don't worry about her,* Kendall assured, keeping Cat in the corner of her eye.

In a bored tone, Kane replied, "It varies, but I've never really liked murdering psychotics, so you're out of luck."

Cat only laughed. "Oh, don't worry. I can make you like whatever I want."

Just a few more feet . . .

"Really." Kane sounded as though he was discussing the weather.

Cat huffed a little. "Boy, don't you know what I am?"

Kane chuckled. "Of course I do. You're crazy—that's all I need to know."

Two feet. Good enough. Bracing her body, Kendall sent a silent prayer heavenward and lunged. The woman sobbed out in relief and lunged for her.

Kendall wrapped her arms around her and whispered, "Hush now, it's okay." Cat hissed and tried to leap for them, but Kendall kicked backward. She grimaced as she landed on her ass, the weight of the woman pinning her to the ground for a moment. The bright sunshine shone down on her face, uncomfortable but not painful yet.

At least not to her. But she squirmed backward before trying to get up, dragging Cat with her. With her hand locked around Kendall's ankle, Cat was slowly forced out of the shadows and into the sun. As bright rays of sun shone down on her hand, the younger vampire hissed with pain. Blisters welled up, and she jerked her hand back.

"You better go put some sunblock on, Catharine dear, if you are going to play with the big kids," Kendall drawled as she rose to her feet and carried the woman over to Kane.

She didn't want to let Kendall go, though. Clinging to

Kendall, she tried to bury her face against Kendall's neck. "It's okay; he won't hurt you."

"Muh-marci," she stammered, her pupils wide, dilated. Going into shock. Kendall looked at one pupil first, then the other, before checking the woman's pulse. Oddly enough, it was much steadier than she'd expected. And Marci's color was normal. She had too much of Cat's scent on her to have just been with the crazy bitch for a little while, but why wasn't she low on blood?

Kendall checked her neck. Two neat little puncture wounds. Frowning, Kendall glanced at Kane. Just one feeding. A short one at that. She glanced at Kane before looking back at Marci. "Marci, you need to get to a doctor, okay?"

Marci shook her head desperately. "No . . . she'll find me . . ."

Kendall sighed. Pushing gently into the woman's terrified mind, she said, "Marci, my friend here is going to get you to the hospital. You need help. Don't worry, you'll be safe."

"But—but—"

Kendall shook her head, glancing back at where Cat stood in the doorway, glaring at Kendall with rage gleaming in her eyes. "Don't worry about her, Marci. She won't ever hurt you again."

Silently, Kendall added, *She won't ever hurt anybody again. I promise.*

Holding Marci's gaze, she asked, "Understand? You are safe."

Marci nodded, her eyes wide, unblinking. "I'm safe." She went to Kane as docile as a lamb and curled against him like he was a big teddy bear.

Lifting her eyes, Kendall stared at Kane for a long moment. Then she turned back to Cat.

"Kendall."

Turning her head, she looked back over her shoulder, staring into his bottle green eyes. "You better be here when I get back," he said hoarsely.

There was a world of emotions inside his eyes and

Kendall found herself wanting to say something, but she wasn't sure what. Instead, she just nodded. "Go."

The rays of the setting sun shone directly into her face and they made her itch, made her skin feel tight and hot, but before she moved toward Cat, she took one last second to lift her face, looking into the glory of the sun. One lone tear trickled down her face.

K ANE moved as quick as he could, hoping and praying nobody that saw him moving through the park would stop him to ask questions. That would just cause more problems.

Marci looked too obviously like somebody that had been hurt and hurt bad.

She had bruises on her, blood, and she was in a state of shock. There were two neat little puncture marks in her neck. But she looked a hell of a lot better than he'd expected for somebody who'd been trapped with an insane vampire.

Just one set of bite marks.

He would have expected to find her drained.

This was the girl he'd seen in that fucked-up dream he'd had. He knew it without a doubt. He also knew that she'd been in the building with Cat since before the sun rose—all day, and Cat didn't look like she'd been feeding as much as a vampire her age needed to.

Yet there had been a ready supply of blood right in front of her and she hadn't taken it.

That nagging voice in his head kept whispering *Hurry hurry hurry* . . .

His feet moved over the pavement and his mind ran in circles. Kendall fighting a psychotic alone. Psychotics always had the edge, because there was nothing they didn't mind doing. Sane people had lines they wouldn't cross. A crazy bitch didn't.

He turned the corner that led out of the park and almost crashed into somebody.

It was a little old woman. She vaguely reminded him of

the Mrs. Claus types he had seen in the malls around Christmas time. She stood there, beaming up at him, a bright smile lighting her face, blue eyes sparkling as she studied him.

"Oh, you are a handsome one."

"Excuse me, ma'am."

He tried to go around her.

"Oh, that is quite all right, boy. Come with me." She ignored the woman he was holding and looped her hand through his arm and tried to turn him around, guiding him back down the way he had come.

Gritting his teeth, Kane forced out, "Ma'am, I'm sorry, I don't know who you think I am, but I'm in a bit of a hurry. This woman needs medical attention."

She rose on her toes, her blue eyes narrowing as she peered at Marci. "Hmmm . . . my." She stopped walking forward and moved around to stand in front of Kane once more, blocking his path. Leaning forward, she sniffed at Marci. Marci turned her head, staring at the old woman, baffled. The old woman smiled at her. "It's all right, child. Everything will be quite all right, you'll see. Why don't you sleep for now?"

"Going to sleep isn't good for shock victims," Kane said, glancing at Marci. As her lashes fluttered down, he barked out, "Stay awake!"

The old woman just laughed again. "My word, you are a bossy one. However is Kendall going to manage with you? Hmmm . . . I smell vampire. Nasty stench. I know that smell. But I'm kind of curious. She doesn't leave victims alive very often."

Kane's jaw dropped.

Behind him, he felt a silent, watching presence.

"Vax, do be a good lad and take this child off Kane's hands. She's yours, anyway."

Kane turned, staring with irritated eyes at Kendall's ex-lover. The dark-skinned man looked every bit as frustrated as Kane felt. "Who in the hell is this woman?"

Vax replied levelly, "A pain in the ass and the most powerful witch the Hunters have. Basically, I'd listen to her." He dropped his eyes to the woman Kane was holding. Kane saw something unreadable move through his eyes before he reached out and took Marci. "Shock?"

"Yes. Cat had her."

Within seconds, Vax had disappeared down the path and Kane was alone with the very odd woman. The top of her head didn't even reach the middle of his chest, and her blue eyes had a weird look to them. Almost like she wasn't exactly from this world.

Crossing his arms over his chest, he glared at her. "You were the one who was talking to me," he said flatly.

She smiled, her teeth white and straight. Very few wrinkles marred her face as she grinned up at him. "Indeed I am. A friend of Kendall's—I told you we would meet."

"Who in the hell are you?"

She sniffed primly. "Don't you young people have better respect for your elders these days?"

"Not ones that go ramming into people, barging into their minds, and bossing me around without so much as an introduction," Kane said with a shrug.

She just arched a silver brow at him. "Lad, after five hundred years, I imagine I can pretty much do what I please."

Kane blinked. "Uh." Swallowing, he tried again. "Uh, did you just say, five hundred years?"

"Hmmm, I did. I was born shortly after Columbus discovered the New World."

The New World . . . Kane realized that theoretically she was talking about America. *The New World.* That was his home. America . . . and this woman had been alive back when it was still a wild, unsettled land populated only by the proud, noble people that would come to be known as Indians.

Laughing, she looped her arm once more through his, and when she started to walk again, Kane went willingly with her. "Don't worry, it gets easier to think about in time."

Faintly, Kane murmured, "Uh-huh."

Her hand, half the size of his, came up and patted his reassuringly. "Oh, it does. Imagine this . . . I had brothers, five of them. Three of them traveled west to the New World.

America. I never met them. I don't even know if they survived the journey.

"But if you are . . . Vax said you're a witch."

She chuckled. "My magick started emerging when I
turned twelve. Oh, I hid it well. An old Hunter found me
right when my village would have burned me. He saved me,
took me to Brendain, the lands the Hunters call home in
England. By the time I had mastered my magick—learned
that I could search for my brothers—I'd found a new life.
When you find a new life, sometimes it's best to let go of the
old one altogether, Kane."

He was quiet for a minute. "You still haven't told me your
name. Or why you are here."

"Agnes. My name is Agnes. I'm the one who found
Kendall after she was Changed into a vampire. I brought her
to Brendain, asked her to become a Hunter. And I'm here to
help."

"Help Kendall?"

As they rounded the final curve in the path, she just
shrugged and gave him an odd glance. "In a way."

The stone storage building appeared ahead of them and
Kane flinched as a muffled thud came from inside. "Fuck."

Agnes just laughed. "Oh, don't worry. That wasn't
Kendall's head crashing into the wall. Cat is getting a well-
deserved thrashing."

K ENDALL backed away as Cat rose unsteadily to her feet.
Blood dripped from her nose and one eye was swollen
shut. "You haven't been feeding much," Kendall said flatly.
It was obvious in the slow healing. Which made Marci all
that much more puzzling.

Cat just sneered at her. "Don't worry. I'll feed from him
before I fuck him."

Kendall smiled. "Kane has better taste than that, Cat." She
glanced at the spot where Marci had obviously spent a great
deal of the day. It was ripe with her scent and traces of blood
still splattered the floor. "Why didn't you feed from her?"

Cat glared at her sullenly. "You already know. You did something to me, damn you. What did you do? I don't know what, but you did something. Agnes, was it her? That's it. Some kind of spell—that old witch bitch cooked it up and put it inside your brain."

The ripple of power that floated across Kendall's skin was the only warning Kendall had as that familiar old laugh drifted across the room. "Now, now Catharine. I don't go putting spells inside people's brains. The brains spoil my spells. And then there are some people—they have no brains, nothing but empty skulls, the lot of them."

Kendall didn't take her eyes off Cat to look at her old friend. "Hello, Agnes."

"Mary, you look as lovely as ever."

Kendall snorted. She was splattered with her blood as well as Cat's and her hair was tangled, thanks to Cat fisting her damn hands in it, so *lovely* wasn't the word she'd use to describe herself. "You're getting blind in your old age, Nessa."

Agnes chuckled. "Actually, my sight is quite fine. Cat, I'm seeing something inside of you that I haven't seen in quite some time. Whatever did you do?"

Cat snarled. "Get the fuck away from me, bitch. Otherwise, I'll make *you* my meal instead of Sexy over there."

Agnes laughed. "Well, Sexy over there would probably taste better than me. It doesn't matter, though. You know as well as I do it's your last meal. Perhaps we should do what the prisons do and let you choose."

From the corner of her eye, Kendall could see Agnes approaching. The witch's slight figure appeared less stooped than normal and her eyes were glowing as she stared at Cat. "My, my . . . it is, it is . . ."

"Get away from me, you crazy bitch!"

"Agnes, this is my fight," Kendall murmured. "I have to finish it."

Agnes smiled, glancing at Kendall. "Cat is fighting herself. She's beating herself more effectively than you ever could." But she slowly backed away from Cat, never once taking her eyes from the younger vampire. "I sense your essence within her, Mary. Did she try to force her mind within yours?"

"Agnes, we're sort of fighting here," Kendall said, circling away as Cat started edging toward her again.

"Oh, posh. I want answers. I'm curious. This is just rather strange." With that, she flicked her wrist, and before Cat could launch toward Kendall, ever-changing rings of fire encircled her. Cat shrieked with rage, turning to hiss at Agnes. Agnes turned toward her, shaking her finger at the younger vampire as though she were admonishing a young child. "Hush, you! I could kill you with merely a thought. And I ought to. But that's not the way this is meant to play out. I have questions, and bloody hell, I *will* have them answered. Now be quiet or that fire will just close up on you and this will be done with."

Kendall turned disbelieving eyes to Agnes. "What are you up to?" Then Kendall just threw up her hands. "Bugger, forget what you are *up* to. What the hell are you doing here? You belong back in England, back in Cornwall. Have you forgotten that you retired? You don't fight anymore, Agnes. Your battles are all well and done."

Agnes whirled around, moving faster than seemed possible for somebody that looked as frail as she did, staring at Kendall with narrowed eyes as she advanced on the vampire. "You hush as well, girl. Been fighting demons and ferals and deranged witches before you were even a speck in your mama's womb. I'll have my answers." Agnes glared at her. Fisting her hands on her hips, the petite woman demanded, "What happened? I want to know why I look at Catharine and see some remnants of a soul. She threw hers away long ago, so why can I sense regret within her now?"

Kendall blew out a breath and counted to ten as she stared at Agnes. "You can be a serious pain in the butt, Agnes, and I have absolutely no bloody idea what you are talking about."

Agnes snorted. "That is because you look but do not see, Kendall. Foolish girl. There was a child here, wasn't there? The girl you sent out with Kane?"

Kendall gave Agnes a jerky nod.

Agnes breathed in, her lids drifting down. "I can smell her. She bled. But why didn't Cat bleed her out? She obviously needed the blood. She looks half starved. Can you tell me you didn't notice?"

Shaking her head, Kendall murmured, "No."

Turning around, Agnes stared through the ring of fire at the captured vampire, studying her.

Cat snarled at Agnes. "I want to snap that wrinkled neck of yours and feel you die under my hands."

Growling, Kendall lunged forward, stopping only when the heat of the fire from Agnes's spell threatened to sear her flesh. "Watch what you say, Cat. I can make your death quick . . . or very, *very* slow."

Cat grinned. "You'll be the one to die, Kendall. But I'll kill her first. Just so you can watch." Her icy blue eyes flicked to Kane then. Leaning forward, she purred seductively, "I won't be killing him, though. I like him. I'll keep him around, for quite awhile. I might even make him like me. He has power ripe inside him. He'll be quite a lot of fun."

Quick as a snake, Kendall struck through the swirling bands of fire and punched Cat in the nose. As blood fountained out, Kendall stepped back, watching Cat clap a hand over her face. "You fucking whore!" Cat screamed.

Behind them, Agnes cleared her throat gently. Turning to stare at her old mentor, Kendall moved away from Cat, fighting to throttle down the rage inside her belly. "What do you want, Agnes?"

Agnes repeated archly, "I want answers. What has happened between you and Cat? I feel something of you inside her, something that wasn't there before."

Driving a hand through her tangled hair, Kendall tersely explained what had happened the night before. "I've been more aware of her ever since. If something happened to Cat, it was likely then."

Cutting her eyes to Agnes, she shrugged. "I don't know what happened—I don't know what *she* did. She thinks you or I did something, but I didn't do anything," Kendall finished up. Flicking her wrist toward Cat, she demanded, "Now can you take Kane and go? I'd like to get this over with. Although I really do want to know *why* you are here. I don't need help fighting my battles, Nessa."

Ignoring the last part, Agnes tapped one finger against her lips. "How interesting. Hmmm . . ." she slid her gaze toward Kane for one long moment. Kendall narrowed her eyes at the pensive look on Agnes's face.

That look made the blood flowing through Kendall's veins chill. Time slowed down to a crawl as she turned her head and stared at Kane. He was leaning against the wall, his thumbs tucked into his pockets, his stance totally relaxed, almost lazy. She knew better, though. He was tensed, ready to spring into action, ready to fight.

God, I love him, she thought suddenly.

And that was when she knew why Agnes was here. It wasn't for Kendall or for Cat.

But because of Kane.

Kane's weird dreams. How he was always able to find her. His resistance to Kendall's mental commands. That ability to fight vampires—no mortal should be able to do that. It wasn't natural. His ability to see through both Analise's and Cat's odd magick. And then there was what Cat had just said . . . *he has power ripe inside him . . .*

A hot tear trickled down her cheek. No. She didn't want this for him. Trapped in this life, no chance at anything normal. He sensed something was wrong and started to shove off the wall.

Spinning away from him, she looked at Agnes. "Nessa . . ."

Agnes turned, cocking her head as she studied Kendall.

Kendall swallowed, shaking her head. "No, Nessa."

"Kendall, love."

"No!" Kendall snapped. Shaking her head, she said, *"Go."* She gave her a pleading look. "Take Kane and go."

Agnes ignored her completely. "She took something of you inside her, Kendall," Agnes murmured, holding

Kendall's eyes. "A piece of you. She's still Cat, but now she remembers what it was like to be mortal. You never did lose your humanity, you never forgot what it was like. Now, she remembers as well, what it's like to be human. To love, to grieve, to hurt . . ."

It was the softest ghost of a whisper that floated through Kendall's mind. *Sometimes, my friend, things are just meant to be.*

"Agnes, please." *Take Kane and go.*

She heard him moving up behind her, felt the warmth of his body against hers as he drew her back against him. Slowly, he turned her around. "I'm not going anywhere," he murmured, putting his hand under her chin and lifting her face to his. Leaning down, he kissed her gently before he brushed away the dampness on her face. "I'm not."

Agnes, take him away, please . . .

There was a soft sigh in the air. "Very well, Mary."

Kane turned his head, glaring at Agnes. "I don't give a damn who in the hell you are to the Hunters, or how fucking old you are, or how long you've been around. I am *not* leaving Kendall."

Agnes just smiled.

Kendall turned to face Cat, unable to look at Kane a second longer. As the whirling bands of fire started to dissipate, she braced herself. But Cat didn't go for her.

And Agnes, damn her tricky hide, didn't get Kane out.

Of course, Agnes didn't get herself out either.

Witch or not, five-hundred-year-old creatures shouldn't be able to move that fast. Kendall heard her. "You feel regret. I sense that inside you. Too bad that is not enough. Because there is still evil inside you," Agnes murmured as she intercepted Cat before Cat could reach Kane.

"Get the fuck out of my way, you bloody old crone!"

"Old, am I? Why don't we just finish what you started with Kendall the other night . . ."

Turning, Kendall watched as Agnes laid one hand on Cat's chest.

Cat fell screaming to her knees, her hands clutching

Agnes's wrist. "No!" Cat screeched, trying to force the witch away from her, but Agnes wouldn't be moved.

A golden glow formed around Agnes's hand, and light slowly filled the entire room. It faded, and when it did, Cat fell back away from Agnes and stood there staring at the witch for a long moment. Agnes smiled at her.

What happened next Kendall couldn't exactly understand. Agnes could handle vampires like Cat blindfolded. She'd left the life of the Hunters behind because she was *tired,* not because she was feeble and too weak to fight.

So why was the broken, battered body of her oldest and dearest friend laying on the floor? "Nessa!"

Cat glared contemptuously at Agnes's huddled body and said, "Your trick didn't work, old woman." Lifting her gaze, she stared at Kane and purred, "You're mine now, lover."

Kendall turned around, feeling as though her heart had leaped into her throat as she saw Cat moving in on Kane. She felt torn. Agnes lay on the floor behind her. And Kane stood in front of her. In his hand, he held one of his knives, a cocky smile on his face as he stared at Cat.

"Put the knife down."

Kane just smiled. "Don't think so, sugar," he drawled, wiggling it a little so that the silver flashed in the dim light. Cat's eyes widened a little, and Kendall tensed as she felt the swell of power rise as Cat increased her focus and pushed harder against Kane's mind.

"So she's already put a mark on you."

"No, I haven't," Kendall said softly.

Cat didn't take her eyes off of Kane. "Don't lie to me, Kendall. It's getting old. That's the only way he could resist me."

"Not if he's like you are," Kendall said. Making her choice, she stepped away from Agnes. *Forgive me, Nessa.* Tears almost blinded her as she inched her way closer, trying to circle around so that she could get behind Kane. She needed to be able to grab him and shove him away before Cat got too close.

Cat laughed. "He's not like me. Not yet. But he will be."

"You can't control his mind. Believe me, I've tried."

The younger vampire just sneered, never once looking at Kendall. "You've always been too weak to try hard enough, Kendall. That's your problem." Kendall had to bite back a scream as the power swelled to a painful intensity that even made her head ache.

Kane staggered. Kendall smelled blood. But when the power broke over them, he was still standing.

Cat stared at him, breathing raggedly. "You won't do this to me, Kendall. You've taken too much from me. Damn it, I'll have him!"

Kane's laughter was cut short by Cat's shriek as she flew across the room. Kendall screamed as Cat grabbed Kane and leaped for the vaulted stone ceiling. Yes, some vampires flew. And Cat, it seemed, was one of them. The rich, ripe scent of Kane's blood filled the air, and the blonde vampire sank her teeth deep inside his flesh.

Kendall couldn't fly, but she sure as hell could jump. Crouching down, she tensed her muscles and leaped. Cat had her face buried against Kane's neck, but she saw Kendall coming and simply flew across to the other side of the room.

They didn't have that much room, but she had enough to outmaneuver Kendall still. Kendall growled as she landed back down on the ground.

Power rippled through the air. Kendall recognized the scent in the air even before Vax spoke. "Get her out of the air, Vax, *now*."

He had already started to act. Fire came leaping from his fingertips as he pointed to her, but Cat was moving already. "You won't have him," Cat hissed.

Kendall watched with dread as Cat pulled away and used her own fangs to tear open her wrist. There were two ragged holes in Kane's neck. Blood was gushing and he was already unconscious. Unable to move, Kendall watched helplessly as Cat held her wrist to his mouth and her blood flowed in.

Nausea roiled through Kendall and she stared in numb horror. The blood exchange—Kane was pale. Dark life blood pumped from his jugular, and Cat's blood stained his mouth red.

That was all it took. He was low on his own blood and now vampire blood was mingling with what little remained of his own.

Had he taken enough of Cat's blood in?

Tears burned their way down her face as she murmured hoarsely, "What does it matter?"

He was already lost to her.

Kendall threw back her head and screamed out in fury.

Next to her, Vax swore furiously. He held out his hand, and Cat screamed as some unseen force yanked Kane from her hands.

Kendall turned her back on Cat, rushing to Vax as the magick moved Kane through the air. Vax wouldn't let Cat near them. She'd take care of Cat after—

After. Closing her eyes, she kept herself from even finishing the sentence in her mind.

Oh, God, she prayed. But she suspected her prayers were already too late.

Vax caught Kane's body and gently eased him to the ground. The second Kane touched the ground, Vax pressed a hand to the wound at his neck, and a golden glow emanated from his hand, the warmth of healing magick passing through the air. When he moved his hand away, the bleeding had stopped and the skin there was healed, scarred skin in place of the ragged wound.

Kendall settled down beside him, stroking his hair back, staring down at him. He was so pale.

And his eyes were closed.

But Kendall didn't need to see his eyes to know what had happened. With just this one look, she knew. He had lost too much of his own blood—and taken in enough of Cat's.

Either the Change would kill him.

Or he would become vampire.

"No," she whispered, shaking her head.

Hot tears spilled down her cheeks.

"He needs more blood," Agnes murmured. Kendall stiffened, looking over her shoulder at Agnes. The witch stood there, quite hale and hearty. Just beyond her, she saw Cat.

And Cat was crouched on the floor, sobbing, staring at her bloodied hands with horror. There was something in her eyes that Kendall hadn't ever expected to see again.

Humanity.

Cupping his face in her hands, she stared down at him. His skin was still warm. "Kane, no," she whispered, lowering her head to press her lips to his.

"Kendall, he has to have more blood," Agnes repeated, her voice hard and firm.

Kendall could hardly speak. Forcing the words past the sobs, she said, "Cat's tainted—she never once brought over a vampire that wasn't insane. Agnes, I can't . . . I can't see him like that."

Dark, warm hands closed over hers. "Kendall, Kane's strong. His strength will bring him over. He'll be whole, he'll be fine."

Kendall's hands trembled as she took them away. "I can't." Lifting her head, she stared at Vax. "I can't . . . don't you see? The one vampire I brought over, the one I have to kill is a raving lunatic!"

Behind them, Cat continued to sob.

Vax smiled. "I know." He shifted a little, reaching behind him, and seconds later, metal flashed. Kendall stared as Vax slashed the blade over his wrist. "That's why I'm here." The scent of blood, magicked blood, filled the air, and Kendall watched as he lifted Kane by gently sliding his uninjured wrist under Kane's upper body, lifting him up. "He'll come through, Kendall. You're here just to guide him over."

Kendall stared, watching as dark red rivulets of blood flowed down Vax's wrist, staining Kane's mouth. Terror and hope both flooded her. God, if they were wrong . . . she couldn't Hunt Kane. She couldn't kill him.

A hand stroked down her head. Agnes murmured wordlessly to her for a moment before finally kneeling down behind her and wrapping a supportive arm around her. Surrounded by the familiar scent of lavender, Kendall gave into the urge to cry and just leaned against Agnes for a minute and sobbed.

Agnes rocked her, patting her head gently. "Reasons, Kendall. There are reasons for every thing under the sun, Kendall. Even for Cat. Her reason, Kendall, was him. She led you to him."

Giving into the need for comfort, she turned into Agnes's embrace and cried. Agnes rocked her back and forth, whispering softly to Kendall. "All will be fine, love. You'll see. All will be fine."

"I don't want this for him, Nessa . . . not for him."

"Hush, love . . . hush, now."

Kendall finally pulled away. When Agnes tucked the handkerchief into her hand, she wiped away the tears and fisted the linen square in her hand as she stared down at Kane. His face was still and pale. "He doesn't deserve this."

"Reasons, Kendall," Agnes reminded her quietly.

Kendall hissed wordlessly. Reaching out, she closed one hand over Kane's. His skin was cooling more and more. "Reasons!" she growled under her breath. "A reason . . . for this?" Closing her eyes, Kendall tried to bury the anger that thought filled her with and couldn't. "I should have just let her die! Better to have let her die as a baby than to have had her grow up and kill as many people as she has killed. And Kane . . ."

The sobs behind them fell silent, and Kendall slowly turned her head, staring into cornflower blue eyes. She tensed, preparing to jump up and fight once more.

But Cat simply turned her head, blonde hair swinging down to hide her face.

Clenching her jaw, Kendall linked her hand with Kane's, shaking her head. "No. There was no reason on earth for this. He deserved so much better than my life."

"It means little, I know."

It was unwelcome, that voice.

Slowly, Kendall unlaced her fingers and stood, turning to face Cat where she still sat on the floor. In her hand, the blonde held the silver knife Kane had held. Fury laced her voice as she demanded, "What?"

Haltingly, Cat repeated, "I know it means little. But I am sorry."

Kendall narrowed her eyes, taking a step toward Cat. "You are *sorry*?"

Cat said nothing.

Turning her head, Kendall stared at Agnes. "What kind of joke is this?"

Agnes lifted one shoulder. "It is not a joke. Cat chose her punishment the night she linked her mind with yours. She started feeling human emotions again. You never forgot them, Kendall. She gave up humanity in exchange for the vampire hungers. When she linked your soul and mind with hers, she opened a window. I merely finished the job."

"Finished what job?" Kendall growled.

Agnes just shrugged again.

"Nessa . . ."

Vax glanced at Agnes and then looked at Kendall, smiling sympathetically. "She did something when she touched Cat, darling. Kane's blood was the key. As soon as she tasted his blood, the spell started and when she fed on him, there was no turning back. Now every single thing she's done since she became a vampire, she's feeling it, remembering it. Her conscience hasn't ever bothered her. Until now."

Across the room, Cat murmured in a hollow voice, "It's not bothering me. It's killing me."

"Good," Kendall spat viciously.

Cat whispered, "Not enough punishment. It's not enough." She lifted her head and said, "What will you do with me?"

Vax glanced at Kendall, then at Agnes. Technically, if a person could be rehabilitated, then there was a trial. It was rare, very rare. Often there was a sentence to be carried out and at the end of the sentence, a very long sentence, the person went before the Council. If the Council felt the person was safe to society, they could be released.

But Vax didn't know if they could let Cat out of here—not with Kane laying on the floor, lingering between death and life as a vampire.

But before any of them could say anything, Cat said quietly, "Kill me."

Kendall stared at her. "What kind of trick are you trying to pull now, Cat?"

Agnes said quietly, "Kendall, it is no trick. This is the woman you once knew."

Cat rose, facing Kendall across the room. Blood smeared her mouth, drying in gory streaks down her neck, painting her hands red. "Please. I can't live with what I've done. I deserve to be judged, and I'll face whatever judgment I must face, but I'll take it from the Almighty."

Kendall stared at her for a long moment. Then her gaze dropped to the knife Cat held in her hand. Cat's hand shook as she held it out. Slowly, Kendall closed the distance between them and reached out, wrapping her fingers around the hilt of the silver knife.

Kane's knife.

"I don't think I can forgive you, Catling."

Cat's mouth trembled. "I understand that, Mary. I certainly can't forgive myself." She closed her eyes.

Kendall clenched her jaw and struck, plunging the knife into Cat's chest, striking her full in the heart. Cat gasped, arching up. Her eyes held Kendall's for a long moment. "It wasn't ever your fault, Kendall," she murmured, her voice a harsh, broken whisper. And then the light faded from her eyes and she fell to the floor.

Black little wisps of smoke rose from her chest.

As Kendall turned away, tears fell down her cheeks.

CHAPTER 14

Vax followed Agnes out into the sunlight. Cat's body was wrapped in a long black cloth Agnes had pulled from her bag. They paused in the shadows of the building as Vax stared back inside.

"I don't feel right leaving her."

"She needs to be alone right now," Agnes whispered.

Vax just shook his head. "I don't understand. I thought Kane was here to save Kendall."

Agnes chuckled. "Boy, he is. Kendall has been dying inside for years. Him coming into her life is the only thing that could have possibly saved her."

Harshly, Vax said, "If it wasn't for Cat, she would have been fine."

Agnes sighed. "Vax, you haven't known her as long as I have. Kendall wasn't ever fine. She's been torn inside so long—her father, the man who Changed her. Kendall was dead inside even before she was Changed."

She glanced back at the building, smiling a little. "She'll be fine now, though. Aye, she will."

*   *   *

SHIT, he was cold.
    Cold all over.
  It was dark.
  Kane didn't know where in the hell he was.
  And he couldn't find Kendall. Where had she gone?
  Kane tried to open his mouth and call her, but he couldn't.
When he tried to talk, it *hurt*. That was one thing that wasn't
cold. It burned like fire along his neck, aching and burning,
and when he opened his mouth to try and talk again, it just
hurt even more.
  What had happened?
  His head was nothing more than one empty, aching husk.
He couldn't remember much of anything. The last thing he
remembered clearly was that crazy bitch trying to pull that
voodoo shit with his mind and it didn't work. He had
laughed—maybe. Was that right?
  Then Kendall did . . . something.
  Everything else was blurry. Something had hurt. He
didn't even want to think about the pain.
  Sick. Got to be sick, he told himself. In the hospital. Made
sense. Explained why he hurt so bad, why he was so cold.
Why it seemed so dark.
  His entire body hurt. The cold got worse. A blanket.
Didn't anybody have a damned blanket?
  But how in the hell could he ask for one when he couldn't
even talk?
  Then the heat started. Icy chills one second and fiery hot
the next. So damned hot, sweat had soaked him before he
could even realize what had happened. Kane groaned as
sweat rolled into his eyes, stinging them. He wanted to wipe
it away, but he still couldn't move. Hadn't been this hot in
Iraq. Sweat rolled down his neck and that *hurt*. Hell, fuck
hurt. It was worse than that. It burned like somebody was
gouging a raw wound with a hot poker.
  He swore and again it hurt, but finally, his voice actually
had a sound.

A cool hand stroked down his hand. "It's okay, Kane."

Kendall. "Kendall," he gasped out. Damn it, was that his voice? It sounded awful, raspy and cracked and entirely unlike his own.

"Shhhh . . ." her voice sounded husky, kind of rough. And she sounded sad. Baby, what's wrong? He wanted to know, but he seriously doubted he could ask.

"I'm here, Kane. Don't try to talk, okay? I know it hurts."

He focused as hard as he could to move his hand. Her hand closed over his, and he relaxed a little. It was still too damned dark for him to be able to see. Why was it so damned dark? Where were they? "Throat hurts . . . sick?"

Something hot splashed on his face. Her fingers wiped it away. "No . . ." she sighed. "You're not sick. Just rest, love, okay?"

He shifted, feeling something soft but firm under his head. Her . . . his head was resting on her thigh. "Have to tell you something, babe," he whispered. Exhaustion was pulling at him and his throat was burning. He could tolerate it though. He could take anything. Kendall was here.

But he had to tell her.

Her hand stroked over his burning face. "Rest, Kane, okay?"

"Tell you, first."

She sighed, and he could almost picture the aggravated look on her face. *You can't always be in charge, sweetie,* he thought tiredly. He'd tell her that—later. Right now, this was the only thing that really mattered. "Tell me what?" she asked quietly.

"Love you, Kendall," he whispered. The exhaustion pulled at him, and he gave into it, falling back into the darkness. It seemed a little cooler there anyway . . .

TANGLING her fingers in his hair, Kendall let her head fall back against the stone wall behind her as tears rolled down her face. He was sound asleep. It wasn't the deep sleep of one struggling through the Change.

He'd already gone through it.

Love you . . .

The words *I love you, too,* burned on her tongue but she'd be damned if she said it to him the first time when he was asleep. He'd struggled out of that sleep to say it to her. She'd say it to him when he was awake.

"Come back to me, Kane," she whispered, curling her upper body around him as he started to shiver again.

He'd alternate between fever and chills as his body adjusted to the Change. He deserved to be someplace better than this underground hole, but she couldn't move him until the sun set.

Tears burned hot, slow tracks down her cheeks. Grief and rage tore through her—at some point, she knew she'd likely mourn for Cat, but right now, she couldn't even dwell on her.

Her entire heart was one aching knot of misery.

Resting her cheek on top of Kane's head, she sighed. "I didn't want this. Not for you."

And she wanted some place better than this while he dealt with the ravaging sleep a body had to go through during the Change. It seemed to be moving so fast for him. A person usually went through the symptoms over three days. Why was it moving so quick for him?

He hadn't had the long, peaceful sleep most new vampires had during the first twenty-four hours. He'd barely rested three before the chills started. Then the fever was on him. Now the fever and the chills were alternating every twenty to thirty minutes. By the time night came and he woke out of his sleep, he would be exhausted.

Tracing her fingers down the worn, tired lines of his face, she whispered, "I'm sorry, love."

There wasn't any warning. But then again, Agnes had been around so long, she'd mastered her magick to the point that she didn't give much warning. Kendall jumped as Agnes spoke out of the cool darkness, "It wasn't your decision, Kendall. This was just the way it was meant to be."

Lifting her head, Kendall stared at Agnes through the tangled mess of her bangs. "Nessa, I'm kind of ticked off at you right now. You might want to leave me be."

"Oh, sweetheart, do you think I don't understand?" Agnes closed the distance between them and lowered herself carefully to the floor, sighing as she sat down. In her arms, she held a blanket, and there was an old bag slung across her shoulders. Cocking her head, she studied Kane. "Hmmm. Going through it rather fast, isn't he? I was wondering if Vax's blood would do that."

Kendall huffed out a breath as Agnes laid the blanket alongside her. Then from a little pouch at her waist, the witch pulled out a little ice pack. She twisted it with a flick of her wrist and laid it on his forehead. Kane sighed in his sleep, and the lines of strain around his mouth eased just a little.

Pursing her lips, Kendall studied Agnes closely. Agnes just smiled serenely back at her. "I'm still mad at you."

Agnes shrugged. "I imagine you are. But this is the way it was meant to be, sweeting." She reached up, brushing Kendall's hair back from her face gently. "Oh, Kendall. None of us would have chosen the lives we live. Ours isn't an easy lot. We certainly wouldn't have chosen it for our loved ones."

"Then why in the hell did you let happen?" Kendall demanded, one hand closing into a useless fist.

Agnes smiled. "Baby, it happened because it was meant to happen this way." Her voice dropped and she reached out, capturing Kendall's fisted hand in her own, bringing it forward and closing her own hands around it. "You stare at me angrily, but I know this. I've seen it for years. It wasn't what you *wanted*, Kendall. But it was what you needed."

Kendall laughed bitterly. "No. No, Nessa. I can't believe this. She was Changed before he was even born. Before his parents were born. How can you expect me to believe that the entire reason she was made, the reason she was Changed, the reason she went insane was to lead me to here . . . to this?"

Agnes smiled, reaching out with one hand to touch her fingers to Kane's brow. "God bless, he is a strong one," she murmured, more to herself than anything. Then she lifted her gaze to meet Kendall's. "Why, Kendall, because you *are* here. And so is he. He is alive. And he is whole. He is still the man you fell in love with."

Kendall shook her head, tears falling silently down her face. "You can't know that."

With a shrug of her stooped old shoulders, Agnes said, "Yes, I can. Kendall, we're the witches. The witches are the ones who know who will Hunt. Who will not. That's why all who wish to become a Hunter are brought to the schools first. They must be seen first."

Agnes cocked her head, staring at Kendall as though she was seeing something that Kendall couldn't see. Her voice was quiet, serene. "There's a color, you see. A color only we can see. A color that surrounds, that goes clear through to your soul. That's how we choose." She reached out, passing her hand over Kendall's face. "It's a color I've never seen anywhere else, and we're the only ones who can see it. It's a lovely, surreal shade of blue, so lovely, so unlike anything you've ever seen . . . if only I could describe it to you. We see this color only in the Hunters. Sometimes we see it in somebody who will become a Hunter—I saw it in your young man the moment I laid eyes on him."

Her lids drooped low over her eyes and Agnes was quiet for a moment. When she looked back at Kendall, her eyes were glowing. "And I still see it, even now . . . Trust me, Kendall. He *will* be fine."

Lifting Kendall's hand, she reached out with her other hand and caught Kane's, pressing their two hands together. Automatically, Kendall linked her fingers with Kane's, pressing her palm to his.

"Together, Kendall. That is how you two were meant to be." With that, Agnes stepped back into the shadows, and her magick took her flying away.

Her words lingered with Kendall and she let the hope fill her.

I t was dark when he opened his eyes, but he could see well enough. Kendall stared down at him and he smiled up at her. "Hey, beautiful," he murmured.

A slight smile twitched her lips, but her face remained solemn. "How do you feel?"

Kane grimaced. "Stiff. Sore as hell." Scowling up at her, he asked, "What in the hell happened?"

"You don't remember?"

Kane closed his eyes. *Cat.* Kendall had told him to get Agnes. Cat had hit her. The old woman had crumpled to the ground like a rag doll. Weird . . . she had seemed a lot more powerful than that. She looked frail, but that was just appearances.

Kane had planned on getting the old woman out of there, stabilizing her if he could. Then get back to Kendall.

But he hadn't ever made it out of the building. He didn't think he even made it to Agnes—

A strangled groan escaped him as his hand clapped over his throat. He remembered now. That psycho bitch had grabbed him. So fucking strong. He'd had absolutely no idea just how much strength a vampire had hidden inside. And fast—

"She bit me," he said flatly. He expected to find a bandage under his fingers.

But there was no bandage.

There was healed skin. And two ridged scars. His lids closed briefly and then he looked up at Kendall. "She bit me."

Kendall swallowed. He could see her throat working, watched as she licked her lips. Her lashes fluttered. "I'm sorry, Kane. I couldn't stop her. I tried . . . Vax got here, but—"

Kane closed his eyes. More bits and pieces of his memory fell into place. "She flies, doesn't she?"

Gruffly, Kendall said, "She *did* fly. She's dead, Kane. I killed her, I just didn't do it in time."

Something hot splashed on his face. Too hot. He opened his eyes and watched as tears fell slowly down her ivory cheeks. "In time for what?" he asked gently.

"In time to save you."

Kane smiled. "Hey, I feel pretty okay. Kind of groggy, but . . ."

She looked away. "You don't understand, Kane. She

didn't just bite you. She fed you, too. Vax got in here fast, but when she bit you, she did it in a way that tore your jugular. You were bleeding out. And while you were bleeding, she bit herself and fed you."

Okay, now *that* part Kane didn't remember. "Fed me."

"Yes." Her face was stark, her eyes dark in the pale circle of her face as she stared down at him.

It took him a minute to put it together. When he finally did, he sat up, closing his eyes. When he opened them, he realized there was absolutely no light inside the building. Nothing.

So why could he see so clearly?

"I'm like you now."

Behind him, he heard an odd clicking sound. A dull thud. The shaky sound of her breathing. Turning, he found himself staring at her face, able to see her almost as clearly as if it were full daylight.

Except it would be another hundred years or more before he could even take a few seconds of dawn. She was staring at him, her eyes dark and gleaming with tears. Her voice was husky as she murmured, "I'm sorry, Kane. I wasn't fast enough—"

A slow smile spread across his face. "I'll be damned," he murmured, shaking his head.

Kendall whispered thickly, "It will be all right, Kane. Eventually. I mean, I know it's hard to take in, but—well, Nessa, Agnes, the old woman that was here, she says you'll be a Hunter and if you don't want to train with me, I'll make sure tha' ya find somebody tha' . . ."

That lilting music of Ireland had slipped back into her voice, and as much as he liked listening to it, he had to muffle her words, laying two fingers across her lips. "Now why would I want you to do that?"

Kendall merely stared at him with dull eyes. "I let this happen."

Somewhere inside, Kane could understand how this had torn her to shreds. "Kendall, you didn't let this happen. It happened because it was meant to. And I'm damned glad it did."

She just shook her head. "It shouldn't have happened. You deserved better than this."

He just snorted. "Deserved what? What did you think I was going to do, settle down and go and find a cute little wife, a house and white picket fence, have three kids? Bowl on Saturdays? Do I look suited to that kind of life?"

At the mention of the word *wife,* he saw her eyelids flicker just a little, but her face remained set and stubborn. "You deserved some sort of normal life after everything you've done."

Kane laughed, hooking his arms over her shoulders. Resting his brow against hers, he murmured, "Babe, I've done nothing compared to the things you've done. But I'll never have anything close to normal. I'm in love with a vampire. The closest thing I'd ever have to normal is living with you until I grow old and die, while you stay as amazingly beautiful as you are now . . . and would you let that happen?"

He watched as her face paled, her eyes haunted in the white oval of her face. She didn't respond at all. "You can't give me an honest answer, can you? You've run from me almost from the beginning—you're terrified of me, because I was human. You have feelings for me. I know it, I feel it, every time you touch me, every time you look at me. You don't want me hurt, not just because you're a Hunter, or because you're a woman with a heart too soft for your own good. But because you are you, and I'm me."

"So you don't know if you'd stay with me or not. You'd be afraid I'd get hurt, get killed, that you'd lose me," he whispered, threading his hands through her hair, arching her face up so that he could kiss her gently. "How normal would my life have been? Either I'd stay at your side, growing older and older, weaker and weaker . . . until I eventually died, or got killed. Or you'd walk away and never give us a chance. And I'd be miserable, loving a woman I'd never get over, one I'd see every time I closed my eyes. I'd be alone. And likely die young, one night when I was out fighting because I wasn't paying attention. How normal is that, Kendall?"

Carefully, he wiped away the tears that streaked down her cheeks. "All I've wanted, practically since I saw you in Louisville, was just to be with you. Forever. Now I can."

Kendall tore away from him, folding her arms around her middle. "Damn it, Kane, don't you understand? You've lost everything now." She fell silent for a long moment, and finally, she wheeled around, her hair flying around her shoulders as she spun to face him, her eyes glowing furiously. "There is no life left within you because of me. And you stand smiling about it. I feel sick inside, and you *smile*."

"No *life*?" he demanded, crossing the distance between them with two strides. Savagely, he jerked her against him, whirling around and slamming her against the wall, unaware of just how hard he had done so. The strength flooding his body was alien, but her words had infuriated him and he could hardly see straight. "Damn it, Kendall, the only way there is no life in me is if you *leave* me. I love you, damn it. And I'm alive because somehow, somebody was here because of you. Vax wasn't here because of me. Vax wouldn't have known I existed if you weren't in the picture. If he did something to save me, it was because of *you*."

"Damn it, Kane," she cried, glaring up at him. She tried to shove him back, but she couldn't. Once she had been the stronger, but now, physically at least, they were equal. "I didn't want this for you."

"I did!" he roared. Closing his eyes, he sucked in a deep breath, trying to still the rage in him. In a quieter voice, he said, "You don't understand, Kendall. I did. I didn't care what it took, I wanted forever with you. And now I can have it."

She didn't get another word out as he pulled her up against him, dragging her down to the cool stone floor as he pressed his mouth against hers. She gasped, startled. Kane greedily pushed his tongue inside her mouth. *Oh, hell . . .* if he had thought she had tasted good before—

A whole new world of taste and sensation seemed to be opening up before him. He could actually hear her heartbeat speed up, smell the scent of her as she got hotter and wetter under the touch of his hands.

Rolling over, he pinned her body beneath him and started to kiss a hot path down the line of her neck. "I wanted forever, Kendall, can't you understand?" he muttered.

"Oh, Kane."

"I would have taken what I could get, but it wouldn't have been enough," he whispered. He tasted salt as he kissed her neck and looked up to see tears rolling down her cheeks. Resting his chin between her breasts, he murmured, "I didn't care that I'd be old and gray in thirty years, if I could still have you with me. But what I really wanted was forever."

Cupping her face in his hands, he whispered, "And now I have it." Slanting his mouth over hers, he kissed her, groaning as she arched up under him, pressing her body against his so that he could feel every long, lean inch of her. Tearing away from her, he shoved to his knees and fumbled with the button to her jeans. "Now all I have to work on is convincing you."

Kendall managed a small smile, lifting her hips to help him slide the jeans down. "Oh, I'm already convinced."

He froze, sliding a look up at her. She stared solemnly at him, her eyes still gleaming with tears, as she met his gaze.

"Huh?"

She shrugged a little. "I was just waiting for you to wake up. I love you, too. But I thought you'd need some time."

His hands clenched around her jeans convulsively as he stared into those golden eyes. They had haunted his dreams for what seemed like an eternity now. How could he have lived this long without her in his life? "Shit," he muttered, as a desperate need flooded him. Looking back down at her jeans, he started trying to jerk them down her legs. They tangled around her knees and again around her ankles.

Kane jerked. Hearing a ripping sound, he muttered, "Sorry," under his breath. Kendall shifted, trying to help him, but all they managed to do was tangle the jeans even more. Finally Kane managed to free one ankle and he figured that was good enough. Shoving her knees apart, he crouched between her thighs.

Tearing his own jeans open, he looked up into her eyes.

The smile there had faded and she was staring up at him with a hungry intensity that matched what he felt inside. "I'm never going to be without you," he whispered harshly, tumbling her back onto the floor.

"Not if I have anything to do with it," she murmured, wrapping her arms around him.

Kane groaned as he pushed inside her, impaling her on his length. Once he was lodged within her sheath, he rolled over onto his back, pushing her up so that he could stare up at her. Kendall smiled down at him, bracing her hands against his chest as she started to roll her hips.

With the flat of his hands, he caressed the silken skin of her thighs. "Part of me hoped for this," he rasped hoarsely. She flexed around him, the inner muscles of her sheath caressing his cock.

Tears filled her eyes. "Kane . . ."

He grinned at her as he cupped her ass in his hands. "I did. All I wanted was a lifetime, or longer, with you." He started to pump his hips, rocking upward to meet her slow, downward thrusts. "Now I have it."

A soft scream fell from her lips, her nails biting into his chest. The hot, sweet scent of her hunger flooded the air. Kane dropped his gaze, staring at where they joined. His cock gleamed wet from her cream, the dark red of her curls brushing against him as they moved.

She fell forward, planting her hands on the ground beside his head. Kane reached up and fisted one hand in the deep red of her hair, dragging her mouth down to his. "Now I have *you*," he growled against her lips. He bit her lip gently before he kissed her quick and rough. "I'm not letting you go. Not ever."

Kendall laughed shakily. "Bloody hell, I hope not," she whispered.

Kane rolled her over again, pinning her on her back, catching her legs behind her knees, pushing them high in the air. With slow, deep strokes, he shafted her, staring into her eyes. "I love you." He trailed his fingers down the soft skin of one outer thigh, down to the soft, plump curve of her ass, back up, then reaching between her thighs and focusing on the engorged flesh of her clit, flicking it lightly until she was panting and squirming against him.

With glassy, wide eyes, she stared up at him. Gritting his teeth, Kane lashed down the need to come as he lightly slapped her clit and watched her explode. She climaxed around his cock, her muscles flexing and convulsing until he thought he'd lose it, until he thought he was going to fall on top of her and fuck her until he died.

But finally, she calmed. Letting go of her legs, he brought them down and lay down on top of her, cuddling against her as she smiled sleepily up at him. With a wicked smile, he whispered, "And guess what?"

Huskily, Kendall asked, "What?"

"You won't always get to be the boss now."

Covering her mouth with his, he started shafting her again, slowly, until he could fell the answering tremor inside her body. This time, when she came, he followed her.

As he came inside her, he collapsed, pillowing his head between her breasts. With a shaky laugh, Kane groaned. "Damn, I feel like putty."

Kendall smiled, stroking a hand down his back. "You really should have gone to feed, not stayed in here for this."

He grunted, shifting just a little so that he could kiss the soft swell of her breast. "This was better."

Seconds later, he was asleep.

Kendall sighed. He needed to feed. And they couldn't stay here. Rising, she stared down at him.

Somebody needed to come up with some sort of fast-food for vamps.

But as she dressed, she was smiling.

That crazy old witch had been right.

It really would be okay.

Epilogue

A FTER SIX weeks, the last person Kendall expected to see on this rocky Maine beach was Agnes.

The craggy old beaches were serene, lovely, and somewhat wild. Maybe they reminded Agnes of home. But why wasn't she home?

Glancing at Kane, she shrugged. Well, they weren't going to spend the night making love on the beach. But that was okay.

"Hey, Nessa."

Perched on a rock, staring out into the water, Agnes looked up and smiled. "Did I ever tell you who first called me that?"

Although some thirty feet separated them, Agnes's voice came to Kendall as clear as day. Shaking her head, Kendall said, "No."

Almost as agile as a child, Agnes hopped down off the rock and started making her way to shore, using sharp, wicked-looking rocks that Kendall definitely wouldn't have considered stable enough to bear weight. As she reached shore, Agnes started to talk. "His name was Elias."

Agnes sighed a little. "We were young. Very young. Fifteen when we fell in love. Not that it was young then. I was already a Hunter. He knew. He shouldn't have. But I didn't keep secrets from him. We were already married." A tear rolled down her cheek, but she didn't seem to notice. She whispered something.

It sounded vaguely familiar to Kendall, but she wasn't certain why.

Agnes's voice was thick, almost harsh as she continued to mutter, *"They quelled him."*

It clicked in Kendall's mind after a moment—English, but a dialect that hadn't been spoken in hundreds of years. Middle English. Taking a step closer to Agnes, she whispered, "Killer? Who? Who did they kill?"

Agnes lifted her head and looked at Kendall. Instinctively, Kendall fell back a step and to her shock, she felt her fangs drop. Without even looking, she knew Kane was at her back and braced to fight.

Agnes's eyes were glowing with the blue flames of rage. *"They* killed my Elias. They stole him from me. After all we had done to protect them."

"Nessa."

Kendall licked her lips, watching as tears continued to roll down Agnes's face, watching as the magick and anger continued to rage within her. Reaching out her hand, she whispered again, "Nessa, they are long dead. It's just us here. Kane and me."

Agnes spun away, her stooped shoulders shuddering for a long moment. Kendall didn't dare touch her though, not until she knew Agnes had that deadly anger under control. "Yes, long dead. Just like Elias," Agnes whispered softly, lifting her head and staring out across the ocean.

Kendall wondered if maybe she was seeing England instead of the water.

"After I finished training at Brendain, I found a new home. Oneoak—a small village about two days away from Brendain. Oneoak had a terrible problem with rogue werewolves. I made my home there. Elias had lost his parents to the rogues. He was hunting them alone. I saved him one night—although he argued that he saved me, called me a silly girl. We fell in love almost from the first moment we saw each other," Agnes murmured. "He always called me Nessa. His mother's name was Agnes, and he said it just didn't suit me right."

Turning back, Agnes faced them. "We married less than a month after I moved there. And in less than four, we had destroyed the pack of wolves terrorizing that poor village. They called it a miracle from God." Agnes shrugged. "It wasn't a miracle. It was my job." She snorted. "Fifteen years old. My job. I didn't think much of it. The people at Brendain were sensible then, as they are now. They make sure you understand why we are given the abilities we have. Elias and I were going to move on. He understood, you see. Knew that I had to Hunt. But, one night, I was seen. I was out Hunting. Had to make certain they'd be safe."

Agnes paused, wrapping her arms around herself. "I didn't like the dark." Closing her eyes, she tipped her head back, staring up at the sky. "I was just like them at heart. Bad things waited for you in the dark. I made fire—the bastard that ran the tavern had his eye on me. I didn't much care for him. He followed me, saw me. They were waiting for me when I got back. And they had Elias. They told me if I passed their witch tests, they'd let him go." A soft, broken sob escaped her. "I can pass their bloody tests. I'm a witch, but their tests were nothing more than rot. I agreed, but as soon as they had me tied—they stabbed him."

As Agnes started to stumble, Kendall caught her, wrapping her arms around her. "Oh, God, Nessa, I'm so sorry."

Leaning into Kendall, Agnes sniffed delicately, her body trembling as she tried not to sob. "Even then, I could control fire. I wasn't quite so powerful then, but I was good with fire. Perhaps too good. I surrounded myself and Elias with it, keeping them away from me, but it raged out of control. I didn't even notice. Elias was dying as I held him. I hadn't learned enough about healing yet to help him. I begged him not to leave me. He did anyway."

Gently, she pushed against Kendall and stepped away. Using her cane to support her, Agnes walked wearily up the beach. "He promised me that he would come back to me. He never did, though. Five hundred years, I've waited. And I'm too old and tired now."

Kendall watched, tears rolling down her face as Agnes started to walk away from them. Then she stopped and turned back around, the wind blowing long strands of silver hair into her face as she stared at Kendall and Kane. "My time is coming, Kendall. I feel it, in my heart, my bones. I'm tired."

Kendall was silent. If she tried to talk, she'd just sob, she knew it.

"I always thought I'd want to be home when it happened, yet something calls me here. But I don't want to spend eternity resting here. I want to be back home, with Elias. Will you take me?"

Kendall nodded slowly. Licking her lips, she tried to force the words out, but couldn't. Kane stepped up behind her and asked quietly, "Where, Agnes?"

Agnes smiled at him. "So well suited you two are. Meant to be. I always knew it would happen for you, Kendall." She reached into her pocket and pulled out a sturdy silver chain. Pressing it against her chest for a long moment, Agnes closed her eyes, her lips moving as she whispered silently. Then she pressed her lips to it. "The New Forest. You know the New Forest, don't you Kendall? Near Southampton?"

Kendall forced a smile through her tears. "Nessa, love, I lived in England for years. Of course I know Southampton. Where around the New Forest?"

Agnes sighed, her eyes drifting closed. "Oneoak is long gone. But it was in the New Forest, not far from where Southampton is now. A road . . . there's a road." She held up one hand and a ball formed there. Kendall stared at it, her eyes watering a little from the brightness of it. A swirling blue fog obscured the ball for a moment and when it cleared, Kendall saw a manor fallen to ruin. She remembered, though, when it had been in its glory. "Do you know the place, Mary, love?"

Kendall nodded.

"Park there. The stone will be glowing a little. It will start to glow brighter when you head south, beyond the manor into the New Forest. You'll know when you get there."

"Get where?" Kane asked, moving past Kendall to stare into the ball with wide eyes. Kendall had to smile a little even through the tears that still stung her eyes. Magick was still very, very new to him, despite the powers that he'd adjusted to with rather phenomenal ease.

Agnes smiled that fey smile. "You'll know," she murmured as she held out the necklace to him. There was a pale white stone in it with just the barest hint of purple in the middle.

Kane accepted it but continued to stare at the ball with perplexed eyes. "How will I know?"

Agnes just smiled. "The stone will tell you, love."

Her gaze dropped to the stone and once more, tears welled in her eyes. Reaching up, she touched her fingers to it and whispered, "You promised you would come back, Elias."

"You picked the wrong girl to mess with."

Leandra said it flatly and hoped the idiot breathing down her neck would get a clue, but it wasn't very likely. This part of Huntington, West Virginia, seemed to have more than its share of fools.

A big, sweaty hand closed over her neck, squeezing tight. "You're a cute little thing . . . mebbe if you're nice, I won't mess up that pretty face of yours."

Rolling her eyes skyward, she whispered, "And there are poor women out there who might actually believe that."

Damn it, she had wanted a night *away* from this. A night where she could just have a drink, or five, and try to forget about that damned haunting dream. Find someplace where she could just be anonymous, where she could put her sorry life on hold for a bit.

Then you should have picked a better place to go for a walk, that sane, evil part of her whispered.

Leandra steadfastly ignored that voice as she stepped away from the bastard holding her neck. He had been holding her tightly—her flesh still ached a bit, but he hadn't been holding her tight enough to keep her from moving. Of course, he was just human. Dirty, unwashed, *thuggish* human, but human nonetheless. It would take somebody more than human to keep her still.

He blinked at his empty hand and then lifted his eyes to snarl at Leandra. She just cocked a brow at him. "If you want me to be nice, all you have to do is ask," she told him.

No reply. He just lunged for her. Leandra moved out of the way easily and watched as he fell facedown in the rubble and garbage that littered the narrow side street. She had to give it to him—he was fast. He leaped back up and whirled, flashing his knife at her. She imagined he was trying to scare her. Leandra smiled coldly.

He had no idea what real fear was.

At least . . . not yet.

When he lunged for the second time, she let him close his hand around her arm, but then she pivoted, tripping him and dislodging his grip at the same time. They ended on the ground, with her kneeling across his chest and staring down into his face. She had his knife hand pinned and she squeezed her hand around his wrist, tightening her grip until she felt bones grind together.

She smiled, letting him see the fangs glinting in her mouth. "So, tell me, friend. How nice am I supposed to be? Do I let you live? Kill you quick?"

He struggled, but she kept him pinned easily as she reached out and trailed the tips of wine-red fingernails down his cheek. Probing his mind, she heard the echoes of screams and whimpers of fear. He liked hurting women. "I don't know that a quick death is what you deserve," she mused. Shrugging, she said, "But judgment isn't mine to give. I'll just send you on to your maker and let him deal with you."

By now, his eyes were wide and glazed with terror and he kept jerking on his arm, trying to free the hand that held his knife. Leandra simply squeezed his wrist a little harder and felt bones snap. He wailed in pain and then began to beg. "Let me go. Please . . ."

Leandra let go of his useless hand, picking up the knife and tossing it aside before she looked back down at him. "How many women begged for that same thing?" she asked soberly as she reached out and clasped his head in her hands. As she wrenched his neck to the left, snapping it cleanly, she closed her eyes.

She'd seen too many lives ended and each one had left a mark on her. Slowly, she rose, staring into his lifeless eyes.

"He doesn't deserve it."

At the sound of that familiar voice, she hunched her shoulders instinctively. Then she forced her muscles to relax. *What in the hell was he doing here?* she thought as she tried to relieve the tension suddenly tightening her entire body.

It wasn't easy—all she wanted to do was hide. Run and hide.

Well, either that or jump him. But she doubted Mike Prescott really wanted her touching him. And Leandra would be damned before she'd let him see he bothered her enough to make her want to run.

As he circled around her, she blanked her features and looked up at him with what she hoped was an unreadable look. "Doesn't deserve what?" she asked.

"Your pity." Mike nudged the dead man with the toe of his boot, his lip curled in a sneer. "I smell the violence on him. He preyed on fear."

"Isn't that what we do?" she asked mildly. Before he could answer, she shrugged. "Life is life. No, he wasn't a good man—his life was a cruel waste. And I pity that more than anything else."

More than most, Leandra understood what it was like to look back on a wasted life and see nothing but blood, evil, and lies.

Turning on her heel, she moved away, keeping to the shadows out of habit. Mike fell into step beside her and she sent him a narrow look. "Do you know that if I wanted company, I would have stayed at Eli's?" she asked shortly.

Mike laughed. "Leandra, I don't think you know what you really want."

You. That simple reply leaped to her mind and it was all she could do not blurt it out. Leandra hadn't ever wanted much in life, but she did want him. Wearily, she sighed, looking down at her feet for a minute. Thick black braids fell forward, obscuring her face and she absently pushed them back.

"Nobody knows what they really want in life, do they, Mike? Why should I be any different?"

You just are.

Whether Leandra liked it or not, she was different. Not because of her exotic, erotic looks, or because of that lilting voice that made him think of beaches and sex. Because of who she was.

He doubted she'd relish hearing that though.

Nobody knew quite what to make of Leandra, this enemy turned comrade-at-arms. A witch who had spent half of her life serving the Scythe, and now she fought as a Hunter, the warriors she had been raised to hate.

She'd been born a witch and she'd die a witch. But in a little over three years, she'd become something more.

Just a few seconds, and her life had been irrevocably changed. She'd been fighting one of the feral vamps that the Hunters dealt with, and he had bitten her, bleeding her out and then leaving her to die of blood loss once he took what he needed to heal himself.

It had been Malachi that had fed her his own blood and brought her over. From what Mike understood, the centuries-old vampire didn't bring people over, nor did he train them.

Yet another way in which Leandra was different. Malachi had sired her and now he trained her. Not too many others were quite suited for the task. Witches didn't often survive the change from mortal to vampire. It was actually very rare—Leandra was the first in centuries.

While Malachi wasn't a witch, he did have powers that went beyond that of a vampire's, so they made a good match.

It kept Mike awake at night, wondering just how true a match the two were.

Trying to shove those thoughts aside before she picked up on his mood, he said, "What are you doing around here? I thought it was your night off. Did Eli send you?"

She flicked him a glance and snorted. "Hardly. I wanted some silence."

"And you came *here*?" Mike asked with a disbelieving laugh.

She just sneered at him. "Perhaps I should have anonymity—and I wanted a drink."

Mike had to smile. "You found a bit more than a drink, baby."

Her lips pursed in a scowl Mike found adorable as she drawled, "Really?"

He started to reply, but a sound caught his ears. Sirens. Distant, but heading their way. "Hell, that was fast," he muttered as he cupped his hand around her elbow and started to urge her into the alley just ahead of them.

She tugged on her arm and pointed down the street to a glowing neon sign. "That is where I want to go—not into another dark alley."

Then she scowled, her head cocking, eyes narrowing as she picked up the sound of the siren as well. Then she glared at him, those amazing eyes sparking as though the sirens were his fault.

Still, she resisted his efforts to guide her into the alley. "Hiding in an alley is an excellent way to not look suspicious, I take it?" she drawled, still glancing toward the bar. "Not a dark anonymous bar."

Mike sighed, shaking his head. "You really want that drink, don't you?"

Wine-red lips curled in a smile. "Yes, I really want that drink."

So he followed her down the road, listening to the sirens as they grew even closer. As the door swung shut behind him, he caught sight of flashing red and blue as the patrol car turned down the street.

Leandra gently disengaged her arm from his hand and he fell in step behind her, watching as she sauntered up to the bar. How in the hell did a woman make a pair of plain old black fatigues look that good? Hell, Mike was pretty damn sure when the military designed that sort of uniform for their enlisted boys, they hadn't counted on what a woman could do to it.

Of course, most women didn't wear it with a form-fitting black shirt that ended inches above the waistband. Even the thick-soled combat boots on her feet looked as sexy as hell.

Man, you got it bad. Shaking his head, he caught up with her just as somebody tried to take the empty seat at her side. The big ugly guy was built like a brick wall, his hair skimmed back in a ponytail that revealed the snarling jaguar tattoo on his neck.

And he was studying Leandra with entirely too much interest. There was a predatory air to him, and even though Mike didn't really sense any serious violence in the man, it pissed him off. Anybody who looked at her like that was going to piss him off.

Mike simply stared at the man for a long moment and the guy shrugged and mumbled, "Sorry," before disappearing into the crowd.

"You don't understand the concept of being anonymous, do you, Mike?" Leandra drawled, studying him with pursed lips.

Lifting one shoulder in a shrug, he said, "I understand the concept. Just don't always see the point." Taking the stool next to her, he met the bartender's eyes. The old man ambled their way, limping.

"The usual?" Conrad asked, his voice raspy from years of smoke.

Mike nodded and glanced at Leandra with a raised brow. "Rum and Coke, heavy on the rum," she told Conrad.

As Conrad limped away, Leandra asked, "You come in here often?"

Mike shrugged. "Often enough. Told you I patrolled

around here. I get thirsty." And desperate to drink her out of his mind . . . this was his chosen den when that was the plan. Conrad didn't water the drinks, and the liquor wasn't so cheap it damn near killed the lining of the stomach.

Plus it was far away from any place he had ever expected to see Leandra.

Not that it mattered much, whether he expected to see her or not. He knew that. Mike saw her everywhere he went, every time he closed his eyes, every time he took a woman and pretended she was the one he really wanted.

And now every time he came in here, he had a bad feeling he was going to remember the image of her straddling the bar stool, her skin smooth and dark as chocolate, that smirk on her lips as she met his eyes in the mirror hanging on the bar.

And her eyes . . . that warm, golden shade of amber, always so sad.

He'd remember that, probably more than anything else.

She had to come to his favorite dive, didn't she?

As Conrad slid their drinks in front of him, Mike stood, intending to lose himself in the shadows and try to dull his mind a little.

She followed him though, and Mike was certain his control would snap before the night was over. He leaned against the wall, staring at the sparsely crowded dance floor as though the dancers there enthralled him.

Even though the air reeked of smoke, sweat, and alcohol, he could smell her. The oil she used in her hair, the lotion she smoothed on her skin, and *her*, that sweet scent that was simply Leandra. She stood at his side, staring out at the dance floor as she sipped her rum and Coke.

Mike couldn't think of a damn thing he wanted more than to touch her. Caress the naked flesh exposed between shirt and pants, thread his hand through the thick wealth of braids that fell down her back, tear those damned clothes away from her so he could feast on that long, sleekly powerful body.

"There's an exit at the back," he said flatly. Not even ten

minutes ago, he had been dying to keep her with him for just a few minutes. But she'd always taken off running in the opposite direction after less than two. He hadn't ever had to lash so tightly on to his control before and it was tearing at him.

The hunger rising in him teased the creature that lay deep inside him and Mike found himself battling both his own lust and the driving hungers of the wolf. The wolf—that odd entity that had placed a mark on him before Mike was even born, marking him as different, giving him the power to shift from man to wolf whenever he chose.

It had been that part of him, that deep, primal part, that had recognized Leandra, years ago That last day, when she had come back to Eli's, prepared to accept her judgment. Prepared to die.

Mike had known it then. She would be his—his mate, his woman, his partner.

Wolves mated for life, and he wanted this woman with everything he had inside him.

Keeping his hands off her was a tougher job than Mike had ever imagined anything could be. And if she stayed so close, he was going to lose control and grab her.

Leandra shrugged. "I haven't finished my drink yet. And I plan on having more than one."

Fuck. Tossing back the rest of his drink, he tossed the bottle into a nearby trash can and gave her what he hoped was a nonchalant smile. "I'll be heading out then."

She cocked her head, studying him. "What is wrong with you?"

Mike forced a smile. "Nothing. I'm gone. Got work to do."

As he tried to brush around her, she shrugged. "Have fun."

But he hadn't even taken two steps when he spun back around, staring at her hungrily. *Fun . . . have fun . . .*

Screw this—keeping his distance when he'd been trying to get close to her for the past three months? Hell, the past four years.

He'd lost count of how many times he almost went after her. He'd always stopped though—a quiet little voice said she still wasn't ready. But if he kept waiting to see that despair fade from her eyes, he'd die an old man without so much as kissing her.

Approaching her, he had the small pleasure of seeing her eyes widen just a little as she fell back a step. "What's wrong?" she demanded, and unless he was mistaken, she was suddenly a little nervous.

Mike just kept moving toward her until she had backed herself into the wall. Lifting his arms, he caged her between the wall and his body, lowering his head to breathe in the rich scent of her skin. "You're what's wrong, Leandra," he whispered, brushing his lips against the small tattoo by her eye. She hadn't ever bothered to have it removed, that sign of what she had once been.

And he imagined he knew why. As a reminder—to punish herself.

That was something she had been doing for far too long.

Her hands flew up, pushing him back. Mike only moved back a breath, staring down into her face as he stroked his fingers down her jawline. "You're what's wrong," he repeated. "I think of you. Night and day. All the time. Wondering . . ."

Lowering his mouth, he brushed his lips against her lips. She gasped, a soft, startled little sound and her hands tightened into fists against his chest. Barely even a heartbeat passed before she tried to shove him back, harder this time. Mike didn't budge, but he did lift his head to meet her gaze. "And what do you think about? Ways to get back at me?" she demanded hotly.

Mike smiled. "No. Ways to get *to* you." Leaning into her body, he pulled her flush against him. He cuddled the throbbing length of his cock against her abdomen and whispered, "Ways to make you feel what I feel. All I have to do is look at you and I ache."

He felt it—that slight tremor in her body just before she started to soften against him. An odd light entered her eyes just before she lowered her lashes, shielding herself from him. "That is something that cannot work," she said quietly.

"Why not?" he asked, sliding one hand down her arm and lacing his fingers with hers. Lifting his hand, he looked at their palms pressed together, her skin smooth and dark as chocolate, his own skin seeming even paler against the warmth of hers. "Because of this?"

A frown darkened her face as she turned her head, staring at their joined hands. Finally, a slight smile appeared on her face, one that looked terribly sad. Gently, she tugged her hand free from his and placed it against his left side, on a scar just below his heart. "No, Mike. That has nothing to do with it—this does."

She'd put that mark on him five years ago as she fired a bullet into his chest just before she kidnapped a child away from him. She'd been blind, fiercely protecting what she thought was right, yet she'd done everything in her power to keep that child safe. When she'd discovered just how wrong she had been, she'd been willing to die to make things right.

Mike covered her hand with his as he lowered his head, scraping his teeth along the elegant line of her neck. "This," he whispered roughly, pressing her hand tighter against him, "is nothing. If I had wanted blood from you, I would have taken it. This doesn't matter to me."

She laughed harshly, trying to tear herself away from him, but Mike just wrapped his arms around her, keeping her trapped against him. "Doesn't matter? You're crazy—I tried to kill you. By all rights, I should be dead."

Mike smiled as he stared down into her eyes. They looked wild, terrified . . . and desperate.

For the first time, he realized she wanted him every bit as he wanted her. *Oh, kitten, you shouldn't have let me know that,* he thought absently as he lowered his mouth to hers. He bussed her lips gently before moving to whisper against her ear, "I don't want you dead. I just want you. And I have for years—ever since Agnes brought you back to us. I wanted you then, and I want you now."

And there wasn't a damn thing that would keep him from it now, not now. Not since he knew his need wasn't one-sided.

"What kind of fool are you?" she whispered weakly, turning her head aside. "I tried to kill you—you nearly died."

"You didn't try to kill me. If you had wanted me dead, then I would be dead," Mike argued easily. Sliding one hand up the length of her back, he closed it around a fistful of her braids. "And it wasn't until I damn near died that I really started to live."

Arching her neck back, he stared into her eyes for a long moment before he said, "I didn't start to live until you came into my life, Leandra. And I'll take another bullet, this one straight to the heart, before I let you go."

Slanting his mouth across hers, he kissed her, pushing his tongue demandingly inside her mouth. For a moment, she did nothing, standing there passively under his hands and he prepared himself for her to pull away.

Instead, she moaned, rising up and pressing against him, her arms winding around his neck. Mike crushed her against the wall, rocking his hips against the cradle of hers, shuddering at the softness there.

He skimmed his fingers up her side, brushing the heel of his hand against the outer curve of her breast. She leaned into his touch and Mike swore, tearing his mouth from hers and pressing his forehead against hers. "I want you naked. I want to strip your clothes away and watch as I push inside you. I want to make you scream."

Her lids drooped and for a second, Mike thought she was going to try to pull away again. But instead, a slow, feline smile curved her lips and she whispered, "So what is stopping you?"